FEAR OF ANY KIND

DI ROB MARSHALL
BOOK 7

ED JAMES

Grey Dog Books

Copyright © 2025 Ed James

The right of Ed James to be identified as the author of this work has been asserted in accordance with the Copyright, Designs and Patents Act 1988. All rights reserved.

No part of this publication may be reproduced, stored in or transmitted into any retrieval system, in any form, or by any means (electronic, mechanical, photocopying, recording or otherwise) without the prior written permission of the publisher. Any person who does any unauthorised act in relation to this publication may be liable to criminal prosecution and civil claims for damages.

This is a work of fiction. Names, characters, businesses, places, events and incidents are either the products of the author's imagination or used in a fictitious manner. Any resemblance to actual persons, living or dead, or actual events is purely coincidental.

Cover design copyright © Ed James

Cover background image copyright © Mike Clark:
www.mikeclarkphotography.co.uk

OTHER BOOKS BY ED JAMES

DI ROB MARSHALL SCOTTISH BORDERS MYSTERIES

Ed's first new police procedural series in six years, focusing on DI Rob Marshall, a criminal profiler turned detective. London-based, an old case brings him back home to the Scottish Borders and the dark past he fled as a teenager.

1. THE TURNING OF OUR BONES
2. WHERE THE BODIES LIE
3. A LONELY PLACE OF DYING
4. A SHADOW ON THE DOOR
5. WITH SOUL SO DEAD
6. HIS PATH OF DARKNESS
7. FEAR OF ANY KIND
8. OUR DEBTS TO THE PAST (coming 2025)

SGT RAKESH SYAL POLICE THRILLERS

1. FALSE START
2. FALSE DAWN
3. FALSE HOPE (coming 2025)

Note: 1 is set before Marshall 1, 2 between Marshall 6 & 7.

POLICE SCOTLAND

Precinct novels featuring detectives covering Edinburgh and its surrounding counties, and further across Scotland: Scott Cullen, a rookie eager to climb the career ladder; Craig Hunter, an ex-squaddie struggling with PTSD; Brian Bain, the centre of his own universe and bane of everyone else's.

1. DEAD IN THE WATER (revised 2024)
2. GHOST IN THE MACHINE (revised 2025)
3. DEVIL IN THE DETAIL (revised 2025)
4. FIRE IN THE BLOOD (revised 2025)
5. STAB IN THE DARK (revised 2025)
6. COPS & ROBBERS
7. LIARS & THIEVES
8. COWBOYS & INDIANS
9. THE MISSING
10. THE LOST (coming 2025)
11. THE HUNTED
12. HEROES & VILLAINS
13. THE BLACK ISLE
14. THE COLD TRUTH
15. THE DEAD END

Note: Books 2-8 & 11 previously published as SCOTT CULLEN MYSTERIES, books 9, 11 & 13 as CRAIG HUNTER POLICE THRILLERS and books 1, 14 & 15 as CULLEN & BAIN SERIES.

Book 10 is a new book starring Craig Hunter combining a new story with expanded material previously given to mailing list.

DS VICKY DODDS SERIES

Gritty crime novels set in Dundee and Tayside, featuring a DS juggling being a cop and a single mother.

1. BLOOD & GUTS
2. TOOTH & CLAW
3. FLESH & BLOOD
4. SKIN & BONE
5. GUILT TRIP

DI SIMON FENCHURCH SERIES

Set in East London, will Fenchurch ever find what happened to his daughter, missing for the last ten years?

1. THE HOPE THAT KILLS
2. WORTH KILLING FOR
3. WHAT DOESN'T KILL YOU
4. IN FOR THE KILL
5. KILL WITH KINDNESS
6. KILL THE MESSENGER
7. DEAD MAN'S SHOES
8. A HILL TO DIE ON
9. THE LAST THING TO DIE
10. HOPE TO DIE

Other Books

Other crime novels, with *Lost Cause* set in Scotland and *Senseless* set in southern England.

- LOST CAUSE
- SENSELESS

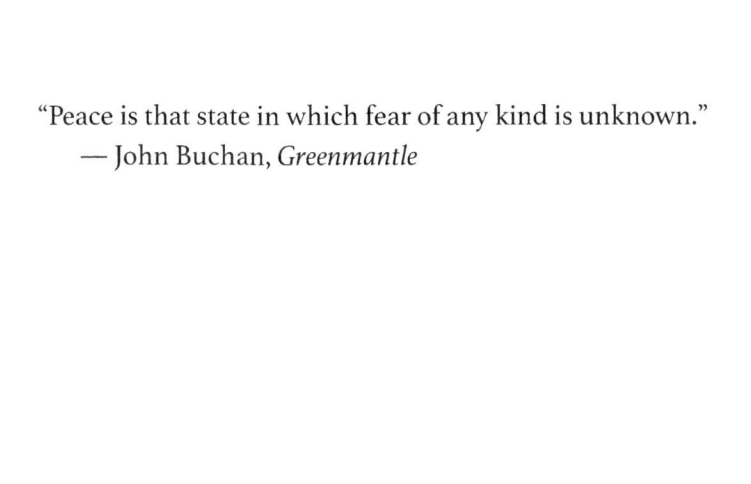

"Peace is that state in which fear of any kind is unknown."
— John Buchan, *Greenmantle*

1

Jake walked along the road in such darkness it felt like it'd swallow him whole.

Not just dark, but cold too – the kind that bit deep into your bones. And the wind blew in harsh gusts of freezing rain towards him, each one the lash of an arctic whip. Felt the cold dig even deeper. No matter how fast he walked, he couldn't outpace the chill.

He stopped to look back the way he'd come. No moon tonight, no soft glow from anywhere. Might as well be in the middle of nowhere. Hawick was sleeping tonight, the lights forming the loose shape of the town, the roll of the hills hidden in the pitch black.

He gave himself a few seconds, counting slowly. As slowly as his heartbeat, a solid pulse that felt like it was slowing to zero. Even with the fast walk.

Nobody had followed him.

Nobody was watching him.

Good.

Jake walked up to the old railings and shifted one to the left, then another to the right – not many knew of this shortcut, but he did.

A final look back the way, listening hard. Hearing nothing. Not even the footsteps of a drunk or a cat.

Jake clambered up and slipped through the railings, into the gardens, thick with cold rhododendron bushes – they'd give him perfect cover from the road. He turned to restore the broken ones, listening again for anyone following. Then he trudged off through the bushes, trying to avoid rustling any but not quite managing. He burst out into the open grounds, pitch black under the thick clouds. Sometimes there would be people in the museum or they'd have left the lights on and it'd made the grass glow, but not tonight. The lawn was wet underfoot, made it feel like a bog. He stepped in a puddle and slipped, sliding forward in the mud but somehow catching himself and stopping himself from going down.

A yelp escaped his lips.

Jesus – anyone could've heard that...

He stopped to look around again, trying to catch his breath. His pulse was definitely quicker now.

He'd got away with that, but he needed to be careful, so he set off again at a slower pace now, inching across the grass to the exact spot. Every step could be another slide, so he planted each foot carefully and made sure it was steady.

He turned around, then took in the museum. A pretty big building that must've been someone's home at one point, back when Hawick was a proper town. Not the kind of place someone like him could get trapped in.

Tonight, though, nobody was there.

Perfect.

Jake took his phone out of his pocket and unlocked it with the code. Time for a selfie. He posed with his tongue and out—

WHO THE FUCK WAS THAT?

Something hit his skull from behind and pushed him over.

He put his hands out to brace himself, but something smacked into his back and forced him face first into the soggy mud. He tasted it, the dirty filth in his mouth. Disgusting.

Something sharp bit into his wrists. His arms were hauled back behind him. Must be a rope or something – tight and cutting into his skin.

Another blow smashed into the back of the skull.

Someone grabbed his hair and jerked his head back. His mouth opened. He tried to speak but it was just a gurgle of noise.

They pushed something into his mouth. Felt like pills, but they tasted sweet – not the bitterness of paracetamol.

They wrapped tape over his mouth.

He could only breathe through his nose

Jake started to hyperventilate – what the fuck was going on?

He swallowed down the pills – didn't mean to.

Jake blacked out.

Then came to.

He'd no idea how long he'd been out – a day or a few seconds.

Felt like the latter – it was dark still and still so bloody cold. He was shivering now. Was he naked? He couldn't see but he felt like he was.

Duct tape pressed against his temple, then hauled over his eyes.

Everything was black now.

He couldn't see his attacker, but they pressed a knife against his skin.

The blade dug into his throat. A dull pain seared in his arse.

What the fuck?

The pain got even worse – what the fuck was going on?

Then a sharp burning near his left shoulder, searing forward through his chest.

Jake couldn't breathe.

He couldn't breathe.

2

MONDAY

Acting DCI Rob Marshall drove his stupid big American truck across the car park, scanning around for a free space. Bloody hell. It was tipping it down – had been since he'd left Gala – and it always felt like it rained much worse over this side of the country.

There.

A single space, sitting under the branches of a tree.

Finally.

Marshall pulled up, then stuck it in reverse and swung back in. But he was taking it too quickly. He slowed and eased forward again. Then reassessed his angles, like a professional trying to break free of a tricky snooker. Or more like a drunk trying to pretend he could play pool. He took it very slowly and eased the truck back into the space, then let the engine die.

Finally here. And he needed to get shot of this piece of crap. It'd seen him through another Borders winter, with its snow and ice, but it'd annoy the hell out of him through the rest of the year.

He opened the door and almost scraped the next car's door. A really tight fit, so he took his time squeezing out. Then had to reach back in to grab his laptop bag from the passenger seat. He shut his door and shimmied along the length of his car, just clearing it as the rain started bucketing down.

The driver of the other car popped her head over the top. DCS Miranda Potter. His old boss.

'Narrow escape there, Rob.' She smirked across the roof of her Mercedes. Her new fringe gave her face a cherubic look. 'Thought you were going to trade that thing in?'

'Wish I could, ma'am.' Marshall breathed in the cold air, then let it out in a rough explosion. 'Trade-in prices have totally collapsed for some reason.'

'All the same, you do need a new car.'

'Hard to disagree.' Marshall gave her a shrug. 'But it all depends on where I'm going to live, doesn't it?'

'Oh?'

'Long story.'

'We've got time.' She grabbed her own laptop bag and gestured for him to go first. 'After you.'

Marshall set off towards the entrance. Gartcosh looked more like a fancy new university or tech company's head office than a crime campus. Whatever a crime campus was supposed to be. 'Just depends on how today goes, really.'

'See, that wasn't such a long story, was it?'

'Guess not.' Marshall followed her inside to the atrium, all glass and concrete. People milled around, heading for meetings, waiting for them or just talking on the phone out of earshot of their colleagues.

Potter swiped her card through the reader and bumped her hip through the barrier. 'Have you revised the slides after our wee chat last week?'

Marshall did the same and, wonder of wonders, his card still worked here. 'Of course.'

'I see.' Potter marched down the long main corridor, then

stopped outside a glass-fronted meeting room. 'You didn't want to run the deck past me first?'

'I'd rather see your reactions in person.'

'Interesting.' Potter raised her eyebrows. 'Confident, eh?'

'Quietly.'

She laughed, then pushed into the room.

Marshall took a second to straighten his tie and check his suit jacket wasn't too damp, then followed her in.

Detective Superintendent John Ravenscroft was messing about with the projector hooked up to his laptop. Early forties and sharply dressed – his greying hair was sculpted into a gravity-defying quiff. 'Can't get this bloody thing to bloody work.' His accent was the softest Scouse you could get, but still reeked of the Mersey.

'Morning, sir.' Marshall got his laptop out of his bag and laid it on the table. 'Mind if I have a go?'

Ravenscroft looked over at him with a sneer, then seemed to notice he was in the room with his boss and his expression softened to a grin. 'Be my guest, Robert.' He stepped back, hands raised.

Marshall plugged his own laptop into the connector and his presentation appeared on the screen.

Borders Major Investigation Team
Strategic Redefinition v1.0
Acting DCI Rob Marshall
2024 02 03

Ravenscroft scowled at him. 'How the hell did you manage that, eh?'

'Magic.' Marshall grinned. 'Been plugging laptops into projectors in many locations for a very long time.'

'All the same. I'd been at that for ten minutes.' Ravenscroft took the seat at the head of the table and examined the screen. 'That "acting" prefix sticks out like a sore thumb, eh?'

Potter shot him a look. 'We're not here to discuss that.'

No, that'd be another entirely separate session for Marshall to endure. He stayed standing, looking at each of them in turn. 'So. We're here today to discuss the Borders MIT. I wanted to share my presentation and get some feedback from both of you at the same time. If there's anything contentious, then we can discuss it here. Or take it offline. You're in charge, so it's all up to you.'

Ravenscroft waved a hand at the screen. 'So why are you at version one, rather than, say, a zero point one?'

'This is just how I like to number things, sir. We haven't worked together very long, but you'll get used to my approach.'

Ravenscroft laughed. 'And if it differs from mine?'

'I don't care enough about it to argue.' Marshall shrugged. 'Your way wins.'

'Robert.' Ravenscroft fixed him with a hard stare. 'I don't need you to kiss my arse here, okay?'

'I'm serious. If you want me to use a different version control system, I'll happily comply.'

'Can we get on with this?' Potter looked up from her phone. 'I'm meeting the chief at ten and I desperately need a coffee before.'

'Sure thing.' Ravenscroft shifted his irritation back to Marshall. 'The floor's yours.'

Marshall cleared his throat, then clicked the button, shifting the slide on.

Summary of Approach

He clapped his hands together, just like he'd learned years ago in some stupid presentation skills training course. 'Okay, so as you've requested, I've pulled together a presentation for how to scale up the Borders MIT to incorporate Behavioural Sciences.'

The screen filled with his PowerPoint deck. On the giant screen it seemed very slick – probably too slick. He should've stuck with the standard format, with its basic font and house style, but he hadn't been able to help himself.

Borders MIT sat in the middle of the screen and each click added in connected boxes:

Behavioural Sciences Unit
Edinburgh MIT
Stirling MIT
Livingston MIT
Dunfermline MIT

He watched them both nod at each box – so far, so good. Then the final click.

Forensics Centre of Excellence

'I've also included a Forensics Centre of Excellence at Tweedbank.'

'Tweedbank?' Ravenscroft laughed. 'Why there?'

'Easy proximity to Edinburgh, sir, where some of the work is presently done, but the bulk of it is here in Gartcosh. Tweedbank offers a significantly reduced cost base in terms of office space. Also, it's reasonably close to Newcastle for—'

'Newcastle?' Ravenscroft glowered at him. 'Are you talking about taking on work from Northumbria Police?'

'Right. It's just over an hour to Newcastle from Tweedbank, sir. Similar time to Carlisle. And if the train line *does* continue to Carlisle, it'll make it even easier.'

'I don't quite see the logic here.'

'Basically, a centre of excellence in the Borders, where things are cheaper, can be a profit centre for Forensic Services.'

'Have you run this past them?'

'Not yet.'

'Good. Keep it that way.'

'Well, I've discussed it with Kirsten Weir.'

'Ah yes. The lead forensic scientist for your area.' Ravenscroft sat back and sighed. 'Robert, I tasked you with cutting costs, not with growing the Borders MIT into some kind of ten-armed homunculus.' He paused to lick his lips. 'Not to mention one that's very convenient for your personal commute and your love life.'

'This is a logical extension of our current situation, sir.' Marshall felt a surge of frustration bubbling in his guts. He tried to stay calm. Tried. 'The Borders MIT sticks out like a sore thumb in your east branch of DCS Potter's Specialised Crime Division.'

'Agreed.'

'We cover a big geographical area, which isn't densely populated. There's no Livingston or Stirling or Inverness down here, just a load of small towns. For instance, Galashiels – where we're based – is only ten thousand souls. Hawick's bigger, but not by much. If we build on the land at Tweedbank, the new police station will have proximity to Gala, Selkirk and Melrose, plus easy routes to Hawick, Kelso and over to the coast, but also Peebles and the land to the west. And it'll be right next to the current Borders railway terminus.'

'The bit I agree with is the low population density.' Ravenscroft sat back, arms folded and thinking it through. 'In my head, it means we don't need an MIT down here. Local uniform and CID can handle the majority of crimes down here just as well and, in the rare occurrences where an MIT *is* needed, Edinburgh can cover. Livi or Dunfermline at a push.' He scribbled down a lengthy note, then looked up at him. 'My problem, Robert, is this proposal is just way too expensive.'

'But I haven't costed it up yet.'

'And you won't. Because I need you to revise your strategy.'

'But I've put in—'

'I do like the COE element, as we're overly reliant on here in Gartcosh. But if that were to be moved to Edinburgh...' Ravenscroft looked over at Potter. 'We have first refusal on a site at Easter Bush Campus in Midlothian, next to the university's veterinary campus.'

Marshall looked around the room and it hit him – he'd been set up. There was no interest in ideas here, just a fixed target he hadn't been warned about. He gave Ravenscroft a smile, but it wasn't genuine. 'Won't that be much more expensive?'

'Sure, but it's probably cost-positive when you factor in the additional transportation requirements of basing skulls down in the Borders full-time and having the associated office space in Galashiels.' Ravenscroft twirled his fingers. 'And can you roll the Borders MIT into Edinburgh, please?'

And there it was. 'So you want to scrap it?'

'I do. It'll save on the DCI salary, for starters.'

'My salary, you mean.'

'You're only acting, Robert.' Ravenscroft shot him a dismissive look. 'To cover the shortfall down there, you'll need to add in Edinburgh MIT travelling down for weekly satellite postings for face-time between with local uniform and CID.' He looked over at Potter. 'That'll give us scope to increase the headcount of DS and DC pairings under each of the DIs. The span of control goes up, so it's more economical.'

Potter nodded, but it was like she wasn't putting her full weight behind it.

'Sir, with all due respect...' Marshall ran a hand through his hair. 'The case for setting up the Borders MIT in the first place is still very valid.'

'Remind me?'

'A murder down by Jedburgh three years ago, where—'

'That could've been run from Edinburgh.'

'It was.' Marshall narrowed his eyes. 'Ended up with a dead cop and an escaped suspect who wasn't caught until local resource was deployed.'

Ravenscroft tapped his pen off his fancy notebook. 'That was an aberration.'

'An aberration?' Marshall sat down between them. 'But that doesn't mention the cases I've worked in my time down there, both within the MIT and when attached to Behavioural Sciences.'

'Robert.' Anger flashed across Ravenscroft's face. 'I'm sure someone with your background must appreciate how statistically unlikely it is to have that many murders in a place like the Borders in, what, two years?'

'Three. That case was January 2022, sir.'

'And you've been there how long?'

'Two and a half.'

'But with over a year here at Gartcosh.' Ravenscroft sucked in a long breath. 'The bottom line, Robert, is you're suggesting we take the opposite approach to the one I tasked you with.'

'Pretty much, aye.'

'Look, mate, I get it. I can see the opportunities. But it's just way too expensive.'

'It costs more because it's better.'

'Better.' Ravenscroft laughed. 'Right.'

'Sir, with all due respect, the next time a major case turns to shit because nobody local was working it from the start, you can expect the lawsuit for investigative insufficiency to start in the millions. Any thousands you save will just look silly.'

Ravenscroft gave him a long, hard look, then he refolded his arms. 'The budget's not there, Robert, and you've clearly misunderstood the remit of this exercise.' He glanced at Potter. 'Would you agree, Miranda?'

'This exercise was open-ended.'

'Sure.' Ravenscroft capped his pen and closed his notebook. 'Okay, Robert, here's how we progress. You change this—' He gave a dismissive wave at the only slide they'd bothered to look at. '—then we can regroup.' He scraped his chair back and stood up. 'The good thing is, all we've wasted is the petrol and diesel to get here, on top of your efforts in pulling this together. I'm heading back to Edinburgh for a session with your equivalent there. Talk about a cowboy...' He smirked. 'Let's pick up at your next one-to-one. Thursday, isn't it?'

'I believe so, sir.'

'Good, good. Well. I'll be in touch. Or my assistant will, at least.' Ravenscroft grabbed his laptop and stuffed it back into its case. 'I'll see you later, Miranda.' He marched off, swinging his bag.

Leaving Marshall with Potter.

Marshall collapsed back into his chair. 'I feel set up there.'

'By me?'

'No. By him.' Marshall let out a deep breath. 'He asked me to come up with a non-specific strategy for reducing costs in his East region, but I've ended up having to sack myself from my own job.'

'Your job's safe, Rob.'

'But he wanted to remove the C from DCI, right?'

'Rob. Your *position* in Galashiels might be at risk, but your job is safe and sound.' Potter yawned into her fist. 'Listen, if you're going to be angry with anyone, be angry with me. I'm the one who's tasked John with cutting costs. But I wanted it done this way because I know how you both think. Sometimes the strengths or weaknesses of an idea get exposed through adversity.'

'Killing the Borders MIT isn't going to save the kind of money he needs, though.'

'But this Centre of Excellence down in Tweedbank? Really?'

'Edinburgh isn't fit for purpose. All of our work goes here. This is xa chance to create a new Gartcosh at Tweedbank.'

'When Edinburgh would be a better location for it.' Potter shook her head. 'I trust him and his process. John's earned the nickname of "the scalpel" for his ability to remove waste at many forces down south.' She raised a hand. 'Or what he terms waste, anyway.'

'Policing is a public service, though. And we're having to cut back on service.'

'It's the nature of the beast.' Potter stared at the table. 'The truth is, I'm not that keen on having to do this, but the directive has come from the very top. We've all got to cut costs and focus on frontline policing.'

'But that'll just push the burden back to us with fewer resources.'

'I understand that concern. But to reassure you, while we're starting with East, John will cycle through to the rainy West then to the frozen North to work his magic there. After a few years, I'll have cut my overall budget by around thirty percent with hopefully no impact.'

'At least I won't have to endure him that long, then.'

'He's not that bad.' Her eyebrow flashed up – blink and you'd miss it. 'But I get it, Rob. Time was, policing was an investment in the security of a nation to underpin prosperity but now it's…' She blew air up her face. 'We are where we are.'

They sat around for a bit, that passive phrase lingering in the air between them.

People passed in the corridor, the sound of their chat leaking into the room, but leaving the content and words back out there.

Marshall unplugged his laptop from the projector. 'When I

agreed to be acting DCI, I thought it was to give me a chance to—'

'Rob. The reason you're acting is because there's a strategic review underway to mark ten years of Police Scotland. We've got to cut costs somewhere.'

'Or bring money in from elsewhere.'

'True, but that's just not going to happen and, even if it did, it'd be precarious and at the whims of other chief constables. And a word of advice – if you're seriously talking about that railway extension bringing in money, when the truth is it's nowhere near even consultation let alone laying tracks on the ground...'

Marshall saw her point, but he also saw the logic in his madness. Everything he did was about the long term – making things right strategically, rather than messing about with tactics that might be outdated in a few months. He looked over at her. 'Level with me here. Are my team all going to end up back in Edinburgh?'

'Not all. A few will stay to join the local CID and some will be reallocated to Livingston or Dunfermline.'

'But most will?'

'I'm afraid so. It was a noble experiment, but you said it yourself – it sticks out like a sore thumb.'

'And I'll be back to my previous grade?'

'Rob, you'll be based in Edinburgh, sure, but I'm challenging you to act like a DCI. If you want this job full-time, then you need to prove you're worthy of it.' Potter waved at the door. 'If you fold every time your super squeaks, I don't want you in that role. But you stood up to him there.' She leaned forward. 'You certainly raised some good points, especially about why this MIT was formed in the first place. But I suggest you build a better mousetrap.'

'What's that supposed to mean?'

'It means...' Potter sighed. 'Your experience is in the

detailed analysis of offenders and strategic profiling. That's priceless. But I need you to develop more political skills.'

Marshall felt like he'd been punched in the balls. 'I'll try my best.'

'You do, Rob. All the time. Thing is, if you act up locally and you excel in the role, we can bump you up elsewhere.' Potter left a pause, pregnant with promise. 'What you said earlier about your car and depending on where you live... Well, you could move anywhere as a DCI.' She shot him a wink. 'Just think about that.'

3

Marshall took the right turn at the roundabout and drove through the thick rain towards the logjam backed up to the traffic lights. Luckily, he was turning left. He passed the Kwik Fit, then pulled into the police station's car park. For once, the DCI's space was free and, even stranger, he managed to squeeze his car into it first time.

Compensation for that clusterfuck of a meeting.

Smashing.

Still, there was work to be done – so many plates spinning and if he took his eyes off one, he'd be cutting his feet on a load of smashed crockery.

He grabbed his laptop off the passenger seat and got out into the cold rain, then trudged across the tarmac, thankful it was cold but not cold enough to freeze – he could do without slipping on his arse, especially not on CCTV.

A patrol car whizzed past him and pulled in by the back entrance to the custody suite, presumably with a suspect in the back.

He sucked in a deep breath, but it was a mouthful of second-hand cigarette smoke. Despite them recently spending a ton of money on the station – not on Ravenscroft's watch – they hadn't relocated the shelter from the perfect location to spread smoke all across the car park.

A Vauxhall slid into the disabled space next to the front door. DI Callum Taylor got out and loomed over Marshall. That cleft chin seemed to grow deeper, like he was mining something deep inside. His hair had been shaved, leaving more salt than pepper. 'Morning, boss.'

'Welcome back, Callum.' Marshall walked over and clapped him on the arm. 'How are you doing?'

'You know how it is.' Taylor shrugged, then looked down at his foot. 'Still hurts like hell, but I'm mobile enough. And I was bored rigid at home so thought I'd better get back to work, eh?'

Marshall led him across the car park and held open the side door. 'You better be fit and firing.'

'Fit, no. Firing? Maybe.' Taylor limped over, badly. Like a waddling penguin, rocking from side to side with each step.

Marshall worried about the onslaught of HR paperwork heading his way if Taylor wasn't indeed ready to return to work. 'Sorry, but that looks pretty bad, I have to say.'

'Feels a ton worse than it looks. Doc had me on so many pills you could hear me rattling, but I've seen too many people get addicted to them. Nothing stronger than paracetamol now.' Taylor brushed past him and stepped inside the station. 'Ah, it's good to be back.'

Marshall followed him inside, then kept pace with him along the corridor leading to their office space, dashing forward to hold the door. For once, the room was busy and full of troops. Not that there was much going on – maybe Ravenscroft had a point…

Taylor did his penguin waddle over to his office, next to Marshall's.

The state of it – boxes and files everywhere, with a light dusting of Greggs wrappers. 'Sorry about the mess, Cal.'

'Not your fault, boss.'

'No, but I should've got *someone* to clear up.' Marshall flared his nostrils, then wagged a finger at him. 'Desk duties, remember? As in, you're not allowed out in the field.'

'Aye, I remember.' Taylor grimaced as he sat behind his desk. 'Never thought I'd make it back here, you know?' He seemed to wipe a tear from his eye – but Taylor was too butch to cry in front of another officer, especially his boss. 'Doc says four hours then home. For the first month, anyway.' He looked around the room, grinning. 'Still plan on taking a full hour's lunch so at least I'll be away from home that bit longer.'

Marshall knew he had a colourful private life, the kind of complex domestic arrangement you could only reach by going through some bad stuff – but he couldn't quite remember the details. 'You don't have to go home, but if you do stay here, you can't work.'

'Understood.' Taylor nodded at the door. 'How's it been going here?'

Marshall shut the door. 'Mostly fine, but it'll be good to have you back up to speed.'

'Jolene's been acting up to DI, right?'

'She has.' Marshall looked around the room. 'This is her mess. Or her team's, anyway. I'll get her to clear it up.'

'It'll give me something to do.' Taylor smiled. 'Is she still hopeful she'll get the gig full-time?'

'Aye, but...'

'But you're going to have to be frank with her?'

'Right. Exactly.' Marshall scratched at his neck. 'Hate this part of the job, Cal. Andrea's away on holiday to Florida, so Jolene's got another fortnight, but then she's back to being a DS again.'

'Even with me only here half the time?'

'Even so.'

'Such is life.' Taylor let out a slow breath. 'Jo's a good cop, Rob, and she knows the deal.'

'Aye, but covering you for the best part of six months means she's got her feet under the table.'

Taylor raised his eyebrows. 'And you've not done anything to dissuade her?'

'The opposite. I've been hard on her, trying to keep her feet on the ground. But she won't listen.'

Someone knocked on the door.

Marshall walked over and opened it.

Jolene burst past him, eager as a small child seeing their new puppy after a tough day of school. 'Hiya, Cal.' She wrapped him in a hug, then broke off to smile at him. 'You look like shit.'

'Aye, because some bastard shot me in the foot and for once it wasn't me.' Taylor grinned. 'I've got so much metal in my ankle they've given me one of those exemptions for the detectors at the airport.'

'Wait.' Jolene frowned. 'So they left a bullet inside?'

'God, no.' Taylor laughed. 'No, they had to put so many screws in my ankle just to hold it all together. It's a miracle I can walk.'

Jolene flashed a kind smile, instead of the sarcastic one. 'Well, it's good having you back.'

'Good being back.' Taylor winked at her. 'Heard you've been acting up?'

'Just until Andrea's back from holiday. Been good fun.' Jolene looked Marshall up and down. 'Any chance we can have a word, boss?'

'Sure.' Marshall smiled at Taylor. 'See you in a bit, Cal.' He walked through the door, then looked back. 'And Jolene *will* clear away the shite from here.'

'It's not that bad, is it?'

'No, but it's not his shite.' Marshall followed Jolene into his office next door.

Just how he'd left it first thing. He sat down and dumped his bag next to a pile of fresh paperwork waiting for him on the desk.

Jolene perched on the front of the chair opposite him. 'So, how did it go up at Tulliallan?'

'Got moved to Gartcosh.'

'As in where Forensics Services are based?'

'Aye, but more like where Miranda's based.' Marshall sighed. 'Let's just call it a disappointing outcome.'

She stared at her feet. 'Oh.'

'There was a bit of a gap between what I was asked to deliver and what I did.'

'In what way?'

'They liked the font, the colour scheme and the graphics.' Marshall laughed. 'The content, though... We're back to the drawing board.'

Jolene sat back in the chair and wrapped her arms around her torso. 'So they're not going for the Centre of Excellence?'

Marshall took his time to consider what to say by getting his laptop out and logging into it. He had to enter his password again but the buggering thing finally accepted it. 'Strictly between us, Jo, but we might get folded into the Edinburgh MIT.'

'Fuck sake.' Jolene shot to her feet, fists clenched. 'Seriously?'

'Costs are getting slashed everywhere. We're deemed too expensive.'

'Meanwhile people still get murdered. Not to mention Gary Hislop still selling drugs to people. And all over Scotland now too.'

'I know.' Marshall pointed at his laptop. 'Potter liked aspects of it and gave me some pointers. I'll sort it out, okay?'

Another sigh, deeper this time. 'So I'm guessing I'll be back to DS when Andrea's back?'

'The only chance is if Taylor can't return to full active duty. But then there's no guarantee it'll be you either. Any permanent DI spot for you could be in Edinburgh or Livingston.'

Jolene shook her head. 'Right.'

'You've done a great job, Jo, and I'll add that to your record.' Marshall gave her a smile, trying to be encouraging and kind. But it felt false even to him. 'As someone said to me – act up locally, get bumped up elsewhere.'

'What's that supposed to mean?'

'It means, you could be in line for a DI gig in Edinburgh. They've got four teams, after all. If this change happens, there'll be a fifth and sixth. And if one of the many DIs there were to be moved on…'

'I don't want to go anywhere else.'

'You might not have a choice. These days promotion comes with mobility.'

'So this is what She Who Cannot Be Named wants?'

'It's not what *DCS Potter* wants, Jo, but it's what her boss—'

Another knock on the door.

Marshall leaned back and sighed. 'We'll continue this chat, okay?'

'Sure.' Jolene stayed there, arms folded.

Marshall got up and walked over to the door. He took a breath before he opened it.

A man stood there, hands in pockets. Stubble, tall, rugged. He smiled at Marshall, but he could only smile on one side of his face – or he just chose to. 'You must be Marshall.'

Marshall stood there – he'd no idea who this was. 'That's me. Yes.'

'DS Douglas Crawford.' He thrust out a hand. He sized up Jolene as she slipped past them. 'Stirling MIT picked up a murder this morning, so John sent me down early, rather than getting stuck into that.'

'John?'

'Superintendent Ravenscroft.'

'I see. But I don't follow. Is this to do with a case?'

Crawford frowned. 'Eh, it's my first day?'

'What?'

Crawford's frown deepened. 'Haven't you been told I was starting?'

'First I've heard of this.'

'Oh, right. Well, apparently I'm here instead of DS Siyal.' Crawford handed him a sheet of paper. 'Here are the orders John gave me.'

Marshall read through it, then set it down on his desk. As pissed off as he was, he grinned and held out his hand. 'Good to meet you, Sergeant.'

Crawford shook it, way tighter than necessary. 'Pleasure's mine, sir.'

'Rob's fine.' Marshall took his hand back. 'And welcome to the Borders MIT. I like to sit down with all new members of the team, but as I haven't been warned of your arrival... I'll schedule some time for a coffee.'

'Sounds great.' Crawford looked through into the main office. 'Seems a bit quiet here?'

'This is a busy day.' Marshall laughed, but it didn't land.

First name terms with Ravenscroft... This was a guy he needed to keep an eye on.

And Ravenscroft could've bloody warned him up at Gartcosh.

'Come on, I'll introduce you to your new boss.' Marshall walked back out into the incident room then rapped on the open door to Taylor's office. 'Cal?'

Taylor and Jolene were chatting in low voices.

They stopped.

Jolene stood up and walked off.

'That's twice now.' Crawford watched her go. 'Something I said?'

'Lot going on.' Marshall gestured at Taylor. 'DI Callum Taylor. This is DS Douglas Crawford. Just joined your team.'

Taylor struggled to his feet and shook his hand. 'Douglas or Doug?'

'Prefer Douglas. Don't mind Doug. Dougie, I will punch you in the face. Make it rhyme with "boogie" and they'll never find your body.'

'Noted.' Taylor laughed. 'Afraid you're going to have to do my running for me for a while.'

'That looks rough.' Crawford grimaced in the direction of Taylor's feet. 'What happened?'

'Got shot. Still, could've been much worse. Much, much worse.'

'I've been shot. It wasn't fun.'

Taylor laughed again. 'That's an understatement and a half.'

'I'll leave you pair to it.' Marshall slipped away, then went back into his office, shutting the door behind him and hoping no other bugger would knock on it.

He sat down and stared at the wall for a few seconds.

It wasn't cool to shoot the messenger – Crawford wasn't to blame – but he could shoot the decision-maker, couldn't he?

He picked up his mobile and called Ravenscroft.

Took a few seconds, but credit to the arsehole – he did pick up. 'Robert, this'll have to be quick as I'm just about to go into a meeting.'

'Can't promise that, sir.'

'Oh?'

'Why have you sent down DS Crawford instead of DS Siyal?'

'Ah.' A slamming door – sounded like Ravenscroft moved to another room. 'Two things. First, Dean Asher requested an extension to Rakesh's tenure to cover some long-term sickness. As you know, operational policing takes precedence *these days*.'

Marshall left a long pause – hopefully long enough to irritate him. 'Why wasn't I made aware of this?'

Ravenscroft's pause was definitely long enough to irritate. 'It's an emerging matter.'

'Did it emerge after our meeting at Gartcosh?'

'Partly.' Ravenscroft sighed down the line. 'The reason I had to dash off so swiftly, in fact. Stirling caught a murder and I was forced into a decision. Stick or twist with Crawford.'

'I prefer vetting new members of the team before they turn up.'

'Would that we had that luxury, Robert.'

'What's the other reason?'

'Ah.' Ravenscroft sighed again. 'It appears Sergeant Siyal sent Miranda an email regarding his tenure. Used quite forceful language too.'

Bollocks…

'Be good to have a word in his shell-like as she's really pissed off about it.' Ravenscroft sniffed. 'Catch you later.'

And he was gone.

Marshall rested his phone on the desk and stared up at the ceiling. The patch of brown water stain was spreading. Felt like a metaphor.

Rakesh…

Why did he have to be such a bloody idiot?

What made him good as a cop was how different his experience and motivations were.

Sadly, it also had a cost.

He picked up his phone and started tapping out a message:

> Need to catch up with—

His desk phone rang.

He set his mobile down and picked it up. 'Marshall.'

'Sir, it's Isla Routledge.' Sounded like she was outside somewhere – somewhere wet and windy. 'I'm down in Hawick.'

Marshall knew her – one of those uniformed sergeants he'd kill to make a DS but who'd treat the concept with abject contempt. But she was based in Gala, not Hawick – meaning something was up. 'What's up, Sergeant?'

'Someone's been murdered.'

4

For once, Hawick didn't seem to be buggered up by roadworks, so Marshall got a clear run past Aldi and Sainsbury's, tracing the path of the Teviot River splitting the town centre off from the A7. The buildings were dull under the thick cover of rain, but it didn't seem to put off the locals, hardened to this kind of weather.

Marshall glanced over at the passenger seat. 'This is my first murder since I moved back permanently.'

Crawford frowned over at him. 'Seriously?'

'Aye.' Marshall rubbed at his chin, already dotted with stubble despite this morning's shave before his presentation. 'Almost six months now.'

'Does it feel better to be leading rather than consulting?'

'Like I never left.'

Crawford pointed to the right, past a country store selling grain and feed. 'This is it here, isn't it?'

'Aye.' Marshall took the turning, then the next left past the furniture shop his mum insisted on buying everything from. Past some nice houses, nice enough he'd consider buying if only they weren't in Hawick.

Another glance at Crawford – he knew a couple of things about him, like his background in the Behavioural Sciences Unit, without being told. Must've come from Ravenscroft – he hoped Crawford wasn't a spy to see if Marshall was up to the job.

Aye, he needed to be careful around this one…

He spotted the row of patrol cars and pulled up behind the last. He got out first, then waited for Crawford to get out before locking it and walking over.

And there he was, securing entrance to the area – PC Liam Warner. Big lad, more tall than strong, grinning wide as he surveyed the scene. Behind him, more cars filled the parking spaces.

Marshall was surprised he was still employed. Talk about a saving that could be made – just a shame he wasn't on Ravenscroft's budget.

'DS Douglas Crawford.' He showed his warrant card. 'Good to meet you. What's the name?'

'Warner. Liam Warner. And good to meet you too, Sarge.' He nodded at Marshall. 'Sir. We've managed to secure the scene.'

'Good work.' Marshall returned the nod. 'Where's your sergeant?'

'She's over by the crime scene, sir.' He pointed through a gap in the hedge.

'Who found the body?'

'Woman who manages the place.' Warner thumbed behind himself. 'Turned up and started making a coffee while the heating woke up and all that. Saw something on the grass and thought it was a bit of crafty fly-tipping. Quite common, apparently. But nope. It was a dead body, sir.'

'Have you identified the body?'

'Not yet, sir. Anyway, she called us in. Me and Stish attended as we were dealing with a follow-up to a breach of the peace just before Christmas.' Warner shrugged. 'And here we are.'

Further down the winding road, Marshall clocked a middle-aged woman giving her statement to a pair of uniforms. She stared into space, still stunned by her discovery.

'Can you at least take her inside out of the rain?' Marshall clapped Crawford's arm. 'I'll see what's what through there while you get a handle on this.'

5

Marshall was now all suited up.

The CSI tent stood below the darkening sky, mere feet from the ceremonial fountain – at least, that's what Marshall thought it was. Wilton Lodge Park was further over, through a wall of trees – they might be bare, but there were still enough of them to block the view.

He looked back across the common approach path around the side of the grass. The middle was boggy and dotted with some footprints – some poor sod was cataloguing and photographing them. Could prove useful, especially if it was more than the victim's.

Hawick Museum lay behind – presumably Wilton Lodge itself. A Georgian remnant of a more prosperous time for the town. A local mill owner would've erected that for his family, far enough away from the mills along the river.

PS Isla Routledge pulled off her cap and shook out her hair, until the curls kinked out. Dark, almost black, and she started tying it into a standard bun. Bare arms, though, despite the temperature. 'Hate doing this.'

'I get it.' Marshall nodded at her. 'Must take ages to tie all that up?'

'Not my bloody hair.' She stopped to glare at him. 'I meant being a CSM. Should be one of your lot doing it.'

'I get it.' Marshall raised his hands. 'I'll get you relieved soon.'

'You bloody better.'

'What are you doing down here?'

'You mean in Hawick?' She sighed. 'Big pile-up on the A7 by Langholm, so the Hawick lot were sent south to manage that and us lot in Gala were told to cover this too. Perfect timing...'

'Well, I'm glad you called it in.' Marshall took a deep breath, then snapped on his goggles and pulled up his mask. 'I'll make sure you're relieved soon.' A final nod at Isla, then he stepped into the CSI tent.

Six figures in there, all hidden by masks and goggles.

'Robert.'

Marshall made eye contact with the one nearest the body. 'Hiya, Leye.'

The Borders pathologist stood up and stretched out his back with a sickening crack.

A teenage boy lay on the ground next to him, naked and in a crucifixion pose, facing up. Silvery duct tape covered his mouth and was wrapped over his eyes.

'That's something you don't see every day.' Marshall took in the grisly sight but couldn't for the life of him figure out how he'd been killed. 'This is how he was found?'

'Naked as the day he was born.' Leye pointed at two figures cataloguing some items. 'Green hoodie was found near him.'

'What about jeans or a T-shirt?'

'Not that I've heard. Shoes missing too.'

Another figure turned around. Kirsten Weir, the lead forensics officer and Marshall's girlfriend. 'Hi, Rob.'

Marshall wanted to reach over and kiss her, but this wasn't the time or place for it. 'Anything so far?'

'We've just got here.' Kirsten rolled her eyes through her goggles. 'But we've found nothing of note so far. And we think we're missing clothes as there were footprints over here. Similar size to the victim's feet.'

'Figures.' Marshall nodded at the body. 'Can you do some analysis on the tape?'

'Will do, once we're cleared to. Unlikely we'll get anything, mind…' She turned away from him and went back to whatever she was doing.

Marshall focused on Leye. 'Do we know when he died?'

'I'm still processing it, but if you want a rough time, then I think between ten o'clock last night and two this morning.'

'Big window.'

'Indeed. I'll get a better idea when I do the post mortem. I'll do a core temperature check but the victim's naked, wet and very cold, all of which will greatly affect my estimate for time of death. Doesn't mean it's unattainable, just means I've got to look up the values when I get back to my desk and perform some calculations.'

Marshall crouched next to the body and cast his gaze across the skin. He frowned up at Leye. 'Are those *messages* carved onto the body?'

Leye pointed at the left arm. 'Any regrets?' He pointed at the chest. 'Scumbag.' At the abdomen. 'Liar.' At his left cheek. 'Poof.'

All Marshall could do was read them. The flesh was scored with twenty or thirty messages.

Leye puffed up his mask. 'Haven't turned him over yet, but I expect more on his back.'

Marshall kept looking at them, transfixed by the subtle knife-work – it took a lot to cut a message into someone's flesh like that. It all pointed to a deliberate act, for sure, and to a motive – revenge. 'What was he lying about?'

Leye shrugged. 'Don't know.'

'Sorry, it was rhetorical.' Marshall stood up tall, but didn't know what to say.

Leye brushed a hand across the victim's skin. 'One thing to note. From the lack of blood, we can tell the carving was postmortem...'

'Jesus...'

Leye gave him a hard stare. 'Please don't take the Lord's name in vain.'

'Sorry.' Marshall raised his hands. 'I didn't think.'

'No, but given the pose...' Leye laughed. 'Relax. I'm just messing with you. But you know how it works – if you end their life first, then there won't be anywhere near as much blood spurting out of the body.'

'And you've more time to carve the messages. No screaming means no witnesses.' Marshall nodded. 'What's the cause of death, then?'

'Knife wound pierced his heart.'

Marshall looked at the body but couldn't see the required wound. 'Are you sure? Because I can't—'

'Interesting fact, but you can pierce the heart from behind as well.' Leye held out an imaginary knife and stuck it behind himself, then pretended to pierce his own heart. 'So if the victim's supine and facing up, you won't see a big gory wound. Meanwhile he's exsanguinated through the wound in his back.'

'I thought you hadn't turned him over?'

'I haven't moved the body, but I had a little look.' Leye looked over to the side. 'Kirsten hasn't found a murder weapon, though.'

'That's our priority.' Kirsten turned around again. 'Could do with some skulls to help out, if you've got anybody?'

Marshall nodded. 'I'll get Cal to allocate some.'

'Taylor's back?'

'Today, aye. Limited duties.'

'Good stuff. How's he—'

'Rob, I need to warn you.' Leye stepped between them and fixed Marshall with a rigid stare. 'There are signs of sexual activity.'

Marshall frowned at the body. 'With him?'

'Well, I didn't mean with me.' Leye laughed. 'Yes, with him. And I can't be sure until I get him on the slab, but I undertook a presumptive piece of work. After we took a few pictures in situ, we rolled the body. Seeing anal tearing is obviously beyond this, but there was lubricant visible on his buttocks. Highly suggestive of sexual activity. Given the slurs, it seemed prudent to check that area.' He grimaced. 'The lacerations don't have any blood in them, so my conclusion is his heart must've stopped prior to it.'

'Fuck.' Marshall shut his eyes. 'You mean he was raped after he died?'

'That, or he had consensual anal intercourse proximate with his death.'

6

'Okay, gather around!' Marshall clapped his hands together and waited for the team to obey. He stood outside the rear entrance to the museum, which was even grander than the front. At least someone had been able to provide tea and coffee to the team.

Crawford was chatting to Kirsten, then he spotted Marshall and walked over to join them.

No Jolene or Taylor, but all the rest of them were there.

'Let's get out into the community.' Marshall locked eyes with Taylor, then DC Jim McIntyre, then DC Ash Paton. 'Ash, can you relieve Isla Routledge from the CSM duties?'

'Sure. Got my training in, so I'm good to go.'

'Excellent. And can we focus on finding out who this lad is and why he was here at that time of night?' Marshall pointed along the road. 'Let's go door-to-door in this area. Crawford, can you take lead on that?'

'Sir.'

PC Liam Warner sidled up like he belonged there.

Marshall ignored him. 'We've got some hold-back evidence, but that's on a need-to-know basis.'

Warner frowned. 'What is it, sir?'

'You don't need to know.' Marshall paused while the unintentional laughter subsided. 'The killer carved some messages onto the victim's body. Only six of us have seen what was written, so I'm keeping it that way, as far as possible. Taylor, you're in charge of collating and assessing all of that.'

'So I'll be the seventh?' Taylor nodded. 'Sure thing, boss.'

Warner was still frowning. 'Why are we not to know, sir?'

Marshall walked over to him, frustration building in his guts. 'We're holding back the actual text written on his flesh, Constable, because only the killer will know exactly what was carved.'

Warner shrugged. 'Right, and?'

'So when the first nutter comes forward claiming to have done it, we can ask them what words were left at the crime scene and what they were written in.'

'Okay, so that means it's a double hold-back, right? The carving and the actual text. Got you.'

'And can you forget I said any of that, please?' Marshall looked around the team. 'Don't go spouting off about that to the public or any witnesses. Am I clear?'

They all nodded as they sipped tea and coffee.

Warner snorted. 'You say that like I'm an idiot.'

Marshall didn't know what to say. 'Constable, I thought you were supposed to be manning the—'

'Rob!' Jolene ran over, waving a tablet in the air. 'Forensics have found a wallet near the body. The photo on the driver's licence seems to match the victim.'

Marshall took the tablet from her and inspected the photo of his ID. Subtract the duct tape on his mouth and eyes, and they had a very good match.

'Kid's seventeen. Name of Jake Turner.'

7

Jolene followed Marshall's car through Hawick as though they were heading back up the A7 to Galashiels and home, but he took the right turn towards Burnfoot. Post-war council houses marched up the hills, facing south to give a glorious view of the Cheviots – at least, they would on a day with better weather than today.

Marshall pulled in behind a red MG SUV and was out and walking by the time she'd even parked.

Jolene managed to catch up with him by the gap in the wall that led up to a pair of cottages. The path had other ideas, though, and kept going to serve two other semi-detached houses. Must be a right bugger lugging up a week's shopping from the parking bay.

Marshall took the path to the best house in a bad street. The others had rough harling, but this one had been rendered in a white bright enough to hurt the eyes, even in today's conditions.

She finally caught up with him at the gate. 'Hate this place.'

Bloody hell, she was out of breath.

Marshall frowned at her. 'What, Hawick?'

'No, Burnfoot. It's Hawick's Langlee.'

'Langlee...' Marshall laughed. 'People should try working in London, then comparing that with those places.'

'Yeah, but the places you talk about down there have got a mishmash of people and are in a massive city. This is in a small town in the middle of nowhere. These people have lived here forever. It's a really tight network. They don't like people from outside coming in. Especially cops.'

'My point is, it's not that bad.' Marshall pointed at the address. 'You can lead in here. I'm just a senior investigating officer.'

'Does that mean I'm the deputy?'

'Cal should be, but for continuity's sake, I can't have a part-time deputy, can I?' Marshall shot her a wink. 'So, aye. You're the deputy.'

'Cool. Thanks.' Jolene felt a tingle of something – satisfaction maybe? 'Guessing that means I've got to attend the post mortem?'

'And all that fun stuff. You want the rank, Jo, you have to do the crappy work that comes with it.' Marshall pressed the Ring doorbell.

It chimed inside.

Jolene peered in the front window but couldn't see any movement. She spotted a couple of other security cameras, though, all pointing outwards.

The door opened and a woman scowled out at them. 'Aye?'

'Police. We're looking for Tracy Turner.'

'And you are?'

'DI Jolene Archer.' She gave a flash of her warrant card. 'This is DCI Rob Marshall.'

'Right.' She folded her arms. 'Have you found him, then?'

Jolene glanced behind her. 'We should do this inside.'

'Shite.' Tracy shifted her gaze between them. 'Is he dead?'
'I said we should—'
'No…' Tracy slid down the wall. 'No, no, no…'

8

The TV dominated the living room, with Sky News playing – the ticker scrolled along the bottom of the screen as a man stood in an airport, talking to camera. The room itself was well decorated, with everything matched perfectly. Just that monster TV. Jolene thought it might've been sixty-five inches, in a room that could handle maybe forty-five at most.

Marshall stood by the window, looking south across the town towards the hills. Just a load of grey shapes on a day like this.

'We just thought he'd...' Tracy sobbed quietly on the sofa. 'Stayed with a pal, you know?'

'I understand, Tracy.' Jolene sat on an armchair, legs crossed, notebook on her lap. 'We need to speak to Jake's father.'

'I called him, but... He's working in his garage. Doesn't often hear the phone.'

The door opened and a big man walked in, rubbing a rag on his hands. He stood there, shifting his gaze between them. He held out an oily hand to Marshall. 'Paul Turner.'

Marshall shook it, despite the grime. 'Motorbike, aye?'

'Right. Got a Honda in a garage around the corner. Thing's older than my boy.' Paul rubbed at his eyes. 'So he was murdered?'

'I'm afraid so.'

'How?'

'He was stabbed.'

'Jesus Christ. And it's definitely him?'

'His identification matches, so there's no doubt in our minds.' Marshall nodded. 'But we'll need one of you to confirm that.'

'Happy to.' Paul grimaced as he sat next to his wife. 'Well. Never want to do a thing like that, do you? But... Aye. We'll do it.'

'I hate this.' Tracy leaned into him. 'We reported him missing first thing this morning. Still haven't spoken to anyone. How's that right?'

'I'm sorry. That's not our department, but we'll have a word with our colleagues there.'

'Make sure you do that.'

Jolene planted her feet on the floor and leaned forward. 'Has Jake ever gone missing like this before?'

'Not like that, no.'

'But he has?'

'A few times, aye.' Tracy shook her head. 'He's been away until, like, three or four in the morning, but never overnight.'

'Jake's a right bugger.' Paul held his wife tight. 'Ever since he was six or seven... he's been hard to contain. And since he was eleven, he'd run off most nights. Cause hell in the town.'

'Doing what?'

'Just the usual, you know?'

'What does the usual entail?'

'Ach, you ken? Always on the edge of trouble but never deep in it. You lot brought him home a few times... Just hanging out with his pals. Boys will be boys and all that. Never knew who with. I was exactly the same at his age, then I got into motorbikes.'

Tracy dabbed at her eyes. 'But he'd always return. Always.' She stared into space. 'And then he didn't…'

'No.' Paul wrapped her hands in both of his. 'So we called it in. Thought you'd find him in some lassie's bed…'

'I'm sorry.' Jolene's forehead creased. 'This must be incredibly difficult, but we have some questions—'

'You've no idea, hen. No idea at all.' Paul breathed out slowly. 'You got kids?'

'A boy.'

'Then I hope you never feel like this.'

Jolene smiled, but her eyebrows remained locked in a frown. 'Jake's body was found at Hawick Museum in Wilt—'

'I know the place.' Paul let go of his wife's hands. 'Why the hell was he there?'

'I was going to ask you the same question.'

'Right. Well, I took him once there when he was eight. Never seen anyone so bored in their puff.'

'So there's no significance attached to that place?'

'None whatsoever.' Paul looked at his wife. 'Right?'

'Didn't even know you'd taken him there…'

'It was after your dad got taken into hospital.'

'Right…'

Jolene waited for them to stop looking at each other. 'Do you mind me asking what you do for a living?'

'Tracy here's a hairdresser. I own a quarry.'

Jolene frowned. 'A quarry?'

'Aye. Not a big one, mind. Wee place, just outside Lilliesleaf.'

'I know it. Between Hawick and Selkirk. Hard business, right?'

'And then some. We're trying to sell up but nobody wants to buy.'

'I want to see him.' Tracy scowled at Jolene. 'I need to see his body.'

Jolene gave her a nod. 'I'll take you to see him in hospital once he's ready.'

'When's that going to be?'

'It'll be a few hours, I'm afraid.'

'And we can't see him until then?'

'I'm afraid not, no... Our pathologist needs to do a lot of preparation work beforehand, not to mention the forensic analysis required at the location.' Jolene gave them a patient look. 'As the parents of a murder victim, we can appoint a family liaison officer, who—'

Paul narrowed his eyes. 'What's one of them?'

'They're specialist officers who... Well, they liaise between the family and the investigation team. A single point of contact for you. They can provide guidance and counselling to—'

'Can't you do that?'

'I'm part of the team investigating his murder, sir.' Jolene nodded along with her words. 'An FLO is specially trained for this kind of matter. They can provide great comfort in times like this.'

'Don't need that.' Paul looked at his wife. 'Do we?'

Tracy shook her head.

'See?' Paul stared hard at her. 'If you ask me what I need, all I want is five minutes in a room with the prick who did this to our boy.'

'We're working on identifying who that is, sir. And your help in the matter will accelerate things.'

Tracy sat back on the sofa, folding her arms. 'What do you want to know?'

'This might sound a wee bit odd.' Jolene stared at Tracy,

reflecting her intensity back at her. 'Did Jake have something he might've regretted?'

'Regret?' Paul barked out a laugh. '*Eh?*'

'Did he do something to cause him regret? Or someone else?'

'Not that I can think of.' Tracy shrugged. 'Why?'

Jolene waited, not answering it. 'Was your son homosexual?'

Paul's eyes bulged. 'Eh?' He spat it out.

'Was he—'

'I heard what you said, darling, but my boy was straight. Why are you asking, eh?'

'It's possible the motivation for the murder was—'

'No. No way.' Paul collapsed into the sofa. To an old-fashioned alpha male like Paul Turner, the concept of his son being gay hit him like a hammer. 'No fucking way.'

Jolene sat there, waiting for him to process it.

'As far as we know, that wasn't his thing.' Tracy stared up at the ceiling. 'But we maybe don't know him as well as we thought... Clearly didn't.'

Paul glowered at her. 'Fuck's that supposed to mean?'

Tracy glanced at her husband. 'Remember Blake, right?'

'Aye, I fucking remember Blake.' Paul focused on Jolene. 'One of his friends from school. Blake Langlands. He's... that way inclined. We had to talk to Jake to find out he wasn't.' He laughed. 'Wee sod played along, saying he was in love with the laddie, but it was just to wind us up. He was a bugger, but not in that way.'

'When you say bugg—'

'Just a cheeky wee sod.' Paul jabbed a finger at her. 'He never did anything too bad, alright? That we know of. And Hawick's that kind of town where you'd hear pretty much before he'd done it.'

Jolene nodded. 'Is Jake still at school?'

'Doing his Highers in the summer.'

'And he's seventeen?'

'Aye. Oldest in the year.' Tracy fidgeted with something, but Jolene couldn't see what it was. 'Can I have his mobile phone?'

'Why?'

'It cost a lot. Got him it for Christmas. Plus…' Tracy sighed. 'Jake was always taking selfies. We'll need a few of them blown up for the funeral and the wake. And I want to build a website to him.'

'I understand that.' Jolene gave her a kind smile. 'I'm afraid his mobile hasn't been recovered.'

'Eh?' Paul lurched forward. 'You saying his killer took it?'

'We don't know. But that's a possibility.'

Paul looked at Tracy. 'Fucking hell.'

It was Tracy's turn to comfort her husband, wrapping her hands around his. 'Had his phone on him all the time.'

'Aye. Aye, he did. Constantly.'

They sat in uncomfortable silence for a few long moments.

Jolene shifted her gaze between them, the feeling of discomfort growing with each passing second. 'What aren't you telling us?'

Paul looked at Tracy, got a shrug, then threw his hands up in the air.

'There's a reason he's only doing his Highers now.' Tracy bit her bottom lip. 'Jake had to repeat a year… Third year. First of his Nat 5s.'

Paul flared his nostrils. 'The daft wee sod got a lassie pregnant, didn't he?'

9

Despite the rain, the Aldi car park was rammed full of upmarket cars. Maybe because of it – get the shopping out of the way.

Marshall parked behind Jolene and got out, just in time for it to start absolutely chucking it down.

Jolene raced over to the store and slipped inside.

Marshall followed at a casual pace – he didn't mind the rain and didn't want to run.

Jolene waited inside the door, wringing her hair like she'd been swimming. She led off through the store, though it seemed like the lights weren't working.

Only a couple of people were smart enough to use their phone torches to search for their products.

Jolene switched hers on and lit up the floor in front of them. 'Feels daft us both driving, but I'll have to go and pick them up, won't I?'

'Soon as Leye calls, aye.'

'Could be any time, though. Could be tomorrow.' Jolene walked over to a man in a store uniform. 'Excuse me, are you the manager here?'

'Kenny is, but this is his day off. Bloody typical the lights would go off, eh? Shouldn't be open but the bosses told me to open up. So here we are.' He smiled. 'Anyway. How can I help?'

'Police, sir. Looking for Casey?'

He rolled his eyes. 'What's she done?'

'Nothing, sir. Just need a word.'

No way did he believe that. 'She's working on the tills the now.' He shifted his gaze between them. 'I'll relieve her.' He walked over to the till and spoke in her ear.

Casey got up and walked over, arms crossed.

Behind, her boss started scanning and chatting to the customers.

Casey sidled up to them. She looked young – barely fifteen, let alone eighteen. Pale skin and small, she seemed to sink into the uniform rather than wear it. 'Mickey said you're cops?'

'DI Jolene Archer.' She showed her warrant card. 'Just need a wee word with you, then you can get back to it.'

Casey glanced over at the door. 'Mind if we do this outside?'

'It's raining cats and dogs.'

Casey shrugged. 'Dying for a smoke.'

'Sure.' Jolene smiled. 'Lead on.'

Casey couldn't move fast enough as she led them outside, pulling out a vape stick and puffing away before she got out the front door. She exhaled as it opened, then stood under the lip of the roof and glared back inside the store. 'That prick's looking for any excuse to do me.'

Marshall frowned. 'Your manager?'

'Mickey's not the boss. Just thinks he is.' Casey looked Marshall up and down. Her eyes were heavily lined – she looked exhausted, like she'd been up all night… She shifted her focus to Jolene. 'So then, DI Jolene Archer. What's this about?'

'We gather you're acquainted with one Jake Turner.'

Casey sucked hard on her vape stick. Then let it out slowly. 'What's he done?'

'We gather you and he were—'

'He knocked me up, aye.' Casey clenched her jaw tight. 'Dropped out of uni because of it.'

Marshall scowled at her. 'But that was a few years ago, wasn't it?'

'Right.' She took another puff. 'Aye.'

'You were fifteen and he was fourteen?'

'Thing is… I buried the trauma. At least, that's what my therapist said I did. I was way too young to have sex. And Jake… He was younger, but he was experienced. That wasn't his first rodeo by a long shot.' Casey took another toot on her vape stick. 'And I'm the one who got pregnant.'

'That's what happens, isn't it?' Jolene nodded along. 'We're the ones who get saddled with the bairns.'

Casey eyed her suspiciously.

Marshall broke the glare. 'Can you tell us what happened?'

'What's there to say?' Casey put her vape stick away in her pocket again. 'When two people love each other very much, they have a very special cuddle.'

'Very funny.' Jolene beamed wide. 'But were you in a relationship, aye?'

'If you can call it that.' Casey shrugged. 'We snogged a few times. Then… He was in with this crowd of older people and they were having a party. Took me and my pal, Kelly, along. Jake wanted a threesome but she wasn't up for it.'

'Were you?'

'Hardly.' Casey got out her vape again and tooted, the damp air misting with the taste of blueberries. 'And we had sex. Just me and him. And after, I realised he hadn't used a condom.' She stared at Jolene. 'You ever hear of stealthing?'

'Where they sneakily take a condom off partway through?'

'Right.' Casey gave a sour look. 'Fuck me, he must be carrying a loaded weapon because I was pretty much immediately throwing up. Told my dad and he took me to the clinic.'

Marshall waited to see if there was anything else, but Casey was just focused on her vaping. 'Did you tell Jake?'

'Of course I did. He wanted to keep it.' She laughed, shaking her head. 'But I couldn't. How the hell could I? And it's my choice, right? But it ruined my head.' She stared up at the sky, wrapping her arms around her torso and drumming her fingers off her arms. 'What I said about burying it... I went to Glasgow uni last year but... Drinking a bottle of vodka every night wasn't helping myself, was it?'

Marshall held the gaze – she would've been in the same year as his niece. 'Sorry to hear that, Casey.'

'I'm better now. Had therapy for it and it's starting to clear my head. I'm going back to uni next year.'

'Back to Glasgow?'

'That's the plan, anyway.' Casey gave a flash of her eyebrows. 'I'll have to redo my first year but actually attending lectures and not drinking every night will be a start.' She tugged her ponytail loose and let her hair hang free. Made her seem that bit older. 'Nothing prepares you for what you'll feel after you let your baby go. I mean, it wasn't an option. Couldn't be... But still...'

Jolene held her gaze. 'I understand.'

'Do you?'

'I wasn't much older than you.'

Casey looked away, then gave her a long look. 'It sucks, doesn't it?'

'It's awful. But I've got a son now. Joe. And he really helps.'

'Wait a sec...' Casey smirked. 'Joe and Jolene?'

'Husband's called Joe too.' Jolene gave a flash of her eyebrows. 'Big Joe and Wee Joe. Seemed like a good idea at the time... Trouble is, you don't fall in love with someone because of their name, do you?'

'True enough.' Casey held her vape stick in front of her lips. 'I want to be a mum someday. Just not now.'

Marshall felt the air thicken – not just with the blueberry vape, but with the sharing of deep truths. Jolene seemed a bit shaken by it.

Casey focused on Jolene. 'Thing is, I blame myself. Not him. I wanted to do it... I was desperate to... to pop my cherry, you know?' She shook her head. 'So stupid. I wouldn't do it now without being on the pill myself *and* with him wearing a condom. Can't trust boys, can you?'

'We're not all bad.' Marshall winced. 'But I wouldn't trust many of them. And stealthing is a crime.'

Casey frowned. 'Is that why you're here?'

'Sorry, no.' Marshall looked away from her, then fixed her with a hard look. 'We found Jake's body this morning.'

'Fuck.' Casey dropped her vape pen. 'Fuck.' She bent over to pick it up.

Then fell over.

She sat there, staring into space.

'I liked him.' She ran a hand through her hair. 'When I was fifteen. But everything was transactional with him.'

Marshall crouched and picked up her vape stick. 'What do you mean by that, Casey?'

'I mean...' Casey took her vape back but didn't stand up. 'I mean he was the most selfish person I've ever met. And I've been to university.'

Marshall smiled at that. 'Here.' He offered a hand.

Casey looked at it, then finally took his hand and let him winch her up to standing. 'Thank you.'

'Do you mind me asking where you were last night between ten o'clock and two?'

'Are you asking me for an alibi?'

'Do you have one?'

'I do.' Casey smiled. 'I was working here.' She pointed inside the shop. 'Doing a stocktake last night.'

'But you're working here today?'

'Brutal, right? Finished at four. Home for some kip, then back on ten minutes ago.' Casey thumbed inside. 'Manager can give you the CCTV.' She winced. 'Just don't ask Mickey.'

'Why, were you doing something you shouldn't on the CCTV?'

'No.' Casey gave another wince. 'Actually, can you tell him I've been helpful?'

'Sure.' Jolene smiled. 'If you keep being helpful.'

Casey shifted her gaze between them again.

'When did you last see Jake?'

'Not for a couple of years.'

'After this incident with—'

'My abortion, you mean?' Casey gave her a stern look. 'I'm owning it. Okay?' She took another suck on her vape stick. 'I didn't hear from *him* after that. Just dropped me like a stone.' She then inspected the stick and rubbed something off the end. 'Actually. That's a lie. I saw him in the shop a few months ago. He was seeing this girl, Emily? She works here. And...' She ran a hand through her hair. 'And he was being sexually aggressive with her.'

Marshall frowned. 'Sexually aggressive how?'

'They were in the freezer section and he was feeling her up.'

'You saw this?'

'The manager got him to clear off. Threatened to call the cops.'

'And did he?'

'Jake? Aye. He did.'

'But?'

'But nothing. He didn't grass on Emily, even though she was seeing him.'

'Do you know her?'

'She's good people.'

The American phrase jarred with the Hawick accent. 'Does she know?'

'About what happened between me and Jake?' Casey nodded, scowling. 'I tried warning her off. Subtly. But Emily said they were in love. Turns out as soon as he'd taken *her* virginity, he was gone.'

'Sounds rough, Casey.'

'It's the game he plays, right?' Casey grimaced again. 'Look, it's weird, but if he asked me again, I would. What the fuck is that all about?'

Marshall had a few ideas, but all of them took him down a path that wouldn't lead to their killer. 'Any idea who might've done this?'

'I heard a story about him. Someone else who works here told me.' Casey narrowed her eyes. 'Said he'd got into something with a teacher.'

'Something sexual?'

'Who knows. With him, it could've been. But I heard it was a male teacher.'

Marshall let out a gasp. The homophobic slurs scratched into Jake's skin... 'Do you know what happened?'

'Sorry. Just something like this teacher did something inappropriate. That's what I heard.' Casey focused on Jolene through a cloud of blue mist. 'You mind if I go back to work now?'

10

Jolene slowed for the roundabout. Right along Buccleuch Street was quiet, but she went left and pulled up on the double yellows outside the hardware shop.

McVicar Home & Hardware.

One that mercifully didn't belong to Gary Hislop. A real outlier in the area.

It looked open, just a pair of old men chatting outside.

Jolene put out her 'OFFICIAL POLICE BUSINESS' sign, then sat there, checking through her messages.

Feeling that dull ache in her stomach.

Why had she told Casey that? And in front of Marshall, of all people?

He was a good guy and someone she'd got close to in her acting-up stint, but sometimes you just needed to keep a secret.

A hard knock on the window.

McIntyre was peering in, hand raised.

Jolene put her phone away and got out into the drizzle. 'Thanks for meeting me here, Jim.'

'Not a problem. Ash said she's meeting Rob at the school,

right?' He left a pause but she didn't fill it. 'What do you need from me?'

'Just need you to stand there and look pretty.'

McIntyre laughed. 'Not sure I can do that, Sarge.'

Jolene climbed the steps and opened the door. The bell chimed as she stepped inside.

A rough old shop, stinking of wood, glue and sawdust. Tuneless free jazz played out of giant speakers facing the tills like they'd been expertly placed to give the perfect sound to the man standing behind the counter.

Eyes closed, nodding in time to the music. Or what passed for it – the kind of atonal squawking and honking Jolene's dad would love.

She walked over to the counter. 'Karl McVicar?'

He opened his eyes and inspected them. He gave McIntyre a tight nod. 'Morning, Jim.'

'Karl.' McIntyre smiled. 'Windows still intact?'

'For now.' McVicar picked up a remote and turned down the music. 'Odd how you never caught the wee bastards that did it. Or the big one.'

'Hard to do that these days.'

'Even with all these cameras everywhere?'

'No. I didn't mean that.'

'Oh, you mean my competitor. The one who keeps trying to buy me out.' McVicar rolled his eyes. 'Aye, I know what you mean.' He tapped his nose. 'I'm hoping this visit is about Mr Hislop.'

Jolene rested her fingers on the counter. 'This is about Casey.'

McVicar stood up tall, but the truth was he was smaller than both of them. A good few inches shorter than Jolene, while McIntyre had over a foot on him. 'What's she done?'

'Nothing.'

'So why are you here?'

'To ask you about Jake Turner.'

'Fuck me. There's a name I've not heard in a while.'

'You know him, then?'

'Aye…' McVicar took a moment, then let out a deep breath. 'You got any kids?'

Jolene nodded. 'A lad.'

'Well, if you had a daughter, you'd make sure you knew all about the little fucking arsehole who'd knocked her up, wouldn't you?'

'We heard about that.'

'Such a… Jake's a wee bastard. Pestered her for sex for ages. And she finally gave in.' McVicar shook his head. 'Wee bastard was a year younger than her too. Took her to a party with a pal when I was away for a weekend. Her gran thought she was at Kelly's but nope. Kelly took Casey along to this party, armed with a bottle of vodka. And she got off her skull.'

'Wasn't your wife there?'

'Hard to. She's dead.'

'I'm sorry to hear that, sir.'

'You're not, but I'll take it.'

Jolene gave him an understanding look – or what would've passed for one. 'That whole thing must've been tough for you.'

'Worse for her, believe you me. *Way* worse. And I'd do anything for my girl. If she wanted to raise the bairn, I would've supported her.'

'But she didn't.'

'Nope. Sat with her while it…' McVicar swallowed hard. 'While it happened.' He swallowed again. 'Hard isn't how I'd describe it. Emotional, sure. Conflicting, aye. Just… awful. Casey was fifteen and pregnant.' He picked up his remote and looked at it, then turned the music down another notch. 'I don't judge the lassies who are in that situation, but it's hard not to feel like I'd completely failed her, you know? You want the best for your kid, but I... I let her down. Failed her. I'd kind of fallen apart after Liz died. First to admit how badly I struggled.' He waved around the space. 'This place almost went to the wall. That's why I want to resist that arsehole Hislop – rebuilding this business was the same thing to me as rebuilding my life.'

Jolene frowned at him. 'What do you mean resist?'

'Keeps offering to buy me out, doesn't he? Increases the offer every time. But I'm a stubborn sod.' McVicar looked at McIntyre then back at Jolene. 'Is Jake working for him, or something?'

Jolene shook her head. 'Jake Turner was murdered last night.'

'Fuck. It wasn't me.'

McIntyre raised his eyebrows. 'Big boy did it and ran away, right?'

'Of course not.' McVicar walked through the shop over to a CD rack. He picked out a Miles Davis album and put it in the stereo. Softer jazz started playing, more tuneful than the atonal stuff from before. 'When are you talking?'

'Around midnight. Plus or minus a couple of hours.'

'In that case, it definitely wasn't me. I was at the jazz club. The one on Chambers Street.'

'Up in Edinburgh?'

'Right. Seeing this band called Blue Giant Orkestar.'

'Blue Giant Orchestra?'

'No.' McVicar pulled out a CD and handed it over. 'Orkestar.'

'Never heard of them.'

'They're really good. Mate's the percussionist in the band. Sort of Balkan folk with a lot of jazz and a bit of metal.'

'When were you there?'

'Got there about ten.'

'At night?'

'Aye. Left about three in the morning.'

'You got any way to prove this?'

'My pal Frazer drove us there and back. I was a bit worse for wear.' McVicar sniffed. 'Today's been a bit of challenge, I have to say.'

McIntyre smiled. 'You got his number?'

11

DC Ash Paton kept pace with Marshall as they walked along the school corridor.

The lunch break chaos was in full flow, tons of kids fucking about in the dinner queue. Not quite a big food fight, but a pair of kids looked ready to start one. Standing there armed with half-eaten burgers.

Another had a fellow student in a headlock.

Maria Ferguson whistled, fingers in her mouth. 'Jayden Harrison! Alfie Simpson! Stop that!'

They dropped their burgers on the floor.

Marshall raised his hands. 'Listen, we can come back later.'

'No, it's fine.' Ferguson whistled again. 'Jack! Let him go first!'

The headlock was released and the lads moved to different tables.

The girls weren't getting involved in that, instead sitting at tables at the far end.

'Noah! I've told you!' Ferguson opened the door to a room at the side of the dining hall. 'In here.'

Marshall let Ash go first, then joined her. First problem was the room was tiny. Second was it had only two chairs. He let them take them and took up a position just by the door, not that it was possible to get far from it.

'Very gentlemanly.' Ferguson took her seat, shaking her head at Marshall in a knowing way. 'So, someone's been arrested, right?' She narrowed her eyes. 'Jake Turner?'

Marshall frowned. 'Is that just an educated guess?'

'I wish.' Ferguson sighed. 'No. It is him, right?'

'Why do you think that?'

'I go through the absence register every morning. Way fewer kids on there than there used to be. Attendance figures are up, which is all the politicians care about, but the troubled kids aren't getting any help, so all they do is come to school and wander the grounds or the school corridors. We call them lappers, because they just do laps of the school. And we can't do anything to them. Can't expel them nowadays.' Ferguson shook her head again. 'All I can do is pretend I'm in control of anything, so I pore through the list of absentees. When I saw Jake was off, it made me wonder.'

Marshall stepped closer and spoke in a low tone. 'We found his body earlier.'

Ferguson nodded slowly. 'It's definitely him?'

'Definitely. His parents reported him missing and we found his identification documents nearby.' Marshall could only offer a shrug. 'His parents have yet to identify him but we're sure it's him.'

'Fuck.' Ferguson looked around the lunch queue, but didn't seem to be focusing on anything. 'Was it an accident?'

Marshall shook his head. 'He was murdered.'

'Bloody hell. In Hawick?' Ferguson let out a sigh. 'Where was he found?'

'Hawick Museum.'

Ferguson scowled. 'Why *there*?'

'We don't know. We've got a few questions to ask.'

She raised her eyebrows. 'You want an alibi?'

'For you?'

'Sure.' Ferguson shrugged again. 'I was with a gentleman.'

'A gentleman?'

'Sounds better than a hook-up from Tinder.'

'Relax. You're not a suspect.'

'Just wanted someone to know I don't just do this job all the time. Feels like it. I mean, I'm in here at six every morning. Some nights, I'm lucky enough to get away and let someone smash my back doors in.' Ferguson rolled her eyes. 'You going to tell me what Jake did?'

'What do you mean?'

'Someone's killed him. Got to be a reason. Why do you think he was killed?'

'Our inquiries have only just started.'

'But you're here.'

'Right. We wanted to ask you about the pregnancy, though.'

Ferguson looked away, sighing again. 'Casey. Right.'

'So you were aware of it?'

'Sure. But the matter was between the two kids and their parents. Casey was a good girl. Smart. But that… He was pushy. Precocious as hell. Casey was smart, academically minded, but a bit naive. And in that situation, it's the girls who pay the price.'

'I gather Jake went off the rails?'

'Jake…' Another shake of her head. 'He was never on them. But yeah, he had to repeat the year, so a different set of kids had to endure him.'

'You don't talk positively about him.'

'Hard to. That wasn't the first time he'd been in trouble on that score. As far as I know, he's been sexually active since he was thirteen. Probably before that even. Boggles the mind, doesn't it?'

'How do you know that?'

'Us teachers might seem like statues but we're not. We listen. And we talk to each other.' Ferguson scowled. 'I mean, I lost my virginity when I was twenty. More than made up for it since. But Jake Turner? He was fourteen when he got her pregnant. And he was already very experienced.' She laughed. '*Fourteen.*'

'Do you know if he still—'

'—fucks anything that walks? Of course. Leopards don't change their spots. Some kids just rush through life, you know? Live eighty years in their first twenty. But then there's nowhere to go. Except prison.' She laughed again. 'Casey didn't let it knock her back, though. She left last year and went to uni in Glasgow. Do you need me to look up her details?'

'We've spoken to her, as well.'

Ferguson frowned. 'So why are you here?'

'She told us she dropped out of university because of what happened.'

'Ah, fuck.' She swallowed hard. 'Well, we can't win them all. No matter how hard we try.'

Marshall let her sit there with that sentiment for a few seconds. Poor woman was already reeling. 'The other reason we're here is we gather there was an incident between Jake and a teacher.'

Ferguson looked up at the sky through the skylight. Muttering something. Then over at Marshall. 'Did Casey tell you that?'

'I'm not going to confirm that.'

'But it was...' Ferguson gave him a sour look. 'What have you heard?'

'Just that there was an allegation of a teacher sexually assaulting a student. A male teacher. Caused some sort of controversy. Was Jake the victim?'

'God, no.' Ferguson barked out a nervous laugh. 'I mean, Jake was precocious but he was extremely heterosexual.'

'You're sure about that?'

'Oh, who knows these days? But I think if he was so inclined we'd have heard all about it. And we had lots of issues with him on that score.' Ferguson took a deep breath. 'The teacher was Christopher Goodwillie. He was Head of History.'

'Was?' Marshall frowned. 'Was he sacked? Or is he dead?'

'You're a smart cookie, Chief Inspector.' Ferguson clicked her tongue as she wagged a finger at him. 'He's neither. There was an investigation into the allegation. He was suspended with pay. And if you want more, you'll need a warrant.'

'Jake was murdered.' Marshall held her stare. 'This is incredibly serious.'

'So? You have your rules, I have mine. I have to protect my staff and students.' Ferguson rested her hands on her hips. 'Hate the game, not the player.'

'Listen, we'll get the details one way or another. But it'd look much better for you if you just told us it straight.'

'Tough guy, eh? Listen, I spend the day outnumbered by teens, so you don't frighten me. At all. This isn't something I can tell you straight. It's an extremely sensitive matter and was never officially signed off. In my position, it would be an ethics breach.' Ferguson gave a subtle wink. 'But if you were to, say, charm my secretary and persuade her to help you... I wouldn't hear about it. She might not know the details, but she could maybe give you the address...'

12

Marshall took the turning before the garage – the opposite way from the shortcut he'd sometimes take to avoid the embuggerment of the A7 going through the heart of Selkirk. He'd found out to his cost this shortcut only worked in one direction, but today he only needed it to access an address along the first turning on the right.

A long row of post-war houses, maybe even Sixties, but around here the decades didn't seem to work like they did elsewhere. Low-slung bungalows with big plots, way more generous than anything built nowadays, and each had their own little quirky extensions at either side – or even above.

'I think...' Ash pointed to the left. 'Think that's it there, sir.'

And the big clue was Jolene's pool car idling by the pavement.

Marshall pulled up behind it. 'Thank you, Constable. That was useful.'

'But I didn't do anything?'

'Your presence was a big help.'

'Sounds like nonsense, sir, but I'll take the compliment.'

Ash gave a smile then got out and held the door for Jolene as they swapped places.

Seconds later, the car whizzed away and McIntyre gave Marshall a curt wave as they headed off.

Marshall killed the engine and got out. 'How did it go with Casey's folks?'

Jolene stood on the pavement, fiddling with her phone. She stopped as he approached. 'Mum's dead. But the dad… Not sure, Rob, but he could have a motive.'

'Anger at what happened between Jake and his daughter?' Marshall waited for her to nod. 'But?'

'But he has an alibi.' Jolene let out a deep breath, misting in the cold air. 'I've asked Jim to investigate it.' She gave a flick of the wrist. 'He's heading up to Gala now to check.'

'Good. Well, not good, but you know what I mean.' Marshall checked out the address they'd been given for Christopher Goodwillie.

Seemingly the only bungalow in the street left untouched or un-extended, if that was a word. The front garden had been paved over, the only feature a quaint bird fountain. Not that any birds were bothering today. The 'For Sale' sign wedged in the barren flowerbed was ominous, though.

Marshall led up the drive and knocked on the door.

The whole street was quiet, but this house seemed to suck in sound like a sonic black hole. The front window looked in on a living room set up to minimise hassle during a sale. Two chocolate-coloured leather sofas forming an L in front of a small TV on an oak unit. Pictures of seaside landscapes, regardless of how far Selkirk was from the coast.

'Nobody in.' Marshall sighed. 'Great.'

Jolene hopped over the wall and walked across the pebbled path to the neighbour's door. She knocked and it was answered by the time Marshall had joined her.

An older woman stood there, fists on her hips, eyes scanning them. 'Can I help, darling?'

Jolene was smiling away. 'Hi, just wondering if you've seen your neighbour today?'

Marshall's presence seemed to make her stiffen, those fists on her hips clench. 'Sorry, who are you?'

'Police.' Jolene showed her warrant card. 'We're looking for Christopher Goodwillie. He lives next door, right?'

'He does, aye.' The neighbour snatched the warrant card off her and gave it a good going over. Took a few seconds before she handed it back. 'I'm afraid Chris is living with his parents.'

Marshall let out a groan – they'd been sold a pup here. Then again, Maria Ferguson shouldn't have passed anything on to them, so he had to be grateful for the precious little they had been given.

Jolene still smiled, though. 'And do you know where they live?'

The neighbour pointed across the road. 'Over there.' She shut the door and bolts started slotting into place.

Marshall followed Jolene over the road to a house the same size, but with a converted loft and a metal-framed conservatory on the side. Two Renaults parked outside, a giant SUV and a little run-around, like mother and child.

She walked up the path and knocked on the door.

Music played out, that old Steppenwolf song. Someone was singing along, almost in tune.

The door opened and a big man loomed there. Tall and rugged, probably in his mid-sixties. His ginger hair had faded to straw, with silver threaded through it.

Jolene gave him a smile. 'Hi, we're looking for Christopher Goodwillie.'

The man glowered at her. 'Mind telling me your rank?'

'My rank?'

'Cops, right?' He shifted his gaze between them, grinning slightly. 'Just trying to gauge how serious this is.'

'DI Jolene Archer.' She still had her warrant card in her hand from across the road, but he didn't seem to want to take it. 'This is DCI Rob Marshall.'

Marshall flashed a smile at him. 'Were you in the job, sir?'

'Aye, but a better one.' He snorted, then humour filled his eyes. 'Hugh Goodwillie. I was a fireman for thirty-five years. Watch commander in Gala. Retired now, mind.'

'Ah, I see.' Jolene pocketed her ID. 'So if we could—'

'I was the commander at that big fire back in 2012.'

'I remember it.' Marshall nodded. Truth was, he'd been nowhere near the Borders at the time, but guys like him lived to share war stories and by sharing, Marshall might get him to open up. Might. 'Must've been bloody tough.'

'Tell you, man, it was brutal. Never got to the bottom of how it started. Worked with some of your lot to investigate.' He frowned. 'Lad called Pringle? Jim, I think.'

'My old boss.' Marshall had to fight to not look away. 'He's… Uh, retired now.'

'Really? Lad was quite young, wasn't he?'

'It's a long story, sir.'

'Aye. Well. Aren't they all, eh? He was a bit of a character, I have to say. Quite the character, indeed!' Hugh cleared his throat. 'But I saw the writing on the wall and got out while the going was good. Could see the way things were going when they merged the brigades together. Just like they did with Police Scotland, eh? Absolute joke, if you ask me. The old Strathclyde lot snatched the reins of power. Riddle me this, what does a daft laddie in Glasgow know about fire safety in Selkirkshire?' He looked at them like they had the answer. 'Sod all.' A wild laugh erupted from his throat. 'Suspect it's the same with your lot, eh? Not sure how that shower ended up top of the pile, but they did. And it was a mess. A total mess. Had to let some *very* good officers go just to satisfy the bean counters. The county's a lot less safe now than it was back then, let me tell you that!'

Marshall gave a conspiratorial flicker of his eyebrows. 'You have my sympathies, sir.'

'Don't get me started, mate. Weegies... They think because they're in a big city that they know everything about the job. Truth is, they don't know the first thing about rural fire management. You try telling them about getting from Gala up to Ladhope in a fire engine while a stolen car's burning out! Or about creating pond relays because there isn't an "H" sign in sight for miles. Tell you...'

Marshall held his gaze, trying to show him he knew. He *knew*. 'I take it Christopher is your son?'

'He is, aye.' Hugh swallowed something down, seeming distracted. 'What's up?'

'We were wondering if we could speak to him.'

Hugh shut his eyes, his lips twisting up. 'In you come.' He stepped aside.

Marshall followed Jolene into a hallway.

The walls were covered in crucifixes, at least seven Marshall could count. An alcove was filled with even more crosses and a Jesus figure.

Hugh showed them through into a bedroom on the ground floor.

A man sat in a chair by the window. He had his dad's red hair, undiminished by silver and violently bright. He looked over at them, but his movements were off. Slow, like he was moving underwater. Spit dribbled from his chin. He was watching children's TV on a small television.

Hugh shot over and wiped it away. 'Ah, Christopher...'

Marshall started to process it all. Why Ferguson had been so cagey, why the house over the road was up for sale... She hadn't been cagey because he'd died, but because something had happened to him, reducing the Head of History to this...' 'Sorry, sir. We didn't know.'

'Fucking scandal is what this is...' Hugh sat on the bed next to his son, then looked over at Marshall and Jolene. 'My laddie was the Head of History at Hawick High for three years. Now look at him! He's got the mental age of a six-year-old. And that's being very fucking generous.'

'Hi there.' Jolene crouched in front of Christopher, smiling with concern and empathy. She got nothing, so she shifted her focus back to his father. 'Do you mind me asking what happened?'

'Course not.' Hugh sighed. 'You want the truth?'

'We do, sir.' Jolene stood up again. 'Of course we do.'

'Hard to believe it, myself...' Hugh took a deep breath. 'Last year, this wee harlot accused him of having an inappropriate relationship with her.'

Marshall nodded along with it, not committing either way. 'Who was she?'

'A student. Daft wee lassie from Hawick. Nonsense. Complete nonsense.' Hugh scowled at them. 'She alleged he raped her on a school trip. And Hawick being Hawick, the rumours spread quicker than a fire across dead wood. Chris insisted he was innocent, but the school acted quicker than a cop grabbing a free cup of coffee. The headmistress put him on suspension. Despite him having done the square root of hee haw.' He was clenching and unclenching his fists. 'Ask me, she was scared shitless about the potential scandal. All anyone cares about nowadays is how things look. Bloody PR everywhere. Same with the fire service, could see where that was going. Nobody wanted to save lives anymore, just follow procedures. Guess that's what happens when you put a lassie in charge of a school like that.' He smiled at Jolene. 'No offence.'

She didn't say anything.

'Like I say, I saw a lot of that as a fireman.' Hugh held up a hand. 'Sorry, I'm being unkind here. It's nothing to do with her being a lassie. Just… Managers, you know? Reputation is everything – and everything is reputation. Especially in the Scottish Fire Service. Old Lothian and Borders, we'd rush into a burning building. Now, you have to sign umpteen forms and ask your boss to ask his boss to ask her boss to get inside, all the while you're listening to the screams of the people dying in the building.' He snorted. 'Same in the police, no doubt.'

'I'm sorry to hear all of that, sir.' Marshall left a long pause, enough to think he was in agreement with the sentiments. A lot of cops would be, but he tried to keep an open mind about things. Or just not get caught. 'Was there an investigation?'

'Aye. Christopher was suspended on full pay, of course. Trouble is, Hawick being Hawick, the court of public opinion decided much faster than the education authority, didn't it?' Hugh went over to the window and looked out onto the street. He waved his hand at the house they'd just visited. 'Christopher lived over the road. Bought his grandparents' old place when they went into a home. Lost the old man a few years ago, but the old dear's still sticking around, bless her. Still got all her marbles too. Nice to have him so close, especially for his mother.' Something seemed to die inside him – the glowing light in his eyes dimmed and his shoulders sagged. 'Then one day, he tried to kill himself. Hung himself in the shed in his back garden.' He turned back to face them. 'House is stuck on the market, though. Nobody wants to buy a ghoulish home like that, do they? Unless someone famous died in it, mind. Or they can pay bugger all for it.'

Marshall held his searing gaze. 'I'm sorry to hear that, sir.'

'But you knew all of it before you got here, didn't you?'

Marshall shook his head. 'We'd heard there was an investigation. We haven't been privy to the details. And we didn't know what had happened to your son. We're both truly sorry you've had to go through this.'

'Happened on a Sunday night too.' Hugh stared at his son for a long few seconds. 'He was supposed to be coming here for his tea, like he did most weeks, but he didn't show up. So my better half asked me to go and see if something had happened. No sign of him inside, but there was a light on in the shed. Can see it from the side, you know? And, me being me, I was never one to back away from a fight, so I charged down the path to give him a piece of my mind about letting his mother down.' He pinched his nose. 'And I found him, hanging there. He'd used this belt I'd got him for his birthday... Good, strong leather... And he was still alive, kicking and jerking. Managed to cut him down. Drove him to Borders General myself. But he'd been like that for five minutes, or so the doctor said.' He clamped his hands on his son's shoulders. 'Hypoxia left him with severe brain damage. They say he now operates at the level of a six-year-old, but I think that's stretching it. Heard it said that's the same level of intelligence as a collie dog, but you don't see him herding sheep, do you?' He barked out a laugh. 'He's thirty-five and the poor bastard is living under the care of his parents.' He gave a dismissive flick of the wrist towards the telly. 'All he can do is watch *Balamory* and *Teletubbies* on the TV.'

'That must put a strain on you.'

'Oh aye. It's brutal. Fucking brutal.' Hugh rubbed at his eyes. 'But you do it, don't you? Because it's your son.'

Marshall stood up tall. 'We needed to talk to your son in relation to an investigation, but... I think we've wasted your time.'

'Time spent chatting to like-minded folks is never wasted.'

Someone crunched up the path to the house and the front door opened.

Hugh looked out of the window. 'Ah, that's his mother. Muriel.' He led them back out into the hall.

A woman was stamping her feet on the mat and tearing off her jacket. Looked about the same age as Hugh. '*Bitter* out there.' Her silvery hair unfolded when she took off her hat. 'In you come, Pam.' She hung up her coat and let another woman into the porch.

Much younger, with long dark hair and thick glasses. A dimple on her left cheek.

'Muriel.' Hugh pointed at Marshall. 'The police are here to ask about Chris.'

'The police?' Muriel nodded slowly, but fury burnt in her eyes. Her accent was west coast, but could even be Northern Irish. 'Does that mean you're finally going to do something about what that little witch put our son through?'

Marshall frowned. 'Who are you talking about?'

'Take it that's a no, then.' Muriel shook her head. 'A pack of bloody lies, that's all it was. And look what it cost him? What it's cost us. That headmistress. Ferguson. She didn't believe a word he'd said. And he told them the truth. Didn't he, Pam?'

The woman smiled at Marshall, offering a hand. 'Pam Campbell. I'm Christopher's girlfriend.'

'DCI Rob Marshall.' He shook it but it was like shaking air – it'd been a while since he'd faced such a weak hand. 'I'm sorry about what's happened.'

'It's... We're coping with it, aren't we?' Campbell put on a fake smile as she squeezed Muriel's hand. 'Anyway, I'd better get on.' She brushed past them into Christopher's room. 'And how are we today, my darling?'

Hugh stared at the open door for a few seconds, then sparked into life. 'Muriel, you're forgetting we've got to head out again, aren't you?'

'Oh, shuffle.' Muriel bent over again and started putting her shoes back on.

Hugh reached past her to grab his coat and smiled at Marshall. 'We're speaking to our lawyer.'

'We're suing the education authority.' Muriel finished lacing up her shoes and stood tall again, though put a hand to her back. 'It's *disgusting* what they let happen to Christopher. There were scores of witnesses on that trip who told them Christopher was never alone with any student, much less a female one, and certainly not for anywhere near long enough to do what that little witch alleged he did.'

'It's a nonsense, so it is.' Hugh sucked in a deep breath. 'Going to need every pound to pay for Christopher's care, as well. Hence us selling his house. My folks lived there since it was built.' He swallowed hard. 'Christopher should be raising a family in there, just like they raised me.'

Muriel nodded along with it as she wrapped herself in her coat. 'It's been so bloody tough. We should be enjoying our retirement. Holidays and grandkids, you know? But we're stuck between generations. Hugh's mum in a care home and my mum in Ayr and Christopher here with us... reduced to *that*.'

Marshall held the door for her. 'How many grandchildren do you have?'

'Oh, none. Christopher was an only child and he never... It's just. Him and Pam never got the chance, did they?' Muriel beamed wide, but it was all a distraction from the deep trauma she faced every day. 'She's a godsend, she really is. Especially after what she's been through. Same as us, I suppose, but she's lost a future too. A life filled with love and with children.'

'Come on, woman.' Hugh patted his wife on the arm affectionately. 'We need to get going.'

13

Jolene exchanged a look with Marshall, but it was clear he was thinking the same thing as her. This house was filled with emotion – mostly anger and rage and fury – but it didn't seem to connect with their case.

Still, they needed to dot all the Is and cross the Ts, so she led him back into Christopher's room.

Pam Campbell was tending to him, dressing him in a grey checked shirt incongruous with his behaviour. She looked over at them and gave a nervous laugh. 'I'm useless at this, I have to say.' She started unbuttoning his shirt again, then doing it up the right way. 'His carer comes in once a day to clean him, but he's so messy he doesn't stay clean for long.' Her accent was local, or sufficiently local. Could be anywhere outside one of the big cities, but seemed to tend west rather than east.

Jolene rested against the windowsill and glanced out as the Goodwillies drove off in the bigger Renault. 'I'm sorry to hear about what's happened.'

'It is what it is, you know? I come here when I can. I'm a teacher, so I'm usually very busy, but I arranged two free periods on a Monday afternoon, so I could come up and help out.'

'You're at Hawick, right?'

'Aye. It's where we met. We were lovers prior to the accident.'

'Accident?'

'Incident, then.' Campbell shook her head. 'I seem to spend more time helping Hugh and Muriel as a quasi-caregiver to Christopher than at the school doing my job... And I'm just not very good at this at all.' She finished buttoning up his shirt and looked over at them. 'Do you mind if I see some credentials?'

'We showed them to Mr Goodwillie outside.'

'All the same, his eyesight's not what it used to be and he was probably boring you with his time in the fire service.' There was steel in her gaze. 'I'm sure you understand, but we've had a lot of vermin journalists here, trying to dig dirt on what happened.'

'I understand that.' Jolene handed over her warrant card again – felt like it'd been in so many hands today that forensics could have a field day grabbing prints from it. 'Was the story in the press?'

'Not so far.'

'Wouldn't it be in your favour if the story was covered?'

'Not necessarily. Who knows what agenda the newspapers have these days? Everything's so sensational now.' Campbell handed back the warrant card, then looked at Marshall. 'And you.'

Marshall handed it over with a smile but Jolene knew he'd be thinking *all* the thoughts.

Campbell took a while checking it. 'A DI and a DCI are here to ask about a failed suicide attempt? Seems like swatting a fly with a toffee hammer. No DCs or DSs free?'

'It's all part of a wider inquiry.' Jolene took Marshall's ID then passed it back to him. 'You seem to know a lot about police rank structure and procedures?'

'I listen to a lot of audiobooks and podcasts.' Campbell shrugged. 'When I started at Hawick, I had a monster commute. Lived in Edinburgh at the time and I had to travel over two hours, door to door. Bus, then train, then another bus down from Gala to Hawick. I moved to Selkirk last year and the bus is pretty quick, I have to say.'

'You don't drive?'

'Never learned. Stupid when you live around here.'

'Why not move to Hawick?'

'Have you *been* there?'

'Grew up there.'

'You've lost the accent, though.' Campbell laughed. 'I *hate* the place. Selkirk is much safer and, well... My boyfriend lives here.' She looked over at him, watching him suck his thumb. 'It's... It's been really tough, you know? I've lost my future. And I wanted to give Hugh and Muriel grandkids, but... That's not going to happen, really. Though...' She looked back at Jolene. 'I've been looking at TESA. Testicular Sperm Aspiration. Basically, extracting his sperm... That way I'll be able to give them a grandchild or two, just like me and Chris had planned.'

That seemed like an extreme step to Jolene – and she was already toiling with looking after one almost-school-age child, albeit one in the body of a full-grown man. But grief did funny things to people and maybe she'd cope with it all. Maybe even thrive. 'We're very sorry about what's happened to him. To you both. But we do need to ask a few questions about it, if you don't mind?'

'What's there to say?' Campbell looked out of the window. 'After what happened at the school, Christopher went into a spiral. It's been the most appalling time. For all of us. I'm just glad I can be here for them. For *him*.' She walked back over to Christopher and held his hand.

He didn't seem to understand, just kept watching the bright primary colours on the screen. 'Oh-oh.'

Campbell frowned at him, her face full of love – and patience. 'What's up, Chris?'

'Duck duck!'

On the screen, a cartoon mother duck and her fluffy babies walked across a road.

Marshall smiled at Campbell. 'It sounds like you're able to help lift the load from them.'

'I hope so. I try to.' Campbell narrowed her eyes at them. 'So, if this isn't a proper investigation into what happened to him, why are you here?'

Christopher waved at the screen. 'Little doggy!'

Marshall's gaze shot over to Christopher, then back to Campbell. 'We're investigating a murder.'

'Oh my God. What happened?'

Marshall took a moment. 'A body was found at Hawick Museum this morning. A young man.'

'Is it someone... I take it you're here because it's someone from school?'

'Do you know a Jake Turner?'

Campbell put her hand to her mouth. 'My God.' She had to sit down on the bed. She sat there, staring into space, shaking her head.

Jolene exchanged a look with Marshall. 'So you know him, then?'

'I'm his registration teacher. I also took him for English in his Nat 5s last year.' Campbell looked up at her. 'What happened to him?'

'I'm afraid we're not at liberty to divulge that just now.'

'Right. I see. But you *can* tell me someone's killed him?'

'I don't make the rules, unfortunately.' Jolene gave a kind smile. 'How's he been recently?'

'Jake?' Campbell blew air up her face. 'I've known him since first year. So that's, what, five years now. No, six – he had to repeat a year, didn't he? Jake... He's never been an easy kid. I mean, he's talented and smart but he lacks focus. And he's one of those precocious kids, you know? Trying to do everything far too young.' Words they'd heard said about him before. 'Jake... He... I think it came from the fact he's quite troubled. They all have their issues, especially nowadays, but Jake had a few more than most. Undiagnosed ADHD, probably. But it seemed like talking to a therapist helped him. Started to unlock his potential. I mean, I had him down as someone who'd fail his Nat 5s and leave after fourth year. What happened to him... It gave him the space to mature a bit and, in the end, he just knuckled down and got very good grades. He did it. And I was so proud of him. Sounds he was on track to do well in his Highers.'

'It sounds like you did well by him?'

'It was nothing to do with me.'

'Why did he repeat the year?'

'It was a matter... Listen, you probably better discuss that with Maria. Maria Ferguson. She's the headmistress at the school.'

'We've spoken to her.'

'I see.' Campbell shrugged. 'Listen... Circumstances were such that I couldn't bear talking with him.'

'Oh?'

'Have you heard about the investigation?'

'We have, yes.'

'Well, maybe you can understand why I couldn't... Because...' Campbell scowled. 'The girl who claimed Christopher raped her was Jake's girlfriend.' She shook her head. 'How could she do that? How could she? Christopher is a kind, gentle man, he wouldn't hurt a soul and everyone knew that. But the pack of lies Emily Borthwick told ruined him. And it's ruined my life too. And think what it's done to Hugh and Muriel.'

14

'Feels like I'm back at school.' Marshall sat in the waiting area, rubbing his hands together to expel the nervous energy. 'Sitting outside the headmaster's office like I'm going to get into trouble.'

'Come on, Rob.' Jolene looked over at him with a smirk. 'You were never in trouble.'

'I was, actually. Went through a phase where I was in shit all the time. My sister... She was a nightmare. And I always got the blame.'

The secretary stopped hammering at her keyboard, then looked at them as though just remembering the police were waiting there. 'I'll go and see where Ms Ferguson is.' She got up and walked off with her mobile, leaving them alone.

Marshall was tempted to go and have a rummage around on her desk, but instead he just sat back with a sigh. 'What did you think of Hugh Goodwillie?'

'As a suspect?'

'Just generally.'

Jolene let out a deep breath. 'Typical buckethead, right?'

'Precisely.' Marshall leaned forward. 'There's a joke that

goes, "how do you know the guy in the pub is a fireman? Wait thirty seconds and he'll tell you".'

Jolene smiled. 'Heard that said about vegans.'

'Probably had a form of that joke since we were hunter-gatherers. Or cavemen. "How you know Ugg is hunter? Wait ten beats of heart and he tell you".'

They sat in silence for a few seconds – Marshall started to wonder if his caveman impression was dodgy in some way and he was about to get cancelled.

Jolene leaned forward. 'Can you imagine a vegan firefighter, though?'

Marshall laughed. 'But that doesn't answer my question.'

'Whether I think he could've killed Jake?' Jolene shrugged. 'He's a grieving father. For a son who hasn't died. I think that's a good enough motive, don't you?'

'It is. And he didn't exactly willingly share the information with us, did he? Trouble is, we don't have any evidence to support him killing Jake, do we?'

The door to the corridor opened and Maria Ferguson stepped in, a flurry of activity, then she stopped and let out a groan. 'Aw, fuck.' Her ire was directed between them equally. 'You're here to see me again, aren't you?' She didn't even wait for a response. 'You better come in.'

'Thank you.' Marshall passed her as he entered the room. 'This is DI Jolene Archer.'

'Pleasure's *all* mine.' Ferguson waited for Jolene to enter, then slammed the door. She took her seat behind a desk stacked with paperwork, even in this modern age of iPads and Chromebooks, and just sneered at it. She shifted it to the side, then looked up at them. 'Is this still about what happened with Christopher, right?'

Marshall nodded. 'We visited him.'

'Well done on charming the address out of Sheena.'

Ferguson tapped her nose. 'So, I take it you've seen the state of him.'

'We have. And it's a bit puzzling why you didn't mention precisely what happened.'

'I told you. There's a level of confidentiality at stake here.' Ferguson kneaded her forehead. 'And when I say "at stake" I mean, it's my arse on the line. And, really, what's there to say?'

'That he tried to kill himself as a result of these allegations?'

'Who knows what motivates a person to do that. Can you say that caused him to do what he did?'

'Really.' Marshall laughed. 'I think it's pretty likely, isn't it?'

She didn't have a response for that, but instead took out her fury on the pile of paperwork.

'Meanwhile, DI Archer and I are investigating the murder of a boy who appears to potentially be involved in this incident. So of course it's relevant.'

'You can't think this was the reason he was killed, can you?'

Marshall paused long enough to make her squirm. Something was being covered up here and he just had to make sure it was the usual arse-covering and not something truly malign. 'Look, I get it. You don't want your dirty laundry aired in public. It's human nature, right? But what happened to Goodwillie was tragic. And what's happening to his family is arguably even worse.' He left another pause, longer this time. 'So you can see, we really need to understand what happened here. So I'm asking you a question – are you going to tell us or are you going to keep hiding it from us?'

Ferguson took a few seconds to think it through, then sat back with a breathy sigh. 'How much do you know?'

'That the allegation was made by a student called Emily Borthwick.'

'Right. So Emily alleged Chris sexually assaulted her on a history trip. Every year in the Easter break, Chris took a group of Nat 5 students over to Ypres in Belgium to cover the

First World War. She claims he raped her on the Tuesday night.'

'Did you believe her?'

Ferguson leaned forward to rest on her elbows. 'It's not my job to believe her, okay? The investigator from the education authority? Sure, it was his job to listen. He was sent in to investigate what happened and to determine the truth. Then they were going to implement any findings they deemed appropriate.'

'But?'

'But what?'

'Did anything change as a result—'

'The investigation was inconclusive.' Ferguson sighed again. 'Chris was going to be exonerated.'

'Seriously?'

'Yup.' Ferguson gave a tight nod, pregnant with regret. 'We had done everything by the book, so of course he couldn't have done anything to her. There were plenty of parents and teachers there as chaperones. Each one buddied up with someone from the opposite sex for safety.' She laughed. 'Believe me, I've been on those trips and there was *much* more likelihood of the chaperones getting it on with each other than anyone with a student.' She pinched her nose. 'The kids were all four to a room, with a parent in the room between them, so how could he have done it?'

'So you're saying you *didn't* believe her?'

'I...' Ferguson drummed her fingers off the table, staring at the wood. 'This is a really difficult situation for me, okay? This has to be off the record.'

Marshall tilted his head slightly, but didn't say anything.

'The truth is, I thought it was unlikely. Which is the polite way of saying "she was full of shite".' She laughed. 'And not just for selfish reasons, okay? I listened to the girl and I just didn't believe her. Also, as far as everyone's told us – and I've no reason to think otherwise – all protocols were followed to the letter. Christopher was a stickler for detail.'

Still reeked of someone trying to cover their arse, but Marshall was glad she was at least opening up about it. 'Had you informed Mr Goodwillie of the decision?'

'I was going to on the Monday morning. We had a meeting scheduled for first thing.'

'Was he aware of it?'

'The meeting, sure. But not the decision.' Ferguson clenched her jaw and looked over at the window. 'I'd called him on Friday and told him about the appointment. As far as I can see, he'd obviously sat stewing on it all weekend.'

'You didn't tell him the outcome?'

'I might be friends with some of the staff, including him, but there are protocols in place which I have to respect. My boss needed to be there for this.'

'You didn't offer him any clues?'

'Had to come from the school board. If I leaked it... You've got to understand – there were lawyers involved in this. And a gag order. Christopher was going to be reinstated but he just needed to be a bit more patient...'

Marshall made a few notes to that effect, but he didn't know what to make of it. Other than it making the whole thing all the more tragic... He looked up at her. 'Do you think Jake Turner made her lie?'

Ferguson crunched back in her chair and folded her arms. 'Jake was a witness. He was the only one who backed up her story.'

'That she was raped?'

'Right. Said he heard it from the room across the hall from hers.'

'And you didn't believe him?'

'Not a case of that. He was in there, alright. But the issue was nobody else heard it. It wasn't exactly the middle of the night. Emily had gone for a lie down – there was a bug going round, but I don't think she caught it, just felt a bit tired from having to get up at the crack of sparrow fart to get the coach on the Sunday morning.' Ferguson leaned forward, resting her arms on her desk. 'Besides, Christopher was seen exercising outside around the time. Big into running. And CrossFit. So it was a case of her word against the word of a few people I trust. And the only tick in her column was Jake Turner. So no, I didn't think he even had the opportunity to do it, let alone the inclination.'

Marshall looked over at Jolene and the slight shake of her head betrayed her shared unease at this matter. He looked back at Ferguson. 'Shouldn't this matter have gone to the Belgian police?'

'They were going to be engaged if we found sufficient evidence.' Ferguson shrugged. 'If anyone had reported the matter to the authorities in Belgium we would've assisted with their investigation. No one did.'

'Sounds very convenient to me.'

'I swear, this is the truth. It was investigated, of course it was, but don't for one second think I didn't do my own. I spoke to every one of them and the difference is I know them. I know the parents, the kids and, most importantly, the teachers. What she alleges didn't happen.'

'And yet the report was inconclusive.'

'I'm sure I don't need to tell you how to investigate a rape, Mr Marshall. I wanted to believe her, but girls that age can be *vicious*.'

'That's one way of looking at it.'

'Oh? And what's the other?'

'That you were terrified of this getting out. You knew how badly this could affect your school's reputation. And your own.'

Ferguson sat there, eyes twitching. 'If you want the truth,

then part of the reason we were going to exonerate Christopher is because Emily didn't give a formal statement.'

'Even though you received an allegation from her?'

'Correct. She sat there, in the seat your bum is in right now, and told me what she thinks happened.'

'But?'

'But... But her mother kept obstructing the investigation.'

'Obstructing how?'

'How do you think?' Ferguson laughed. 'Getting in the way. Speaking to people she shouldn't. Sitting in with her daughter for every interview. Not letting her answer even the most basic question. And making her leave when things got difficult.'

'Let me get this straight...' Marshall looked through his notes, trying to mask his growing frustration. 'Emily alleged Christopher Goodwillie raped her whilst on this trip. And Jake Turner backed up her version of events. But her mother had been speaking to others on the trip and... what?'

Ferguson snorted. 'She was... It was like she was trying to get them to lie for her.'

'Like it? Or it actually was that?'

'I didn't have anything concrete, but...'

'Do you have the names of the people who might or might not have lied for Emily?'

'I don't, no.'

Marshall sighed. 'In that case, can we speak to Emily?'

15

Marshall drove them past the Turner home, but didn't slow any. Three other cars were parked outside and it looked like their occupants were inside the house.

'People always go on about how bad these areas are, but look at that.' Jolene pointed up at it. 'Friends and family looking after the bereaved.'

Marshall looked over at her with a grin. 'You were the one who was going on about how bad it was.'

'Was I?' Jolene laughed. 'I talk a lot of shite, don't I?'

'No comment.' Marshall sped on up the hill, passing a long green bank he was surprised hadn't been built on. Like some kind of demilitarised zone between the town and Burnfoot. 'Any word on when they can see the body?'

'Not yet, no.' Jolene clutched her phone in her hand. 'I've chased Leye twice now, but you know what he's like.'

'What's that supposed to mean?'

'He avoids me.'

Marshall pulled out to overtake a lorry laden down with wood and scaffolding poles. 'Does he?'

'He does.' She waved her phone around. 'He's doing it right now.'

Marshall frowned. 'Need me to speak to him?'

'I might only be an *acting* DI, Rob, but I can fight my own battles.' Jolene checked her phone then pointed to the left. 'That's it there, just past the Co-op.'

Marshall parked outside two semi-detached houses, identical in plan to the Turner home, but nowhere near as refined. A black Audi sat outside. He looked over to Jolene. 'Listen, the offer's there – if you need me to speak to Leye, I'm more than happy to.'

She got out without a word.

Marshall struggled to stifle his sigh, then followed her out onto the street.

She was already at the door of the left-hand house, hammering the buzzer.

The door opened and a woman stepped out, her face all chewed up, her hair hauled back in a ponytail. She got in Jolene's face. 'What?'

Jolene stood her ground. 'Looking for Emily Borthwick.'

'I'm her mother.'

Jolene smiled as Marshall joined her. 'Leanne Borthwick?'

'Aye.' She stepped back and folded her stick-thin arms. 'Who are you, like? Cops?'

'DI Jolene Archer.'

'Right. Well. I'm just heading out, so can we do this in the morning?'

'You mean tomorrow?'

'That's what that means, aye.'

'Then, no.' Jolene shook her head. 'This is an urgent matter.' She looked over Leanne's shoulder. 'Is Emily here?'

'What makes you think that?'

'The headmistress told us she'd left school at lunchtime.'

Leanne sniffed. 'Said her period's bad.' She reached inside

for a cigarette, already burning away, then took a deep drag. 'Ask me, I'm not even sure she's on the blob, you know? Or that it gets *that* bad. Little madam's just looking for an excuse to sit on her arse and watch TV.' She took another drag and sprayed it over Jolene. 'Why do you want to speak to her, anyway?'

Marshall stepped forward. 'It's regarding an urgent matter.'

'Aye, aye. Aren't they all...' She reached back in for an ashtray and tapped her cigarette off the side, liberating a chunky pipe of ash. 'Are you going to tell me what it's about?'

'Just need a word with her. It's important.'

Leanne dug the cigarette into the ashtray then swapped it for a high-end Samsung smartphone. She tapped the screen then put it to her ear, holding up a finger. 'You're not getting in, by the way. Stevie?' She turned away from them. 'Hi, it's Leanne. Aye, listen – something's come up so I'll be in a bit late the day. Sure thing, aye. I'll drop you a wee text when I leave. Cheers, Stevie, you're the best.' She turned back and tapped her finger off the screen. Her nails were dusted with orange varnish, each one with a slightly different pattern. 'Fuck my life. I'm working three fucking jobs, seven days a week, just for *her*. And I get fuck all thanks for it, let me tell you. Work for the council up in Newton St Boswells every morning, six until two. Just got back the now. Then I'm driving a cab four till late. Usually when I'm so tired that I'm a danger to myself or to others, so I bring myself home. And I work in a shop at the weekend. Never ends. Never fucking ends.'

'Which shop's that?'

'Aldi.'

Marshall nodded – it explained how Emily had got the job there. A few things started slotting together, like why she'd been in Aldi for Jake to get a bit sexually aggressive and how Casey knew about Emily. 'Does her father help out?'

'He's fucking dead.' Leanne sparked her lighter and got the

cigarette going again. 'Anyway. What's this about? That shite with the teacher?'

'What can you tell us about that?'

'Fucking hell. You're actually finally looking into that?' Leanne took a deep drag. 'Took all of my money to get her onto that fucking school trip... Thing is, as much as I talk shite about her, my daughter shows promise. She'll amount to way more than I have in my life. She loves history. Lives for it. Gets that from her late father, along with a congenital condition which has a predisposition to a brutal form of cancer.'

'I'm sorry to hear that.'

'Those are just words.' She tapped off ash again, but this time over the slabs. 'Did all these tests a while back. Emily has it, which means she's getting a preventative op in the not-too-distant future. Poor girl. I wouldn't want to go through that, like, but it'll save her life.'

'I imagine she has a lot of time on her own, then.'

'What are you saying? That I can't look after my own kid?'

'She's seventeen. It's not a crime to leave her home alone.'

'Damn fucking right it's not. And aye, she *had* plenty of time, until I got her that job in Aldi. Took *ages* to persuade her to take it, but it's been good for her. Getting out, speaking to people. Getting mates who aren't her age or in her class, you know? Broadens the mind.'

'We gather there was an investigation into what happened on the trip?'

Leanne looked away with a scowl. 'Waste of time.'

'I'm sorry you feel that way.'

'Well it fucking was!' Leanne shook her head, teeth bared. 'Complete fucking waste of time. They didn't get to the bottom of what happened to my girl.'

'That wouldn't be because you impeded the investigation, would it?'

Leanne sniffed, her eyes narrowing. 'What the fuck do you mean by that?'

'It's been alleged.'

'Well, fuck whoever *alleged* it. And I've got a *very* good idea who.' Leanne sniffed again. 'Truth is, I've no faith in the justice system. You're all corrupt, aren't you? Looking out for your mates. And after what happened to her father...'

Marshall frowned. 'You said he died of cancer?'

'Did I fuck.'

'You said...' Marshall flicked back a page. 'He had a rare congenital form of cancer. Which you've confirmed Emily has inherited.'

'I said he had cancer, aye, and he was undergoing treatment.' Leanne rolled her eyes at him. 'But he died in a car crash.' She took another long drag from her cigarette and cast her gaze across them. 'One morning, he was taking a fare from up in Gala over to Berwick because the trains were all buggered and this guy needed to get to London for some important meeting. Frosty, but Tommy was an experienced driver and, around here, you get used to the frost. The lorry driver wasn't. Smashed into him just outside Lauder on the A696. Dead on impact. The passenger walked away with a cut.' She stared off into the distance. 'I took over his cab to make ends meet.'

'That's rough.'

'Don't you fucking talk to me about what's rough, you prick. Nobody can have *any* idea what I've been through. *Nobody*. You hear?' Leanne's furious glare made Marshall stay his hand – sometimes you just needed to let them get their anger out. 'Fucking cops investigated that, just like the school investigated what happened with Emily. They said it was Tommy's fault for overtaking. But I know that road and it's *fine*. Done it myself *hundreds* of times.' She glowered at Marshall. 'So you can see why I don't want my daughter reliving what happened with that sick nonce, eh? Either to the school or to the police.'

'As far as we're aware, this matter wasn't raised with ourselves.'

Leanne nodded. 'Aye.'

'And that didn't bother you?'

'Don't know.' Leanne sucked a drag deep into her lungs. 'What I do know is I'm using what little money I have to sue the education authority for breaching their duties and not safeguarding my fucking daughter on a fucking school trip. Lawyer says I'll get fifty grand. Not a lot, but it'll help out. Let me replace the car. Pay towards her university, assuming she still wants to go. Assuming she's able to. But the most important thing for me is I need to send a message. Nobody messes with my girl. And I mean nobody.'

Marshall just nodded and let her rant.

'Emily's doing fine now, at least academically.' Leanne looked down at her cigarette and saw it had gone out, so she sparked her lighter again and got it going. 'And I heard that Goodwillie creep tried to kill himself, so good fucking riddance to him. Talk about justice, eh? I mean, if he does that, he's *obviously* guilty, right?'

Marshall gave her a moment to think he agreed with her. 'We really do need to speak to her.'

'Of course you do.' Leanne stepped forward and pushed a hand against his chest, but he didn't move. 'But I don't see why I should let you.'

Marshall had to give her it – no way were they getting inside otherwise. 'Someone connected to Emily was found dead this morning.' He paused to soak in her reaction. Nothing. 'Name of Jake Turner.'

'What?'

'At the museum.'

'Fuck.' Leanne took a long drag from her cigarette. 'I tell you, there's another one. Talk about messing her around… Wee toe rag.'

'So, we need to speak—'

'Why? You think she killed him?'

Or Leanne herself...

Marshall smiled at her. 'We really do need to speak with her about it, one on one.'

'Good for you.' Leanne laughed. 'You can either talk with me there or you can pound salt up your arsehole.'

16

Emily was in the living room, watching a different kind of TV to Christopher Goodwillie a few miles north in Selkirk.

Some weird thing on YouTube, where a kid ran around a busy train station somewhere in England, stopping to smack people on the arse.

A red-faced man raced after him and he ran through the car park, smacking his fist off the wing mirrors of every car he passed and cackling.

Leanne reached for the remote off the coffee table and turned it off.

'Mum!' Emily looked around at her with a vicious snarl. She had her mother's physique, all bones and nothing much else – even her skin-tight leggings were loose – but her ash-blonde hair must've come from her father. 'I was watching that!'

'Didn't look educational to me.'

'Fuck sake. Taking a *break*.'

'The police are here to speak to you.'

Emily sat back, arms folded. 'Better than speaking to *you*.'

'Charming.' Leanne stood there, arms folded, nodding at Jolene. 'Go on, then.'

'Emily, we need to ask you a few questions.' Jolene perched on an armchair, facing towards her. 'We need to hear your side of what happened.'

'Eh?' Emily shifted her gaze between Jolene and Marshall. 'What do you mean, what happened?'

'With Mr Goodwillie.'

'Right.' Emily nibbled at her lip. 'Why?'

'Because it's potentially related to another investigation.' Jolene left her a space, but Emily didn't fill it. 'We found Jake's body this morning.'

Emily looked over at her, then at her mum. She slumped back on the sofa and Leanne sat down to comfort her.

Jolene waited until she got a look in her vague direction. 'Jake was your boyfriend, Emily, wasn't he?'

'Not anymore.'

'No.'

'Broke up with me.'

'Bet it's still upsetting, though, right?'

'Maybe.'

'When did that happen, Emily?'

'Didn't last long. Like, three months?' She shook her head. 'First and only serious boyfriend. I mean... He sent me a message on fucking *Snapchat*. Then he blocked me.' She leaned into her mother, acting a lot younger than her seventeen years. 'Saw him at school, but he just, like, totally blanked me. Hard to take. After what we did.'

Jolene tilted her head to the side. 'What was that, Emily?'

'What do you think? We had sex!' Her words rattled around the room. She leaned forward, nibbling at her thumbnail. 'My first time.'

'Was this after the... incident?'

'What incident?'

'The allegation you made against—'

'What?' Emily looked over at her mum, mouth hanging open. 'Are you hearing this?'

Leanne nodded. 'Sooner you help, the sooner they'll leave.'

'*So* unfair.' Emily slumped back in the sofa. She might've had a tough time already – losing her father, being raised by a mother who was clearly struggling and facing her own high risk of contracting cancer – but she had the sense of entitlement all those Gen-Z kids seemed to have. 'Sake.'

'You alleged Mr Goodwillie raped you on a school trip.'

The starkness of the words rattled around the room.

Emily stared at the floor. 'He did.'

'Do you want to tell us what happened?'

'No.'

'It's important we hear your side of—'

'Why do you want to re-victimise me?'

Jolene sat back.

That kind of technical term wasn't exactly in regular use in a town like Hawick. And it probably wasn't common parlance in school friend groups.

But you could get inundated with them if your YouTube or TikTok algorithm led you down a particular rabbit hole and kept recommending self-help videos.

'Interesting choice of phrase there.' Jolene leaned forward again. 'That's a very strong technical term. Re-victimise.'

'So?'

'Just wondering where you heard it, Emily.'

The girl shrugged. 'Watch a lot of TikTok.'

And there it was.

The biggest-ever social experiment in the history of the world was being carried out on developing brains. A few massive tech platforms shovelling literally anything at them and seeing what stuck, then doubling down on that. Tripling down. Quadrupling. Until everyone just watched stuff, all day long.

'My TikTok feed is all about cats being cute and monkeys.' Marshall smiled, but the joke didn't land – probably shouldn't have tried it in the first place. 'I love monkeys. How's yours got that in it?'

Emily shrugged. 'I watch videos from women who've been through what I have.'

'Which is?'

'I was *raped*, you dick!'

Marshall let the rage wash off her – best way to get her to keep opening up.

Jolene sat back and let him take over this.

'Do you not understand that word?'

Marshall nodded. 'I do. But do you find those videos help?'

Emily's mouth hung open. Then she snapped it shut. 'They do. Aye.'

'I understand that.' Marshall ran a hand through his hair, leaving a bit sticking up at the side. 'As hard as it is to go over that experience again, we really need to know what happened to you.'

Emily tugged at her own hair, as if picking up on a cue from Marshall. 'Why?'

'Because Jake is dead and—'

'What does that have to do with me?'

'Because if he put you up to—'

'What the fuck?' Emily's mouth hung open again. 'Seriously?' Her exaggeration was even more extreme now, even more put on, even more fake. 'You think I'd lie about that?'

'Sorry, I didn't mean to imply that.' Marshall raised his hands. 'We just need to know what happened.'

'Is that your thing, eh? Listening to women talk about being raped? Eh?'

'No.' Marshall held her gaze. 'We're just here to listen to you. If it didn't happen, it's safe to tell us.'

'Didn't *happen*?' Emily looked around the room, anywhere but at Jolene or Marshall, then settling on her mother. 'Mum, can you *hear* this?'

'Em, just tell them what they want and they'll bugger off. We both know you've not done anything wrong so just let them get on with it and they'll piss off soon enough.' Leanne checked her watch. 'Need to get to work, so please…?'

'Fine.' Emily hugged herself tight. 'I went to sleep. Woke up just as he was finishing.'

'As in, when he was—'

'Cumming? Aye.'

Marshall nodded slowly. 'And what did you do?'

'Nothing.'

'You didn't try to stop him?'

'How could I? He's huge. As big as you are.' Emily scowled at him. 'I… I was scared so I just went back to sleep. Tried to forget the whole thing.'

'And you waited until you got back to report it?'

'Right. I felt ashamed.'

'I understand that.'

'Bullshit. You going to say you've been raped?'

'No. But I know shame.' Marshall locked eyes with her and held it until the girl looked away. 'Emily, did you make it up?'

'What the fuck?' Leanne shot to her feet. 'How fucking dare you?'

Marshall raised his hands. 'I'm sorry, but we've got to ask these questions.'

'No you don't!' Leanne lurched forward like she was going to punch him. 'You come in here, to *our house*, and you accuse her of fucking *lying*?'

'Nobody's accusing anyone of anything.' Marshall clenched his jaw. 'I can see you absolutely believe it, Emily, but the trouble is there's not much proof. Except for Jake Turner.' He paused. 'And he's now dead.'

'You think I didn't get raped, don't you?'

'What I think is irrelevant. If you—'

'I've been traumatised by what he did to me. And you... You just want to reactivate my trauma and victim-shame, don't you?'

'Emily. That's not what's happening here. If you say you were raped, then I will believe you.' Jolene locked her in a hard stare. 'Were you?'

'Fuck you!' Emily got up and stormed off out of the room. She thundered over the floorboards, then slammed a door.

'See what I mean?' Leanne sparked away at her lighter, taking a few goes to get her cigarette relit. 'You're not interested in her wellbeing. You just want to score points for your mates in the school. You don't care about her or what she's been through. You're all corrupt.'

Jolene felt the rage thudding inside her head. 'We're investigating a murder here. I don't care about anything other than the truth.'

'You think *she* killed that wee bastard?'

'I've seen weirder things.'

'She's got an alibi.' Leanne shrugged. 'I had a massive argument with her when I got back from work last night. Little madam was shouting at me. Screaming. I was so tired and I couldn't handle it. I get no time to myself. None. I couldn't even dream of dating someone. But no, she wants me to give even more. Pay her money so she doesn't have to work. Screaming at me, about how I hate her and how I'm totally ruining her life. Fuck sake, I give *everything* to that girl and I still try to give more.'

'But that doesn't prove anything.'

'Eh?'

'You said that was an alibi. It's not. Can anyone back this up?'

'Oh, right.' Leanne took a deep drag on her cigarette. 'Our neighbour came around to check she was okay. And she was. Of course she was.'

'Which neighbour?'

'Brenda. Lives next door.'

'Thank you.' Marshall narrowed his eyes at her. 'How do you know when Jake was killed?'

'You said he was found this morning, so I'm thinking last night.'

'Okay.' Marshall took Emily's seat on the sofa. 'Do you believe her story?'

'About the rape?'

Marshall nodded.

'I do. Of course I do. She's my girl and I'd do anything for her.'

'Including killing him?'

'Are you joking?'

'No!'

'Of course not! I was here with her. Are you deaf or something?' Leanne stubbed out the cigarette again. 'Answer me this, though. Do you think she's lying?'

'I don't know, but I don't think it's relevant to our case.'

'Great.' Leanne rolled her eyes at him. 'So you've just upset her for nothing. I'm the one who has to pick up the pieces here. And put her back together. Not you. You get to go home to your nice house and your nice wife and your lovely family. Meanwhile, we're stuck here.'

'Clearing her of involvement in a murder case isn't nothing.' Marshall reached into his pocket and produced a card. 'If you think of anything else, can you give me a call? Anytime, day or night.'

Leanne looked at it, then tossed it onto the coffee table. 'Don't get your fucking hopes up.'

17

Outside, Marshall sat in his car, staring into space. The only thing he was aware of was holding his phone.

He didn't like being lied to – nobody did – but that just felt like a professional insult. A mother covering for her daughter.

But why?

Why had she done it?

The door opened and Jolene crunched down on the passenger seat. 'Well, the story checks out with the neighbour.'

'Figured it would.' Marshall put his phone away and looked over at their home. 'Leanne was very eager to raise the fact Emily had an alibi, wasn't she?'

'Too eager. Probably sees the lay of the land, right? Her kid's ex-boyfriend turns up dead, so of course they're going to be suspects.' Jolene gave a harsh laugh. 'As much as you can be an ex at that age, right?'

Marshall looked away, tasting something bitter in his mouth.

'Forgot to say...' Jolene held up her own mobile. 'Jim McIntyre called me. Said he and Ash checked out Casey's dad's story. He was definitely in Edinburgh when Jake was killed.'

'Okay. That's good.'

'Not really. I thought Casey's dad was a good candidate.'

'Me too. There's a solid motive there, that's for sure. With what Casey went through, sometimes the true cost isn't apparent until years later. Took Casey four years for her life to spiral out of control when she left home. School is heavily structured and regimented, with lots of support in place. University, though, is a sink-or-swim environment – especially living somewhere reasonably far away like Glasgow.'

'Sinking a bottle of vodka every night.'

'Right. Exactly. Almost a shame to exclude someone so strong.' Marshall frowned. 'You said midnight?'

'Right. Well, that's when Leye said. I called his secretary, but the body *still* isn't ready for the PM. Said it took ages for forensics to release it.'

'Keep on it and try to nail down that timeline.' Marshall looked over at her. 'Anyone else we can remove from suspicion?'

'Not to my knowledge.' Jolene folded her arms. 'What have you been up to?'

'Just thinking through some stuff.' Marshall got out his phone again. 'Just made some notes for a mini-profile.'

'A *mini*-profile, eh?'

'Helps to get things pointing in the right direction.' Marshall waved his phone around. 'What do we know about the perpetrator?'

'Eh… Aren't you the profiler?'

'Just want to see how much my expertise has rubbed off on you.'

'Right. As long as that's all that's rubbing off on me.' Jolene grinned at him but it soon faded, her forehead creasing as she thought it through. 'For a start, our killer is obviously male.'

'Why's that?'

'Well. Because of them being strong enough to overpower a healthy seventeen-year-old male. Then you factor in the post-mortem rape.'

'Okay. Good. What else?'

'I'd say it's someone with a grudge against Jake.'

'Not his parents?'

'Don't see it. Why, do you?'

'No, I think I agree, but I try to not rush into things.'

'You think it might be revenge against his dad for not selling the quarry?'

'I think that's a bit of a stretch. But we clearly need to dig into them as much as we do him.'

'Fine. I'll see what I can conjure up.'

Marshall waited, but she didn't continue. 'Well?'

'Well what?'

'More of your mini-profile...'

'Right... Well. It's someone with a fair amount of time on their hands. Because they seem to have got in and out without anyone noticing, which makes me think they'd been tailing him or knew his movements sufficiently well.'

'Good stuff.'

'Why there, though? That's the bit I don't get.'

'Sometimes, a location is chosen for no reason.' Marshall shrugged. 'His parents didn't think it held any significance for him.'

'Right, but they don't seem to know much about him.'

'True. What else?'

'Eh... It's someone with a bit of knowledge of police procedure.'

Marshall frowned at her. 'Why's that?'

'This murder is pretty methodical, right? They'd taped over his mouth and wrists, which shows they know how to contain someone. And that if the victim screams, it'll attract attention.

But it's also been done far enough away from prying eyes. Sure, it's not out in the countryside, but it might as well be. No houses back onto that part of the park or museum grounds, so it's not overlooked.'

'Okay. What else?'

'Not sure what to make of the crucifixion pose.' Jolene shrugged. 'Could be something. Could be nothing. Could be everything.'

'Explain?'

'Well... It could just be a joke, right? Or a distraction. Or it could be the killer uses religious symbolism, right? Maybe it's to do with all the sins Jake perpetrated?'

'I can buy that.' Marshall nodded. 'Anything else?'

'Not off the top of my head, no.'

'Okay, so armed with that... Do you have any suspects that could match?'

'I think Hugh Goodwillie seems a good fit. All that Catholic stuff in their house. So many crucifixes and that shrine to Jesus in their hall. But we don't know if that was Hugh's doing or his wife's.'

'Does it make a difference?'

'Well, yeah. He's male, she's female.'

'You don't think she could've done it?'

'Very, very unlikely. She lacks the requisite appendage. But with him? Pretty likely.'

'Hard to disagree with that assessment.'

Jolene looked over at him, eyebrow raised. 'But you said earlier, just after we left, that you didn't think he did it?'

'At the time.' Marshall tapped his phone case a few times. 'But I hadn't thought enough about it. And besides, I hate jumping to conclusions.'

'I'm confused now, Rob. Do you or don't you think he could've done it?'

'I do think he could've done it, aye. Even if Emily was telling the truth about what happened, it just takes Hugh Goodwillie to feel like her or Jake stitched up his son. So of course he's got a solid motive. And I don't want to sound bleak, but something like that would be ideal. A quick result. And no serial killer shite like I've had to deal with for years.'

Jolene laughed. 'Serial killer shite.'

'You know what I mean. A nice simple case, where we can pin down a suspect and get them to confess, without me having to spend hours and hours on a mega-profile.'

'Just want a quiet life, eh?'

'Exactly. Thought returning to the Borders would give me that.' Marshall cleared his throat, in case Jolene jumped back in and started asking more about his proposal for the Borders MIT. 'Anyway. Let's focus on what we know. Sounds like Jake was a little rascal.'

'A wee rascal...' Jolene chuckled. 'That's putting it mildly.'

'Exactly. But someone like Jake... We've all known kids like that. He must've done something to someone.'

'Oh aye. Several times over.' Jolene looked over at him. 'But something that got him killed?'

'Could think of a hundred things he could've done.' Marshall thought it through. 'Way I see it, Jake is a free-range kid. His parents gave up on trying to contain or control him long ago. At seventeen, he's probably now involved in some petty crimes, like theft, damage, fire-raising, animal cruelty, drugs. You name it. He's feral.'

'We don't know that.'

'We do.' Marshall held up his phone. 'For once, I got something useful out of PC Liam Warner. He picked Jake up a few times while he worked in Hawick. Clip round the ear kind of deal. Never stopped him. Stands to reason it's still happening.'

'And Warner didn't recognise him?'

'Said the tape over his eyes and mouth confused him. Typical Warner, eh?'

'How is he still employed?' Jolene shook her head. 'Okay. So you're saying he's—' She sighed. 'What are you saying?'

'I'd describe Jake as morally indiscriminate. The motivation isn't "why?" so much as "why not?" Comes from boredom or just a feeling that the rules don't apply to him.' Marshall leaned forward. 'But if he was crossing the line with girls at a young age, then why not with boys?'

'His dad didn't think so.'

'Aye, but he's a typical small-minded small-town man. Probably never knowingly even met a gay man. Or it'll be an air steward with a bit of wink-wink, "backs against the walls, lads" joking thrown in. The idea his son could be gay or bisexual repulses him.'

'And you think the scars on his body point in that direction?'

'Exactly. And the fact there had been anal intercourse near to the murder... It adds a bit of fire to that. Maybe his parents don't know anything about him. And it makes me wonder whether his parents *do* have a better idea of what he's been up to. They might open up after they see his body. I want you there when it happens.'

'I'm planning on it. If and when Leye bothers to call me back...' Jolene stared at her phone. 'But the trouble with all that is he got Casey pregnant at a young age.'

'True.' Marshall scratched at the stubble on his chin. 'Throw the promiscuity we know about into the mix, along with a possible gay thing, and Jake could classify as sexually indiscriminate. The classic try-sexual. Boys, girls, whatever feels good to him.'

'Variety is the spice of life. Lock up the dog when nobody else is around.' Jolene laughed, but it soon turned to a frown. Whatever she was thinking of, she didn't voice it.

'Listen, Jo, I had no idea about your experience.'

'It's fine.'

'It's not fine. How old were you?'

'Fifteen.' Jolene let out a deep breath. 'A bad mistake. I don't regret it.' She squeezed her hands tight. 'I mean, I do. Obviously I do. But the thing is, I can barely raise wee Joe now. Back then, I was a total mess...' The air in the car misted with her breath. 'I can buy that theory. Maybe his dad found out.'

She'd snuffed it out like a candle.

'Jo, if you ever want to—'

She pointed over to the Borthwick house. 'What do you make of Emily's story?'

Marshall sat back and looked at the house. They were both still in there, despite Leanne's suggestion she was due at work. 'As a white, heterosexual male, it's not a great look for me to doubt her story.' Marshall laughed. 'So I'll ask you what your take is.'

'As much as I hate saying the words, I find it hard to believe her.'

'I'm the same.'

'I'm keen to hear your why, Rob. I'll let you off with your white privilege for once.'

'The last thing I feel is privileged...' Marshall blew air up his face. 'The problem I have with her story is it had no connection to the real world.'

'What do you mean?'

'It was just a statement. There was no context before or after.'

'I sort of understand...'

'Think of it like this. Imagine a cheesecake... A victim who can give you a slice with very neat margins, like a slice of cheesecake you'd see in a high-end café, where there's nothing before, during or after is most likely lying. True recollection is like a handful of cheesecake where all the sauce squirts out and the biscuit base is crushed and spread all over the carpet... If anything there's *too much* detail, both relevant and irrelevant. They're literally leaking the truth and can't stop doing it.'

'I can see that. She didn't mention any talking between them. Didn't say how it made her feel.'

'It was like was reciting something she'd memorised.'

'Right. Exactly. And there were no witnesses.' Jolene raised an eyebrow. 'Except for Jake.' She tugged at her hair. 'Do you think he put her up to it?'

'It's possible. Or she put him up to confirming her account.' Marshall paused to think. But nothing connected to that theory, certainly nothing concrete and nothing they had evidence for. 'But the way he just dumped her afterwards makes me wonder, though. That would've been the time for her to come clean about it.'

'True, but it was after Christopher Goodwillie… did what he did… to himself, I mean.'

'You think the guilt over that was too much for her to confess to what she'd done?'

'Right. In circumstances like that, sometimes it's best to just double down.'

'Have seen that happen.'

'How do you want to play it?'

'Let's leave it for now. Then come back to it later. I don't think us pushing it any is going to help the case.'

'Okay.'

Marshall's phone rang.

He got it out of his pocket and checked the display:

Leye calling…

'Here we go.' Marshall answered it. 'Leye, you okay?'

'No.' Sounded like he was in a tiny room, full of hard surfaces. 'Why isn't DI Taylor at the PM?'

Marshall checked the dashboard clock. 15:30. 'Cal's on restricted hours, so he's left for the day.'

'Well, I really need one of you here.'

'I told you to call Jolene.'

'Did you?'

'And she called your secretary.' Marshall looked over at the passenger seat, where Jolene was rolling her eyes. 'I'll send her over now. She was going to bring Jake's parents.'

'No need. They're already here.'

18

Jolene had seen Jake Turner's body before, back at the museum. All prostrate on the lawn, staring up at the skies, except for the tape covering his eyes – and his mouth.

Now, he lay in a similar position but he was at least freed of the duct tape.

And he looked a lot younger in death than she'd imagined, based on all the conversations she'd had about his short life. Almost cherubic, that slicked-back blond hair and those pale blue eyes.

Leye picked up a scalpel and cut into a fresh section of the torso, leaking blood onto the slab. 'So Callum Taylor's finally back, then?' Spoken like they were waiting in the coffee queue in Starbucks.

'First day back today, aye.' Jolene watched him work with care and precision. 'Not too far off being on your slab all those months ago.'

'Indeed.' Leye laughed, a warm eruption of sound totally in contrast with the surroundings and the other attendees. 'Today has been a baptism of fire for him, eh?'

'Just like a born-again Christian getting dunked for the second time.'

Leye looked up at her, fire in his eyes. 'That's not something you should joke about.'

'Surely everything is.'

'Racism? Sexism? Homophobia?'

'If you can use humour to show racists, sexists and homophobes for how stupid and illogical, then why not?'

'I beg to differ.' Leye rested his scalpel on the dish at the side. 'Well. That's enough done now to confirm the sexual assault on the victim. Anal rape, both before and after death.'

'*Before*?'

'Upon further inspection, I uncovered some minor bleeding and some contusions in his anus. Neither would be possible without a beating heart. Ergo, still alive.'

Jolene jotted it down. 'Could it be historic?'

'Not historic, no. These were fresh injuries. Given the lack of healing, they were within, say, six hours of his death, but most likely very close to the time of death.'

'Okay.' Jolene made another note again – she needed to get it right, otherwise Marshall would be right on top of her. 'Any sign of him having sex around then, though?'

'You mean consensual anal intercourse with appropriate precautions and preparation… Hard to tell. But if this wasn't his first anal rodeo, he'd been very careful at the previous rodeos and got himself all lubricated. But this time was very much an unprepared rodeo, with minimal precautions taken. Or an extra level of force to which he was unaccustomed.'

Jolene struggled to stifle a laugh.

And failed.

Leye picked up a different scalpel and held it in front of her. 'Something wrong?'

'I'm okay.' Jolene focused on the dead body, trying to deflate the rising need to laugh and ignore the others staring at her.

What was it about the worst possible situations that caused the most inappropriate reactions? 'Just please stop talking about anal rodeos.'

Leye nodded, but didn't seem to find the same humour in it.

She pointed a gloved hand towards the body. 'Any semen in there?'

'We're not so lucky.'

'So the attacker wore a condom?'

'We found traces of spermicide, so I'd say so.'

Jolene took a few seconds to process it. 'Okay. This is helpful.'

'It wasn't a bareback anal rodeo.'

'Leye!' Jolene raised her hand and stared up at the ceiling. 'I swear...'

'The cause of death is exactly how I described at the scene.' Leye pointed at the body. 'A stab wound to the heart, from the rear. Happened just before midnight.'

'Can you be precise on the timeline?'

'I can. Ten to midnight, plus or minus twenty minutes.'

'Anything about the type of knife?'

Leye clicked his tongue a few times. 'I have a few ideas, but I'm going to have to work with Kirsten Weir to consolidate a list. You can then track down retailers of the knives.'

'Talk about a poisoned chalice...'

'I know. Believe me, I'm glad it's not part of my remit.' Leye sighed. 'During my time in London, I saw how fruitless that can be. But we got a result in both cases. And there are a lot fewer knives up here. A lot fewer of everything. Except hills.'

Jolene made another note. 'Have you done the blood toxicology?'

'You're in luck. Because he was in situ for such a long time before we transported him here, we were able to process that in parallel.' Leye left the body and walked across the room to consult his notes. 'He had a high level of temazepam in his blood.'

'Meaning he'd been sedated?'

'Indeed. Whoever attacked him didn't want him to struggle. There were undigested pills in his stomach contents, which implies he was force-fed them. I'd also suggest this is outside of typical recreational use, but in the realm of an attempted suicide.'

'Consistent with him being murdered?'

'Indeed.'

The door opened and Leye's secretary charged in, shaking her head. 'Leye, his parents are kicking off.'

19

Jolene knocked on the door to the family room and entered.

Paul Turner was spitting angry, shouting and jabbing his finger at him. 'Why can't we see him?'

'Sir, I've been over this.' McIntyre was struggling to contain him. 'If you'll just be patient for a few—'

'Patient?' Paul squared up to him. '*Patient*? We've been nothing but!' He pressed a finger into McIntyre's sternum. 'Our boy's *dead* and you're giving us that *shite*?!'

Jolene cleared her throat. 'Sir.'

Paul turned around. He looked at her – her mere presence seemed to calm him down.

'It won't be long until you can see him, Mr Turner.' Jolene smiled at him. 'The pathologist is just finishing up now.'

Behind him, Tracy was sitting on the sofa, staring at her feet.

'Right.' Paul didn't sit next to her, just stayed standing. 'We just want to see our son. That's all. And this gorilla is lying to us.'

'Gorilla?' McIntyre swallowed down the words. 'Sir, all I'm trying to tell you here is there's a process and we've got no choice but to follow it.'

'Fucking bullshit!'

'Mr Turner, I can't imagine what you've been going through.' Jolene walked over and got between them. 'Like I said, it won't take long now.' She pointed at the spot on the sofa next to his wife, like she was trying to control an unruly dog. 'It'll be a few minutes, so if you could just take a wee seat...'

'And if it's not?'

'It will be. I promise.'

Paul took a few seconds to stare at her before – wonder of wonders – he did as he was told and sat down. 'When I get my five minutes in a room with the prick who did this.'

Jolene stood there, not giving it any oxygen.

Paul looked right at her. 'Have you found him?'

'Not yet, sir, but we're doing everything we can to find your son's killer.' Jolene took the seat opposite, then tried to let the silence soothe them. No sign of Leye's secretary coming in to update them, but it seemed like all Paul Turner wanted to do was to rant. 'We spoke to Casey.'

'Did she kill him?' Paul narrowed his eyes at her. 'Is that why you're not saying you found him? Because it's a her?'

'No.' Jolene shook her head. 'Ms McVicar had an alibi.'

'Right.' Paul sat back and took his wife's hand. A brief moment of tenderness passed between them. 'Her old man could've done it, right?'

'Similarly, he had an alibi for the time in question.' Jolene held his gaze until he looked away. 'At present, we don't believe what happened to Jake is related to that incident.'

'Right.'

'We were going to help look after the baby.' Tracy loosened her husband's grip, but her eyes lost their focus. 'Even though

Jake was far too young for it. They both were. We still would've done everything we could to help out. Hell, we would've taken it from them and... I've got very strong views on it. I would've raised him or her as my own.'

'Still raging about that whole thing.' Paul shook his head. 'That lassie's basically raped my boy and got herself knocked up in the process.'

Jolene almost laughed, but caught herself. 'What do you mean?'

'Our lad was fourteen. She was older.'

'Casey was under sixteen at the time, so it wasn't technically a crime.'

'Aye, aye. But she was the aggressor in that.'

'Are you sure?'

Anger flashed across his face. Then it shifted to a frown, then he just collapsed back on the sofa and let his wife cuddle him.

Jolene leaned forward, gripping her knees tight. 'We heard there was an incident at the school, involving a teacher and a student.'

'Eh?' Paul jerked forward. 'Are you talking about that history teacher raping a lassie on a school trip?'

'That was the allegation, yes.' Jolene nodded. 'You heard about it, then?'

Paul returned the nod. 'Goodwillie, wasn't it? What a name...' He snarled. 'No excuse for what he did to wee Emily, though.'

'You know her?'

'Jake went out with her.' Tracy grimaced. 'Even brought her home once. I thought he might settle down a bit, but no.'

'We also understand your son was involved in it.'

'Jake? No. HE wasn't involved in that.'

Jolene held her gaze. 'He was a witness.'

'What?' Tracy looked over at Paul. 'Did you know?'

'Nope.' Paul shook his head. 'We didn't even know he was seeing Emily until he brought her back to ours. Next thing, he says he dumped her weeks ago. She's sort of a plain girl and not really up to Jake's standards, if you know what I mean.'

'That's not nice, Paul.' Tracy cuffed him gently on the arm, then stared into space. Her focus snapped onto Jolene. 'Can we see our son yet?'

Jolene looked over at McIntyre. 'Jim, can you check if they're ready?'

McIntyre gave a nod then left the room.

'This is a joke...' Paul sat back, arms crossed. 'You seem to know a bit more than you're letting on about what happened.'

'I'm just asking questions pertinent to the investigation, sir.'

'Are you saying you think that teacher bummed him?'

'No. I'm just saying...' Jolene thought it was interesting how he'd brought that up – it sparked a connection with her earlier discussion with Marshall. 'Is it possible Jake might've been party to the investigation because he couldn't voice his own assault?'

'So you *are* saying he was bummed?'

'No. I'm asking if you think it's possible he was sexually assaulted by—'

'No.' Paul clenched his teeth. 'You're asking if he was gay. And if a teacher raped him?'

Jolene knew she had to tread carefully here. 'I'm not saying your son was gay.'

'Fucking asking enough questions about it for someone who doesn't think that!'

'I'm asking if it's possible he was raped by—'

'He *wasn't* raped!'

But Tracy was shaking her head, looking uncertain. She looked up at Jolene. 'Have you found his phone?'

Jolene grimaced. 'It appears to be missing.'

'So someone's taken it?'

'We don't know.'

'Please. Find it.'

'We're doing everything we can.'

'What about his rings? He had these two sovereign rings.' Tracy pointed to the forefinger and pinkie on her own left hand. 'Got them from my father. And he had a fancy wristband with these letters... You could write something on it, like... Well, anything. He put football scores on it.'

'He was a Man United fan.' Paul rubbed his hands together. 'He'd have their last score on it, but that's been not so great recently. Or he'd have their next opponent. Pretty much the only thing I ever saw him doing with any regularity. His grandfather got him it when he was wee.'

'My father.' Tracy brushed at her eyes. 'He was from Manchester. We moved to Carlisle when I was fifteen. That's where I met Paul.'

'Was working down there. Big quarry on the Solway coast. Then I bought my own, you know?'

The door opened again and McIntyre popped his head around. 'They're ready now.'

Paul shot to his feet. 'Finally!'

But Tracy didn't move. 'I can't.' She looked up at her husband. 'Paul, I can't look at our boy!'

'Come on, darling. We've come all this way to—'

'I can't!'

'Okay.' Paul leaned back down and pecked her on the cheek. He nodded at Jolene. 'Fine. I'll do it.'

'Thank you, sir.' Jolene led him through to the observation area, a large area separated by a clear screen.

Leye stood there, mere feet away from them, next to Jake's body on the slab, all covered up by a white sheet.

'It's okay, sir.' Jolene rested a hand on his arm. 'Just take your time.'

Paul brushed her hand away. 'I'm *fine*.'

Jolene nodded at Leye.

Slowly, he eased up the sheet and exposed Jake's head and shoulders.

Paul took one look at him. 'That's my boy.' He rubbed tears from his eyes. 'That's my fucking boy.'

20

Marshall stood in his office, looking over the whiteboard he'd finally got mounted on the wall rather than resting against it. A little groove had been worn into the magnolia, though. He'd covered it with details about the case, connections of people:

Jake.
His parents.
Goodwillie's parents.
Pam Campbell.
Maria Ferguson.
Casey and her father.
Emily and her mother.

And he might as well have not bothered, because he had no idea what any of it meant. Maybe he was just knackered – it'd been a long day, after all – but he felt like he should have at least *some* inkling of where to take this next.

Shouldn't he?

He walked over to his desk and slumped into his chair.

Couldn't help but look at the whiteboard, as if the distance might make some difference to his thinking.

Nope.

All he had was a deep, frustrated sigh.

Someone knocked on the door.

An even deeper, more frustrated sigh escaped his lips. 'In you come.'

The door cracked open and DS Crawford popped his head in. 'Evening, sir. I was just heading.' He scratched his head, then entered. 'Didn't manage to get that coffee today, did we?'

'No, we didn't.' Marshall noticed he was still holding the marker pen, so he re-capped it and set it down on the desk. 'You certainly hit the ground running today.'

'Aye. Have to say, DI Taylor's been great. Hard to believe he's been shot through the ankle. The foot's one thing, but the *ankle*... Not to mention it being a joint, but there's all those bones in there... That he's able to work so soon afterwards is pretty bloody impressive...' Crawford cleared his throat. 'Anyway, thought you'd like to know my team have been busy. We've reviewed the CCTV from Aldi. Emily and Casey were both working at the time of death, so they're excluded.'

Marshall glanced over at the board. 'Emily was?'

'Definitely.' Crawford nodded. 'Spoke to the manager and got all the names ticked off on the footage.'

'Huh. She told us she was at home, arguing with her mother.' Marshall walked over to the board and scored out her name. 'Guess that explains why she had to go home from school today. Must've been shattered.' It left her mother, though. That rush to provide an alibi, one that didn't seem to cover the time in question... 'What about her mother?'

'Eh... From what DI Archer told me, it sounds like the argument ended around eleven. Then Emily's mum was driving her taxi.'

'Any chance you can—'

'Already done it, sir. On the rank at eleven. Had a fare to Tweedbank to catch the last train up to Edinburgh, then went on the rank in Gala to cover the last train *from* Edinburgh. A couple more, but she ended up with a trip back down to Selkirk.'

'You've backed this up?'

'As well as we can, sir. Checked the GPS on her phone and the satnav in the car. Got drop-off addresses but I don't hold much hope for them even if we find the passengers. I mean, who remembers their taxi drivers? Unless they're regulars, but this was all fares off the rank. And not in Hawick. Nothing against cabbies, but it's an intentionally forgettable profession. All baked in, right?'

'I disagree, but I see your point.' Marshall checked the board again. He scored off Emily's mum, Leanne, then looked around for other options, trying to see what else that scratched off – or added. Nothing came up. 'What about Casey's dad?'

'Right. Because Jake had got his kid pregnant, it stands to reason he'd want to kill him?' Crawford frowned at him. 'Didn't Jolene speak to him?'

'She did.' Marshall sighed. He now remembered forgetting. 'But I was talking about his alibi.'

'Oh. Hang on.' Crawford scribbled a note, then flicked through his notebook. 'Jim McIntyre cleared him regarding his alibi, sir.'

'Right. The jazz bar in Edinburgh. Did we back that up?'

'We did. McIntyre spoke to them and got CCTV showing him there at the time in question. Left at three, a wee bit worse for wear.'

'Got it.' Marshall scribbled a note next to their names. 'Can you run a check against the ViCLAS database?'

Crawford scowled at him. 'Wasn't that what Cal was doing?'

'It was. But you work for him, so I'm expecting you to know.'

'Sorry, sir. I didn't get a chance to speak to him before he left.'

'Well, can you run a check for me before you head home, please?'

'To Falkirk?' Crawford shrugged. 'Fine. But do you think it'll give us anything?'

'No, but there's a very remote chance it might. There's certainly lots of behaviour we can analyse. Victim left out in the open or hidden. Naked versus clothed. Night-time. Post-mortem sexual activity. The crime occurred in situ. Taped over mouth and eyes. Sedation. Plus the unique signature of carving messages into the body. That, and the Jesus Christ pose.'

'Is that the hold-back information?'

Shite.

'Yes. Part of it.'

'Sure.'

'And the crucifixion pose... Have we got someone questioning anyone from a religious background?'

'Wasn't the last big case down here along those lines?'

'Doesn't mean they can't both be.'

But Crawford didn't leave. He just stood there.

Marshall raised his chin. 'You have used the system before, right?'

'Few times, aye. Just not hopeful, sir.' Crawford sniffed. 'Do you really think it's a serial killer?'

'How many dead bodies have we got here?'

'Eh, one?'

'Right. Then, if nothing else, you'll go home tonight knowing if you don't have three, you don't have a serial killer.' Marshall gave a hard scowl. 'Not every murder is by a serial killer, Sergeant. In fact, very few are.'

'Right, right.' Crawford gave him a nod then finally got the message and scurried off into the office space.

Leaving Marshall alone again.

He clocked Crawford taking a few goes and a lot of swearing to log into his machine.

Aye, Marshall had been sent a useless sod there.

He reappraised the board based on Crawford's update, but it wasn't getting him any further forward. No magical insights leapt out from it.

'I'm sure if you think hard enough you can make it lift off the ground.'

Marshall swung around.

Jolene was standing there, smirking. 'How's it going?'

Marshall felt himself deflate, like a pricked balloon.

'That good, eh?' Jolene joined him at the board. 'Not getting much further forward, are you?'

'Nope.' Marshall re-capped the pen and rested it on the lip below the board. 'Managed to persuade Maria Ferguson to send through the investigation report.'

'How did you manage that?' She winked. 'A wee bit of flirting?'

'Hardly.'

'Still, she's definitely into you.'

'Well, I'm off the market.'

'What does the report say?'

'Bugger all other than what I just said. It repeats the initial allegation and... Remember what I was saying about slicing into a cheesecake and getting a neat triangular portion?' Marshall brandished the print-out. 'Her explanation in here is consistent with either a dream or a fabrication. But the fact the only verification came from Jake makes me think it's the latter.'

'So we need to dig further into it, then?'

'Right. We need a list of his mates.' Marshall gave her a bitter smile. 'Doubt his parents can provide one, right?'

'Exactly. Spoke to them and he's like a stranger to them.'

Marshall tapped on Emily's name. 'But the upshot is, the investigation *was* inconclusive, mainly due to the lack of a formal statement from Emily, so they decided to reinstate Chris

Goodwillie. And it's like we were saying about Emily. I just don't believe her.'

'Like you, Rob, I hate to doubt victims, but it does happen.'

'This whole thing could be related to a different incident with him.'

'Another school trip?'

'Or just anywhere. His house. Hers. She's had a lot of time on her hands. Time on her own. Have seen it happen.' Marshall scribbled it down on the board. 'Another explanation is both could be true.'

'I don't follow.'

'She was raped, but not by him. The SOG defence.'

'SOG?'

'Some other guy... in other words, Emily had sex with someone then got worried she was pregnant and felt compelled to blame it on some other guy. Chris Goodwillie.'

'And you think Jake is the guy who'd been having sex with her?'

'He was. We know that. But I'm not sure the timelines match. And it sounds like the sex they had was consensual. He was pushy, sure, but I don't think he ever raped her. But she could also do this because her history grade was poor... Blame a teacher for a serious crime, then get them kicked out. Could also be she's just an attention seeker – after all, she's an only child who lost a parent at a young age. Not to mention going through a serious medical assessment. Or it could be mental illness or just a grudge... you name it.'

Jolene looked across the board and seemed even more mystified than Marshall was. 'Anyway, the PM was just like we expected. Except... As well as after, he was raped before death.'

'Jesus.'

'I know. Leye's hopeful he can get a list of knives that could cause that particular penetration pattern. He's going to work with Kirsten on it.'

'Right. Good.' Marshall looked across the board. 'Which leaves us with—'

Crawford stormed back in. 'Sir!' He waved around his laptop. 'Found a case on ViCLAS that matches.'

Marshall laughed. 'That was way too quick.'

'That's what I thought, but there's a pretty bloody solid match.' Crawford set the laptop down on the desk, then started fiddling with the cable to attach it to the TV hanging from the wall the previous occupant had installed to watch the Euros. 'Three young men were raped and killed near Applecross.'

Marshall frowned. 'Up in the Highlands?'

'Aye. Wee place on the coast, kind of near Skye.' Crawford pulled it up on the big screen. The standard ViCLAS report – pretty much unreadable on the screen, even one that big. 'Happened between 2013 and 2015. All three victims were males aged seventeen.'

'Three?'

'Aye, as in the minimum number needed to call it a serial killer. Very similar MO to Jake Turner. Stabbed through the back into the heart. And the clincher?' Crawford pulled up the photos. 'Someone scored messages into their flesh.'

The screen filled with postmortem photos of pale skin.

> You little poof
> Why, Kieron?
> Any Regrets?

'Oh fuck.' Marshall tasted bitter bile. 'Our hold-back information.'

21

Marshall found Kirsten in the lab, leaning over a desk while she frowned and scowled at a machine. 'Evening.'

She jumped and jerked around, clutching her chest. Then let out a breath and shook her head. 'Rob!' She walked over and punched him on the arm. 'You gave me a right fleg there.'

'Sorry.' Marshall leaned in to kiss her, but she moved away. Okay...

She sat back down at her desk and went back to work.

It'd been a while since he'd seen her without her crime scene garb on and he hadn't even known she'd had her hair shaved short on one side.

He should raise it.

Or he could just let it go, like everything else.

'What are you up to there?'

Kirsten didn't look up at him. 'Working.'

'Right. Working. I'll just go, shall I?'

'Rob...' Kirsten sighed. 'If you must know, I'm trying to recreate the knife blade from the imagery Leye sent through.

Seems like an impossible task, but sometimes stuff like that solves the case, right?'

That piqued Marshall's interest. 'You think you can do this?'

'It's worked before. And then it's just a case of narrowing it down to suppliers and seeing if anyone in the case has been buying very sharp stabby knives.' She winked at him. 'Stop me if I get too technical for you.'

'Anything in this world is way too technical for me.' Marshall took a moment to look around the lab, but it was empty, save for them. Meaning he *could* ask her what the hell was going on between them. 'Clothes?'

Kirsten scowled at him. 'Clothes?'

'Have you found them?' Marshall cleared his throat. 'The lad was naked, after all.'

'Well, we can't find them. Did a fingertip search of the whole museum grounds. Took ages. And all we really got, aside from bottles and crisp packets and cans, was that hoodie.'

So the killer definitely hadn't just taken the phone, then.

Or at least, that was Marshall's supposition. 'How are you getting on with Jake's phone?'

'His phone?' Kirsten stared at him then shut her eyes. 'Right.' She reopened them. 'We're nowhere, Rob. We don't have it.'

'But you've—'

'We've pinged it, aye. Of course we have. Trouble is, it's off.'

'Do you have the last-known location?'

Kirsten sifted through some paperwork – as high-tech as her area was, she was one for printing stuff out. Anything. Everything. 'Last-known location is Hawick Museum, or nearby. So I'd suggest it's either broken and lying in an off state somewhere nearby we haven't searched, or the killer took it.'

'Right. And I'd suggest the latter is much more likely. Especially as most of his clothes are missing.' Marshall leaned back against the workbench, resting his arse against the cold metal.

'If someone lured him there, then stealing his phone – or destroying it – is a good way to cover their tracks. Particularly if there was something on the phone the killer didn't want revealed.'

'Hardly. We can access his phone records.'

'Have you?'

'I have, aye.' Kirsten ran a hand through her hair. 'I've requested a dump of his phone calls and texts from the network but don't get your hopes up, Rob – he's seventeen, so it'll all be apps and stuff.' She leaned forward to make a note. 'It's extremely unlikely we find anything useful.'

'Speaking of extremely unlikely...' Marshall cleared his throat. 'We've found a possible connection to a case in Applecross.'

Kirsten looked up. 'Up in the Highlands? Wow.'

'Right. Wow, exactly. Best part of three hundred miles north of here. Seems to be a decent match, though. Sexual assaults before and after death. Messages carved into the flesh, like we saw at the museum. Clothes and phones missing.'

'Christ...'

'So you can guess what's coming, right?'

'You want me to dig out the old forensics and see what I can find...'

'Know that saying... If you don't look you don't find.'

'Don't get cute.' Kirsten rolled her eyes. 'Do you think it's connected?'

Marshall took a few seconds to think it all through – since Crawford unearthed it, he hadn't actually stopped to consider whether it might not be. 'I'm not sure if it is but, me being me, I need to check it out.'

'So, this your way of saying you're spending tonight poring over the old case file?'

'I'm going to visit. Planning on heading up there tonight.'

'To *Applecross*?' Kirsten glowered at him. 'In this weather?'

'Well, to Inverness tonight. Case was one of the first the MIT there worked after Police Scotland was formed.'

'Can't you just look at the photos in the case file like a normal human being?'

'I could, but I'm not a normal human being. You know that.' Marshall grinned but it didn't work. 'And you know me – I prefer to see things with my own eyes.'

'Including the SIO's eyeballs, no doubt.'

'Right. Exactly.' Marshall stood up tall, trying to stretch out. 'I spoke to her briefly. Still working, still in the same job. Obviously, she's not happy about me digging into her case, especially one from the dim and distant. But I'm going to head up and we'll speak to them first thing and get a handle on the old case, then visit the dumping grounds. Maybe even speak to the old witnesses.'

'We?'

'Taking Doug Crawford with me.'

'Crawford?'

'New DS I've got on loan from Stirling.'

'What happened to Rakesh?'

'They're keeping him in uniform at Craigmillar.'

'I didn't know that.' Kirsten stared into space for a few seconds, her eyes twitching. 'Rob, you do remember we've got a flat viewing, don't you?'

'Sorry.' Marshall checked his watch – she still had plenty of time to get up to Edinburgh in time, even if he didn't. 'I can't do anything about this. It needs to be the SIO heading up there.'

'Fuck sake. You could *not* go. There's nothing in your procedural handbook saying you need to visit. It's fucking miles to Inverness and then even further over there. This is you just being weird and running away from your problems, isn't it?'

Marshall stood there, fizzing with rage. It was okay for her to say that shit, but the second he dared criticise her... Nuclear war. 'Kirsten, a lad's body is sitting on the slab over at BGH. The sooner we eliminate this case from the scope of ours, the sooner we can find out who killed him.'

'That doesn't follow.' Kirsten poked her tongue into her cheek, making the skin bulge. 'But you should make sure you polish your shining armour before mounting your white horse, Sir Galahad.'

'Don't be like that.'

'Why not? I'm pissed off!'

'Well, I'm sorry.' Marshall folded his arms. 'Ravenscroft wants me to head there.'

'Your King Arthur.' Kirsten gave a shrug then went back to work. 'King Arsehole, more like.'

Marshall stood there, feeling like a twat. Feeling angry as a bear. But also as lost as a wee laddie. 'This isn't about that, is it?'

'Don't.'

'I mean it, there's something—'

'I said, don't do that. You always try to pin something you've done on me. Like I'm not allowed to get pissed off with you for doing something. There's got to be some hidden layer to it, right?'

'Come on, Kirst. Things have been a bit weird between us for a while.'

'Rob…' Kirsten slammed her laptop shut. 'You're buggering off up to the Highlands on some stupid flight of fancy when we've got a viewing in the calendar that's been booked for a week. You know how difficult it's been to even get viewings for my flat.'

'I do. Which is why I've been there for all the other ones.'

'Look, just because your flat in London sold in two days, but mine is stuck on the market doesn't mean you can slacken off, okay?'

'Didn't say it was.'

'I mean…' She nibbled at her lip. 'A two-bed in Gorgie really should've sold quickly but I've had sod all interest, other than those chancers from Aberdeen putting in a very low offer. You had, what, forty grand more than you expected?'

'Right. But that's not my fault. I was just lucky. The market in London's still ridiculous. Edinburgh's tough just now.'

'Don't do that.'

'Do what?'

'That. Being smug.'

Marshall felt the rage fizzing away. The wee laddie was gone and the bear was taking over. He *hated* it when she belittled him. 'Kirsten, I'm not being smug. Remember that your solicitor suggested you lower your price to get multiple offers. Once you get into that situation, they shouldn't mind coming up in price, assuming they've fallen in love with it. Otherwise you need to be prepared for it sitting on the market for a while. Sticking to your guns is noble, but—'

'I know what it's worth. And you're being smug.'

'I'm not being smug...' Marshall took the seat next to her and tried to calm himself down. 'Look, there's no rush.' He wanted to put his arms around her, but didn't. 'I know us living with my mum isn't that great but it's not *that* bad, is it?'

'Do you really want me to answer that?'

'It's just... You haven't been there in a while, have you?'

'Nope. I haven't.' Kirsten grabbed her laptop and stuffed it in the case, then got to her feet with a sickening cracking in her back. 'I'd better head up to Edinburgh now, seeing as how I'm doing the viewing on my own.' She left the room without even a backwards glance, not to mention a farewell kiss.

Or a hug.

Or even a wave.

And Marshall was back to feeling like the wee laddie again.

22

The more industrial parts of Inverness whizzed past in a dark blur. The sleet hadn't developed into full-blown snow like he'd feared, but the road was a slushy mess, glowing orange under the streetlights.

Marshall reached up to grab the oh-shit handle over the door and felt himself pushed in the opposite direction from the one the lizard part of his brain told him he should be going in.

Crawford was going way too fast for this stretch of road, especially in all this shitty sleet. 'Made good time, right?'

'Indeed.' Marshall reached down to pick up his notes from the footwell, still grabbing the handle. 'And not just because we drove through the evening.'

'What's that supposed to mean?'

'You drive pretty fast, Douglas.'

'I do, but are you saying I'm a *bad driver*?'

'Just fast.' Marshall went back to reading his documents, but the constant shoogling was making him start to feel like throwing up. And he never got car sick.

'Are you prepared to admit you were wrong about the serial killer?'

Marshall looked over at him. 'We've not established the connection yet.'

'But it looks good, right?'

'Not yet.'

'Even after reading those files for the last few hours, you're not prepared to even discuss it?'

'Let's have this chat tomorrow.'

'Suit yourself.' Crawford slid off the road to the right, into a hotel car park.

It didn't bode well – Swankie's was a few sheets of corrugated iron painted navy and welded together. Some rooms even had windows. At least it was cheap enough to get through Ravenscroft's tight fist on expenses and it promised a twenty-four-hour kitchen.

Marshall stuck all his papers together and stuffed them alongside his laptop. He got out into the bitter cold and bits of sleet got everywhere, coating him in seconds. Tasted like petrol too. He walked around to the boot, but it was locked.

And Crawford was taking his time getting out.

Marshall peered in and saw he was messing about with his phone.

Bloody hell...

Crawford finally got out, still tapping away at his phone and whistling to that tune that'd played on the radio as they whizzed past Pitlochry, yet another town they hadn't stopped at on the way up in his rush to get there. 'Instead of that coffee you promised, how about we have that chat over food once we've checked in?'

Marshall grimaced at the cold. 'Sounds like a plan.'

'Just to say I won't be staying up for a session with the new boss, though, if that's what you've got in mind.' Crawford winked at him. 'Early to bed, early to rise.'

'I hadn't thought of it.' Marshall grabbed his overnight case and extended the handle. 'You going to be alright without clean clothes?'

'Got a bag stashed here.' Crawford pulled a rucksack out of a storage box hidden below the boot, probably where a spare tyre should be. 'You manage to glean anything from the old case file on the way up?'

'Just a ton of questions, to be honest.' Marshall started walking over to the hotel. 'Thing I can't fathom is what could possibly connect them. Applecross and Hawick are hundreds of miles apart and pretty different towns. Applecross has a population of like five hundred and Hawick thirteen thousand.'

'You ever been to Applecross?'

'Once, when I was little. Mum took us there on holiday. Granddad had a friend who had a place in Plockton, I think. We visited for the day and all I remember is being bored shitless all week.'

'Tell me about it.' Crawford laughed. 'Didn't go there as a kid, but had one of the worst weekends of my life there. Worst of anybody's life.'

Marshall didn't want to ask too many searching questions – the reason would come out in due course. 'Anyway. Applecross is a tiny wee place, pretty far from civilisation. And Hawick isn't particularly civilised according to anyone from any of the other Borders towns. Used to be a mill town that did pretty well until the Sixties but has struggled since. Hawick is still a textile town, but doesn't have much else.'

'Why are you looking at the locations?'

'Location is as important as anything. At least. Think about it, Douglas. The killer lived there. So did the victims. If these cases are linked, then those data points are crucial.'

'Guess I can see that.' Crawford held the door open for Marshall. 'The North Coast 500 goes through it, right?'

'Exactly. Hawick doesn't even have tourism.' Marshall entered the hotel.

The interior was much fancier than he'd expected, given the outside looked like a factory. Stripped stone walls and polished marble floors. A long queue snaked towards reception, hidden under a mezzanine level with a bar upstairs.

'So my room will give me a view of *Edinboro* Castle?' A tall American stood at the head of the queue, dressed in several layers of green, tearing off a Green Bay Packers cap and slapping it back on. He didn't seem to care he was holding up five people. Five people desperate to check in and get to their rooms. 'Or it won't?'

'This is Inverness, sir.' The receptionist stood her ground with a polite smile. 'The hotel *can't* afford any views of Edinburgh Castle because it's in Edinburgh.'

'But see, I paid a bomb to you assholes on the understanding my room would have a view of Edinboro Castle.'

'Then you'll need to travel down to Edinburgh, sir. There's a train—'

'You don't seem to understand.' He gave a polite, patient smile. 'I paid good money to have a suite looking out onto Edinboro Castle. It's in the goddamn brochure.'

'Sir, the brochure covers the whole chain, which includes two sister hotels in Edinburgh. The Princes Street hotel affords views of the—'

'So you're saying you can't give me that here? That's *fraud*.'

Crawford rolled his eyes. 'What do you fancy eating?'

'Whatever's on the menu.'

'Starters?'

'Don't mind.'

'Got quite a sweet tooth.' Crawford tugged at his tooth and gave a cheeky grin. 'Of course, you owe me a pudding.'

Marshall didn't want to rise to it – but he was tired, cold and hungry. 'Why's that?'

'A massive slice of humble pie. Because these cases are connected.'

Marshall gripped his arm tightly. 'No shop talk in the queue, Sergeant.'

'Right, sorry.' Crawford looked around, blushing. 'Didn't think.'

Marshall's phone rang.

He dropped his bags and fished it out of his pocket.

Kirsten calling...

He looked up but the loud American was still hogging the queue.

'Better take this.' Marshall walked over to the area in front of the lifts and answered the call. 'Hey, how's it going?'

'Good.'

'Good?'

'The viewers seem very keen.'

'Oh, that's brilliant.'

'And they're going to pay pretty much what I'm asking.'

Marshall felt his eyebrows shoot up. 'Pretty much?'

'Well. I'll have a tidy profit.'

'Great stuff.' Marshall smiled. 'So you're feeling justified?'

'Great, so even when I've got good news, you're scoring points...' Kirsten sighed down the line. 'Aren't you happy?'

'Of course I am.' Marshall made eye contact with Crawford – he was at the front of the other queue, alongside the noisy American. 'It means we can put an offer in on that place in Melrose.'

'Let's discuss that in person.'

Crawford walked over, brandishing a key card.

'Look, Kirst, whatever it is, this is great news.' Marshall smiled as he took the key from him. Room 214. 'Sorry, I better go. I'll call you once we've eaten. Starving.'

'Bye, Rob.'

'Bye, Kirsten.' Marshall ended the call and held up his key

card. 'Cheers, Douglas. I'll obviously get Cal to sign off your expenses.'

'Sure.'

'Do y'all take real money here?' The big American was still at the counter, using the tried and trusted system of shouting at the receptionist – like that'd get him anywhere. 'Is there anyone here who speaks real English?'

The lift pinged and Crawford stepped in, reaching over to hold the button.

Marshall entered and leaned back against the side.

Crawford hit the button for the second floor and the lift started rising. 'Was that Kirsten Weir?'

Marshall nodded. 'Why do you ask?'

'Heard she was working down here. Or there. I gather you're an item?'

'Who told you that?'

'Callum Taylor. Hope this doesn't affect us working together.'

'Why would it?'

Crawford held up his hands. 'Full disclosure, Rob. We used to be a thing.'

It hit Marshall like a hammer. 'You went out together?'

'Not very seriously. But aye. Not a big deal, I hope.'

The lift door opened.

Crawford clapped Marshall on the arm. 'See you in the bar in fifteen.'

23

The room door clicked shut. Marshall stuck his card in the slot and the lights came on. He felt pretty weird, like he might throw up at any moment.

He dumped his bags on the stand, then sat on the bed. Feeling even more weird.

Sod it, he had to do this, didn't he?

He got out his phone and called Kirsten.

'Hey, Rob. You all checked in?'

The line was quiet, like she was in a room somewhere, rather than driving.

'Aye.' Marshall kicked off his shoes and lay back on the bed. 'Listen, you know Douglas Crawford, right?'

Silence filled the line, swelling in his ears.

'Why?'

'He seems to know you.'

Another long pause. 'Is that what he said?'

'It's just... I mentioned his name earlier.'

'And?'

'He just said you and he dated.'

'Dated?' Kirsten laughed. 'Rob, we didn't *date*. We might've shagged a few times when we were both pissed, but we most certainly didn't—'

'*Shagged*?'

'Rob... Come on...'

Marshall sighed. 'You didn't think to warn me?'

'So we're playing that game, are we? I'm allowed to have a sex life before you.'

'Didn't say you weren't.' Marshall didn't know what to say. Somehow she'd manoeuvred this so he was on the back foot here. Maybe he was being a bit pissy, but still... 'Look, I'm not trying to be difficult here. I just don't like secrets. Or surprises.'

'Must've slipped my mind.'

'What, when I mentioned him by name?'

Silence.

'Kirsten, I saw you talking to him at the crime scene.'

'Fuck sake, Rob. I thought we weren't playing that game?' She spat out a sigh. 'I'm surprised Douglas even mentioned it. Happened years ago and he wasn't much of a lover, if I'm being honest.'

Marshall jerked upright on the bed. 'Bloody hell.'

'What, that's too much information?' Kirsten laughed, all bitter and coiled up. 'Come on, Rob. Grow up, eh?'

'Look, I'm not going to make a big thing of it.' Marshall ran his hand down his face. 'I'm tired and hungry and I... I'm just a bit surprised, that's all.'

'I get it, Rob. It's like whenever that Liana lassie rocks up.'

Marshall gave a patient sigh. 'There was never anything between us.'

'Same story here, Rob.'

'Except you said you shagged.'

'There was no emotion in it. It was just... Functional.'

What the hell could he say to that?

Marshall sat there in silence for a few seconds, tapping his foot on the floor. 'Look, I know my love life has been non-existent until you, but...'

'You mean you lived like a monk?'

'That's a bit harsh.'

'Tell me it's not true, though.'

Marshall couldn't.

'Rob, I get it. It's okay. I suggest you get yourself fed and watered, then we can try and chat about it like rational adults later or we can discuss this when you get back.'

'Sure.' Marshall stepped into his shoes again and started lacing them up, cradling his phone between neck and shoulder. 'Are you on your way back to Melrose?'

'I'm staying here.'

'Oh. Again.'

'Don't be like that, Rob. I've texted your mum. It's all okay. Night.'

And she was gone.

Marshall sat back and stared at the phone's lock screen – a selfie of him and Kirsten in bobble hats halfway up a hill.

He had no idea what the hell was going on with her.

24

Marshall found Crawford at the bar, taking a foaming pint of lager from the barmaid.

'*Detective* sergeant. World of difference.' He tapped his temple and gave her a crafty wink. 'Means I have to use the old grey matter.'

What a bloody cliché he was...

'Right. Sure.'

'Unless you prefer a man in unifo—' Crawford spotted Marshall and stood up tall. 'Boss. What can I get you?'

Marshall inspected the beer taps. Typical hotel bar – lager, lager, lager, cider, lager, Guinness. He smiled at the barmaid. 'Pint of Guinness, please.'

'I'll bring it over once it's settled.' Spoken like any of that mythology about a "lovely pint of Guinness" had been true since the Eighties and it wasn't identical everywhere.

'Cheers, Mandy.' Crawford gave her a nod, then took his pint over to a table, the only one which had been set for dinner. 'We're the only ones dining, so we should be quick.'

Marshall perused the menu and it didn't take long. He folded it again and dropped it. 'Haggis pizza.'

Crawford did the same, then took a long sip of his pint. 'Veggie pizza.'

'You a veggie?'

'Vegan, actually, but you try getting anything vegan north of the central belt.'

Marshall smiled, recalling his joke with Jolene. He needed to send her a text about it.

Crawford wrapped his hands around his glass. 'Or west of the industrial garter.'

'The what?'

'The industrial garter. That bit up through Fife and Dundee up to Aberdeen.'

'Never heard it called that before.'

'That's because I coined it.' Crawford waved over to the barmaid.

She didn't notice.

'Back in a sec.' Crawford walked over to the bar and chatted to her – Marshall hoped he was ordering their food rather than asking for her phone number. He walked back and placed Marshall's pint of Guinness in front of him with a grin. 'Safety pint, eh?'

'Didn't fancy any of the lagers.'

'All taste the same, eh?' Crawford took another long sip. 'Ah, that's better.' He was fizzing with all the energy of a toddler who'd destroyed a bag of sweeties. 'How likely is it I'll be in the Borders long term?'

'I don't know. Lots of things up in the air.'

'So John was saying.'

'Aye?'

'Aye.' Crawford hid behind another sip of beer. 'So, you're hoping to get this Shunty lad I keep hearing about back, aye?'

'That was the plan, aye. But there are other things in play.'

'Word is they're shutting down the Borders. That true?'

'Not that I've heard.' Marshall took a dent out of his pint.

Been ages since he'd had a Guinness and it was actually pretty decent. 'That come from Ravenscroft?'

'Just heard a few things.' Crawford leaned forward and dipped his head. 'Like how She Who Cannot Be Named brought in the Scouse pilchard to cut her team in half.'

'Where did you hear that from?'

'Him. Thing with being in Stirling is it's not *that* far from Tulliallan, right? It means they come to us first to grab DCs and DSs for their various wee projects and flights of fancy. I've had four spells there in the last three years, usually a few weeks each. Grinds different gears, you know? Weirdest thing is the high heid-yins don't seem to notice who's listening to their chats in the coffee queue. Or care.'

Marshall could've mentioned he'd been guilty of the same loose-lipped behaviour in the queue here, but didn't want to. 'Go on. What have you heard?'

'Word on the street is the Borders MIT is first off the rank to close. It's barely three years old, so it's easiest to get rid of. Dunfermline's next. Plan is to merge the staff both into Edinburgh. And Livingston's fate is up in the air too.' Crawford took a long sip of beer. 'That tally with what you're hearing?'

'Not really.'

'Well, in response to my question of whether I'll be down there long term, that'll be a no, then?'

'All depends. I'm working on a few new angles to keep the MIT going.'

'So it is at risk?'

'Like you say, Ravenscroft has been brought up here to cut costs.'

'You think I'm thick with him, don't you?' Crawford sniffed. 'I'm not. Believe me I'm not. He was one of the worst for leaking stuff he shouldn't. Guess it's his way of showing how close to power he is. He slashed the analysis team up there in half. Sixteen DCs redeployed to local CID in Edinburgh and, worse, to uniform.' He held Marshall's gaze. 'Want to run your ideas past me?'

Marshall sat back and took his time, sipping his ice-cold stout. He could just talk openly, see what happened. It was likely to get back to Ravenscroft, but did he care? Could he care?

He sat forward again and rested his beer on the mat. 'I've proposed building a new station at Tweedbank to house the MIT but also incorporate a centre of excellence for forensics. Means they could take on work for the East divisions of Police Scotland that currently goes to Gartcosh, but also take on work for Cumbria and Northumbria Police.'

Crawford cast his gaze around the room, then settled it back on Marshall. 'Look, I'm not one for finance or politics but that seems a bit far-fetched. It's going to cost a bomb. And why *there*?'

'Why *not* there? The land is cheap – way cheaper than in Edinburgh or Glasgow. And it's right next to the train station and not far from both the A68 and A7, so it's got decent transport links.'

'Sure, but transport links to places nobody wants to go. And people will need to move. People *hate* moving.'

'You've moved.'

'Temporarily. And I'm not people.' Crawford laughed at his own joke. 'Besides, I haven't moved. That commute from Falkirk to Galashiels is going to cripple me, I just know it. This whole proposal isn't because the fragrant Miss Weir is based down here, is it?'

Marshall raised his eyebrows. 'Fragrant?'

'Rob, I'm sorry about that.' Crawford sat back, raising his hands, palms outwards. 'I thought she would've told you.' He reached over and took a sip of beer – not much left in his glass. 'But I'm not working in Gala to move in on Kirsten, okay?'

'Didn't think you were.'

'No, it's just when I told you, you acted all weird. Half expected you to not come down to meet me for dinner.'

'But you did ask for this role?'

'I did, aye. I worked for Ravenscroft when he scythed through the analysis team, so he owed me a favour.' Crawford clicked his fingers a few times. 'You know Sheila Crawford?'

'Beat cop in Selkirk?'

'That's my mum. She's legendary. Gets her thirty next December so she's going to retire in a few years.'

'So you're saying you requested a move down here to spend time with her?'

'That's the plan. That commute to Falkirk won't be happening that often. I'll stay with her.'

'You haven't got family there?'

'Nope.' Crawford finished his pint. 'Ex-wife and two kids live in Polmont.'

'But you didn't stop in on the way up?'

'Not really welcome. Besides, Jenny's taken them away skiing to France for the school holidays with her new bloke. We all get on fine, but just don't ask me to say anything nice about him.'

Marshall nodded. 'So you're single?'

'Single and ready to mingle.'

The waitress walked over, carrying their meals.

25

TUESDAY

07:20. Still no sign of Crawford.

Marshall waited in the hotel lobby, luggage at his feet. Tempted to reach down and get out his laptop and do a bit of work. Checking out was adventurous, but he doubted they'd need to stay another night. And the way Crawford drove, at least they'd get back to civilisation quickly.

Sod it. He got out his phone and tapped out a text to him:

> So much for 'Early to bed, early to rise.'

He sent it and felt like a passive-aggressive twat. This wasn't a holiday – they were here to work. And their work was solving a bloody murder.

Aye, he'd been sold a pup with him.

He sipped at his coffee. He should tip it out and try to find somewhere open at this time that made something that tasted like real coffee. He should've brought his own AeroPress, but he'd left that locked in his drawer back in the station in his hurry to leave. But he was desperate and needed the caffeine – the tea looked vile.

Still, the sun was sort of up, or at least giving a flicker of blue to the clouds. Hopefully it'd stay that way, leaving yesterday's rain and sleet as yesterday's.

He picked up his phone again. Nothing from Crawford. He should call, but he decided he'd let him simmer on that single-text warning, so he called Jolene instead.

It rang.

And just kept on ringing.

'We're sorry but the person you're calling is unavailable. Please leave a message after the tone.'

Beeep!

'Jolene, it's Rob. Give me a call when you get a minute. Just want an update from the briefing. Nothing to worry about. Thanks.'

He ended the call and looked around.

The lift door opened and Crawford tumbled out, alongside the American from the previous night. He didn't look like he'd found *Edinboro* Castle.

'There you are.' Marshall tapped his watch. 'You missed breakfast.'

'Eh?' Crawford dumped his bag at his feet. 'Thought it was served till eleven?'

Marshall grabbed his bags and got to his feet. 'I mean we're leaving now, whether you've eaten or not.'

'Oh, right.' Crawford scratched at his neck. 'Only ever just a coffee for me, Rob.'

'Have you had it?'

'A bit of instant in my room. Otherwise, I thought we could get one on the way?'

'You'll have to wait until we get there. And you're driving.' Marshall raised his eyebrows. 'Assuming you're fit to?'

'What are you saying?'

'I left you in the bar at half past ten, but you didn't go to bed then, did you?'

'Got chatting to these Americans. One of them insisted Edinburgh Castle was in Inverness. Wouldn't listen. Wouldn't even accept videos of it. Or Google Maps. Insane.'

'When did you finish up?'

'Around midnight.'

Which Marshall knew meant two in the morning.

Aye – Crawford was someone with a drink problem.

Marshall held out his hand. 'Keys.'

'But I thought you wanted to work while I drove?'

'And if you were up till midnight, I don't want you risking getting caught being over the limit.'

'I wasn't—'

'Keys.'

Crawford stared at him for a few seconds, then handed them over. 'I had two pints with you, that was it.'

'You were just drinking soft drinks until midnight?'

'Pint of Indian tonic water. Sober as a nun by the time I got to bed.'

'A likely tale...' Marshall set off towards the pool car.

Crawford ran to catch up with him. 'Did you check out?'

'If we need to check in again, then we can. But it'll save money this way.' Marshall got in the car, then started adjusting everything. The greatest downside of pooling cars was how the last driver did literally everything in the exact opposite way.

Well, the worst was the state the last driver always left the car in, treating it like a bin on wheels.

Crawford was tapping away furiously on his phone. Up close, he didn't smell too boozy, so maybe he had gone to bed when he said he had.

Marshall plugged in the address for the station into the satnav – not far from the hotel at all.

Arrive in less than five minutes.

Marshall powered across the car park. 'Could've walked there while you were suffering from your hangover.'

'I'm not hungover.'

26

Jolene clutched her giant cup and took a sip. Yet again, she regretted it. She hated the taste of whatever passed for tea in this thing, bought from that new drive-through place on the way in. Had some weird herbs or spices in it, rather than just tea. And there was so bloody much of it.

The incident room was full, almost the whole team of officers, plainclothes and detectives. Just Marshall and Crawford missing, on their jolly up north. And Taylor's shortened shift hadn't started yet.

Still no sign of anyone from forensics, though – she hoped that wasn't a slight on her authority...

Ash Paton was in the middle of giving her update and Jolene realised she hadn't been paying attention.

Idiot.

She set her giant cup down and waited for her to finish. 'So, in summary?'

Ash frowned. 'Weren't you listening?'

'No, I was.' Jolene felt herself blush. 'But I want to make sure we're all on the same page.'

'Well, like I just said, we've unearthed nothing much overnight, I'm afraid. Plenty of canvassing being done, but Hawick's a quiet town to outsiders. Especially to us cops.'

'But not to each other.'

'No. So we're hoping something comes up. But for now...' Ash gave a shrug. 'That's all she wrote.'

'Okay, thanks for the update.' Jolene looked around the room. 'Now, you've all been allocated tasks, so let's get on with them. And if you haven't, please speak to myself or to DI Taylor. And just to remind you all that his shift starts at ten o'clock, but can you please make sure you update me first, okay?'

A few nods and grunts.

'Off you go.'

Not the most engaging of ra-ra speeches, but at least it was over.

Aye, that'd be something to add to her development plan for the next year, on top of all the other stuff...

The crowd broke up and Jolene walked over to the sink in the corner of the room. She tipped out her cup of tea, then went into the fridge for her tin of WakeyWakey, marked with her name on the lid. At least nobody had stolen it or done anything to it. Certainly nothing she could see. Then again, it was watermelon and parmesan flavour, so maybe she was the only one daft enough to want to drink it.

She cracked it open and took a gulp. Somehow it was even more disgusting than you could possibly imagine. Her heart started thudding almost immediately. Wretched stuff, but it sure hit the spot.

Ash Paton slouched over to her and gave a flash of her eyebrows. 'Just before I head down to Hawick to supervise the door-to-door work, what was that about? Were you saying I was rambling?'

'Nothing of the sort.'

'But you think it.'

'Ash, you were fine.'

'Right.' Ash leaned in close. 'Just to say, you look like you've seen a ghost and the ghost stuck his finger up your bum.'

Jolene laughed, then took another glug from her can. 'I hate talking in front of people. Just glad Rob wasn't here to see that disaster.'

'You did fine.'

'Aye, but half of the team will be laughing at the way I called the victim "Alex Turner".'

'I didn't notice.' Ash frowned. 'He's the singer in the Arctic Monkeys, right?'

'Big fan. Hence me slipping up.' Jolene drained her can and was almost sick. Never again. Something was throbbing in her temple. 'Did you see Weirdo at the briefing?'

'You mean Kirsten Weir?'

'Aye. She wasn't there, was she?'

'No. She's in the station, though. I saw her arrive just after me.'

So Kirsten *was* avoiding the briefing.

Jolene patted her on the arm. 'Thanks.' She dumped her can into the recycling then left the incident room and charged along the corridor.

The forensics lab was heaving and seemed to be having their own morning briefing.

'That all okay?' Kirsten was in the middle of it, looking around at the team. 'Then let's get to it.' She clapped her hands, then the team burst into action, dispersing from the meeting to go to their machines.

Jolene stood there, fizzing from the ultra-dose of caffeine but also seething at the cheek.

Kirsten might be Marshall's girlfriend, but she was just taking the piss here. Just because he'd delegated the briefing to her, didn't mean it suddenly became optional.

And of course, she couldn't say these things to her face,

could she? And going to Marshall behind her back would be even worse.

Bloody hell…

Kirsten sat down at a machine and started working away at it.

Taylor was sitting opposite, looking through some paperwork.

Jolene sidled up to him. 'Thought you weren't in until ten?'

Taylor looked up at her. 'Busted, eh?' He rubbed at his ankle. 'Couldn't sleep because of the pain, so I thought I'd come in early.'

'If it's that bad, are you sure you should be here?'

'It's not that bad, just… Not taking anything for it, so it decides to get all achy in the night.'

'You missed the briefing.'

'Sorry, Jo. Didn't want to cramp your style.' Taylor shifted his papers away. 'How was it?'

'Honestly? We're getting nowhere.' Jolene ran a hand through her hair then looked around the room. Kirsten was still there – and she didn't seem to have spotted her. 'What are you up to here?'

'Find it easier to work in here rather than in my office.'

'I promised I'll clear it once this case calms down a bit.'

'It's not that. I'm way messier than you, Jo, it's just…' Taylor picked up the papers. 'Kirsten's retrieved the call records for Jake's phone so I thought I'd go through them now.'

Kirsten glanced over, then looked back at her work without saying anything.

Jolene grabbed a chair and sat next to him. 'Have you found anything?'

'Nothing.' Taylor sighed. 'Like with all kids, everything's done in apps, right? So whatever he's been up to, whoever he's been messaging or calling, it's all hidden in the mobile data, not in the phone calls and texts.'

'So there's nothing?'

'Correct. The only texts I've got are the usual ones from his mum. "When are you coming home?" Which he seems to have ignored. And he's received calls from her, but never called her himself.'

Jolene nodded along with it – she'd seen that behaviour with her own son, despite the fact he was almost too young to have his own phone. 'So we actually *do* need his phone?'

'Right.' Taylor pointed at the screen. 'Kirsten got me this. This is WhatsApp.'

Jolene leaned over and checked through it – just weird characters in no sense of order. 'This is just gibberish, though?'

'Exactly. Way I understand it, everything's end-to-end encrypted, so unless you get one or other phone unlocked, you've got nothing. And with kids that age, all the juicy stuff is in WhatsApp or Snapchat or other things we don't even know about. WhatsApp is encrypted, so all we'll get back is this gibberish. And Snapchat deletes the messages as soon as they're seen, or they do in most cases. This is worth doing, though – like Kirsten said, if you don't look, you don't find. He could've been the sole teenage boy who uses SMS messages.'

'But he wasn't.'

'No.'

Jolene nodded at the screen. 'Can't you see who he's messaging, though?'

'How can you do that?'

'Pretty sure you can, aye. It's just the message contents that are encrypted. You can see when it was sent, who it was sent to, and all that.'

Taylor looked over to the side. 'Kirsten?'

'Mm?'

'Do you know who these messages are between?'

Kirsten looked up and gave Jolene a warm smile. *Finally.* 'Request's in with the RiPSA team to provide it from the services. At the moment, all I can get you is network traffic, which is gibberish.'

'Why didn't it go to the services first?'

'Because they take ages. Whereas the networks don't. I spoke to Rob about it last night. He said it was worth the gamble.'

'Busted flush, though.'

'Right.' Kirsten went back to her machine. 'Exactly.'

'By the way, why didn't any of your team attend—'

'Bingo.' Kirsten clicked her fingers and stood up. 'His phone's on! I've just got a ping on the location!'

27

Marshall pulled into the entrance and drove across the car park. 'Did you actually speak to her?'

'Aye. Said she'd see us at the back door.'

'And where the hell is that?'

The Inverness MIT's base looked like it'd been built sometime between Galashiels's Sixties brutalism and Gartcosh's twenty-first-century chrome-and-glass. If someone had told him it used to be a call centre, he'd have believed them. But it all looked like front, nothing like back.

A woman stood by an entrance, talking on the phone. Her gaze followed them over and she waved at them. Must be her, then.

Marshall pulled up in a guest parking space. 'I'm leading here, okay?'

'Sure thing.'

Marshall got out and walked over to her with a wide smile. 'Janice Shearer?'

She was no longer on her phone. Late forties. About five foot six, her dark hair threaded with silver. And the most hardcore stare Marshall had been on the receiving end of since high school. 'Take it you're Marshall, then?'

'Guilty as charged, aye.' Marshall offered a hand. 'Thanks for waiting here for us.'

'You're lucky, Marshall. I prefer to make the calls to my superior outside. Fewer hungry ears. And I was going to clear off if you took another five minutes.'

Marshall shot a glare at Crawford. 'Well, we're here.'

Crawford joined them with a polite wave. 'Hiya, Janice.'

'Dougie Crawford, as I live and breathe.' Shearer gave a long slow laugh. 'Wow. Thought you were told not to return here?'

'We cleared that whole business up.' Crawford held her stern gaze. 'It wasn't *my* jobbie that burst the pipes.'

'A likely tale.' Shearer laughed, then wrapped him in a warm hug. 'Good to see you, Dougie.' She clapped him on the back, like she would a small child. 'How about you go inside and catch up with Steve? I've briefed him – he's expecting a full grilling over the case.'

'Sure thing.' Crawford looked over at Marshall. 'Assuming that's okay with you?'

That wasn't how Marshall had intended it to play out. He pictured them driving across Highland moors to find remote dumping sites in desolate bogs.

Marshall gave him a nod, then watched him hurry inside the station, before switching his focus to Shearer. 'You've worked with him before?'

'Few cases over the years, aye. Dougie's part of the Stirling MIT and we have regular interactions with them, due to a sort-of proximity. Well, as proximate as you can get from the Lowlands to the Highlands.' Shearer narrowed her eyes at him. 'But what intrigues me is how you're based in the Borders?'

'That's right.'

'They've got an MIT down *there*?'

'Long story.'

'One I'm sure you've told many times.'

'It's not any weirder than having one in Dingwall or Fort William.'

'Come on, we've only got this one up here and you know it.' She cleared her throat and it sounded like something had got stuck in there. 'Anyway. Like I said on the phone, I was the SIO on the case you called about. And also, like I said on the phone, I'm a bit wary of you travelling all this way just to pick up a chicken.'

Marshall laughed at the reference to the old TV advert. She might try to defuse this with humour, but he could tell she was wary of his presence. He raised his hands. 'We're not here to open up the old investigation.'

'No, but you sniffing around in our old case might shoogle something loose.'

'That's far from my intention here.'

'You know how the law of unintended consequences works.'

Marshall nodded – he knew, alright. 'You said you were confident about your conviction.'

'We have a conviction, based on a confession and solid testimony.' Shearer sighed. 'But there's always the risk of an appeal. Always. Especially these days. Convictions from the Eighties can be overturned at the drop of a hat nowadays...' She looked down her nose at him. 'We don't need someone from the *Borders* suggesting "some other guy did it".'

'I'm not here to do that. It's most likely we're looking at a copycat. We need to find out what's the same and where the two cases diverge.'

'I don't disagree.' Shearer set off across the car park, but kept glancing back the way. 'Are you the Marshall who was working for She Who— for DCS Potter?'

'For my sins, aye.'

'Okay, good. Then I know you have previous for digging into old unsolved cases for some nonsense unit?'

'Behavioural Sciences.' Marshall laughed, trying to disarm her. 'It's still going and the only thing nonsense about it is the name, which I hated.'

'Big fan of those films. Or *The Silence of the Lambs*, anyway. Pretty much the reason I got into this game.' Shearer stopped by a grey Dacia car. 'You never caught a Hannibal Lecter, did you?'

'Caught a few serial killers, though. And the thing with Hannibal Lecter is he doesn't exist.'

'Of course I know that.' She rolled her eyes at him. 'A character from a book and film...'

'It's not that. What I meant is someone like that can't exist. Most serial killers are of very low intelligence. No fava beans and Chianti or leading FBI agents on merry dances. They're desperate loners with desperate urges they can't control. Sometimes they collaborate with similarly minded people. But they always make mistakes.'

'Know a thing or two about it?'

'Interviewed a ton of them, aye. For my PhD and afterwards, before I joined the police.'

'Well.' Shearer looked across the car park. Almost like she'd misjudged something about Marshall and expected him to confront her and try to bully her. 'The truth of the matter is, we caught ourselves a real-life serial killer, that's for sure. A pair of them, in fact. The male half is still in custody. And he didn't really speak, so I've no way of saying if he's of low intelligence or if he's ordering his fava beans by the ton.'

'But she's not in custody?'

'That wasn't in your research?'

'Haven't had time to review the case file in any great detail, unfortunately.' Marshall shook his head. 'Managed a quick read as we drove up here but I was focusing on MO and victimology so I could better prove or disprove any connections between our cases.'

'Well, in my book, biography is just as important as anything ending with -ology. The one thing we do know about them is Dominic Hayes coerced his accomplice into committing these crimes. Nicola Grant served her time.' Shearer grabbed his bags and stuck them in the boot. Then she dangled her keys in the air. 'So, where do you want to start?'

'Like I said, I've been through the case file, so we can chat on the way to the dumping site and you can give me your take.'

'My take?'

'DCI to DCI.'

'Rob. I'll be honest with you, *DCI to DCI*. My boss is having kittens about this.'

'That's pretty much all supers do, right?'

Shearer laughed. 'Exactly.' She opened the driver door and got in.

Marshall got in the passenger side but the seat was really far forward, like she'd had a gorilla in the back. Took a few goes to figure out how the controls worked but he managed to slide it back a bit. 'Were you speaking to your boss while you were waiting for us?'

'Right. He's really not in favour of you visiting, *at all*. But DCS Potter and someone called Ravensby persuaded him to let it happen.'

'Ravenscroft. He's my super and, believe me, he's having kittens of his own.'

'Okay.' Shearer brushed her hair out of her eyes. 'The dumping sites were very near the murder sites. And there was only one, so that's probably as good a place as any to start.'

'Sounds good.'

'Buckle up, Marshall, this is going to be a long drive.'

28

Jolene turned right, taking the sign heading towards Cavers, and managed a few hundred metres before she spotted the pool car.

Ash Paton was already there, talking to someone on the phone. She clocked Jolene and waved at her.

Jolene parked alongside her and wound down the window – she'd be buggered if she was getting out into that squall. She waited while Ash finished her call, taking in the area.

The road ahead led down, deep into wilderness – she thought it would end up near Carter Bar on the border with England, but she couldn't be sure. There was so much nothing all the way down to Carlisle. In that hinterland, the few people who lived there wanted to get away from everything – or just a specific something.

Behind her, the road ran between Hawick and Jedburgh, two troubled siblings constantly in a rivalry with each other. Hills climbed up both sides of the valley, but nothing too dramatic.

'Bloody hell.' Ash put her phone away, shaking her head.

'What's up?'

'This.' Ash waved her hands around. 'It's... Just a wide area in the countryside.' She spun around. 'No obvious addresses screaming "a murderer lives here".'

'No, but there *are* addresses.' Jolene pointed up the road as a car whizzed past them. 'There's a road there at that gatehouse. Must be a few houses down that lane.' Then she pointed over the road. 'Another similar thing over there, right?'

'Right.' Ash stared up at the granite sky. 'Feels futile, though.' She pointed at a mobile phone mast over the road, in the shape of a tree. 'It pinged *that*.' She waved a hand into the distance. 'And that other one. That's a huge distance. All we've got is a phone turning on then off again in a kilometre-radius area near here.'

'Okay.' Jolene got out into the drizzle and clapped her hands together. 'Let's get a door-to-door going around here and see if anyone recognises Jake or not. Okay?'

'Sure, but you don't think he's been here?'

'He's dead.'

'No, I mean... Maybe he left his phone before...'

'No. His last-known location was at Hawick Museum, just before he was killed.' Jolene spun around to the west and pointed. 'Which is a few miles that way. So he took it with him there. Meaning someone's stolen the phone off him, brought it here and turned it on. Then off again.'

'Right. With you now.'

Jolene smiled at her. 'Just ask, Ash. See what you can find.'

'Sure thing.'

'And keep me updated.' Jolene got back in the car, trying to hide her own disappointment.

As much as Ash had joked about it, Jolene had been hoping they'd maybe actually just turn up and find someone kneeling in the road with a sign reading:

I killed Jake Turner

Like the case would be that simple...

She got out her phone and checked it for messages.

A missed call and voicemail message from Marshall.

She hadn't even heard it ring – must've been when she was driving through the badlands down from Selkirk.

She tried to return the call to Marshall but it went straight to voicemail – he was in similar badlands up north. Or he was just another person intent on ignoring her.

Then it rang in her hands.

Taylor calling...

She hit answer and put it to her ear. 'Hi, Cal.'

'Alright, Jo.' Taylor yawned down the line. 'Anything?'

'We're here but there's nothing obvious.' Jolene hoped her voice sounded positive and upbeat despite the crushing dead end she'd just smashed into. 'I've got Ash leading a team to go around the area and see if we can find it.'

'Sounds positive.'

'No, Cal, it sounds like a needle in a haystack job. And we don't really know if the needle's here anymore.'

'True enough.' Taylor coughed. 'Listen, I've been through Jake's phone records and found an interesting call from four months ago...'

29

Shearer drove them down the zigzag down the mountain, along a single-track road up the coast. 'See what I mean about it being a long drive?'

'I do.' Marshall was holding on to the handle for dear life. 'Feels like it's quicker to drive to Inverness from home than to here.'

'Not far off. Especially if this road's shut. Which is pretty much whenever it rains in winter. When this is closed, you're fucked.'

'That a technical term, aye?'

'Takes forever to get around on the coastal road. Beautiful, but... A royal pain in the arse.'

The morning was clear – the view across the sea was stunning. The waves rippled in the early sunshine. He thought the land to the north was more mainland, but wasn't sure. But what was certain was Skye lay across the bay, mostly obscured by its little sibling – Raasay, just a wall of rock and stone. The Cuillins on Skye were visible up a long bay, lurking like some spiky creature.

Just looking at the island made Marshall want to explore it

again. It'd been years since he'd last been to Skye and the sheer beauty was a fading memory. He had vivid memories of driving the length of the island, with each turn opening up a fresh vista even more beautiful than the last.

But heavy rainclouds loomed over Skye...

Shearer took her left hand off the wheel to point now – the road was as straight as it got on the descent. 'They only opened it in the Seventies, so this would've been cut off for a good chunk of the year.'

Marshall couldn't spot any coastal road. Couldn't spot any road. 'How does that happen?'

'What do you mean?'

'A town like that getting cut off?'

'Well, Applecross isn't a town. And think about it. Back in Viking times, the various seas were the roads. The Inner Sound there, for instance. Takes maybe half an hour to sail there, but to drive there? You need to head back down to the Kyle of Lochalsh, which is a couple of hours, then drive for a good hour until you get to the ferry. And then you're on the wrong side of the island.'

And seeing the sea...

The one thing the Borders didn't really have – or Marshall's part of it, anyway. 'Feels pretty far from home here.'

'Really?' Shearer glanced over at him. 'A few years back, we had to head down to Dumfries for a case. Felt like I'd just got to Dingwall.'

'Dumfries is pretty far from home for me. Good hour and a half away.'

'Never knew that.' One final dogleg, then they were heading down towards the shoreline. A vast rocky beach spread out.

Shearer took the right turning, away from the village then a fork at a copse of trees, bare for the winter, and followed the sign for Applecross Walled Garden, trundling up a long twisty road lined with a single column of trees on one side and a whole wood on the other. 'Why are you here, Marshall?'

'I told you. We think there's a—'

'No. Why are *you* here? Could be anyone else in the team. You should be holding the fort, shouldn't you?'

'Long story.'

'Couldn't a DI have done it, instead?'

'Well, the reality is I like to see things for myself. And one of my DIs took a shot to the ankle a few months back.'

'Jesus.'

'Thought he was dead.' Marshall felt a trickle of sweat run down his spine, despite how cold she had the car. 'Ended up losing another officer that day too. Struan Liddell.'

'Heard about that.' She winced. 'One's bad luck. Two would be careless.'

'One is on me.' Marshall spotted a glorious old white mansion through the trees – presumably Applecross House. 'Well, it was on him. He was up to something.'

'Oh?'

'We think he'd been playing both sides. Ended up being less smart than he thought he was. And it caught up with him.'

'Ain't that the way?'

'Anyway. Cal came back to work yesterday on reduced hours, so it makes sense for him to run the ship. He's a good officer, too. One I inherited.'

'Like Dougie Crawford?'

'He's just come into my world.'

'And you've brought him here to assess him?'

'Not quite. He found the connection on ViCLAS.'

'*Him*? He can barely use a crayon, let alone a laptop.'

'Well, he's to blame for us finding out about your case.'

'Noted.' She pulled into a car park – enough spaces for twenty, but only two here. 'Here we go.' She took one at the far side and got out first.

Marshall followed and had to stretch out – two hours in the car over from Inverness was way longer than he'd expected. He'd been needing a pee since Dingwall, but hadn't said anything. Not quite bursting, but not far off. 'Must've been a nightmare running this case from Inverness. All that driving back and forth.'

'We rented a few cottages and rooms in B&Bs, so it was actually not bad. Felt like a holiday at times. Missed my kids, though.' Instead of heading to the walled garden, she took a side path towards a thick wood.

Marshall spotted why – the café had a Closed sign up. Presumably everywhere up here shut down from October to March.

He had to jog to catch up with her – she walked at a brisk pace, even in those chunky boots, charging up through a thick wood, though the trees were bare. Shearer walked further through the woods. Marshall followed her but didn't find it as easy going, his feet squelching in the mud. Must be a river nearby because it was very boggy and his shoes were already caked in mud. They walked in silence for a few minutes – mostly because Marshall couldn't breathe and talk at the same time.

She stopped in the thickest patch of the woods then pointed at a gate in the corner of a deer fence. 'Happened right here.'

Marshall took in the vicinity, but it was just like any woodland anywhere. Seemed maybe a bit older, like the trees had lingered around a bit longer than elsewhere and avoided the chop of the lumberjack's axe. The only thing distinct about it was the salty taste of the breeze rattling in from the bay, stirring the copper leaves on the beech but still not shaking them loose. He frowned. 'What's the significance of this place?'

'Our killers… Their first date was a hike up there.' Shearer pointed up the hill to the side. 'They had sex at the top, apparently. The only time Dominic had been able to ejaculate in her presence without the use of pornography.'

'I read something about that in the file.'

'Right. It's very twisted.' She let out a slow breath through her nostrils. 'They brought Lewis here and Nicola filmed them having sex. Halfway through, though, Dominic flipped out. Got *really* angry. Totally lost his shit. He beat Lewis to a pulp.'

'And you've got this video?'

'Yep. Her phone's in the evidence store. The video files are all backed up to our servers. The poor jury had to watch the whole thing. Left half of them bawling their eyes out and the rest sick to their stomachs.' She ran a hand down her face. 'Lewis was clinging on for dear life when Dominic smashed his face in with a shovel. Then he raped him again, this time to climax.' She pointed over to the side. 'They buried Lewis's body in a grave over there.' She opened the gate, then walked over to a patch of ground. She pointed to another mound, covered in grass and moss. 'The others were over there. Heads were bashed in. Skulls practically detached from their torsos.' She shook her head again. 'Horrible.'

Marshall felt the bile climbing his throat just imagining it. What those poor lads had been through. 'But that's a difference. Our victim's head was still intact.'

'In his Jesus Christ pose.'

'Right. Exactly.' Marshall crouched by one of the three patches of ground. 'Okay. So my first observation is they had a shovel. Does that mean they planned to bury him?'

'Neither would answer that question but I think we can surmise they did. Or it was just in case.'

'Second, they buried the bodies, while Jake was left on display.'

'See, Marshall – this is yet another reason why this *probably* isn't your case.'

'Didn't say it was. Just need to understand what happened here.'

'But it's also why I'm really worried about you being here. In his interview, Dominic said they'd watch the video while having sex. The only way he was now able to climax was while watching himself murdering a seventeen-year-old boy.'

'Bloody hell.'

Shearer shook her head. 'Sick as fuck, right?'

Marshall looked around the secluded area. He'd seen enough. More than enough.

Then the rain started, stiff rods of the stuff.

Shearer looked up at the heavens. 'Come on, let's go to the pub.'

30

Shearer drove them towards Applecross, the rain now hammering off the roof.

A café and shop – shut – opposite a petrol pump that didn't seem to be connected to anything. Then a row of cottages, followed by trees hanging over the road.

And that was it.

'Doesn't seem very big.'

'And with good reason.' Shearer pulled up outside the first cottage, which seemed to be a pub. 'This is Shore Street. Locals call it the Street. What people think of as Applecross is this, but it's really seven or eight villages over about ten miles.'

'Seven or eight?'

'Can't remember if one's part of Applecross or not. Think there's local disagreement.' She got out into the rain, then disappeared inside the Applecross Inn.

Marshall took his time getting out, then followed her inside.

It might've been chucking it down outside, but the pub was a haven. A bar on the left, stocked with local beers, then a roaring fire at the far end heating the place up.

Shearer was being led to a table by a waitress.

She looked Marshall up and down. 'I'll bring your tea over.' Her accent was very far from local – Marshall could pin it to a North London postcode from his time down in the Met.

Shearer sat by the fire and warmed her hands. 'Might be the only place open at this time of year, but this is my favourite pub in the Highlands.'

A couple of locals sat at separate tables, locked in a very quiet conversation, pints of the local beer in front of them.

Marshall hoped they lived in one of the cottages, otherwise they were in for a long drive. Not that there were any cops to pull them over for drink driving, save the two senior detectives. 'Could do with some soup.'

Shearer tapped the menu. 'Cullen Skink or sweet potato and ginger.'

'Can't stand Cullen Skink, but the other sounds decent.'

'Here.' Shearer handed him a file. 'Those are my personal notes.'

'Thank you.' Marshall took it from her – he hadn't seen her bring it with them. He sifted through it, focusing on her scribbles rather than the text he'd already read.

But the victims deserved for their names to be remembered, so he read them out.

'Lewis Morgan. January 2013. Scott Wilson. July 2014. Kieron Grant. February 2015. All aged seventeen.'

'Haven't heard those names in a long time.' Shearer looked across the pub, letting out a slow breath. 'These weren't exactly crimes of passion. They were calculated, premeditated and planned carefully.'

They didn't deserve their names to be read aloud, but Marshall still voiced them.

'Dominic Hayes. Twenty-three at the time. Nicola Grant was his partner and accomplice, just twenty-one.' He looked over at her. 'Any relation?'

'I'll come to that.' Shearer focused on the waitress as she put their tea pot in front of them. 'Can we get two soups?'

'Of course.'

Marshall didn't know what to say to that – if he hated anything, it was being kept in suspense like that. He just hoped it had some kind of payoff. 'I did a fair amount of reading on the drive up, like I said. My understanding is Dominic coerced her into helping him. Right?'

'See why I'm wary of you being here?'

'You mean, you don't know if he did?'

'No, we do. She said he did.'

'And him?'

'Dominic said nothing. Certainly about that. But he was very expansive on other things, especially after he was allowed to speak to a therapist for clinical depression. From what we gathered from their interviews, Dominic used to fight his homosexual urges.' Shearer raised a finger. 'Nothing wrong with being gay, obviously, but a lot of the people who live around here who don't work in the tourism industry want their privacy. And Dominic grew up in a very religious household, as far south as you can drive. His father caught him messing around with a friend from school one day and he beat the living shit out of both of them. Obviously, that made Dominic suppress the urges.' She swallowed hard. 'But when he left home he'd occasionally give in and meet up with other teens in notorious cruising places. But from what he told us, he hated himself for it afterwards.'

'Do you mean places like the walled garden?'

'No. That isn't a cruising place. It's the car park for a very nice café.'

'Was it always teens?'

'That we've been able to ascertain, aye. We think it was all to do with that youthful indiscretion with his friend. Trying to normalise it. Or just accept it in his head.'

'When Dominic left here, where did he move to?'

'Inverness. He studied at the University of the Highlands and Islands. The Raigmore campus, not far from the station. He was there when it got university status in 2011.'

'What was he studying?'

'Nursing. Thought it was a niche people would always need. And a way out of his home life.'

'But?'

'Those urges started taking over. You've probably seen it a lot – killers can be people who obsess about stuff. With Dominic, he obsessed about sex. Dominic was very dominant, sexually. And, sure, he could meet other students who were gay. I don't mean to be homophobic, but in nursing there were a few and that generation were a lot more open than even ours was. But a lot of it for him was about the thrill of the chase. Going out and finding lads to have sex with.'

'That figures.'

'And then it started to escalate. He dropped out of uni after second year due to his grades being spectacularly bad. He was going to fail his degree, so they kicked him out before it happened. Dominic tried staying in Inverness, but he soon ran out of money. He got a job working in the garage in Lochcarron. Not far away from here. Same place his dad worked. You can imagine the environment. Lots of testosterone. Birds, beer and football. All lads together.' Shearer stopped.

Marshall didn't say anything, just let her continue at her pace.

'Picking up young lads at cruising areas wasn't enough. No, he needed to exert control. Power was what got him off.' She put a clasp between her teeth and bunched up her hair, then tied it up. Seemed to take years off her. 'He'd been a decent footballer, apparently, even had trials at Ross County and Inverness Caley Thistle, but they didn't take him on. Hence him studying nursing. But at the weekends, when he was back from his job and staying with his folks, he needed to get out of the house and get away from them. Especially his father. So he started coaching a young lads' football team. Under-sixteens on a Saturday. Sixteen to eighteen on a Sunday.'

'Don't see a lot of people, let alone enough for a football team.'

'There's two hundred-odd people in the village and, sure, most of them are getting on a bit, but the primary school has seventeen pupils, so people are moving here.'

'What about for high school?'

'Sixteen poor souls, all down in Plockton.'

'That's... a decent drive away.'

'Aye. An hour and a half if Bealach na Bà is open. Two if it's not. They stay over Monday to Friday.'

'Bloody, that's rough.'

'Isn't it? But they're back at weekends and are desperate to play football. Well, the laddies are. If you add in the lads from up to Sheildaig, you get a decent team.' She gave Marshall a sour look. 'He used that cover to identify vulnerable kids.'

'So he targeted lads in his team?'

'No. God no. Dominic didn't shit where he ate. Or where he worked. He didn't target the lads under his charge, but he used them to identify what he called "prospects" in the wider area. The lads in his team were all alphas, right? They'd compete with each other to the exclusion of everything else, but they might have older brothers who were, for want of a better word, gay. Or open to the conversation, anyway.'

'What, so he'd be listening for stuff like, "here, John, your brother Neil is a total bender", that kind of thing?'

'Exactly. Or "your cousin Tony is a bit soft". And Dominic was *always* listening. See, it's one thing if he were to attack a player on his team. They might not say anything. But if there were a few, then they'd very probably talk. The more of them he attacked, the more likely it was to come out. He understood that from his time in Inverness, which was more tolerant. In the wilds around here? No chance. But if it was family, though, then no young wannabe alpha lad is going to know their brother or their cousin had been abused, much less compare notes with a teammate.'

'I didn't read this in the case file.'

'Exactly. It's why I'm sharing that with you.' Shearer nodded at the file. 'But it's all in the detailed interview transcripts, in case you think I'm pulling a fast one.' She shot him a wink.

'I didn't think that.'

'Good.'

'Okay, so he'd identified these vulnerable lads. What happened next?'

'During the week, Dominic was working in the garage in Lochcarron and he'd drive back up every night to stay in a cottage he was renting. But quite often, he'd drive down to Plockton to follow these lads. Definitely at weekends. He'd build up a list of their movements. He'd observe them. Monitor their patterns. Then he'd know when they'd be alone. He'd determine when the optimal time was. And then he abducted them and raped them. And he'd dump them in an area like we saw, gambling on the fact they were unlikely to even report the crime.'

'I get it. And I take it he's doing this out of season?'

'It's pretty quiet outside of summer, aye.' She gave him a knowing look. 'Sure you see similar down in the Borders?'

'Similar, aye. There was this case where a man was date-raping men in pubs in Melrose and Galashiels, but they didn't catch him because they didn't want to talk. Just woke up in his home.' Marshall reflected her look back at her. 'But I see what you mean about it being premeditated. Do you know how many men he raped?'

'Eight.' She locked eyes with Marshall. 'Then he met Nicola.'

'When was this?'

'Late 2012. Nicola was a local lass from Applecross, while he lived a few miles inland. Thing is, like I said, this isn't a wee village. It's spread out across a few miles. Everyone wants distance from their neighbours. But this pub is the heart of the village. And the community hall too. They met at a dance there and hit it off. First as friends.'

'But not as lovers?'

'Nope.'

'I thought they were? Having sex on that walk?'

'Right. But they only became lovers after a few months. But Dominic couldn't consummate their relationship. He was only able to climax to videos of men in violent sex acts. And she started showing him them. And they had a sex life.'

'So she began to share the fantasy?'

'Sort of.'

'Sort of?'

'It's complicated. We had to bring in a forensic psychologist to consult on it. Based in Durham.'

'Jacob Goldberg?'

'That's him. You know him?'

'I used to work for him. He trained me. Taught me a lot. I'd say it's everything I know, but I've forgotten half of it.'

Shearer smiled wistfully. 'How is he?'

'He passed away.'

'Sorry to hear that.' She blinked hard a few times. 'Anyway, Goldberg said there wasn't much shared about their passions. Dominic wanted power over men, while Nicola wanted power over him. And he was still attacking these lads.'

'This was still just rape at this point?'

'At this point, aye. A total of five lads over a period of eight months, all the way from Tongue on the north coast down to Fort William. And then there was a pause while they got together. Then he started up again.'

'How did she find out?'

'We don't know.'

'You don't know?'

'My, this pub has a really bad echo.' Shearer rolled her eyes at him. 'Neither talked about it. So there was always a gap to him abducting and raping men solo and with her helping. Neither would fill it.'

'But she started videoing the assaults on her phone?'

'That's right. And they'd watch them in bed and it'd help him get off. That power dynamic, right?'

'Right. I get it. They're both after control.' He fixed her with a stare. 'How did it escalate?'

'Like so many of them, by accident.' Shearer winced. 'Harry Morgan played for a team down in Plockton, but he knew a lad in Dominic's team. Their parents were friends, I think. They talked about his brother, Lewis. How his dad caught him watching gay porn on his laptop.' She looked away. 'Dominic and Nicola's plan was to sexually assault him, like all the others. They'd set the wheels in motion by planting false stories on Facebook to further isolate Lewis from his friends. Not just about what he'd seen on the laptop, but stuff about him getting caught in a clinch with a lorry driver. Fake photos posted. Once they were sure Lewis was sufficiently vulnerable and isolated, they lured him into a meeting at night in a secluded spot.'

'How?'

'The promise of sex with Nicola. She was posing as a seventeen-year-old girl.'

'I thought they were targeting gay kids?'

'Dominic had been. But they weren't. Nicola suggested they just target vulnerable lads, regardless of sexuality. A bigger population to look for.'

'What about the gay porn?'

'Dominic overheard the truth – it was straight porn. But

pretty adventurous stuff. BDSM. But the gay stories spread and took on a life of their own.'

'Okay, so they lured him here?'

'No. God, can you just let me finish?'

'Sorry.'

'They got him to go a spot a few miles up the coast road. A beach called Sand, right next to the submarine base. Promised a caravan with candles and all that shit.'

'But he didn't get it.'

'Nope. Anyway, Dominic was waiting. He attacked Lewis and they overpowered him. Held him down and drugged him.'

'Temazepam, right?'

'Right. Stuffed it into his mouth. Nicola had stolen it from her grandmother. Lewis was completely out of it by the time they brought him here. But what's worse is the video soon stopped having the required effect. So Nicola knew she needed to up the stakes. She found Scott Wilson through someone at her work. A cousin who'd been to the same university in Inverness as Dominic. He'd confessed to someone about having a crush on a friend. A male friend. They repeated the act, distancing him from his friends. But this time they went straight for the kill. No messing about.'

'Right. And I take it they watched the video of Scott until that stopped working.'

'Correct. But even sooner this time. They moved on to Kieron, who we believe was identified by her again, and they repeated the act.' She pointed to another patch. 'Kieron was going to be buried there, but they didn't get around to it. This time, they were interrupted by the owner of the restaurant who was walking his dog. They ran off. He found Kieron's body.'

'So Kieron was left on display?'

'See why I'm concerned?' She snatched back the folder. 'This is stuff that isn't in your copy of the file. The Procurator Fiscal didn't want us to leave it open for just anyone to access on the system.' She held out a photo of Kieron like a crucifixion – the exact same way Jake was. 'So, Mr Behavioural Science, what's your take on it?'

'Trouble is, Janice, I'm seeing a big connection here. This fits the FBI classification of a serial killer. Three victims, tick. Cooling off time between them, tick. Sexual motive. Signs of escalation. Clear motivation.' Marshall stared at the file. 'When some killers escalate to three victims, they have to do stuff differently each time because the magic wears off. Seems like that's not the case with these two. She's used it to have sex with him which is how she controlled him. For him, it normalises what he perceives to be deviant sexual behaviour by allowing him to have sex with a woman. But the magic doesn't last. So she's had to think of other things to keep it going.'

'You're not the average SIO, are you?'

'No. Obviously, the discovery prompted a massive police investigation and you caught them, otherwise they'd still be doing it.'

'Dogs found the other two bodies pretty bloody quickly, so we naturally included Lewis and Scott in the scope of the case.' Shearer tossed her head to the side. 'Your friend Jacob Goldberg persuaded us to include any unsolved rapes in the scope. And so we put out a call for others, which is how we got hold of both of Dominic's solo rapes and the ones Nicola pushed him to do.'

'How did you catch them?'

'DNA evidence showed the same man was responsible for all three. We had rape kits done for two of the sexual assaults. Some had taken a few months to report, which, while unfortunate, is typical with male-on-male sexual assault.'

'And Dominic wasn't on file, right?'

'Nope.' Shearer flipped back to the start of the document. 'To answer your earlier question, Kieron was Nicola's younger brother. So we questioned her. And her alibi at the time was

Dominic. We were able to loosely connect him to several of the rapes through his football coaching. And that's when they fell apart. Nicola betrayed Dominic. She testified against him in exchange for a lighter sentence. And he folded under interview. Admitted to it all. She got nine years, versus life for Dominic.'

'Sounds like she's as liable, though?'

'She who talks, walks. Still, she's on the SO register for life.'

'I'll ask you this once and once only. Are you one hundred percent sure it was them for all of the crimes?'

'Of course. They both revealed the same info we held back. The cutting of messages onto the victim's skin. We had a forensic handwriting expert in, who thought it was the work of two people. And so it proved.'

'Right. When was the trial?'

'Eight years ago.'

'And she's out?'

'Right. Released last year.'

'Serving eight of nine.' Marshall frowned. 'She can't have been well behaved inside.'

'Not part of my scope, sorry.'

'I have to say – and you're going to hate me for this – but this is a good match. Homophobic insults and messages scratched into the skin. Stabbed through the heart from behind.'

'Victim lured?'

Marshall frowned. 'Actually, we're not sure about that last part.'

'Great.' Shearer laughed. 'This is going to open up my case, isn't it?'

'Sorry, but I just have to follow the path of justice.'

'The path of justice?' Shearer laughed again. 'Seriously?'

'I mean I'm following the facts.'

And right then, the waitress reappeared with two steaming bowls of soup.

31

Jolene pressed the bell again. 'Come on, come on, come on.'

'I can see they're in.' McIntyre stood alongside her, arms folded. 'Sure you need me here rather than searching with Ash?'

'I wouldn't have asked you if I didn't.'

The door opened and Hugh Goodwillie looked out at them. His smile faded to a scowl. 'What's up?'

Jolene smiled at him. 'Could do with a word, sir.'

'About what?'

'A continuation of what we chatted about yesterday.'

'Who is it, Hugh?' Muriel's voice wafted out from deep inside the house.

'Nobody, love. Can you feed Chris for me?' Hugh stepped out into the cold dreich. Despite his advancing years, he was still a big guy, and still physically intimidating. His arms were like muscular pythons. 'Let's hear it, then.'

Jolene looked over at McIntyre, nodding for him to take lead.

'Four months ago.' His voice was a thin rasp. He cleared his throat. 'Four months ago, Jake Turner's mobile called the landline at Christopher's house.'

Hugh glowered at him. 'Fuck are you talking about?'

'The call lasted twelve minutes. Not long after, Christopher tried to kill himself.'

'Eh?' Hugh squared up to him, like he was going to punch him. 'Say that again?'

McIntyre stood his ground. They were about the same size and strength, but he had the advantage of youth – and being a cop rather than an ex-fireman. 'Did you know about that?'

'No.' Hugh seemed to deflate. He stepped back, shaking his head. 'It's news to me.'

'Any idea why Jake would be calling your son?'

'No.' Hugh frowned. 'Only thing...' He focused on Jolene, rather than McIntyre. 'I told you how we thought Jake was behind the allegations, right? That he'd put her up to it?'

Jolene nodded.

'Well...' Hugh covered his mouth with his hand, like he was trying to stop the truth from coming out. 'I spoke to him in the street.'

'When was this?'

'Before Chris...' Hugh swallowed something down. 'Before my boy did what he did. I wanted that bastard to confess to what he'd done. Cheeky wee sod acted like he'd done nothing.' He pinched his nose. 'But I knew what he was up to. The wee shite was seeing the lassie who reported my boy. Stands to reason, doesn't it? This whole fucking thing wouldn't have happened if she'd not done that.'

'Do you think he might've been calling about that?'

'If so, I doubt he'll have been admitting to anything, right?'

Jolene agreed with that. Nobody alive knew the contents of the call, but they could assume something along those lines.

'But it was all a pack of lies. I don't have anything to back that up, but I know my son.'

'And you don't believe a young woman's story?'

'Young woman? She's a daft wee lassie.' Hugh took a long breath. 'The reason I don't believe her isn't because I'm a sexist pig, okay? It's because I asked Christopher and he told me nothing happened between them. Nothing. So whatever people think about my boy, the truth is he was a good man who did nothing wrong. And he might've been many things, but he's not a liar.' He waved into the house. 'And take a fucking look at him now. I found him hanging in his shed. Just hanging there. Legs not even kicking. Just the faintest fucking pulse. Pulled him down with my own hands.' He held them out. 'Sometimes I think that wasn't the right thing to do. What happened to him is *her* fault. And I think it was *his* doing. But… I couldn't leave him dangling there. It's like not being able to go into a building and save someone.'

Jolene nodded to show her understanding, but mostly to keep him talking. 'Do you know what they discussed?'

'How could I? But if you want my best guess, then I suspect the wee prick was goading my lad. No idea how he got his number. It's ex-directory. Then again, you can find anything out on the internet these days.'

'Did you speak to Jake after the incident?'

'If I did, we'd be having this chat in a prison.'

Jolene nodded again. 'You saying you would've harmed him?'

'I would. If I'd known about this phone call.' Those hands were clenched fists now. 'And he would've deserved whatever I did to him. Break his arms and legs. Smash out his teeth. Leave him lying there, bleeding out, unable to move. Because that's what he did to my son.'

They stood there in silence, just the swoosh of a car going past and the soft drumbeat of the rain.

McIntyre broke the silence. 'What were your movements last night?'

'Why? You think I killed him?'

'Where were you, sir?'

Hugh thumbed behind him. 'I was here.'

'Can anyone validate that?'

'The wife was staying at her sister's in Ayr.' Hugh took a deep breath. 'Only got back when you lot showed up yesterday afternoon. Their mother's in a home and they had to be at the home first thing to sign over power of attorney. Easier for her to stay over there rather than travel all that way first thing, especially this time of year. Weather wasn't that great, was it? Got a clear run afterwards. Far as I'm aware, the meeting went fine but she's declining. She'll be ninety next year.' He gave a bitter laugh. 'They call us the sandwich generation. Supposed to be living our best lives, but we've got to look after our parents *and* our kids. Me and Muriel have it way worse than most.' He pointed inside, his steely gaze trained on Jolene. 'You saw what we have to contend with, didn't you? Christopher's a fucking vegetable. And don't give me any shite about that being cruel language. He's suffering. I'm suffering. We're *all* suffering. All because some wee prick got his lassie to lie about him.'

McIntyre nodded along with the words, but his eyes twitched. 'So you're saying you don't have an alibi for last night?'

'Why should I? I haven't done anything.'

'This doesn't look good for you. You see that, right?'

Hugh took a moment to think it all through. Scratching his head. Staring into space. Then he focused on McIntyre. 'Look. When Muriel's away, I usually open a bottle of wine. Sometimes I open a second. Before I know it, I've arsed the lot and fallen asleep in front of the telly.'

'That's what you're sticking with?'

'It's what happened.'

'There's nobody who can back it up? A neighbour, say?'

32

Marshall stepped out of the toilets and looked around for Shearer, but he couldn't see her. The Inverness station might've looked alright outside, but inside it was just as battered and bruised as any other, with worn-down carpets and people.

Marshall stepped into a big office space, twice the size of the incident room back at Gala nick.

And there she was, pouring coffee from a filter machine into two chipped mugs.

He walked over and nodded at her.

'Your bladder is weaker than mine when I was expecting my twins.'

Marshall laughed. 'Getting worse the older I get.'

'Yeah, well, I've just turned fifty, so you've got that to look forward to.'

'You thinking of retiring soon?'

'This job isn't what it used to be.' Shearer laughed. 'That, or *I'm* not.'

'Tell me about it.'

'You don't look that old, though?'

'I'm not.' Marshall took the one with 'Over The Hill Club' stencilled on the side. 'I'll be getting one of these next year.'

'A DCI and you're not even forty...' Shearer slurped at her own coffee, the pink mug marked with 'It's Wine O'Clock Somewhere!!' then seemed to reappraise him. 'Heading for the top, are you?'

'Oh, I peaked a long time ago.' Marshall wrapped his cold fingers around the heating porcelain. 'Been a DI over ten years and this is just an acting gig.'

'They don't give you an acting gig unless they think you can do it permanently.' Shearer reached into a buggered old beer fridge and pulled out a carton of milk. She had a sniff, then scowled, but tipped some milk into her mug anyway. 'I was acting super for best part of year, but that was a long time ago. Think I've topped out at this level. And that's fine. I like being an SIO.' She threatened to pour some into his mug.

Marshall moved his mug well away from that milk – it absolutely reeked. 'Prefer it black, thanks.' He sniffed the coffee and it didn't smell too bad. 'The question that's been going through my head all the way back from Applecross is what happens if we prove this is the same killer?'

'Oh no, you don't.' Shearer leaned in close. 'Don't go down that path, Marshall. If we reopen the case, I will...'

'You'll what?'

Shearer stepped back. 'We've got a conviction.' She took a long drink of coffee. 'And what have you got? A body. You haven't even got the murder weapon, have you?'

'It's a knife. Stabbed from behind, like the last two of yours.'

'But not the first.'

'I'm comfortable with that, given your escalation path.'

But he understood – she thought she could use her experience against him, the daft new guy who was only acting up in the role. Push them away down a rabbit hole that led away from her blowing her conviction wide open.

Marshall looked around the room – anywhere but at her and those fierce eyes.

Crawford lurked in the corner, leaning against the wall near the vending machines. Phone to head. Red eyes and the hard look of the hungover. 'Cheers, Kirsten.' He walked back to a desk and sat next to a grizzled-looking old cop.

Shearer walked over to Crawford and his mate. 'Need a word, Steve.' She blitzed past them towards the offices lining the far end of the room, just like in their office space in Gala.

Steve got up with a wince. 'See you later, Douglas.' His London accent jarred, but then again so many from Marshall's old stomping ground had moved up here – and who was he to criticise someone moving away in search of their own way of life?

'Aye, it's been good catching up.' Crawford watched him go.

Marshall took Steve's chair, still warm. 'How's it been going here?'

'Slowly.' Crawford shrugged. 'How was Applecross?'

'Worth the journey.' Marshall watched Shearer slam her office door. 'Just about. Barely stopped there. Seemed lovely. I'd think about heading for a holiday.'

'Did you find something?'

'Nope.' Marshall sighed. 'But it was useful seeing the sites. Brings the victims to life, if you know what I mean? But I've got nothing concrete.' Another glance over towards the offices. 'I did get a few bits of info out of Shearer that I didn't get from the case file, which means this has all been worthwhile.' He yawned into his fist, then focused back on Crawford. 'How about you?'

'Nothing much.' Crawford blew on his coffee. 'Dominic only found out Kieron was Nicola's half-brother after the murder.'

'That tracks with what I heard.'

'It's the thing that stood out to me.' Crawford shuffled

through a stack of papers that didn't seem to be in any particular order. 'Mostly been looking through Kieron's murder, to be honest. Even though he was four years younger, he'd been physically stronger than Nicola for years. He used to humiliate her.'

Marshall sat forward. 'Sexually?'

'Nope.' Crawford stared at his coffee but still didn't drink any. 'Apparently there was never anything sexual between them, but who's to say? One's dead and the other never talked about it. According to Dominic, Kieron was their mum's baby, whereas Nicola was the second of three. Like me. Being a middle child is rough.'

'So you're saying it could've been a revenge thing?'

'Maybe.' Crawford took another sip of coffee, then spat it back out. 'That's rank!'

But Marshall wasn't thinking about coffee. The gears inside his head were grinding against each other. 'Anything else?'

'The murder weapon from the second two Applecross murders is in the secure storage in Bishopbriggs near Glasgow.'

'And?'

'Well. It means it's not the same knife.'

'Okay.' Marshall chanced a sip of his own coffee and it wasn't too bad. 'I didn't think it was.'

'Kirsten told me they might match.'

Marshall frowned at that. Something deep in his gut reacted too. 'Might? Or they do?'

'Same blades. Same model.'

'I'll need to speak to her about that, then.'

Steve came back to his desk, shoulders hunched.

Marshall smiled as he got up, grabbing his mug. 'Here you go.'

'Cheers.' Steve crunched into his chair and went back to work.

Marshall walked away from the desk and spotted Shearer in

her office, looking out at them while she talked to someone on the phone.

Crawford joined him, clutching his coffee like it had just bitten him. He spotted him spotting her. 'Janice is probably squawking to her super trying to get your super to shut you down. Or onto their mutual chief super.'

Marshall smiled at him. 'Just as well I'm on first name terms with Miranda, then.'

'You know She Who—'

'Bit of advice, Sergeant. Don't call her that. She *hates* it.'

'Noted. Probably not a big fan of Harry, either?'

'Don't.' Marshall laughed. He took another sip of coffee – there was no chance he was going anywhere near that milk. 'You know Shearer, right?'

'Not well, but aye. I've been up here a few times. She's always seemed fine to me. But she's been around the block a few times.'

Shearer was walking over to them. 'We've got a bit of an issue.' She led Marshall away from Crawford back towards the coffee machine. 'I've just been speaking to my contact in the Public Protection Unit to locate where Nicola Grant is at present.'

'And?'

Shearer bit her cheek. 'They don't know.'

'What?' Marshall glowered at her. 'How the hell do they not know?'

'Long story.'

And one she didn't seem to want to get into.

'Okay.' Marshall finished his coffee and set the mug down in the metal sink. 'So that opens up the possibility Nicola Grant is killing again.'

'Which would be a good result for me as it maintains my conviction.'

'But?'

'But nothing.'

'Feels like you're spinning me a line here.'

'That's not what's happening here, Marshall.'

'Okay, but how the hell can your PPU lot not know where a convicted murderer is now?'

'They do know. Of course they do.' Shearer refilled her mug from the filter jug. 'As a nationwide service, they know precisely where she is. But our issue is that Nicola's no longer in the Highlands and Islands jurisdiction.'

'So where is she?'

'I don't know. Her location is only available to supers and above.'

'So what the hell do we do?'

'I don't know. I've escalated, but I can think of someone who might be able to help you.'

33

Maria Ferguson stopped to look behind herself again, like she didn't believe Jolene and McIntyre still had their visitor lanyards on. She took a left down another corridor.

Jolene had lost track of where they were – and she'd been a pupil here.

She glanced into a room on the left. 'I went to school here.'

Ferguson glanced back the way. 'What year was that?'

'Left in 2006.'

'And after what year?'

'Fourth. I hated it. Went to college.'

Ferguson frowned. 'And now you're a cop?'

'Hated that too.' Jolene shrugged. 'Happens more than you'd think. Nothing like a job you hate to make you find a calling.'

'And being a cop is your calling?'

'Wouldn't go that far, but it's a decent job and I feel like I'm doing good. Surely you must feel that way?'

'Only when I don't want to boil a whole year group in the swimming pool.'

Jolene laughed. 'You've got a swimming pool here now?'

'No. We use Teviotdale over in the town. But I reckon you could build a massive element and treat the pool like a giant kettle.' Ferguson stopped outside a classroom. 'Why do you want to speak to Ms Campbell again?'

Jolene smiled, trying to disarm her. 'It's nothing pertinent to the school.'

'Even so.' Ferguson clicked her tongue a few times. 'This is happening on my time.'

'And we appreciate you letting us speak to her.' Jolene pushed past her into the classroom.

Pam Campbell sat behind the desk, alone, head down in a book. She looked up and frowned at them. 'Can I help you?'

'Sorry, but Ms Ferguson said you had a free period.'

Campbell looked over at the door. 'Thanks, Maria.'

Ferguson took a long look at them, then strolled off along the corridor in search of another fire to extinguish.

'I might have a free period.' Campbell shut her book and sat back in the chair. 'But I was catching up on some marking. As you know, my evenings are pretty busy with looking after Christopher. So if we could make this quick?'

'We'll try.' McIntyre grabbed a seat and sat opposite her. 'We need to corroborate an alibi.'

'For me?'

McIntyre didn't react to that. 'Where were you on Sunday night?'

'What? You think *I* killed Jake?'

'No.'

Campbell let out a gasp of relief. 'Good. Because I didn't.'

'So where were you?'

'I was at a concert in Edinburgh. Well, a live podcast show. You know. One of those things where they record the show then it'll be released later?'

'Been to a few of those myself. Even with stuff my husband likes.' Jolene smiled. 'Was it good?'

'Aye, it was grand. Long night, though. Second-last train back to Gala, then I had to get the bus home.'

'And then where did you go?'

'Where do you think?' Campbell frowned. 'I went to put Christopher to bed.' She grimaced. 'He'd... He'd soiled himself.'

'I'm sorry to hear that.'

'You get used to it. I hate it, but it is what it is, right? I was there for a while.'

'What time was this?'

'Well, it was the second-last train, like I said.' Campbell leaned back and stared up at the ceiling. 'Had to wait for the bus for a few minutes. So, what, about midnight?'

'Did you see Hugh Goodwillie?'

Campbell shifted her gaze between them. 'You think *he* killed Jake?'

'We're just trying to exclude people from our inquiries.'

'Well, Hugh was snoozing in front of the TV. I just came in, put Christopher to bed, cleaned him up and left. I was there about half an hour? Maybe a bit longer. Then I walked home and went to bed. Paid for it since. I didn't sleep much.'

'Sorry to hear that.' Jolene made a note of it, more for Campbell's benefit than anything else. 'Thank you for your time.' She gave a final nod then went back out into the corridor.

Ferguson was lurking a couple of doors away.

Jolene stopped and rested her hands on her hips. 'Thought you were busy?'

'Up against it, aye.'

'But you can wait for us?'

Ferguson shrugged. 'Someone has to guide you outside and make sure you actually leave, and Pam's got a ton of marking to catch up on.'

Jolene followed her along the corridor again, but kept quiet. She'd clocked Ferguson as someone who liked to keep an iron grip on things. Whether that was because there was something to hide... She hadn't made up her mind yet.

'Did you get what you needed?'

McIntyre smiled at her. 'Pretty much.'

'Level with me here, Jim.' Ferguson stared deep into his eyes. 'Is Pam involved in this?'

'Pam Campbell?' McIntyre laughed. 'God, no.'

'Well, that's a relief.' Ferguson held open a door. 'If you keep to the path, this'll take you back to the car park.' She stepped away from the door and let them out. 'I'll maybe see you around, Jim.'

'You too, Maria.' He set off along the path, crunching over the pebbles.

Jolene followed him, then watch the darkened windows that shadowed their route. 'You know her from your time in uniform?'

'Me?' McIntyre looked over at her, then away just as quickly. 'No. I matched with her on Tinder a few months ago.'

34

The visitor centre in HMP Barlinnie had been cleared for them.

Marshall sat with his back to the long, wide window overlooking the car park, which gave that tantalising glimpse towards the outside world for the inmates.

Crawford sat at the end, messing about on his phone.

Marshall cracked his knuckles in the most disgusting way he could think of. 'You getting anything?'

'Nope.' Crawford flipped his phone over and left it face down. 'Think I should chase them up?'

'It's fine.' Marshall smiled at him. 'We're dealing with one of Scotland's worst killers – it's going to take a bit of time for them to bring him through from his room.'

'Guess so.'

Marshall yawned into his fist. 'Wish I'd finished that coffee up in Inverness.'

'You really don't.' Crawford burped. 'Swear that milk was off.'

'I *know* it was, which is why I took mine black.'

'And you still let me drink it?'

'You chose to drink it, despite the reek. Still, I'd rather have finished it. Feel like I might faint.'

Crawford picked at his teeth. 'Could've stopped on the way down.'

'You'd have had to slow to below ninety for that.'

'True enough.' Crawford gave a gleeful smile.

Marshall got out his phone and called Ravenscroft. He kept his eyes on Crawford as he listened to the ringing tone.

'We're sorry but the person—'

Marshall killed it. He sighed, then checked through his phone for messages.

A text from Shearer:

> Still nothing from either boss. Must be meeting to discuss us.

Well, that would explain it...

Best part of three hours to drive back – way shorter than it should've been thanks to Crawford's lunatic driving – and they were still locked in a meeting.

He tapped out a reply to Shearer:

> Thanks for update. And for your time today. I know it's not easy but you were helpful.
> Cheers, Rob

He pocketed his phone and looked over at the door – still no sign of movement. Crawford was back to messing about on his phone. He motioned towards the recording equipment. 'That working?'

'Aye.'

'Can you check it?'

'Cool your jets, man. It's already recording. Just need to unpause it when he gets here.'

Marshall nodded – he was the one feeling nervous here. And he was the one who'd been in hundreds of interviews with serial killers, with people even worse than Dominic Hayes. 'Can you be bad cop here, Douglas?'

'Sure thing.' Crawford rested his phone down. 'How bad are we talking?'

'Nasty.'

'Sure about that?'

'Really bloody nasty.'

'Because I can get—'

The door cracked open and two giant guards lumbered through. Big lads, bulked up and with lithe torsos. The thin man they escorted was almost lost between them as they walked him over to their table.

He nodded at them. 'Dominic Hayes.' No visible tattoos. The normal kind of haircut you'd see anywhere, rather than a clippers and Bic razor job. His eyes were hollow, though – nothing going on inside that skull, or he was giving no clues as to what was. He offered his hand to Crawford. 'Nice to meet you.'

Crawford didn't shake it.

'DCI Rob Marshall.' He shook his hand, loosely, smiling wide. 'Mind if we call you Dominic?'

'Please do.' Dominic was frowning at Crawford, like he'd never had anyone be rude to him before in his life. 'And you are?'

'This is DS Douglas Crawford.'

'Can you not speak or something?'

'Just choose not to speak to arseholes like you.'

The guards both raised their eyebrows, like they were in some synchronised competition.

'I see.' Dominic winced as he sat between them. 'Sorry about this, gents, but I can't stay long.'

Marshall tilted his head to the side. 'Oh?'

'I've become something of a mentor to the new fish, as they

say. One lad is really struggling and I want to make sure he's given sufficient time.'

Crawford laughed. 'Still picking off the weaker ones, eh?'

'Excuse me?'

'You heard. That kind of thing sounds like a great way for you to find new victims.'

Dominic looked genuinely puzzled. 'What do you mean?'

'A shy young lad who's in for robbery. Or some lad who was over the limit and killed his mates in an accident, then ballsed up his case. Or a drug dealer who's only doing it to pay his mum's rent. Sounds like an easy way for you to get close to them and then strike.'

Dominic held his gaze for a long time. 'I'm a changed man.'

'Sure.' Crawford laughed. 'Of course you are.'

'I am.' Dominic's eyes flickered, then he looked at Marshall. 'They told me why you're here. You want to ask about what I did, don't you?' He licked his lips. 'The thing I want you to understand about me that I'm at peace with who I am, but not what I did.'

Crawford scowled. 'Fuck's that supposed to mean?'

'It means...' He licked his lips again. 'My homosexuality was something I viewed as evil and sinful. I was raised that way. But since I was arrested, I've had a lot of time to think and to consider my actions. And I've had extensive psychotherapy too. Being gay is part of me. A *huge* part. I've realised I was weak, but not in the way you might think I was. I let my parents drive my actions, not myself. I heeded their world view and didn't form my own.'

'Interesting.' Crawford nodded along with it. 'Still, I imagine prison is like Club 18-30 to a guy like you.'

'Of course it's not. What I did was shameful and I need to repent for those sins. Beyond shameful. Disgusting. Filthy. Degenerate. That's the part of me that's wrong and broken and needs to be fixed, not my sexuality.'

'And yet, you're still given the opportunity to identify potential new targets.'

'It's called peer counselling. It's all sanctioned and I fully disclose my orientation even though, ethically, abstaining from interaction with clients is all that's required. I choose to do both.'

'Sure. I believe you. Thousands wouldn't.'

'I want to help people like me. It's why I'm training as a therapist. I know it's not going to happen, but it means I can better help the younger lads in here who feel the way I do.'

'But that doesn't exactly contradict what I said, does it?' Crawford laughed. 'You'll spot them a mile off, right? Little lad who—'

'Listen. It's a macho environment in here. Just like it was when I worked in a factory. And being gay isn't so much frowned upon as a death sentence. And how I was raised...' Dominic smiled. 'But I'm totally at ease with it now and I'm trying to show a positive example to lads like I used to be.'

'Nobody's like you.'

'Way more than you'd think. Sure they didn't charge over the lines I did, but I'm far from unique.'

'You're right on one thing, dickhead.' Crawford sat back. 'We're here to talk about what you did back then. When you killed those lads. Lewis Morgan. Scott Wilson. Kieron Grant.'

They sat in silence for a while.

Dominic looked up at the ceiling, but it was like he was staring through it – at the sky. 'Look.' He gave a deep sigh. 'To cope, I had to bury my lust and try to act like a normal person. But it had to spill out somehow. It could just have easily been young women, though, because the darkness was nothing to do with my sexuality. It was something deep inside of me. And my lust... It's disgusting. Makes me sick to think about it.'

'But you didn't work alone, did you? You worked with a young woman.'

'I did. And Nic... She encouraged me to... unleash the demon, she called it. But it was all twisted up with the trauma I'd experienced as a child.'

Marshall nudged Crawford's knee with his own to shut him up. He'd done incredibly well in riling him up and getting him to talk. But it was all just preamble to let Marshall earn trust. 'And Nic would be Nicola Grant, right?'

'Right.'

'And you were romantically involved, weren't you?'

'I mean... Sort of.' Dominic blew air up his face. 'The truth is, she was my beard. That's what people call it when a gay man has a wife, right? Having an attractive girlfriend meant nobody at the factory would think I was gay. And Nic was... Stunning. Got so many comments from the lads. I mean, they were all repulsively vulgar, but you know... If nothing else, it showed it worked.'

'You liked her.' Marshall blew air up his face to mirror the body language. 'So it wasn't just a transactional thing.'

'Right. I mean I did like her. A lot. And she... Nic loved me. Like, was head over heels. And I don't know why, but she was.' Dominic bit his bottom lip. 'And she figured out pretty quickly what was lurking inside me. And she... she still loved me.'

'How did she find out, Dominic?'

'I wasn't very good at hiding it. I thought I was, but she... She was better.'

'So you didn't tell her?'

'No. She caught me.' Dominic scratched at his hair. 'Every so often, I'd disappear to meet up with these men I'd found online. We'd meet in these chat rooms, mainly, and most of them were just looking for the thrill of the chat, but the occasional one wanted to meet. A lot of them were lorry drivers. That's not to say they're all gay, far from it. But the ones who were and were doing a run over to, say, Skye or to the Western Isles... Well, I'd arrange to meet them. They were older guys just looking to get their cock sucked by a young lad like me. And Nic...' Something twitched in his eyes. 'She followed me once. Watched me brutally sexually assault a thirty-five-year-old builder from Aberdeen. Poor guy was working away from home. He'd got drunk in a pub and he was in the wrong place at the wrong time.'

'That doesn't sound like your usual type.'

'Sometimes you have to strike when opportunity presents itself. I'd been due to meet up with this lad. I'd met him before. But I saw the state of him, so I shoved him in the back of my van.' Dominic fixed Marshall with that dead-eyed stare. 'But you're right. Most of the time, I found young guys who lived remotely and thought that was how you found love. So fragile, so desperate and so, so lonely. And then that's all I could think about. Those young guys. How vulnerable they were. How trusting. Show them a bit of affection and they'd do anything for you. *Anything*. Sixteen, seventeen, eighteen. Nothing younger. Sometimes older. But they were just like I was. But the trouble was, it was hard to find them. And I got desperate.'

'Did Nicola confront you?'

'Did she...?' Dominic looked around the room, like he was searching for the truth. 'Nic just wanted to love me. Poor Nic. She just wanted to love me and she tried to understand me. No, she didn't confront me, not in a negative way. She was concerned about me being caught. The crimes I'd committed, the risks I'd taken... If she could catch me, who knew who else was aware. She wanted to help me. And I let her... And that corrupted her. I know she'd have done anything for me and I was wrong to do what I did.' His eyebrows met, deep regret flashing in that simple gesture. 'I feel so bad for her having to go to prison.'

Marshall sat there, glad the recording equipment was working. The one thing he'd learned that Shearer hadn't – the missing link in the chain connecting it all together.

How Nicola Grant got involved.

Sounded like she was just as thirsty for violence as he was. She might not have committed any of it, but the hunger was still in her.

'We understand you heard about some lads through the football team, right?' Marshall waited for a nod. 'Vulnerable kids, not directly connected to you.'

'I can't disagree with that.'

'You knew they wouldn't grass.'

'Right. I knew they'd keep their secrets because the secrets they'd shared had got them into so much shit with their brothers and cousins and friends, or even secrets shared about them.'

'But having consensual intercourse with them wasn't enough, was it?' Crawford leaned forward, his voice harsh and low. 'You had to start raping them to get the same thrill, didn't you?'

Dominic just stared at him, keeping calm.

Crawford sat back now. 'I gather Nicola made you kill her wee brother?'

'Well. Aye. There's that part, I suppose.'

'You killed her brother without knowing who he was.'

'No.'

'No?'

'I just... I saw him as a piece of meat. Someone to... to do what I did. To be the vessel for my lust. I didn't care who he was.'

'You killed him without knowing who he was?'

Dominic shut his eyes. 'You know something? I'm grateful that car pulled up near us. We ran away, Nic and I, but it's how we were caught. I could still be doing it and I wouldn't have paid the price for my crimes.' He shook his head. 'I hated it. Hated myself. I was sick. I was damaged. I despised what I'd become. I despised what I was doing to Nic.'

Crawford laughed. 'And now you're fixed, aye?'

'No, but I know I can't be with anyone else. And I know prison is the best place for me.' Dominic tapped the desk. 'Thing is, I've undergone so much psychotherapy in here to figure out what makes me tick and how to stop others like me. When I was raping and killing those boys... The truth is, I was doing it to myself. Not to my father. *Me*. I was trying to kill myself.'

'Would've been better for everyone if you'd just jumped off the Skye Bridge.'

Dominic's eyes flashed into life, deep fury burning away in them as he glowered at Crawford. 'You're very brave, coming in here and talking like that to a serial killer.'

'Aye, I am. Because you're in here.' Crawford gestured at the pair of guards. 'These boys are here to protect you from me. You're pathetic, Dominic. Whatever you've done in the past, you're no threat to me or anyone now.'

Dominic stared hard at him, for what seemed like minutes. The fire burned cold and he blinked away the embers. He gave one last look at Crawford, then shifted his icy focus to Marshall. 'I know what you're doing.'

'And what's that, Dominic?'

'He's antagonising me until I tell you the truth. But I've told everyone the truth, all along. Since I was arrested. So I don't understand what else you want from me.'

'The reason we're here, Dominic, is because we're investigating a murder.' Marshall let the word sit there. Watched something form in Dominic's eyes, then flicker out. Watched the guards exchange a look. 'Someone was killed in Hawick on Sunday evening. The murder shared a very similar methodology to the three you committed.'

'Someone else is doing what I did?'

No hesitation. No delay. Just straight in there.

'What you *both* did, Dominic.' Marshall left a gap. 'Was there someone else involved, other than you and Nicola?'

'No.'

'It was just you?'

'Just us. Always just us two. And, really, it was all me.'

Marshall nodded. 'So the obvious thing here is, could Nicola be doing this again?'

'I don't know. Maybe.'

'When was the last time you spoke to Nicola?'

'Years ago. I haven't had any contact with her since... I don't know. Five years? And that was a letter I'd written to her. She didn't reply.' Dominic sighed. 'Thing is, I told the cops to exonerate her. I wanted to take all the blame for what we did. It's *my* sickness, not hers. I was the one who raped them all. I was the one who killed them all. It's all on me. Nic's only crime was loving me.'

35

Crawford pulled into the station and started yawning. Then kept going and made a sound like he was going to start yodelling professionally. His lips slapped together. 'Well, did that scratch the itch?'

Marshall stretched out and caught his yawn. It just kept on going until he felt like he was actually crying. He finally stopped and rubbed at his eyes. 'Not really.'

'But you've got to go through the motions, right?'

'Indeed. It's been a hell of a journey, but I don't regret it.' Marshall looked over at him. 'Listen, I've been meaning to say since we left there, but you did well back there.'

'Really?'

'Not many people can sit in a room with a serial killer like him and act like such a bastard.'

'Had loads of practice at that in my marriage.'

'I mean it. Have you done that sort of thing before?'

'I've been in rooms with psychos since I was eighteen. He's killed three people for pretty tragic reasons, to be honest with you, but he's not that different from some animal you pick up in Stirling on a Saturday night for beating up his girlfriend.'

Crawford got out first and continued his stretching, like he was doing tai chi.

Marshall stayed in the car. Aye, anyone who wasn't ruffled by someone like Dominic Hayes had a lot going for him.

He checked his phone.

Still nothing from Ravenscroft.

He tapped out a text to Potter:

> Hate do this, but I need to speak to John and he's not answering me.

He sat back and didn't send it.

Because he hated doing that. He hated people who did, always copying in line managers as though that was a way to make things happen. And Marshall might be many things but he hoped he wasn't a dick.

Instead, he got out and joined Crawford by the car boot.

'Here you go.' Crawford handed him his bag and laptop case. 'Listen, I'm going to get on with it.'

'It's six o'clock, Douglas. Your shift's over.'

'Still want to see what's happened here. Then I'll bugger off back up the road.' Crawford ran a hand over his stubbly chin. 'Though when you go to the shops, I prefer pecan to maple syrup.'

'Eh?'

'Humble pie.'

'Ah. Right. With you now.'

'Willing to admit they're connected?'

'Not sure they are. But I'm starting to think there might be something. And pecan it is.' Marshall walked across the dark car park, alongside him but neither in the mood to keep chatting.

Crawford swiped through to the incident room and was engulfed in yet another yawn.

'I'll see you in a bit.' Marshall swiped into the forensics lab instead, hoping to find Kirsten.

Only Jay Thomson was there. He looked over at Marshall, his dyed-orange hair almost glowing in the darkened lab. 'Sorry, Rob, you've just missed her.'

'Cheers.' Marshall got out his phone, but there was nothing from Kirsten either. He looked over at Jay. 'You got anything to report?'

'Me?' Jay's eyes widened. 'Nothing of note, sir, no. Been one of those days. Slower than me running.' He frowned at the clock. 'Christ, is that the time?' He got up, grabbed his coat and rushed off out of the door.

Leaving Marshall alone in the lab.

So much for this being a priority investigation.

He walked through to the incident room and clocked Crawford in a huddle with Ash Paton and Jim McIntyre, then went into his office and finally hit dial on his phone.

Kirsten answered immediately. 'Oh, hey.'

Sounded like she was driving — her car must've been one of the many they passed on the A7 as Crawford hammered it down.

'Gather I've just missed you?'

'Oh, aye. Got another viewing tonight.'

'Another one?'

'Market seems to be picking up a bit. Know how it is — it's dead around Christmas and over the summer holidays. Now we're into February, things are getting into gear.'

'Right.' Marshall slid behind his desk and started plugging in his laptop. As ever, the dock was playing silly buggers so it didn't work first time. Or second. 'Fingers crossed, eh?'

'Indeed.' She paused. 'How was Inverness?'

'Not sure, really. Need to unpack my thoughts.'

'Was it worth going?'

'Always worth it, you know? Applecross itself was beautiful. We should go there for a weekend.'

Nothing.

'Hello?'

'I'm still here, Rob.'

'Okay...' Marshall sat back and felt a queasiness in his gut. 'Gather you matched the knives, though?'

'Douglas told you?'

'He did, aye.'

'Well. Ninety-five percent chance they're the same make and model of knife.'

'He said it was a hundred percent.'

'Which is why you need to discuss it with specially trained people like me or Jay before you go blabbing to bosses.'

'I haven't spoken to anyone about it.'

'Good.' She laughed. 'Haven't got the name to hand, but it's one of those anti-zombie knives.'

'Get a lot of zombies in the Borders, so you can see why.'

Kirsten laughed again. 'Listen, I'm going to spend the night here at the flat.'

'Again?' The sourness climbed his throat. 'I can't remember the last time I spent the night with you.'

'Friday.'

'Okay. But it's Tuesday now.'

More silence.

'Do you want some company?'

'You choose, Rob. It's a long way.'

'That sounds like you don't want me to come up?'

'It'll be a waste of time. The viewing's at seven. By the time you get here, it'll be over.'

'Right.' Marshall sat there, thinking it all through.

Her choice of language was the bit that got to him – spending the night together would be a waste of time in her book.

'Listen, I'm pretty tired, so I'll head back to Mum's.' Marshall reached into his drawer for a protein bar. Last one, so he needed to get another pack next time he was in Aldi. 'Even though she's threatened to have Jen over and, as you know, she's not speaking to me.'

'Still?'

'You know my sister.'

'I do.' Another uncomfortable pause. 'Well, Rob, I'll let you get on. Have a good night.'

'You too.'

But he was talking to a dead line.

Marshall sat there, a cocktail of emotions churning through him. None of it was good. He struggled to figure out what was the dominant one – feeling pissed off or just sad?

There'd been so much going on and they really needed to clear the decks with it. And just hadn't found the time. Even when things were quiet.

He finally got his laptop to dock and it started syncing with the network.

Perfect.

Someone knocked on the door.

Jolene stood there, hands on hips. 'Evening.'

'Evening yourself.'

His bloody laptop had already stopped syncing. Hadn't even connected to the network, so he had to fiddle around with the settings.

'Going to remind you joking about this being a basic murder and tempting fate.' Jolene sat opposite him. 'Then for tearing Crawford a new one about ViCLAS.'

'Might still be basic.' Marshall sat back with a smile. 'Well, not basic. But I don't think it's the same case.'

'We'll see about that.' Jolene took a drink from a can of WakeyWakey. 'Why did you bounce my call earlier?'

'Difficult to talk up there. I was in a car with my opposite number in the Highlands. And reception wasn't so much shocking as non-existent. Even worse than down here.' Marshall laughed. 'Perfect place to commit a murder and get away with it.'

Jolene winced. 'You get anything?'

'Just whiplash from the way Crawford drives.' Marshall finally got the bastard laptop on the network, but it still wasn't syncing. 'That was a lot of travel for what could've been done over the phone, but sometimes you just need to see the location. And quiz the SIO face to face.' There it was – the little synchronising wheel. Marshall looked over at her. 'Sorry I didn't get back to you. Ravenscroft's been avoiding me, so I know how crap it feels. What were you calling about?'

'Weirdest thing.' Jolene gave a flash of her eyebrows. 'The night of Chris Goodwillie's incident, Jake Turner phoned him. They spoke for twelve minutes. And then he tried to kill himself.'

'Now that is interesting.'

'And I just had to travel to Hawick for that. Not Inverness.'

'Touché.'

'We spoke to his father. Hugh had no idea about the call. And he didn't give an alibi.'

'Good stuff.' Marshall got up and walked over to the board. 'So you're saying Hugh has a plausible motive and no alibi.'

'Trouble is, we spoke to Pam Campbell, who *did* give an alibi for him. He was drunkenly sleeping on the sofa when she got back late to put Christopher to bed.'

'Bugger.' Marshall took in the full extent of their suspects, which was far fewer than he'd like at this stage of an investigation. 'Anyway. Let's regroup in the morning.'

Jolene stood up and finished her can. 'I'll see you tomorrow, Rob.' With a final nod, she left the room and pulled the door shut behind her.

36

Marshall stood by the board and looked over the last hour's work. All he'd done was confuse himself.

He was so bloody tired.

He needed to get home and get some of his mother's cooking. Then early to bed, early to rise – as Crawford had said.

Or he needed to just drink the coffee he'd made for himself and plough on with it. Get rid of the confusion. Way too late for coffee, but it was going to be one of those cases, wasn't it?

Someone knocked on the door.

'There you are.' Ravenscroft charged in like he owned the place. He stopped next to Marshall and cast his gaze over the surface of the board, like he could decipher anything on there. He moved over to the desk and leaned against it, eyeing up the mug steaming away on the desk. 'Oh, is that fresh? I'm absolutely gasping.'

'I haven't touched it yet, sir.'

'Excellent.' Ravenscroft took a big drink, then clattered the mug down on the table. 'Oh, that's fantastic coffee. Where did you get it?'

'I made it myself.'

'As in you roasted the beans yourself?'

'No, I buy them online. What I meant is I didn't get it from a café.'

'Well, if the policing goes to shit, then you've got another vocation, eh?' Ravenscroft lifted the mug and took another deep glug. 'Not that I'm saying that's likely, you know?' He laughed. 'I'll need to get a list of your equipment.'

'Just an AeroPress.'

'A what?'

'It's a thing.' Marshall held up the plastic piping that didn't look like much. 'You make coffee with it. I'll send you a link to buy it online.'

'You do that.' Ravenscroft looked at him like he'd solved quantum computing. 'Anyway. Where were we?'

'Been trying to call you, sir.' Marshall took his seat again. 'Texted you a few times.'

'So I saw.' Ravenscroft perched on the edge of the desk. 'Anyway. Thought I'd come down from Tulliallan to do this face to face.'

'How did you know I wasn't still up in Inverness?'

'Because it's about that.' Ravenscroft folded his arms. 'Word is, you were speaking to Dominic Hayes in Barlinnie?'

'That's right. Did I do something there to—'

'No, no, no.' Ravenscroft held up his phone. 'I had the misfortune of a lengthy conference call from my opposite number in charge of the Northern section of SCD. Chris Godfrey. The guy can talk, that's for sure. Turns out you ruffled more than a few of DCI Janice Shearer's feathers.'

'I'd say something like you don't make an omelette without cracking a few eggs.'

'And you'd be right. I approved that little expedition, so I've got your back.' Ravenscroft reached over to clap Marshall's arm, like they were old mates. 'How much did it cost?'

'The trip?' Marshall shrugged. 'Haven't totted it up, but it won't be much. Two single-night stays in the most basic motel on an industrial estate and two tanks of petrol.'

'Good stuff.' Ravenscroft rubbed his hands together. 'Submit the expenses tonight, if you can.'

'I'll see if Douglas can manage it.' Marshall sat back, but he'd already seen Crawford leave. 'We drove back from Inverness via Glasgow in the time it took for you to have that call, so I've told him to head home.'

'I wasn't on the phone all that time. Had to get fitted for a new suit for the press conference. Got to pay through the nose for the tailoring to be done by first thing tomorrow. A scandal.' Ravenscroft checked his watch. 'Listen. I dealt with Janice Shearer many years ago when I was in West Mercia police. She's the kind of cop who still operates in the playground and thinks her super can beat up your super. Trouble for her is I was able to *see* her super and raise her a chief super. I've cleared the way for you with Miranda.'

'Nothing to be cleared, sir.' Marshall folded his arms. 'I was just doing my job.'

'I know.' Ravenscroft sank into the chair and looked at his phone. He put it away with a bite of frustration. 'Level with me here, Robert – is there *any* risk of this opening up her case?'

Marshall looked at the board and tried to assess it all in an easily digested chunk someone like Ravenscroft could understand. 'Maybe a ten percent chance.'

'*Ten* percent...' Ravenscroft drummed his thumbs off the desk, thinking it through, then looked at his watch again. 'So you honestly think there's a possibility the same person who killed those lads up there could've killed this Jake Turner kid?'

'*Could* is the operative word, sir. Ten percent is a very low probability.'

'But it's not nothing.'

'No. But it's not ninety percent. Isn't even fifty-fifty.'

'You know that won't look good if—'

'I don't care how it looks, sir. I just want to find the truth.' Marshall struggled to contain his frustration. 'The reason we were at Barlinnie was to speak to Dominic Hayes. Obviously, he couldn't have done it, what with being inside.'

'But?'

'But either someone's copied him, which I'd say is the likeliest outcome, or his collaborator is back doing it.'

'Nicola Grant, you mean?'

'So you do read my messages?' Marshall left a pause. All Ravenscroft did was check his watch. 'She was released last year but we've no idea where she is now. One of the reasons I was calling was to—'

'Indeed. That's why I'm here to do this in person, Robert.' Ravenscroft ran a hand down his face. 'The call from Janice's super wasn't just a two-way thing. We had a senior friend in the Public Protection Unit. The central lot, based over at—'

His phone blasted out the basic old-style telephone ringtone.

He checked the display. 'Ah.' He walked over to the door and yelled, 'We're in here!'

A medium-height man followed him into Marshall's office. Immaculate hair, like he'd just been to the barber's, but his suit had seen better days. 'DI Patrick O'Brien.'

'DCI Rob Marshall.' He shook his hand but looked sidelong at Ravenscroft. 'What brings you here?'

'I head up the PPU for Lothians & Borders. My remit excludes Edinburgh City, naturally, but I do spend a lot of time down here.' And he looked the opposite of a cop, more a bank manager or an accountant. 'I just so happened to be in Greenlaw approving an environmental scan for a new release when I got a call from the super to come here and meet a John Ravenscroft and a Rob Marshall. So I came. And here I am. What's up?'

'Thanks for attending.' Ravenscroft grinned wide. 'I was on a lengthy conference call with your superior officer, regarding a Nicola Grant and why she isn't on the list for the Highlands. Apparently you've been approved to divulge that information?'

'That's right, sir.' O'Brien rested against the chair back. 'Nicola's now living in Hawick under the name of Isabelle Ward.'

37

Isabelle hated this dead time. She hated the waiting. Sitting in her cottage, feeling the walls close in, watching the clock as it ticked forward.

She'd rather be anywhere else but there were rules, weren't there? And when there were rules, there were people to enforce them.

There – ten past six. Time to leave.

She grabbed her keys from the bowl and walked over to the door. She stepped out into the freezing air and looked around as she locked it. At least it wasn't raining anymore.

But the pitch black hid them. They were watching her, twenty-four-seven. She just couldn't see them tonight.

She put the keys in her bag, next to her phone, and scanned the trees again. All dark, shimmering in the wind.

She knew someone was hiding in there, watching her. Looking at her. Documenting what she did. When she left. When she had guests – who were they? Why were they there?

But they were good at covering their tracks. Literally. She'd never found a boot print – or even a shoe print – but if you were any good at watching someone, you'd have ways and means.

Wouldn't you?

She hadn't seen them for months, but she knew that was just because they were getting better at not being spotted.

The only thing she could see was light from the farm, a quarter of a mile away.

Maybe they had a telescope. Or a pair of very good binoculars. Those night-vision ones.

Isabelle didn't have a choice, though. She just had to get on with things. The cost of what she'd done. She walked over to her car and opened the lock with the key.

She caught a flash of something over the road.

Someone watching her?

She rushed over to check.

And lost sight of it.

She got out her phone and switched on the torch, then cast the glow across the damp grass.

Had she imagined it?

No – there.

But it was just a can someone had chucked from their car. WakeyWakey. That toxic brand of energy drink.

But maybe that's what they wanted her to think... Make her stop looking for the surveillance so they could be better at it...

She picked up the can, then crossed back to the cottage and dropped it in her recycling bin.

One final look around, then she got into her car and drove off.

∽

Isabelle parked in Hawick, down a side street. A few hundred metres from her usual spot, but they were still watching her from here.

Someone was always watching her.

She locked her car and walked along the street, feeling their eyes on her.

They knew.

They *knew*.

She turned the corner and the high street was quiet. As quiet as it got, anyway. She wasn't wearing her thick coat, so the cold nibbled through the thin fabric. Daft – but she'd left in a hurry, even with all that time sitting waiting. Watching the clock and its incessant ticking.

She walked past the horse statue and tilted an imaginary cap to the rider.

Next to it, the Teribus Arms glowed in the darkness, but the windows were misted from within and it didn't exactly look welcoming. The old bastards drinking in there couldn't be spotted from out here. A real den of iniquity.

She pushed through the door and went into the warmth.

Busy for a Tuesday night.

A few old men were at the tables dotted around the bar, sitting on their own with their own drinks in front of them – a hauf-pint of lager and a wee hauf of whisky each – but they chatted across to the other tables, like they were all around the same one.

Nobody was playing pool yet, but that was likely to change.

That sense of peace settled over her for the first time all day.

They were all looking at her, the filthy old perverts, and she didn't care because she knew why. They just wanted to ogle a younger lassie bending over or showing a bit of tit. They weren't keeping an eye on her because of what she'd done.

She could rest here.

Mike Teviot was bent over, emptying the dishwasher. He stopped and did a double-take. 'Ah, Issy. Can you finish this off?' He straightened up but his distended belly just seemed to keep on plunging. 'Bloody back's killing me.'

'Sure thing.' Isabelle shrugged off her coat and hung it in the back room. 'Just let me get my coat off, eh?'

'Of course.'

She nudged him aside, then crouched to continue his job of emptying it.

Mike just stood there, twatting about on his phone and grunting. 'You hear about this laddie getting murdered down at the museum?'

Isabelle looked up at him. 'What?'

'Saw some shite on Facebook about it.' Mike waved his phone around. 'Brutal.'

'That's not the kind of thing that happens around here, is it?'

'Nope. It's not.' Mike gave her some side-eye, then whispered. 'Auld Eric's been telling us a story about some murderer living in a halfway house in Burnfoot for weeks now. Must be him did this.'

'Burnfoot?' Isabelle laughed. 'They're not likely to house anyone there.'

'Serve them right, though.' Mike bellowed with laughter. 'Living there'll be worse than jail, eh? Only place worse would be in Gala!'

He got a disconnected laugh from across the pub. The old buggers weren't following the chat, but were just primed for certain keywords – like anyone slagging off Galashiels or Jedburgh.

Isabelle finished emptying the dishwasher then stood up again.

'Half of lager, wee tot of whisky, Mike.' Auld Alec chapped on the bar. 'Make sure it's a quarter gill. None of your half measures!'

Isabelle smiled at Mike. 'I'll pour it.' She grabbed a glass from the rack above her head and started pouring the half of lager.

Auld Alec scowled over at the tills. 'Why the hell are you selling tote bags?'

'Eh?' Mike looked around, then gave him a shrug. 'Getting in the merch game.'

'Merch?'

'As in merchandise.'

'Aye, I ken that. My grandkids are always going on about merch this, swag that. Question I'll ask you, Mike, is who's buying a bag with the logo of this place on it to go around the shops with? Eh?' Auld Alec gave a big laugh, but a sneering one. No kindness in it. And nobody joined in, so he just licked his lips a few times. 'Eric was saying there about this boy in the halfway house in Burnfoot. You hear that?'

'Heard it.' Mike nodded. 'Don't believe it.'

'Oh, I do. Can believe anything, Mike.' Auld Alec shook his head. 'It's not right. Someone kills someone, they stay in jail. End of. Shouldn't get let out back into the community, should they? See this shite here.' He waved at the TV. 'Bet you a hundred quid that's him did that. Once a murderer, always a murderer. Should just let the prick rot in jail. Feed him bread and water.'

'We've been over this, Alec.' Mike rolled his eyes. 'You know it's not that simple.'

'It is, Mike. It is.' Auld Alec's hungry eyes looked over at his beer. 'Actually, you know what? You kill someone, you should die. Stands to reason, doesn't it? An eye for an eye and all that? Should bring back the death penalty, if you ask me. World's gone to shite since they got rid of it.'

Isabelle stood up tall, but the old bugger still towered over her. 'Trouble with that thinking is you have to be one hundred percent sure of a conviction. Otherwise you're risking killing an innocent man.'

'Away wi' ye.' Auld Alec dismissed it with a flick of his wrist. 'Havering nonsense there, doll. That's what happens when you let women speak, eh?' Another sneering laugh. 'Who cares if there's one dead wee bastard who didn't do it but hundreds of people left alive. Eh?'

'Sounds a bit extreme.'

'Is it hell, lass. It's just common bloody sense.'

'Common sense, eh?'

'Aye! Way I see it, if someone's up for murder, then it's obvious they've done *something*. Might not be that murder, of course, but they'll have done *something*. Or they'll be likely to do it. And who cares if there's another one off the street if we're protecting good people? Convicted is guilty in my book. Better to lock 'em up and hang them than risk even more decent folk getting in harm's way.'

Isabelle grinned at him, but inside she was seething. 'And you get to decide who the decent folk are?'

Auld Alec nodded. 'Got a good idea of who's good and who's bad, lass, aye.'

Isabelle waited until Mike handed him his whisky, then spat in his half pint.

38

Marshall sat in the passenger seat of O'Brien's car as he wound through the outskirts of Hawick, avoiding the roadworks plaguing the centre.

His phone chimed and he checked it – the photo message had finally popped up and he now had a photo of Nicola, AKA Isabelle Ward. More recent than her release. Dark-haired with icy blue eyes. A black dragon tattoo crawled up her arm and chest, with its tail lashing across her neck. A bold look, for sure.

Marshall put his phone away again. 'Take it you've met her?'

'Isabelle? Obviously. Have to speak to her regularly. First year, she meets with me every month. Parole officer weekly.'

'How was she the last time you saw her?'

'Wouldn't know she'd done what she's done, if you catch my drift.' O'Brien's nostrils started twitching. He stopped at the lights and glanced over at Marshall. 'Thing with Public Protection is it's basically offender management. How we reintroduce them into society, once they've served their sentence. Trouble is, most of our time is spent dealing with difficult cases like Isabelle's.'

'You use her new name.'

'Right. They've paid their debt to society. We're trying to make sure they don't incur another one by showing them respect. These are sex offenders. Child molesters. And my geography's vast. Feels like I cover half of Scotland at times. Jenny in Edinburgh has a whole city, sure, but you can get between any two points pretty quickly.' O'Brien dragged his hand down his face. 'Half my time's spent in West Lothian, then a quarter down here. Midlothian and East Lothian combined are the final quarter but, of course, they still have their issues, don't they?'

'And what were Isabelle's issues?'

'Less than you'd think, but we still assessed her as a level 3 risk.' O'Brien blinked hard a few times. 'At that level, it was my super who chaired the MAPPA, not me.'

'That's a Multi-Agency Public Protection Arrangement, right?'

O'Brien nodded. 'Of course.'

'Just like to check these things. I'm not a fan of initialisations being used willy-nilly.'

'I get it. Sows confusion, right?'

'Right. And division. Wouldn't be the first time something in the Met was called something entirely different up here.'

'You work for the Met?'

'No. Sorry.' Marshall raised his hands. 'I did. See what I mean about confusion?' He laughed. 'Spent ten years there, so all my terminology is still mostly theirs, but I've been working for Police Scotland almost three now and I'm starting to acclimatise.'

'Okay. With offenders like her, we have to assess three risks… First, is she a risk to the community? We deemed her a low risk on that score.'

'Even with a connection to three murders?'

'Even so.' O'Brien nodded. 'She wasn't the killer, was she?'

'True, but—'

'I know what you're going to say, but she'd have to find someone else with homicidal tendencies *and* anti-social sexual pathology. That represents less than a percentage point of the known offenders.'

'But there's always a risk she finds an unknown.'

'Absolutely. But we're talking finding a needle in a barn full of haystacks. Second risk – is there a risk *to* her from the community? Could be active threats online or in person. We found nothing, but there's always a risk so we have a team to constantly monitor social media for that kind of thing. But it's part of the reason we stuck her out here in the wilds.'

And it felt really wild – they were on the road to Jedburgh now, not quite a trunk road but nowhere near as winding as some in the Borders. And at least it had two lanes. 'And the third risk?'

'Is there a reputational risk to Police Scotland if we fuck up?' O'Brien laughed. 'But that's my cross to bear. Bottom line, Isabelle was deemed very low risk of reoffending by representatives from all agencies.' O'Brien leaned back in the seat and ran a hand through his hair. 'Why are you interested in her?'

'You haven't been briefed?'

'Nope. I got a call up from the super who told me to get down to Gala to meet John Ravenscroft. And yourself. You know the drill – when your super calls and tells you to meet another super, you don't ask questions.'

'No. I get it. I've just got back from the Highlands, where I was speaking to DCI Janice Shearer, who was the SIO on those murders in Applecross. And Janice didn't know where she went after her release.'

'Right.' O'Brien dug his fingers into his hair and scratched at his scalp, but still kept on driving. 'The details around Isabelle's case is super and above, because of what she did.'

'Direct involvement in three murders. Surprised you took on someone like that.'

'Wouldn't normally or if we were in control, but we were desperate.'

'Oh?'

'We had an ex-DS who'd been done for voyeurism.' O'Brien gave a flash of his eyebrows. 'Based in Edinburgh, but he lived in Midlothian. After he retired, he started following nurses home from the hospital. He'd watch them from outside their windows, masturbating. Until he got caught. Lucky sod got off with a suspended sentence, but he's on the SO register for life.' He smiled at Marshall. 'That's the Sexual Offences register.'

Marshall laughed. 'I know what that one is.'

'Given he'd put away so many people, we obviously couldn't rehome him in Edinburgh, the Lothians or even down here in the Borders.'

'So you looked for someone to swap with?'

'And we found them. The Highlands and Islands were looking to get rid of Isabelle/Nicola because, for obvious reasons, she couldn't be rehomed there. The case was pretty public and all over the news.'

'Thing is, she was sentenced to nine years but served eight. That means her behaviour inside wasn't that good.'

'I know. But like I said, we were *desperate*. And we both needed a win.' O'Brien stared at him. 'So how about you tell me what your interest in her is, then?'

'Have you heard about that murder at Hawick Museum?'

'Heard something about it on the radio. You think *she* did it?'

'Maybe.'

'I'm here on a maybe?'

'So much of what I do is based on maybe. Or a could be. First, it's almost a carbon-copy of the original murders up north. Second, she just so happens to move here to Hawick and someone copies the exact MO... So yeah, we're seriously considering it.'

'*Almost* a copy?'

'Ninety-five percent chance the knife is the same make and model. But other than that... Victimology is a match. Body left out in the open like the third. Stabbed from behind like the last two. Perimortem and postmortem rape like all three. Messages scored into his flesh'

'Bloody hell.' O'Brien shot him a look, betraying the fear he was going to get into deep shit over this. 'I see why you're desperate to speak to her.'

He took the turning to the right, then drove down a lane in the middle of nowhere. Dark, with the wind blowing the car so hard he had to correct for it. Then another right turn, through the gates of a cute lodge house, long since converted into a home. Half a mile, then he slowed to pull up opposite a battered old cottage that was far too close to the road.

A farm glowed in the distance, but that was the only source of light nearby. Even in the dark Marshall could see the trees, lashed around by the gusts of wind. 'Bit out of the way, isn't it?'

'A farm cottage a few miles from Hawick. Perfect location.' O'Brien nodded over at the house. 'Arranged it for her myself and environmentally scanned it personally.'

Marshall almost laughed – cops loved to tart up what they did as if it was the most technical set of tasks anyone could do. 'And what's an environmental scan when it's at home?'

'It means we assess the vicinity for anything that would breach the conditions of her release.' O'Brien pointed over to the distant farm. 'Two kids live there, but they're both girls and under ten so we deemed them low risk. Everyone else nearby is thirty-plus.'

'So you wouldn't put her in a town?'

'Not if we can avoid it. If you put a sex offender in a council house, you've got a recipe for complete disaster there. Talk about a powder keg waiting to explode... Or just a time bomb. Soon as word gets around, game's a bogey. And in a town like

Hawick, word has a habit of getting around.' O'Brien sucked in a deep breath. 'Let's see if she's in, shall we?' He got out and waited for Marshall to join him, before walking over to the dark cottage.

He pressed the bell and something chimed deep inside.

No signs of life in there. No music, no cooking smells.

Marshall stepped to the side and peered in through the cottage window, grimacing. 'She's not in, is she?'

'Not looking good, I have to say.' O'Brien checked his watch. 'Probably at work.'

'You don't have her shift pattern?'

'Nope. We don't need to see it. Her parole officer does.'

'Does she have a car?'

'Aye, and we've plumbed it.' O'Brien checked his phone then tapped out a message. 'Got my team to run a check on where it is right now and, before you start, she's only just got back to me.' He set off back to his car. 'It's parked in Hawick.'

39

Isabelle finally managed to finish stacking the dishwasher again. Both lunch *and* tea plates sitting there. Not quite enough to put on, but sod it, she wasn't paying the bills, so she ran it again. Not that there were enough old buggers in tonight to need the glasses to be stocked up again.

She yawned, already tired – and most of her shift still to get through.

Not sleeping...

And nothing worked... Pills, potions, lotions. She'd tried it all. And still she'd just lie there, looking up at the ceiling.

Made her long for prison at times – at least the nocturnal screams and shouts meant you knew you weren't going to sleep.

Two of the old timers were playing pool, but it was painful watching them take ten seconds just to bend over enough to take the shot.

Hell, even a game of pool was an extreme sport at that age.

She got out her phone to check the news, but the battery was very low. Stupid. In all that worry about being watched, she'd really not paid attention to the basic stuff.

She found the correct cable behind the bar and stuck it on to charge, then looked around the bar.

Nobody wanted a drink and she didn't have her phone.

Maybe she should stick a 50p on the edge of the table and give one of them a game – after all, she could pour a pint in the time it took them to take a shot. Not that they'd be pocketing much.

Most of the punters were watching the horse racing.

'Fucking told you that was a stupid bet. Should never have listened to you.'

'Surprised you ever shut up long enough to hear what someone else was saying, Stevie!'

Mike was behind the bar, folding his arms across his chest. 'Last time, those two broke four pool cues over the other's heads.'

Isabelle pointed at the stack of cues over by the table. 'Did wonder why you've got forty of them.'

'Remind me to put you on a Friday or Saturday night shift.' Mike laughed, but it soon slipped away. 'If this gets any worse, I'm calling the cops.'

'*Seriously?*'

'I know these idiots, Issy. Can spot where it's going a mile off.'

Last thing Isabelle wanted was the cops in here. They'd ask questions – and they'd wait for the right answers too. 'Mind if I take my break early?'

Mike raised his eyebrows. 'Still smoking, I take it?'

'Didn't get on with those patches. They made my heart race like I was on speed. You mind?'

'Aye, fine but just serve this customer first.' Mike walked off through the pub towards the two arguing punters, both on their feet and squaring up to each other. Hands up, he started to pacify them.

A man was waiting at the bar. Red-faced. Skinny. Slicked-back hair, way too dark for his age, with a sharp widow's peak that almost reached down to the top of his nose. She sort of recognised him, but couldn't place him.

Isabelle walked over with a smile. 'What can I get you, pal?'

He rested on the bar and leaned forward. 'I know what you did.'

A brief spark of fear rushed through her, making her heart race.

But he was just some old arsehole trying to wind her up.

So she smiled at him. 'And what did I do, eh?'

'I. Fucking. Know.'

40

O'Brien parked on double yellows, but he didn't seem to mind so Marshall didn't either. He pointed over the road. 'That's it there.'

A red Fiesta sat under a cone of light. Old enough to be in consideration for a police pool car.

Marshall got out and walked over to it, shining his torch inside. No sign of Isabelle and the bonnet felt cold. 'I hope she's not run away.'

'Not the type to. She wants to put down roots here. Young enough to start again, you know?'

'Does that mean she's talked about starting a family?'

'They all do. It's a way of showing how normal they are now. How little of a threat they represent. Truth is, if they do have kids, it makes them significantly less likely to reoffend.' O'Brien started walking along the street. 'Come on.'

Marshall kept pace with him, passing the town's famous horse statue. It'd come up in a case a couple of years ago, but he couldn't quite remember how or why. Just that it had.

O'Brien stopped outside the Teribus Arms. 'AKA The Terie to the locals.' He frowned. 'Took me a while to work it out, but it's in the town's motto. "Ye Teribus ye Teriodin". No idea what it means, though.'

'An ancient rallying call used in battle.'

'Right. Never knew that.' O'Brien nodded. 'And now it's just a grotty pub where old buggers fight each other with pool cues.'

Marshall followed him inside and tried to act like a pair of blokes out for a pint in a pub they didn't normally drink in.

The place was pretty quiet. A long bar down one side of the room, with a huddle of old drinkers at the far end watching the horse racing on the wall-mounted TV.

This side, two old guys played pool, but were arguing over something with raised voices, drowned out by the shouting over the racing.

Forty pool cues were stacked up next to the table and Marshall clocked it as being one of *those* pubs.

O'Brien nodded to the barman. 'It's Mike, isn't it? Mike Teviot?'

Teviot glowered at Marshall. 'Depends on who's asking?'

'Police. DI Patrick O'Brien.' He tossed his warrant card onto the bar, like he didn't care if anyone picked it up to examine or not. 'This is DCI Rob Marshall.'

'Then I'm the Easter Bunny.'

O'Brien smirked. 'Aye, good one.'

'Aye, I own the place.' Teviot let out a long sigh, then replaced it with a professional smile. 'How can I help you, gents?'

'Looking for Isabelle.' O'Brien looked around the bar. 'Thought she might be on, but I don't seem to see her?'

'What, you just want a quiet word, do you? A DI and a DCI?'

'Trouble with all these books and cop shows is everyone's an expert on police procedure these days.' O'Brien nodded. 'How is she doing?'

'Great worker, even comes in early to clean every couple of

days, which saves me a packet. Punters love her too. Never hear any complaints.'

'How's she getting on, really?'

'She's been fine, *really*. I knew what I was getting myself into by hiring her. I know she served time.' Teviot leaned forward. 'Everyone could do with a second chance. Been there myself.'

'You heard right. And you're doing a good thing by employing her and letting her rebuild her life.' O'Brien looked around. 'Is she on tonight or not?'

'She is, aye.'

O'Brien smiled at him. 'So where is she?'

Teviot pointed to the side door. 'She's on a break now.' He pretended to smoke a cigarette.

'I'll go.' Marshall walked outside into a car park. He couldn't for the life of him figure out how you'd get in here in a car, but there was no sign of her. He found the path through to the road but he wouldn't want to drive anything up there, certainly not anything he owned. Probably just suitable for smoking, drinking and fighting. He went back inside. 'She's definitely on a break?'

'Started smoking again.' Teviot shrugged. 'Maybe she's gone to get some more fags.'

Marshall winked. 'How about you ring her, eh?'

'Fine.' Teviot sighed then picked up his phone and put it to his ear. He kept his gaze locked on Marshall, then pulled the phone away and tapped the screen. 'She's not picking up.' He walked over to the till, where something was rattling, and scowled. 'Fuck's sake.' He held up a phone. 'Her phone's bloody sitting here.'

41

O'Brien drove down another back street, heading towards the river.

Marshall gripped the handle, even though O'Brien was a much calmer driver than Crawford. Trying hard to not jump to conclusions.

And failing.

O'Brien stopped by a nondescript block of Victorian flats, with a shop and office on the ground floor, then got out.

Marshall followed him and joined him by the door.

O'Brien knocked on the ground-floor door. Whether this was the first time or not, Marshall didn't know.

The door opened and a man scowled at Marshall. Big, tall and ugly enough to have played rugby to a good standard but kept up the drinking long after it was good for him. 'What do you want?'

O'Brien stepped forward. 'Evening, Brendan.'

'Oh, it's you.'

'Aye, it's me. Mr Brendan Sullivan.' O'Brien pointed to the side. 'Meet DCI Rob Marshall.'

Just like with Mike Teviot back at the pub, the rank seemed to spook him, making him eye up Marshall again.

O'Brien smiled. 'Working late, I see?'

'So much paperwork these days. Worse than when I had a proper job.' Sullivan shifted his gaze between them, but he seemed to focus more on Marshall. 'What do you want?'

O'Brien took a step forward. 'Can we have a word, Brendan?'

'A word, eh?' Sullivan stood his ground. 'Depends what it's about.'

'No. It really doesn't.' O'Brien slapped his hands together, then motioned inside. 'Shall we?'

Sullivan gave a withering look, then let out a sigh. 'In you come, then.' He stepped back into the building and let them past.

Marshall followed O'Brien into an office. Files everywhere – on the floor, the windowsill, the collapsing bookcase. Seemed to be some semblance of order to it, but it'd take a team of forensic accountants to decipher precisely what.

Sullivan sat down and offered them both the only free seat.

Neither took it.

'Suit yourselves.' Sullivan cracked his knuckles like he was a hard man, but it seemed to cause some pain. 'So. Which one of my clients is it?'

'Isabelle Ward. AKA Nicola Grant.'

'Right. Her.' Sullivan looked away, shaking his head. 'What's she done?'

'Accomplice to a serial murderer, but you knew that.' O'Brien smirked. 'When did you last hear from her, Brendan?'

'Friday of last week. Usual time we meet.'

'In here?'

'In here.'

O'Brien looked around like he didn't believe him. 'How's

she been keeping?' Spoken like he was asking about his dear old mum.

'Fine. Not heard any complaints from any of the usuals.' Sullivan drummed his fingers on the desk. 'Until you pair show up.' He stopped drumming and started tapping the desk with a silver pen. 'Come on, mate, what's she done? And no sarcasm, please, I'm up to my oxters in it.'

'You were on her MAPPA, right?'

'I was. Wasn't sure it was a good idea taking her, given what she's been convicted of.' Sullivan started sifting through a stack of paperwork then pulled out a bulging file. 'But she's actually been fine. No hassle. All her appointments are prompt. All the checks I've done on her work and home have been exemplary.'

O'Brien tilted his head to the side. 'But?'

'But nothing.'

O'Brien reached over for the file but Sullivan slapped his hand away. 'Any idea where she could be?'

'What, you mean now?'

'Yes, now.'

Sullivan frowned then looked through the file, running a finger down a page. 'She's working, isn't she?'

'That's the thing. We've just been to the Terie. Her phone's there, but she isn't. Seems to have buggered off.'

'You're still tracking her phone?'

'We don't track people's phones, Brendan. Never have.'

'But you've plumbed her car, right?'

'Standard procedure.'

'What about her house?'

'First place we looked.' O'Brien sat down in the chair and leaned forward, making a loud creak. 'Listen, Brendan, you and I have always got on pretty well. It'd be a great help to us if you could point us in her direction.'

'Okay, but what's she done?'

'You hear about this murder at Hawick Museum?'

'Right?' Sullivan's frown deepened. 'You think she did that?'

'Similar MO to her old crimes.' O'Brien pointed to Marshall. 'Rob here is the SIO on the case.'

Sullivan crunched back in his chair. 'And you just assume she's involved in this?'

'We're not assuming anything.' Marshall smiled. 'That's the whole point. We just want to speak to her and eliminate her from our enquiries. Sure you can understand that, as part of standard procedure, we'd need to speak to someone like her.'

'Someone like her.' Sullivan shook his head. 'Mate, she's paid her debt to society.'

'Oh, if only it was impossible for someone to do the same crime after they'd served their sentence.'

'Cheeky prick, aren't you?' Sullivan leaned forward, cracking his elbows off the desk. 'I'd love to help, but I honestly don't know where she is.'

'I see.' Marshall walked around the room and started pissing about with his files to see if that would get him to play ball. 'Going to need a list of her known assoc—'

Right then, a woman ran in through the door. 'I need help.' She rushed over to hide behind them. 'Someone's after me!'

She wasn't exactly dressed for the elements – her white vest top exposed a dragon tattoo climbing from her arm up to her throat.

Isabelle Ward…

42

Marshall sipped at his tea. He knew he shouldn't have it this late, but he was absolutely shattered. Hard to believe he'd been in Inverness just that morning.

O'Brien rested his own cup on the windowsill, overlooking the car park, and rubbed at his eyes. 'Sure you're happy with me sitting in on this?'

'Unless the D in your rank doesn't stand for detective?'

'It does, aye.' O'Brien picked up his cup again and slurped at it. 'Been a while since I've done a proper interview like this.'

'Were you ever in mainstream CID?'

'Lothian & Borders CID as a DC and DS, then I moved over to the Edinburgh MIT when they messed it all up and created Police Scotland.' The side of his lip curled up. '*Hated* it. This other DS... Total cowboy, but everyone called him the golden child. Heard now he's a DCI but that could just be a rumour.' His smiled turned to a snarl. 'Anyway... This gig came up in PPU, so I took it.'

'Promotion?'

'Aye. Haven't regretted a second. Got a brilliant team and I feel like we're doing good work to make the place safer.'

'Well done. That's as rare as hen's teeth.'

'Isn't it just...' O'Brien finished his tea and looked around for somewhere to put his cup. 'What about you? You were in the Met, blah blah blah. How long have you been a DCI?'

'I haven't.' Marshall sipped his tea. 'It's just acting.'

'Ah. One of those, eh?'

'Lot of it going around.'

'Horrible situation to be in.' He picked up his tea cup and looked in – clearly forgotten he'd just drained it. 'They dangle a big carrot in front of more than one horse for as long as possible and see who they like best.'

Marshall looked around the corridor, but no sign of any movement, so he stared out of the window over the A7 heading out of Hawick. A steady stream of traffic in and out of the town. 'This station should really be my base. Biggest in the area.'

'But it's in Hawick?' O'Brien winked. 'I get it.'

'Hawick's not that bad. Gala's just more central and easier for meetings elsewhere.'

'You mean up at Tulliallan?'

'And Gartcosh.'

O'Brien nodded slowly, like he knew what went on there, but Marshall doubted he'd been there.

The door opened and a young male uniform stepped out. 'Ready for you now, sir.'

'Thanks, son.' O'Brien stood up tall and adjusted his clip-on tie as he gave Marshall some side-eye. 'So, do you want me to be good cop?'

Marshall smiled. 'Just need you to sit there and let me lead.' He pushed into the interview room.

Isabelle sat there alone, sipping her own cup of tea. She wouldn't look at either of them.

O'Brien took the chair diagonally opposite and rested his

paperwork on the table in front of him, all prim and proper like his posture.

Marshall stayed standing, taking his time to finish his tea as he assessed her body language, his own papers crumpled and bunched up.

He'd been in many interviews with serial killers before – Dominic Hayes was the most recent. All of them had enacted their own crimes, squeezing life out of victims with their own hands, plunging knives into hearts with their own hands or, God knows, drowning people in their own baths then filling them with acid.

Isabelle Ward – AKA Nicola Grant – was a different beast entirely.

While she hadn't plunged the knives herself, she'd coerced or enabled Dominic's murders. Or just documented them to enable him to have sex with her.

Took a particular mind to do that.

Marshall took the seat opposite her and sat there, slowly sipping his tea. Waiting. Smoothing out his papers to iron out the creases.

Isabelle looked over at him, frowning.

Marshall smiled at her. 'You reckon someone was after you.'

Isabelle nodded. 'They were.'

'Thing is, I went back outside Mr Sullivan's office and nobody was there. Just an empty street.'

She shrugged. 'He must've run off.'

'Nobody was chasing you, Isabelle, were they?'

'They were right behind me. Must've lost them down by the river.' Isabelle sucked in a breath and seemed to examine Marshall, like she was assessing prey. 'Who are you?'

'DCI Rob Marshall.' He gave her a kind smile. 'I'm neutral here, Isabelle. Okay? If you tell me the truth, I'll believe you. But I need to stress that I'm looking for truth backed up by facts. Level with me and I'll be your best friend. Lie to me and I'm gone.'

She frowned at him, then nodded. 'Okay.'

He gave her a stern look. 'Let's start with who was following you.'

'I... I don't know.'

'We need a description. Was it a man or—'

'A man. I told you.' Isabelle looked around the room, desperate, but her eyes didn't focus on anything. Then they locked on to O'Brien. 'Someone's found out my identity, haven't they?'

Marshall frowned at her. 'Your identity?'

'Don't pretend you don't know.' Isabelle pointed at O'Brien. 'He knows.'

'Knows what?'

'He *knows*.'

'Isabelle, what does he know?'

'Who I was.' Isabelle looked down at her lap. 'Who I used to be. Nicola...'

'Care to enlighten me?'

'This man, he...' Isabelle looked up at him with fire in her eyes. 'He hounded me. Shouted at me. Chased me out of the pub, chased me down to the river.'

'What was he hounding you about?'

'I can't say.'

'Can't or won't?'

She shrugged. 'Take your pick.'

'Was it about what happened in Applecross?'

'So you know?'

'I do, aye. Was it about that?'

Isabelle just shook her head.

'Who was he?'

'An older guy. Don't know his name.'

'A customer?'

'I think so. But not a regular.'

Marshall sat back. 'After we got you secure, we visited the Teribus Arms and—'

'The Terie.'

'Okay. The Terie.' Marshall smiled at her. 'We talked to an Alec and Eric in the pub.'

'It wasn't them. I just told you he wasn't a regular.'

'Eric did tell us something interesting, though.' Marshall leaned forward. 'Said he saw you spit into Alec's beer.'

Isabelle let out a deep breath. She looked at O'Brien, as though pleading for him to take over and let her off with this. But she got nothing from him, so she looked back at Marshall. 'You know what? He deserved it.'

Marshall laughed. 'He deserved you spitting in his beer?'

'Of course.' Isabelle shrugged. 'He's a prick.'

'But he wasn't the man who approached you?'

'No. But it was about that. Probably thought he could get some free drinks out of knowing.'

'So why did you run?'

Isabelle shrugged.

'Is it because of the murder?'

Isabelle frowned. 'What murder?'

'We found the body of a young man at Hawick Museum yesterday morning.' Marshall paused, watching her reaction. Almost like a normal human being. Almost. Widening eyes, softening of focus, a brief flash of eyebrows, a slight opening of her mouth. 'You know the place?'

'Been there once. Wasn't my scene.'

'Your scene, right.' Marshall smiled. 'The victim's name was Jake Turner.'

Isabelle shrugged again. Seemed to be a habit with her. 'Never heard of him.'

'Sure about that?'

'Told you. I don't know who he is.'

Marshall held her gaze, but she wouldn't look away. Whatever the truth was, she believed what she was saying. And he'd met enough world-class liars to recognise one. But Isabelle was different – there was a fragility to her he hadn't expected, but also an inner strength. He pulled out a sheet of paper. 'Jake was a seventeen-year-old boy.'

Isabelle flinched – she knew precisely why they were speaking to her.

'He lived in Hawick. Parents still do, up in Burnfoot.'

Another flinch. But he didn't think it was anything to do with Jake.

'We don't know why he was there, though. Parents don't either. It's possible he might've been meeting someone there. But it's also a similar location to where you killed your victims in Applecross.'

Isabelle snorted and glared at him. Gone was the lost woman – he'd awoken a demon. She blinked and the demon went back to sleep again. 'I didn't kill anyone.'

'Okay. Sure. Let's say it's a similar location to where you assisted Dominic Hayes to murder three young men.'

Isabelle looked away, shaking her head.

'I visited the location you killed them, you know? And we met him. Dominic.' Marshall paused again, letting the name reverberate. Let it rattle around inside her head. 'Dominic seems to have finally accepted himself.'

Isabelle was still shaking her head, like she was trying to cast the name back out through her ears.

'When did you last speak to him, Isabelle?'

'The day we were arrested. Other than through our lawyers, I mean.'

'You didn't talk to him in prison?'

'Hard to.' Isabelle laughed. 'I was in Peterhead. He was in Barlinnie.'

'Considering you haven't spoken in years, you seem to know a lot about him.'

'Do I?'

'You do. Like the fact he was in Barlinnie, for a start.'

'I was able to ask the guards questions, you know?' Isabelle rolled her lips together. 'And Dom wrote to me. Several times, in fact.'

'Did you reply?'

'Why would I?'

'Remorse, maybe?'

'For what?'

'For what you did, Isabelle. For what you both did.'

'Here's the thing, Detective Chief Inspector Robert Marshall, I gave evidence against Dom. Evidence which convicted him. You wouldn't have got that if it wasn't for me. And the truth is, I was appalled by what he'd done. He'd coerced me into doing it with him.'

'That's your repeated refrain, isn't it?' Marshall sat there, nodding along. 'And almost exactly the same words as I read in the case file just this morning.'

'What do you mean?'

'You're repeating a set of phrases, Isabelle. I assume your lawyer helped you craft that.'

'So? It doesn't mean it's not true.'

'Sure, but that's not all of it, is it?' Marshall raised his eyebrows. 'Because you used Dominic to kill your brother. Didn't you?'

'He killed who he wanted to kill.' She shook her head again. 'I had nothing to do with it. And if you think I did, then you should acknowledge that I've paid my price for it. Eight years I was inside. Eight years. It was hell. Nobody deserves to go through what I did. Nobody.'

'Come on, Isabelle. That's not true, is it? You pointed him in Kieron's direction.'

She shut her eyes, like that would make him stop. 'No, I didn't.'

'Did Nicola, then?'

'What?'

'If Isabelle didn't, then did Nicola?'

'Don't try to use language like that. It won't work.'

'Did killing Kieron make you feel good?'

'You don't know what you're talking about.'

'Come on, Isabelle. He was your *brother*. Or Nicola's brother.'

'Told you…' She reopened them and shot him a fiery glare. 'I'm not here to answer questions about the distant past.'

'Fine.' Marshall rolled his shoulders. 'Let's talk about the very recent past, then. Where were you last night?'

'So you are trying to frame me for this kid's murder, then?'

'I'm just asking you where you were last night, Isabelle. Nothing more, nothing less.'

'I can't go back inside. I won't.'

'Nobody's talking about that, Isabelle.' Marshall splayed his hands on the table. 'Just need to know your movements around midnight last night.'

'An alibi…' Isabelle sucked in a deep breath. 'The truth is, I was with my boyfriend.'

'What?' O'Brien rifled through his own documents. 'Isabelle, as part of your care package, you're supposed to pass on the names of your associates to your parole officer.'

'Aye? So?'

'We don't have the name of a boyfriend listed on your recent submission, which you provided just last week.'

Isabelle held his gaze. 'That's not true.'

'Eh?'

'His name's on there.'

43

Brendan Sullivan was on his hands and knees, scurrying about on the floor of his office. In the intervening time, he'd at least tried to get some semblance of control over his files, now loosely stacked, rather than just cast across the floor. He looked over at the door and winced when he saw them enter. 'Knew I should've bloody locked that.'

'Need to discuss something else with you.' O'Brien clicked at the desk – aside from the files, it contained the keys to a Volvo. 'Sit.'

'I'm not a fucking dog. And I don't report to you.'

'Okay, but you'll want to help us here. Because if you don't, it'll look worse for you... it's already going to be bad.'

'Wanker.' Sullivan sprang to his feet with a grace belying his years, then sat behind his desk. He picked up a document and started reading it instead of paying attention to them.

'So, Brendan, you need to remind me.' O'Brien leaned forward to rest his hands on the desk. 'When did Isabelle provide her latest submission, again?'

Sullivan looked up and scratched at his neck. 'Last week's meeting.'

'Okay.' O'Brien tapped a finger on the desk. 'What day?'

'Friday.'

'Friday.' O'Brien reached into his pocket and pulled out a sheet of paper. He looked at it for a few seconds, then handed the page to Sullivan. 'How many people are on there, Brendan?'

'Do you need to go to Specsavers or something?' Sullivan's laugh faded as he read through it, tongue wedged in his cheek. He rested it on his desk. 'Eleven.'

'Eleven.' O'Brien nodded. 'See any mention of a boyfriend on there?'

Sullivan sat back and sighed. He shifted his gaze between them, then looked back at the paper. Like he was looking for some kind of lie he could spin to get out of this. Instead, he gave up and let the page fall onto the desk. 'What's she been saying?'

'We asked her for an alibi for where she was two nights ago. Said she was with her boyfriend.' O'Brien pointed at the page. 'Now, my eyesight might not be as good as it used to be, but I can still read. And I can't see the name of a boyfriend on there.'

Sullivan picked the page up again, then put it back down on the desk. 'So?'

'Care to explain why she hasn't listed her boyfriend?'

'No idea. Sorry.'

'You know...' O'Brien looked over at Marshall with a cheeky grin on his face. 'It's funny when people talk about being boyfriend and girlfriend at our age, isn't it? You kind of think you grow out of those playground names. But then again, *partner* sounds so cold and formal.' O'Brien stared hard at him. 'And you're a married man, Brendan, aren't you?'

'I am.' Sullivan reached into the drawer for a photo. He handed it to Marshall. 'See?'

Nice trick – handing the photo to the senior officer in the room, like he could curry favour.

The photo showed Sullivan somewhere hot, wearing a vest

and shorts, his arms around a red-haired woman and two kids who shared their mother's hair.

'Lovely photo.' Marshall handed it back. 'But what my colleague meant was you're not married to Isabelle.'

Sullivan stared into space for a very long time, then swallowed something down. He wouldn't look at them. 'She told you, then?'

'She did.' O'Brien took the seat. 'How long has it been going on, Brendan?'

'A while.'

'So you admit you've been—'

'—screwing her, yeah. A real moment of weakness.' Sullivan scratched at his neck. 'Which led to a good few weeks of madness, let me tell you.'

'This isn't funny.' O'Brien shook his head. 'What the hell were you thinking, man?'

'What, because I'm a fat bastard in my forties and she's a goddess in her late twenties?' Sullivan laughed. 'Of course I'm going to smash that. Telling me you wouldn't?'

'Of course I wouldn't!' O'Brien smacked a hand off the desk. 'Our jobs aren't that different, Brendan. We're entrusted with looking after these people. They might have done terrible crimes, but they're also vulnerable in so many ways. Especially someone like her. Besides that, there's a huge power imbalance in your relationship. Not to mention that it's a fundamental breach of care.'

Sullivan shifted his focus to the paper. 'She's damaged, sure, but I can handle her.'

'You can handle her. Right.'

'And fuck me – she could suck-start a fucking lorry. And the things she does with her—'

'Brendan... I'm warning you.'

'I'm being serious here. This isn't what you think. I'm in love with her. And I think she loves me. We've even talked about having kids.'

'You absolute fucking moron.' O'Brien laughed. 'You'll be lucky if you don't lose your job for this.'

'Hardly. I'll just need a transfer, that's all.'

'You stupid, stupid bastard. Did you think you'd be able to just shack up with her and it'd be totally cool?'

'I... Maybe. I mean, she'll get a new parole officer, right?'

'Idiot.' O'Brien tapped the photo. 'What does Emma think of this?'

'Why do you fucking think I'm staying in here?'

'Eh?'

'I'm staying in my fucking office.' Sullivan nodded past O'Brien. 'Tiny wee room back there. Kicked me out, didn't she? Won't let me see the kids.'

'And you're still seeing Isabelle?'

'Of course I am. Have you not seen her or something? Anyone who says they'd have done differently is either a liar or... bats for the other team.'

O'Brien stared hard at him, shaking his head at him.

Then his phone rang.

O'Brien sighed as he checked the display. 'Better take this. Back in a sec.' He stood up and left the room. 'Hi, boss. Sorry. I was with him.' The door shut, cutting off his conversation.

Leaving Marshall with Sullivan.

Sullivan wouldn't make eye contact with him, just kept his focus on his desk, like he was inspecting the wood grain for quality.

'Where were you at midnight two nights ago?'

Sullivan looked up at him and briefly made eye contact. 'Shagging her.'

'Sure.'

'I was.'

'You were with her but you were actually assisting her in murdering Jake Turner.'

Sullivan's mouth hung open. 'Why the hell would I do that?'

Deflection, rather than denial… Interesting.

'It's very obvious to us that it happened, Brendan. We just don't understand why you're involved. So you need to tell us.'

'Last night?' Sullivan shrugged. 'Aye. Like I said, she was sucking my—'

'How long were you with her?'

'All night.' Sullivan gave another shrug. 'Might be getting on a bit, but I've still got stamina in buckets. And when that runs out, there are pills you can take these days. May not be able to see it without a mirror but it works well enough.'

Despite the professional calamity awaiting him, Sullivan clearly took great pride in keeping up sexually with a woman over a decade his junior. Must've made him feel like a real man.

'You know if you insist you were with her all night, you're saying you were involved in everything she did.'

Yet another shrug.

'Have you got any way of proving this, Brendan?'

'Have you asked her?'

'We have, yes.' Marshall nodded. 'Which is why I'm asking you now.'

'So she told you I was with her, right?' Sullivan smiled at him. 'I know how this works, mate. Believe me – more than anyone else, I know how this works.'

'If that's the case, then why have you done something so stupid?'

Another shrug.

'Did you think you'd get away with it?'

'I have, haven't I?'

'For now.'

O'Brien barrelled back in, rubbing his hands together.

Marshall pointed at Sullivan. 'He shares her claim.'

Sullivan nodded his confirmation.

'That's funny.' O'Brien laughed. 'Because we've got evidence to the contrary.'

'Eh?' Sullivan shifted his gaze between them. 'What are you talking about?'

O'Brien took his seat again, resting his feet on the desk. 'Why don't you just own up, eh?'

'We were here!' Sullivan pointed through to the back room. 'Fuck this.' He got up and tramped over, then hauled the door open. 'Have a look, if you don't believe me!'

Marshall popped his head in.

Not exactly an upmarket apartment, but not as bad as he'd feared. A large bed lay in the middle, pressed up against the wall and on one side. Candles were dotted around the floor, running along the edge of the skirting. At least he'd made the bed. A big bin lay next to the door.

'Very romantic.' O'Brien was shaking his head, then he turned to block off the office's door, but Sullivan didn't seem to be intent on trying to escape. 'You helped her kill Jake Turner, didn't you? Lured him there, then did the deed.'

'Fuck off!' Sullivan pointed at the bed. 'We were here all night! You can check the logs on her car.'

'We did. That was the call. Her car didn't move from her cottage.'

'Fuck.' Sullivan shut his eyes. 'I dropped her off there and took her back here. Fuck, fuck, fuck.'

O'Brien laughed, then it softened to a hard glare. 'What if I told you she said you killed Jake while she watched?'

'No!'

'Seems to be how she rolls.'

'I didn't kill anyone!' Sullivan slapped the duvet, dimpling it in the middle. 'I told you! We were here!'

'Come on, Brendan, we've worked together for a few years

now.' O'Brien smirked. 'At least do me the honour of telling me the truth.'

'I am!'

'You're lying.' O'Brien held out his phone. 'ANPR says you're lying.' He winked at Marshall. 'Stands for Automatic Number Plate Recognition.' He sucked on his teeth. 'Quite fancy, isn't it? Gives us a list of cars that have been caught by the cameras along a road. As you know, the A7 winds its merry way through Hawick town centre as it heads down to Carlisle and further afield. One of the main trunk roads in southern Scotland, even if it's only a single carriageway. But as such, there are several cameras placed strategically along that stretch, including four in Hawick alone.' He held the phone up to Sullivan. 'Brendan, your car was caught at half past eleven, heading in the direction of Hawick Museum. It didn't hit the next camera.'

'That's bullshit! We were here!'

'No, it's not.' O'Brien smiled. 'Brendan Sullivan, I'm arresting you for the murder of—'

44

Marshall stood in the doorway to the reception area and watched Fergus, the custody sergeant, processing Sullivan. 'Do you understand?'

Sullivan just stared at his feet.

Marshall left them to it, heading outside into the car park, staying under the little porch – not that it blocked the worst of the elements. Absolutely tipping it down now, with a cold wind cutting through the rain.

He scanned across the car park, searching for Ravenscroft's Audi, but there was no sign of it.

He got out his phone and checked the last message.

RAVENSCROFT:

Will be there around half past.

Marshall checked the time – 21:34 – and reckoned he should head back inside and give him till quarter to before he called.

'DCI Marshall?' A woman's voice. Someone was walking towards him through the murky gloom. Pam Campbell.

Marshall frowned at her, but softened it to a smile. 'Hi there.'

She wasn't alone – Emily Borthwick stood next to her, looking all uncomfortable.

Marshall smiled at her. 'Hi.'

She didn't look at him.

Marshall smiled at Campbell. 'Horrible evening, isn't it?'

'Isn't it? But you get used to it living around here.' She brushed a hand down Emily's arm. 'We were in Gala and she asked to speak to you.'

'To me?'

Campbell nodded.

'Okay, well – here I am.' Marshall focused on Emily but she wouldn't look at him. 'What's on your mind?'

'I, uh...' She looked up at him with those huge eyes. 'I wanted to say sorry.' Despite the cold, her cheeks were reddening. 'You were just doing your job the other day and I was horrible to you.'

'I'm sorry I made you feel that way, Emily.'

'Aye.' She shrugged.

They stood there in silence for a few seconds.

Campbell nibbled at her lip. 'Sorry. Have you got a minute?'

'Sure.'

'Just a sec, Emily.' Campbell moved them over to the side, but kept facing the girl, like she was worried she'd run off. She looked at Marshall. 'Sorry. This must seem a bit weird us being here. Well, Emily's seeing a therapist here. Her mum refused to take her tonight because of all the bad blood between them this week. And I go to a book club in Gala so I offered to take her...'

'That's very kind of you.'

'It's nothing, really. Like I said, she's a good kid. Just had a rough time.' She nibbled at that lip again. 'Thing is, she asked to see you.'

'Why me?'

'Like she said, she felt guilty about the way she'd treated you and your colleague. It was... She said she was rude?'

'It's natural in the circumstances. I've had way worse. Sure you have too.'

'I have, aye.' Campbell laughed. 'But she fixates on things, so I thought it'd be good to just, you know, come here and speak to you. Get it off her chest and see she doesn't need to bottle things up so much.'

'Well, you're lucky I'm still here.' Marshall smiled at Emily. 'Listen, if you ever need to talk about what happened, if there's anything you need to clear up, I'm happy to listen.'

Emily frowned at him but didn't say anything.

'Take it the case isn't going well, then?'

Marshall smiled at her. 'I can't say anything.'

'I get that. Ongoing investigation and all. But I heard you've charged someone?'

Marshall was once again impressed at how quickly the jungle drums could beat in the Borders. 'Again, can't comment on that.'

Ravenscroft's car slid into the car park, him doing some one-handed palm-first steering as he navigated into a space.

Marshall took out a card and scribbled his personal mobile on it.

'Nicola and her probation officer, right?' Campbell was still staring at him. 'Manipulating him into killing for her. Crazy, right?'

Marshall handed the card to Emily, then frowned at Campbell. 'Where did you hear this?'

'About what she'd done?' Campbell shrugged. 'Online.'

'Online, eh?'

'You know. Facebook and that. Plus you hear whispers at the school. Melody Stapleton told George Maidment that Brendan Sullivan was handcuffed and in the back of a police car. No secrets in a small town, especially Hawick.'

'I get it.' Marshall stuffed his hands into his pockets. 'Well, you know we can't comment on ongoing investigations, especially to unrelated parties, but I'd appreciate it if you could help us find out who is talking about it online.'

'Truth is, there isn't actually loads of stuff online about it. Whispers at school and in the shops. I'm more than happy to assist in any way. I could talk to others and see what the actual source is.'

'That'd be great.'

'I just...' Campbell bit her lip. 'It must feel good to get a result, right?'

'Long way to go with it.'

'It's awful. There's no justice in the world. A good man like my Christopher gets framed for something he didn't do and... Jake was a poor lad. He was troubled but no one deserves that... I don't envy you, Rob. No wonder PTSD and suicide are so common amongst people in your profession.'

'Thank you, Pam.' Marshall gave her a look of concern, hoping he creased his forehead just enough. 'I hope you get closure with what happened.'

'Hard to, isn't it?' Campbell stared him out – not many could manage that. 'It's for Hugh and Muriel, really. To know that... To... I don't know. If they *could* get closure on what happened, then it'd make their lives a lot easier.'

'Of course. But I'm not sure how this would achieve that?'

'Well.' She leaned in close so the girl wouldn't overhear her. 'We all think Jake put Emily up to it.'

'Okay. Listen, thanks for your concern. Hope you have a good evening.'

'Not much chance of that, is there?' She looked at Emily. 'How about we get back home?'

Emily shrugged. 'Fine.' She gave Marshall a final look, then followed Campbell over to a car on the street and drove off.

Leaving Marshall standing alone and perplexed.

Two women traumatised by different sets of events.

Pam Campbell was struggling with what happened to her boyfriend.

Aye, that was enough to send anyone a bit bonkers. As Marshall knew personally.

Not to mention the pressure of teaching in a time when discipline wasn't allowed, coupled with what had happened to her boyfriend.

And Emily Borthwick… Poor girl…

He got out his notebook and jotted down a few notes – that felt weird.

Ravenscroft walked over to him, grinning from ear to ear, and clapped Marshall on the arm. 'I am very, very happy with this. *Very* happy.'

'Let's go inside, sir.' Marshall led him over, looking over his shoulder to see if Pam Campbell had overheard anything. He led through the reception area into the incident room, but it was empty. 'Aye, we've arrested them both for the murders.'

'Excellent work. Excellent.' Ravenscroft shook his head, his lip curling up. 'Getting off on killing people together… It beggars belief, doesn't it?' He focused on Marshall as they stepped back into the station. 'Have you ever seen anything like it in all your cases, Robert?'

'I have, sir. Seen worse. So bad you don't want to know.'

'Worse?' Ravenscroft looked him up and down. 'What could possibly—?'

'You *really* don't want to know.'

'Take your word for it.' Ravenscroft leaned back against the wall. 'This evening's been a bit of a challenge, I have to say. One of those where you just think you're going to be in for hours and hours. I've personally faced a lot of flak from Potter and Shearer for enabling your behaviour.'

'My behaviour?'

'Heading up there, risking reopening a case where we've got a tight conviction.'

'Sir, that was never my inten—'

'I know, I know. And the thing is, we've solved our case and maintained their conviction, haven't we?' Ravenscroft focused on Marshall. 'I stuck *my* neck on the line for you, Robert. Managed to stave them off. Because I believe in you, Robert. I believe in you. I need people on my team I can count on.'

'Thanks, sir.' Marshall shrugged it off, but he was reminded yet again of the truth — Ravenscroft was a wanker. 'It's a team effort, sir. You know that.'

'Oh, come on. Don't give me that.'

'It's true. Patrick O'Brien's team were very quick to assist – we wouldn't have been able to arrest Sullivan without their swift analysis of the CCTV in Hawick. And if we'd let him go...'

'He'd be in the wind. I get it.' Ravenscroft sighed. 'I am concerned that this is going to complicate Dominic Hayes's conviction. Or at least his sentence.'

'Does that mean you're assuming Nicola was the real culprit back then, right?'

'That's what's being hauled up the flagpole, yeah. What do you think?'

'Well. It's looking more and more like she's either the ringleader or that Hayes and Grant were equal partners in the murders. In which case, Hayes sentence was appropriate but Nicola got off lightly. It happens, but we can address that in the future prosecution. Certainly Hayes has always maintained he was the prime aggressor.'

'Was he lying then or is he lying now?'

'Either way he's a liar. It's clear to me she's heavily involved in this.' Marshall flicked a wrist in the general direction of the processing area, where Sullivan would be led away to the cells. 'Manipulating daft bastards like Brendan Sullivan or desperate men like Dominic Hayes to kill for her. And getting him to cover up the true nature of her involvement.'

'That seems to be the case, for sure.' Ravenscroft frowned. 'Where is she, by the way?'

'Isabelle? She's in custody in Hawick. Holding her overnight to ruminate, then we'll interview them both formally, first thing in the morning.'

'Okay, good stuff.' Ravenscroft clapped his hands. 'You've travelled far and wide today, but I don't need to tell you that. Listen, it's gone half nine now, so you get yourself home and back in here for a solid early start.'

Marshall yawned.

Then kept on yawning.

'Thank you, sir.'

'Meanwhile, I've got a news conference to arrange for tomorrow.' Ravenscroft set off then stopped and frowned back at Marshall. 'Which station do you think is the most photogenic?'

Marshall took a few moments to compose himself. Aye, he was a total wanker. And a total wanker who was out of his depth here. 'Neither, sir. But Hawick is pretty close to the location of the murder.'

'Right, right. Of course. Speak tomorrow, yeah?' Ravenscroft left the incident room, then skipped off through towards his car, putting his phone to his ear by the time he'd reached the door.

Marshall watched him go, processing what had just happened.

He'd solved a case without fucking up another too badly.

And potentially not fucked up at all... Nicola got off lightly, Dominic got what he deserved.

Aye, that was a decent result. Something to celebrate, anyway.

Marshall got out his phone and called Kirsten.

She didn't answer.

Time to head back to his mum's...

45

Marshall managed to just about get his stupid truck into the space outside his mum's house. Just about – he was sure he'd be dangling over the line at the back, but tomorrow morning he'd be gone by the time the wardens came to Melrose. Assuming they still did nowadays.

If only his mother would park her wee Fiat with less than five metres of clearance at the front...

Starving.

He grabbed his bags from the passenger seat and walked over to the house. The door was unlocked – no matter how many times he warned her, his mum wouldn't listen...

He went inside and Zlatan rushed over to greet him.

Marshall dumped his bags by the door – the washing could wait until the weekend – and crouched down to cuddle the wee rogue.

Zlatan purred as he rubbed his head against him. Then, just as quickly, he scurried through to the kitchen and started rattling his bowls with his paws that were like furry fists.

Marshall followed him over and saw the problem – both

were empty. He refilled the water from the tap and spotted the note stuck to the cupboard door.

Gone to bed.
Sausage bake in fridge.

Perfect – he didn't need to think about food. And no chips from down the hill...

He shook some biscuits into Zlatan's bowl then switched on the air fryer. He grabbed the leftovers from the fridge – three chunky sausages resting on a load of veg – and tipped them into the device to reheat.

Perfect.

He checked his phone, listening to Zlatan crunching away at his biscuits. Nothing from Kirsten.

What the hell was going on?

Sod it. He sat down at the kitchen table and called her.

'We're sorry but the person you've—'

He hung up.

Could leave a voicemail. Could try again, even.

But he was starting to get the message, even if she didn't want to put voice to her words.

He sat there, thinking it all through. Too much caffeine – he'd struggle to sleep tonight, even with this level of exhaustion.

Then his phone actually rang.

Kirsten calling...

He answered it. 'Hey, it's you.'

'It's me.'

'What's up?'

Kirsten paused. Didn't sound like she was driving, so probably still in her flat. 'Just saw you'd called me.'

'I did.' Marshall felt a bit hurt she didn't just want to call him. 'How was the viewing?'

'It was fine.' Kirsten yawned down the line. 'Listen, I'm pretty tired. Could we catch up tomorrow?'

Marshall took the drawer out of the air fryer, gave it a quick shoogle, then stuck it back in. 'Feels like you're blowing me off here.'

'Rob... Seriously. I was in early trying to process that knife for you while you were away on a jolly up to Inverness...'

'A jolly?' Marshall laughed. 'It was hardly a jolly. We had a pint with our dinner, then I had to drive for hours to—'

'Okay, I get it and I take it back. You weren't on a jolly.'

Marshall let out a slow breath. 'Mind if I ask you one question?'

'Depends what it is, doesn't it?'

'Listen, you worked with Crawford before—'

'Rob. I'm not going to get into that again.'

'It's not that. It's...' Marshall sighed. 'Does he have a drink problem?'

Silence.

'Hello?'

'I'm here.'

'Did you hear what I said?'

'I did, aye. I'm just thinking about it.' Kirsten sighed now. 'Possibly. I don't know – don't most cops have issues with alcohol and coffee and mistrust?'

'So I've been given an officer who *possibly* has a drink problem?'

'You know how it goes, Rob. When you're a line manager and you get given someone, they're usually someone else's problem passed on to you.'

'Wise words. I wanted Rakesh.'

'And you're supposed to have Rakesh. But that's not happening just now, is it?'

'No.'

'I spoke to him earlier.'

'Rakesh?'

'Right.'

Nice to see she could pick up the phone to someone...

But Marshall didn't say that. 'How is he?'

'You know him. He's a bit annoyed about being stuck there. You should call him.'

'I will, when I get a moment.'

'You had a few moments up there, didn't you?'

'Not on my own, I didn't. And the reception was terrible. Did you hear what he did?'

'Said he got into shit just for sending an email?'

'Right. It was a bit more than that. He asked Potter why he wasn't getting promoted. She's not someone who appreciates insubordination like that.'

'Typical Rakesh.'

'Typical Rakesh. Meanwhile, I'm saddled with Crawford.'

'He's not that bad.'

Marshall laughed. 'You just said he has a drink problem.'

'He's not... It's... Rob, it's more a socialising problem. He's not sitting in his pants, drinking bottles of supermarket vodka every night.'

'But he does drink a lot, right?'

'He goes to the pub most nights, aye. Probably why he got divorced.'

'Okay. That's useful.' Marshall cleared his throat – Crawford had only been down here two days, including a stint up north, but he'd managed to reveal his marital status to an ex-lover. Probably just human nature and Marshall didn't want to read too much into it. But it didn't stop. 'Sorry. I was only going to ask you one question and here we are, chatting away.'

'Rob, I've got to get to bed...'

'Are you okay?'

A long silence.

Long enough for Marshall to give the air fryer another shoogle.

'Are we okay?'

'It's just me and work and... circumstances. I'm so busy, Rob. Not just your case, either. I've just been given a ton of stuff from Edinburgh. And this flat not selling is really starting to get me down.'

'I can understand all of that, it's just... You seem distant. And I want to be able to help.'

'You do help. Sleep tight, Rob. I'll see you in the morning.'

She hung up before he could say anything.

Marshall stood there, ready to give the air fryer another shoogle, but he just couldn't be arsed now.

What the hell was that all about?

He hated the way she could just ghost him like that. Pretend he didn't even exist. He knew it could be a form of abuse, but he didn't think she meant it that way...

Or he hoped she didn't.

Either way, it felt like they were moving apart.

He looked through his other messages.

One from his father, along with a photo of him standing somewhere he presumed was Egypt.

Finally got to see it!

Marshall wasn't sure what was so impressive about a lump of rocks. It wasn't the Sphinx or the Great Pyramid.

The man he was standing next to looked about the same age as Dad, just in much better shape. Dad wasn't one to share details of his love life – not with Marshall anyway – but if he was indeed seeing him, then all power to him.

Marshall smiled at that, but a hollowness hit him.

Aside from Zlatan, there was nobody in his life. Not really.

The wee sod started rubbing away at his ankles.

His sister wasn't speaking to him. Mum was annoying. All his colleagues at work were just that, colleagues. Maybe Jolene was starting to thaw and become a mate, but it could just be her angling for a promotion. Rakesh was up in Edinburgh and pissed off at Marshall for what was going on with his career.

Aye, he had sod all. Maybe he should've stayed in London.

A knock at the door.

Marshall walked through to the hall.

'Who is it?'

The disembodied voice came from Mum's bedroom upstairs.

'I don't know, Mum. I haven't answered it yet.' Marshall opened the door.

Cath stood there. His and Jen's half-sister. 'Hi.' She nibbled her bottom lip. 'Need a chat.'

46

'Do you want to come in?'
Cath shook her head. 'Can we go to the pub?'
'Give me a sec.' Marshall walked back through and switched off the air fryer – typical, the sausage bake was looking *perfect*. He grabbed his coat from the hall, then called upstairs, 'I'm heading out for a bit.'
'Okay. So, who is it?'
'My sister.'
'Jennifer?'
'The other one. Bye.' Marshall opened the door again, then stepped out into the freezing rain without letting Zlatan squeeze past. He locked the door and smiled at Cath. 'The bar in Taylor's do?'
'Don't really know it, but okay.' She set off down the hill into Melrose, not that it was far.
'It's been a while, Cath.'
'Right. Sorry. I'm not good at staying in touch with people.'
'You didn't want to, if I recall correctly.'
'Right. Sorry. I know.'

Marshall turned the corner, tasting a sour sickness in his mouth. 'Just got a message from Dad. He's in Alexandria.'

'Probably sent me the same photo. Was he with Nigel?'

'Is that the guy he's with?'

'Aye, his new bloke. Lives in Edinburgh.'

'I hadn't heard he was seeing someone.'

'Sorry. Maybe I shouldn't have said anything.'

'Not your fault. Dad's the one who sent it to me.' Marshall smiled at her. 'And I'm glad. So long as this Nigel is a good bloke.'

'He is. He's a psychotherapist.'

Marshall laughed. 'He's got his work cut out with this family, then.'

But she didn't say anything, just stuffed her hands in the pockets of her thin coat.

'Are you still staying in Gala?'

'Right. Still in the same place.'

'Are you working in the same place too?'

'What, since you got me sacked from my last job?'

'You can say that, but at least you don't work for Gary Hislop anymore. And you really don't want to.'

'I'll work for who I like.'

'Of course. But I can still give you advice.' Marshall held the door for her, then followed her through the hotel entrance into the bar at the back.

And it hit him – this was where he had first got together with Kirsten a couple of years ago…

So much water under the bridge since then.

And it felt like Kirsten was driving a bulldozer into the bridge.

'Rob! It's been a while.' Dean stood at the bar, grinning wide. 'How have you been?'

'I'm fine.' Marshall gave a mock scowl. 'I was in on Saturday, remember?'

'Never seems often enough.' Dean gave Cath a sour look. 'And who's this fine young thing?'

'This is Cath. My sister.'

'I didn't realise you had two sisters.'

Cath smiled at him. 'I'm Rob's half-sister.'

'Right. I get it.' Dean gave a flick of the head. 'Not sure why I didn't hear about this fine young lassie when we were at school?'

'He didn't know.' Cath smiled at him. 'We only met a couple of years ago.'

'I see. Well. What can I get you both?'

All Marshall could think of was his rumbling stomach and the sausage bake sitting in the air fryer back at his mum's. 'Is the kitchen closed?'

'Sorry, Rob, but it *is* after ten.'

'I know, I know. It's just... I'm starving. And it's been a total bastard of a day.'

'I could rustle up a sandwich?' Dean's husband, William, shrugged a shoulder. 'It's no biggie.'

'That'd be great.'

'Cheese and pickle do you?'

Marshall grinned. 'You know me well.'

William looked at Cath. 'What about you?'

'I'm fine, thank you.'

'Sure. Back in a mo.' William headed through to the kitchen.

'You owe him, Rob.' Dean nodded at them. 'What can I get you to drink?'

'Coke Zero or Pepsi Max.'

'Pepsi, it is.' Dean patted the tap for it. 'And you, Rob?'

Marshall inspected the selection of beer on offer, but remembered his chat with Crawford that morning. 'Pint of tonic water.'

'Last of the big spenders, eh?' Dean waved a hand across the room. 'Grab a seat, guys, and I'll bring them over.'

'Cheers.' Marshall took a seat at the far side, underneath the TV showing the night's news – aerial footage of Hawick Museum playing alongside a muted commentary of events.

Cath sat opposite the screen and kept looking up at it. 'You said you're tired?'

'Been a long day.' Marshall yawned. 'Woke up in Inverness, drove for a few hours while I was up there, then all the way back home via… via Glasgow. Didn't get a great sleep either. Never do when I stay away from home. And now I'm back here.'

'We can do this another time, if you want?'

'We're here, aren't we?' Marshall smiled. 'So. What's up?'

Cath didn't take her eyes off the screen. 'Dad's having fun on his holiday.'

'You've come here at this time of night and dragged me away from my dinner to talk about Dad's holiday?'

Cath focused on him now. 'I know things haven't been great between you guys. You and Jen. And him. But he's a good guy, Rob. He's done a lot for me.'

'So I gather.'

'That's a bit… passive aggressive.'

'Sorry. I don't mean it to sound that way.' Marshall got out his wallet and rested it on the table – he hadn't paid yet. 'But Dad did bugger off out of our lives when me and Jen were children. We didn't even know you existed until a couple of years ago. It's… It's just been a pretty hard experience for us. And he acts like it's all totally fine.'

'You don't know how happy he is to have reconnected with you and Jen.'

'Well, I do – he keeps banging on about it.'

'There we go, guys.' Dean walked over with their drinks. 'William will be through with your sanger soon, Rob.'

'Cheers.' Marshall handed him a tenner. 'Here you go.'

'Oh, cheers.'

Marshall watched him go, then sipped his drink and let the ice clink in the glass.

The place was quiet, just a table with a group having an animated discussion about something, but they were good at keep their voices low.

Cath stared into her drink. She looked at him for a few long seconds. Seemed like she was going to say something.

Then William came over with Marshall's sandwich. 'Here we are.' He rested it on the table along with a few coins' worth of change. 'Can I get you anything else?'

'Should be good, William. Cheers.' Marshall looked at it and it looked very nice indeed – a rough sourdough with grated cheddar spilling everywhere and a dark pickle oozing out. His mouth started watering at the sight of it. 'That looks perfect, thanks.'

'Enjoy.'

'Cheers.' Cath watched him go, then took a sip of her cola. 'How is Jen?'

'I don't know. She's not speaking to me.' Marshall bit into his sandwich.

'What did you do?'

Marshall finished chewing his first tangy bite. 'It's more what *she* did. But even so, the thing with Jen is she's not the forgiving sort. Even when she's at fault.'

'I can see that.'

'Really?' He set his sandwich back down. So, what's up?'

Cath took another long drink. 'Not sure how to start...'

'So just blurt it out.' Marshall took another bite and raised his eyebrows.

She didn't blurt out anything.

He finished chewing. 'Come on, Cath. Whatever it is, I want to help. Wouldn't be here if I didn't.'

'I'm just short of cash.'

Marshall felt a sting of nerves. Not a good thing when someone came calling like that... 'How much?'

'Did you know I'm working at the hospital now? As a porter.' Cath shrugged. 'Not the best job in the world, but it's okay. Helps pay the bills.'

'Do you see Jen there?'

'I do. But I haven't spoke to her in months, if you catch my drift.'

Marshall laughed. 'Oh, I can well imagine...'

'Look, I better go.' Cath downed her drink. 'Thank you.' She got up and cleared off.

'Cath!'

She turned and blew him a kiss. 'I'll see you later.' And she left the bar.

Marshall watched the door trundle shut.

Bloody hell.

Definitely something going on there, but he had no idea what it was or what it even could be.

He stared at the sandwich he didn't want but was really enjoying, then took another bite. He got out his phone and sent Cath a text:

> Whatever it is, Cath, I am more than happy to listen. Call me. Rob x

After he sent it, he immediately regretted it. She was after money and he didn't feel good about it.

He texted their dad:

> Just had a weird chat with Cath. Is she okay?

He sent it, then copied the text and sent it to Jen as well.

He sat there, eating and craning his neck to look up at the TV but it had moved on to cover the latest in Ukraine.

His phone buzzed.

He picked it up. Text from Jen:

> Bugger off

Charming.

Marshall sat there, chewing. He couldn't fix everyone's problems and he had more than enough of his own.

But at least his sandwich was pretty nice. And the sausage bake would heat up again.

47

WEDNESDAY

'On this cold Wednesday morning down here in the chilly Borders. But at least it's not snowing, though that is forecast for next week... Coming up next is Jon and Kate with *The Breakfast Show* but, first, the news at six o'clock.'

Three beeps rattled out of the car's speaker, making it sound all farty. Another thing wrong with this heap of crap.

'Thank you, Sarah. Police in Hawick are investigating the murder of a seventeen—'

Marshall clicked off the radio and drove on through Gala. He was tempted to head to Starbucks for a coffee, but he kept going – he'd have time to make his own. He turned left at the roundabout onto the bridge, then again onto the street with the station. Past the Kwik Fit and into the station.

Bloody hell, the car park was full.

And some sod had taken his DCI space. A sod in an Audi.

Bloody Ravenscroft.

Already?

Marshall parked in the nearest space and got out.

Kirsten's car was there already and she was over with a team of forensics officers standing around another car, an old Fiesta.

Marshall got out and walked over. Despite being annoyed, he plastered on a smile. 'What's up?'

Kirsten looked around at him. 'Finally managed to get the tow company to deliver her car here so we can process it.'

A tow truck belched out crude exhaust smoke, parked across three spaces. No wonder it was chaos in there.

'Right. Good stuff.' Marshall tried to make eye contact, but she avoided him. 'Can we have a chat today? Maybe grab some lunch?'

'Do you honestly want to?'

'Of course I do.'

His phone rang.

'Sorry.' He got out his phone and checked the display:

Ravenscroft calling...

Marshall shut his eyes. 'Ravenscroft's calling me already... He's unreal.' He refocused on her. 'Please will you at least think about lunch?'

'Aye, aye. But first deal with your micro-manager...'

'Good. Let's say twelve?' Marshall walked away and answered the call. 'Good morning, sir. I see you've—'

'Robert. Glad you answered my call.'

'I'm at the station, sir. Just saw your car is in my space.'

'Listen, I'm in your office so can you come here?'

Marshall stopped dead, despite the teeming rain. He wasn't going to get the wanker to move the car, was he? And he'd be buggered if he was going to march to his beat. 'Sorry, I'm in the middle of something. What's up, sir?'

'I want to make sure we're prioritising this case.'

'You've seen the car park. Everyone's here and it's just turned six. I'm not sure what else we can do.'

'I want to be able to announce that we're charging them when I do the press conference.'

And Marshall wished he was a billionaire…

'We've booked them, sir. Ready to interview. It's all fine.'

'I know, but I've been stitched up here by the shower in Inverness.'

'Oh? What's happened?'

'Sometimes you just wonder why you bother, right?'

'I just try to do the job, sir.'

'I get it. But the politics isn't your strong point, Robert, so I'm not sure I should take advice from you…'

Marshall wanted to throttle him. 'What's happ—'

'Come see me. Let's do this face to face.'

Click and he was gone.

Leaving Marshall standing alongside a car illegally parked and an instinct to just fuck off for the day and let someone else run those interviews and get the convictions over the line.

Who was he kidding? He'd do it. Run both of them. Make sure they confessed to murdering Jake.

Some excitement erupted over by the CSIs.

Marshall walked over and stood by Kirsten.

One of Kirsten's CSIs was photographing two suited-up figures pulling something out of the boot of Isabelle's car.

A tote bag, by the looks of it.

Marshall squinted and saw the Teribus Arms stamped on the side.

The bag was soaked in blood.

A CSI reached in a gloved hand and removed a vicious-looking knife.

48

Marshall carried a tray of coffees into the forensics lab. 'Sorry, but I couldn't find my AeroPress.'

Kirsten and Crawford were locked in a chat.

Crawford clocked Marshall, then stood up tall. 'I'll get on with it.' He set off towards the door.

Marshall stopped him.

Crawford looked him up and down. 'What's up, sir?'

'Here's your coffee.' Marshall raised the tray. 'Americano. Milk and two.'

'Cheers, boss.' Crawford took it and raised it in thanks. 'I'll see you in the briefing.'

'Not sure we're going to have one today.' Marshall checked his watch. 'Certainly not at seven. Can you get Cal to arrange it for nine?'

'Sure thing.'

Marshall watched him go, then passed a coffee to Kirsten. 'Oat milk latte.'

She took it absently while she worked away at her machine. 'No idea where it's got to.'

'Mm?'

'My AeroPress. Someone's pinched it from my drawer. Left the coffee beans and the grinder, though. Had to go out to fetch these.'

'Mm.'

'And you're not listening, are you?'

'Mm.'

Marshall stood there, sipping his coffee – nowhere near as good as the stuff he made, even if he did say so himself. 'What did Douglas want?'

Kirsten finally looked over at him. 'Just something to do with the case.'

'What exactly?'

'Why don't you ask him?'

What the hell was that supposed to mean?'

Marshall sat down. 'What's going on?'

'I'm processing the blood from—'

'Not that. Between us. You and me. You're being weird. You've been weird for weeks.'

'Weird?' Kirsten shot him a furious look. 'You knew when we started that my nickname was weirdo.'

'That's because your surname is Weir.'

'Weird by name, weird by nature.'

'Kirsten, I'm being serious here. You're avoiding me.'

She huffed out a sigh. 'Rob...'

'You won't even say what you were discussing with Crawford. And you won't say why you've slept at your flat rather than at—'

'Rob. I *really* don't have time for this.' Kirsten pointed at the device she was using. 'Now *my* team has recovered the murder weapon for your fucking case, I've got to process it as well. And there's a hair on it.'

That stopped Marshall in his tracks. 'A hair?'

'A hair.' Kirsten shifted to the side and let him use the microscope – sure enough, there was a tiny hair stuck into the hilt of the knife. 'Now, I'm far from the expert on this, but it's probably from your killer. Or from the victim...'

'That's...' Marshall took a slug of brutally bitter coffee and gasped. 'That's a good thing, right?'

'Right. So can you just leave me in peace to—'

The door rattled open with a squawk from the security system. Ravenscroft stood there, glowering at the machine. He charged over to them. 'Any idea how I—'

'On it.' Kirsten reached over to press a button on the wall and the alarm stopped. 'This is why you need to swipe in here, sir.'

'I see.' Ravenscroft looked at their coffee cups, his eyes twitching, then focused on Marshall. 'How's it going?'

'It's fine.' Kirsten went back to her machine. 'I'm just processing the knife now, sir.'

'Right.' Ravenscroft clapped his hands together. 'Excellent stuff. Can you compare the knife with the Applecross murder weapon?'

'Already done that.'

'You mean you did that based on what Leye sent you or—'

'No, I've compared this exact knife with the exact knife in Bishopbriggs.'

'Definitely?'

Kirsten drank some coffee through the lid. 'Exact match. Same make and model.'

'That was quick.'

'Not that quick.'

'Excellent work anyway.' Ravenscroft looked at their cups again. 'Is there a spare one going?'

'Sorry, sir. Someone's nicked my AeroPress from my office, otherwise I'd make you one like last night.'

'I appreciate the thought, anyway.' Ravenscroft grabbed a seat without asking and perched on it. 'Okay, so what about the clothes?'

Kirsten scowled at him. 'Clothes?'

'Jake was naked, remember? Were his clothes in the bag with the knife?'

'No, they weren't.' Kirsten shook her head. 'I was just telling Rob, we've found a hair on the knife.'

Ravenscroft frowned. 'From the killer?'

'We don't know.' Kirsten shrugged. 'We didn't make the cut-off for Gartcosh to process it today.'

'When will they get around it?'

'We'll have all of the biology prepped today, but it'll be tomorrow at the earliest it gets processed.'

'This is unacceptable!' Ravenscroft tapped at his watch. 'It's seven in the morning!'

'There's a lot of it, sir, and to be frank, that's standard operating procedure.'

Ravenscroft scraped his chair back and stood up again. 'This isn't good enough.'

'And I don't report to you. We do the best we can with the technology on offer. It's almost like you need to build that centre of excellence at Tweedbank...'

'Enough of that.' Ravenscroft scratched at his stubble – unusual for him not to have shaved. Then again, maybe he wanted a perfectly fresh one for the press conference. 'Listen, I've got to brief the media on our progress at eleven, so I need you to process the big stuff by then, okay?'

'By *eleven*?' Kirsten laughed in his face. 'That's not going to happen.'

'This isn't the attitude I expect, Kirsty.'

'Kir*sten*.' She rested her fists on her hips. 'And I'm just telling you like it is. It *can't* happen by then, no matter how many skulls you throw at it.'

'Sure about that?' Ravenscroft rubbed his hands together. 'I've been around the block a few times, Kir*sten*, and there's always something that could expedite things, if you just think that little bit more creatively. So...?'

Kirsten looked over at Marshall, nostrils flaring, then reached into a drawer and pulled out a form. She rested it on the table and laid her pen on top. 'Sign this.'

Ravenscroft sat down to inspect it, his lips moving as he scanned through it. He looked up at her. 'And what is this when it's at home?'

'An expedited manual DNA processing form. Needs to go to your cost centre, sir. Superintendent and above.'

'How quickly expedited are we talking?'

'Puts us to the front of the queue in Gartcosh, so drive time up there, then an hour's worth of preparation, then hopefully a phone call once it's done. And it's your only shot of making it in enough time for you to add to your news at eleven.'

'Fine.' Ravenscroft signed the form and handed it over, but pocketed the pen.

'Thank you.' Kirsten held out her hand again. 'Pen.'

'Excuse me?'

'You just put my pen in your pocket.'

'Excuse me?' Ravenscroft reached in and held out the metal Parker. 'I think you'll find this is—'

'—inscribed with KCW. My initials.' Kirsten nodded at Marshall. 'Rob got me it for my birthday.'

'Ah, I see. Apologies.' Ravenscroft handed the pen over. 'Got one just the same.'

'I believe you...' Kirsten took it and stood up. 'Jay!'

He looked round, his face obscured by a mask. 'What's up, Kirst?'

'Got a wee job for you.' Kirsten grabbed a packet from inside the machine and walked over to his workbench. 'Can you drive this knife to Gartcosh and get them to process the biology using the SCD credits?'

'Drive to Gartcosh?' Jay flipped his mask up onto the top of his head. 'Are you sure about that? Because I'll be—'

'Yes. I'm sure.'

'Fine.' Jay got up, grabbed the packet and the form, then buggered off.

'I'm not joking, sir.' Kirsten looked around at Ravenscroft. 'We really do need that centre of excellence over this side of the country. If it's not here, then it needs to be—'

'We've got our killers.' Ravenscroft ignored her and started doing up his jacket. 'Just make sure you close the deal, Kirsty. You've got until eleven.'

'That won't happen. Jay's just leaving now.'

'But you said—'

'I said that's the only chance you've got. He'll not get there until about nine, and that's if he's lucky with traffic. Hopefully they'll start processing it not long after, but I don't control the queue there.'

Ravenscroft sat there, eyes twitching. He pointed a finger at her. 'Make it happen.' Then he shifted it to aim at Marshall. 'I'm heading down to Hawick to ready the press conference.'

'Do you need me?'

'I'll advise you once I've formalised my strategy.' Ravenscroft buggered off, already putting his phone to his ear by the time he reached the door. He managed to get through this time without setting off any alarms.

Kirsten watched it slowly shut. 'He's not exactly chilled, is he?'

'Welcome to my world...' Marshall frowned. 'What are the chances of them getting the work done by eleven?'

'Sod all. Costs a fortune, too, but he signed the form and I saw a chance to wind him up.'

'I'll be the one who pays for that, you know?'

'Mm.'

They sat in uncomfortable silence for a few seconds.

Marshall hadn't noticed the lab empty out, but it had. Just the pair of them in there. 'Kirst, are you annoyed at me because you've been having to do the flat viewings on your own?'

'This again...' She pinched her nose. 'Got another one tonight.'

'I'll try and be there.'

'Try... Great.'

Marshall sat there, gritting his teeth.

'Look, Rob. I need you to help me here. We can't let our lawyers keep stalling or the purchase will fall through.' Kirsten went back to work.

'Is that what you want?'

'Is what?'

'The purchase falling through.'

'No.'

'But we have options to—'

'Told you, Rob. Don't have time to discuss this.'

'Why?'

She looked around the lab. 'Because we're at work.'

'But you won't talk about it when we're not, either. Don't even answer the phone half the time...'

'Oh, just because your flat sold and mine hasn't...'

'So it *is* about that?' Marshall sighed. 'Listen. I have the cash to buy that place with a mortgage. We can do that.'

'So I won't own it, then?'

'No. But once you've sold up, you can buy out the mortgage. I'll get one without an early repayment fee, so it's an easy process. And we can draw up an agreement, if you want.'

She went back to work again, slowly shaking her head.

'Kirsten, if you've got cold feet, then—'

'Cold feet?'

'Are you denying it?'

She ignored him, just keeping on analysing.

'I wish you'd just say what you want, then we can both know where we stand.'

'I don't have cold feet, Rob.' She sat back and looked up at the ductwork on the ceiling, which seemed to be much more interesting than a chat about their future. 'But... I want it to be fifty-fifty. We're supposed to own that place outright. No mortgage. And now you're talking about buying it yourself *with* a mortgage?'

'Just to make things less stressful for you!'

'I just...'

'Kirsten. It's to take the pressure off your sale. Let you hold out for more, because that's what you seem to want to do.'

'What if I don't want that?'

'So you *have* got cold feet.'

'Rob... It's...' Kirsten sighed. 'It's complicated.'

'I need to know you're on board, Kirsten. Either you bring in the equity from your flat sale or we sign a mortgage document.'

Kirsten took a moment to think it through, then looked up at him. 'I can't commit to that.'

'What's that supposed to mean?'

'The agreement needs to be fifty-fifty, Rob. Sure, you have more than me, but how do you think that makes me feel?'

'It's okay.'

'No, it's not.'

'What's the big deal?'

'I don't ever want to be indebted to anyone.'

Marshall felt like he'd been punched in the gut. 'Wow.'

'I don't mean it like that. I just hate debt. My parents lost their house when I was wee. And my ex...'

'Keith.'

'Right, Keith. He fucked everything up. I was lucky to get away with keeping my flat and a massive mortgage. I don't want to be back there again.'

'I totally get that. Come here.' He wrapped her in a big

cuddle. 'It's okay, alright? You don't have to do anything you don't want to.'

'I know.' She broke away from him. 'It just... It feels like a lot of pressure.'

'There's no pressure from me, okay? All I'm suggesting is we draw up a contract, so we spell it all out in black and white.'

'Oh, so this is a business arrangement now?'

'Tell me what would make it work for you, Kirsten, because I'm sick of suggesting the wrong thing.'

Kirsten stared at him with teary eyes. 'I need to sell my flat before I can commit to anything, Rob.'

49

Marshall arrived in Hawick and parked behind the row of three pool cars. The joy of it being a much bigger station with a decent amount of parking. No sign of anyone, though. He checked his watch – he was still a bit early.

The town buzzed around him. Two women walked along the street, one pushing a double pram, but it only contained one small kid.

Like during the whole journey down from Gala, Marshall kept going back to the discussion with Kirsten.

'I need to sell my flat before I can commit to anything, Rob.'

He wished she'd been able to tell him before now...

Crawford walked towards him, clutching yet another coffee.

And there it was, as clear as day...

Kirsten was rekindling their old romance and she couldn't bring herself to break it off with Marshall.

He wished she could just talk to him like they used to.

Ash Paton and McIntyre were following along behind him, chatting animatedly about something.

Marshall got out and walked over to the team. 'How's it all going?'

'Hard to say, boss.' Crawford stopped to take a sip of coffee. 'If only we'd had a briefing...'

'Things are moving too quickly just now. We need to do, rather than talk. But how about you just tell me what you've got and we can take it from there.'

'Fine.' Crawford rested his coffee on the bonnet of Marshall's car, then started flicking through his notebook. 'Okay, so we finished *our* search of Isabelle's home, after Kirsten's lot decimated the place. Nothing.'

'As in, forensics took it all?'

'No. As in, there's nothing there. She doesn't seem to own *anything*.'

'Then again.' Ash smirked. 'She was in prison for yonks, so she probably got used to not having stuff. Means nobody can take it from you, right? And you can just run pretty easily.'

'Guess so. What else?'

'Eh...' Crawford scratched his head. 'Forensics aren't getting anywhere. The place is spotless. Like, freaky cleaning. Obsessive. Looks like she scoured the place yesterday. There's not even a toast crumb on the counter or a stray pube in the shower.'

Ash winced. 'Gross.'

'Sorry.' Crawford flipped the page, not seeming particularly sorry. He reached over and took another sip of coffee then set the cup down again. 'Sullivan's office, on the other hand, is a different matter. Total pigsty.'

'Okay. But I'm not sure what we're expecting to find in there.'

'I thought if we could prove she hadn't had sex with Sullivan there, then we can—'

'You can't prove a negative, Douglas. Just because there are no signs they had sex at hers or his, doesn't mean they didn't go to a hotel to do it or have sex in either car.'

'Aye, but he told us they did.'

'And people get things wrong all the time.'

'Still, but if there's no sign of this…' Crawford flicked through his notebook. 'Where did she say it happened?'

'She didn't.' Marshall folded his arms. 'Just said she was with her boyfriend. It was Sullivan who told us it was in there. And he's at best a complete liar.'

Ash smirked. 'You think they weren't banging?'

'Not sure. Do you?'

'Don't know.' She shrugged. 'Can see it.'

'But do you think it's a lie?' Crawford put his hands on his hips. 'Like he's just giving an alibi for her?'

'No, I think there's something in it. He's left his wife for her. But whether they killed Jake Turner…'

'You found the knife in her boot, didn't you?'

'That's true. But still, we need to back up these stories with additional evidence.' Marshall didn't want to nod, but he did, automatically. 'Have you got her laptop?'

'Doesn't seem to have one. No charging cables or anything. But part of her conditions of release, according to O'Brien on account of her luring young men to their meeting place online, was she wasn't allowed to have a computer. Or a smartphone. The mobile we've got is *basic*.'

'Okay. That's good to know.'

Crawford gestured at Ash. 'DC Paton has been in charge of door-to-doors. Have you got anything else?'

'I have, aye.' Ash frowned. 'Her cottage is within the radius of the phone ping from yesterday.'

'So you think she has his phone?'

'If she does, we can't find it. But the way it went on then off again makes me think she's tried to get into it then, when she's failed, she's switched it back off. Maybe chucked it in the river.'

'Right. Makes sense.'

'And we've got multiple reports of a male in his teens wearing a green hoodie at both addresses.'

'Which addresses?'

'Sullivan's office and Isabelle's cottage.'

Crawford scowled at her. 'That should've come straight come to me.'

'Well, I'm giving you it now, Sarge.'

That seemed to just rile him up even more. 'So you're saying Jake Turner was spotted at both addresses?'

'Not sure.' Ash shrugged. 'But someone who looked like Jake was spotted, for sure. Same green hoodie we found next to his body.'

'Have you got anything to back this up?'

Ash held out her phone. 'Got it from a doorbell camera in the street opposite his office.'

Marshall leaned in to inspect the image – like most of those cameras, it was pretty far from a professional shot and nothing like if it'd been taken from a stable CCTV shot. Grainy video in low light.

But it certainly looked like Jake Turner.

'That certainly does look like him.' Crawford took his time checking it. 'So what the hell was he doing there?'

'That's what we need to find out next.' Marshall nodded. 'The cases up in Applecross showed no direct interaction between the perpetrators and victims prior to the murders. Dominic told us he basically stalked them to understand their movements. But this...'

'It looks like Jake was watching Sullivan?'

Marshall smiled. 'Now you're catching on.'

'So what does it mean, then?'

Before Marshall could even think about it, Warner walked over to them, grinning at Ash Paton. 'Mind if I have my lunch now?'

She frowned. 'It's nine o'clock. Time for Cal's briefing.'

'YEAH, but I've been on since five, so it feels like the middle of the day.'

'What were you doing at five?'

'Training. So, I can go and get my lunch, then?'

'That's up to your sergeant.'

'Okay. Don't see her, though. Feeling quite hangry and it's pasta day today. Know what they say – more spaghetti, less upsetti.' Warner looked around the team like he'd made the funniest joke ever. 'Can I update you, Sarge?'

Crawford rolled his eyes at him. 'Sure.'

'Okay, Sarge. I've just been at the social worker boy's office and they had me going through the bin, which was disgusting.' Warner seemed to shiver and shake with revulsion. He held up a case file, smeared with something brown and sticky. 'This looks like the working file on Isabelle.' He thrust it out to Crawford.

Crawford didn't take it. 'What do you mean, working file?'

'This is the file he shared with DI O'Brien, Sarge.' Warner held up the file and shook it. Then he held up another. 'And this is the one I found in the bin.'

Crawford snapped on a pair of gloves, then snatched the files off him and started flicking through the pages. Stopping every few seconds to compare.

Warner gurned stupidly at Ash. 'So, can I get my lunch now?'

'No.' She shook her head. 'Your lunch is twelve.'

'Would rather go at ten, if it's all the—'

'Okay. This is good.' Crawford held out the files. 'You're right, this is an early draft and it appears he's changed the document substantially.' He stared at Marshall. 'I need to go through it in more detail, but it appears like she was initially very problematic and struggled a lot. To the point where he was going to escalate up the ranks, but then in this version she's suddenly the golden girl. Right after they started shagging.'

'Could be she got wind of getting a bad report, so started trying to manipulate things in her favour.' Marshall frowned. 'How does he define "initially problematic"?'

'Well, she was caught propositioning young lads in the pub she worked in.'

'The Terie?' Ash laughed. 'Young men in *there*?'

'I can see it.' Warner shrugged. 'It gets pretty jumping on a Friday and Saturday night. It's got a late licence and all the old boys clear off about ten, to be replaced by their grandchildren. They have a DJ spinning some tunes.'

'Wonders will never cease...' Ash looked over at Crawford. 'You want us to head over there, Sarge?'

'Sure.'

Ash patted him on the arm. 'Warner, you can come with me.'

'Great.' Warner sniffed. 'But you know someone threw a brick through the Terie's window last night, right?'

Ash rolled her eyes. 'Because of Isabelle?'

'Search me.'

Crawford nodded at her. 'Will you speak to the owner about both things, will you?'

'Sure thing.' Ash made a note, then walked away.

'On it, Sarge.' Warner saluted. 'I'll get my lunch after.' He buggered off after Ash, whistling the tune to that Ed Sheeran song, the one that made Marshall's teeth itch.

McIntyre watched him go. 'How is he still a cop? Worked with him in uniform and he just seems to get *worse*.' He shook his head, then focused on Marshall. 'I was in Brendan's flat with him and he didn't share that with me... Weird little place. It's basically a room in his office.'

Marshall nodded. 'Aye, I was there last night. He was kicked out of his family home.'

'Right. Well, anyway. It was an absolute pigsty, but it's where they'd been making the beast with two backs.' McIntyre frowned. 'Learned the other day that was first coined by Shakespeare in *Othello*.' He looked around but nobody seemed particularly impressed by his etymology lecture. 'Weirdest thing, though. Forensics found loads of used condoms in a bin.'

Crawford winced. 'Gross.'

'Aye. I've seen my fair share of dead bodies, but that was the worst thing I've seen in a crime scene. Sullivan's been having a *lot* of sex and not emptying his bathroom bin. It's disgusting.'

50

Jolene sat there, trying to keep calm. She wasn't Rob Marshall – sitting opposite a serial killer was just another day for him.
Not for her.
So what if Isabelle Ward hadn't been convicted of the murder – she'd still been involved in multiple slayings.
Or Nicola Grant had been.
And here she was, facing questions over another.
Hard to decide whether a leopard could change its spots, or if they just stopped acting on their worst instincts.
Isabelle smoothed out her hair. 'No comment.'
'You keep saying that.'
'Because I don't have to say anything.'
Jolene smiled at her. 'That's not nothing.'
Isabelle rolled her eyes. 'No comment.'
Jolene recognised a woman who'd been through the criminal justice system and come out the other side, knowing precisely how it worked. 'Come on, Isabelle. You persuaded Brendan to lie for you after you started sleeping with him.'
Isabelle shook her head. 'No comment.'

'It's true, though, isn't it?'

Isabelle shook her head again. 'No comment.'

'Okay, so the thing is, Brendan Sullivan has been caught lying.' Jolene leaned forward. 'He knew what you'd been doing in the pub.'

Isabelle frowned at her. 'What am I supposed to have been doing?'

'The Terie gets quite busy at the weekend, right?'

Isabelle's frown deepened – she had no idea where this was going, did she? 'I don't know. I only work there through the week. Monday to Thursday.'

'Well, we're checking on the veracity of that. But I gather the place attracts a very different crowd after about ten o'clock on a Friday and a Saturday night. People looking to party who can't be bothered with heading up to Edinburgh or even just to Gala. And we're not talking about the old guys, the kind of bloke whose beer you'd spit into. No, Isabelle, we're talking people our age, who are looking for a fun night.' Jolene left a pause, but it didn't get filled. 'And then there are underage drinkers.'

'No comment.'

'Most publicans these days would give them a clip round the ear and send them packing. But at that time on a Friday or a Saturday, especially if it was really busy, it must've been pretty tough. But you didn't do that, Isabelle, did you? No, you started propositioning them to have sex with you.'

'No comment.'

'And we're talking young men. Seventeen. Eighteen. You've certainly got a type.'

'No comment.'

'Did any of them take you up on the offer?'

'This is bullshit.'

'So you're denying propositioning young men?'

'Damn right I am.' Isabelle shot her a glare. 'I work as a barmaid in the Terie. Nobody underage drinks there. Nobody.

There are other places for that and Mike doesn't have the interest. He's very fastidious about it. And yes, I flirt with the desperate sods who drink in there. But it's a fucking pub. Adults go to pubs. When they get there, they get drunk. Some even arrive that way. A few of the men tend to hit on the barmaids over the course of a night. And any savvy barmaids will show them they have an inkling of a chance, just so they order more beer. Sometimes they'll even tip the barmaid. "Get one for yourself, darling". Well, that drink doesn't get poured, does it? And the money's going into my back pocket.' Isabelle glowered at her. 'But like I told you, I don't work at the weekend, so your story's kind of broken, isn't?' She smiled. 'End of story. Move on. And quickly, please – I'd quite like to get out of here. Barely slept a wink last night in that cell.'

Jolene sat back. She'd got her talking. Finally.

But where to take it next...

She could prod away at the web of lies she'd spun...

The door to the side opened and Marshall stepped into the interview room. He stayed at the side, giving a flash of his eyebrows, like he was just here to watch rather than participate.

Aye, Jolene definitely wasn't like him – she'd rather be anywhere in the world than in here, given a choice. She shifted her focus back to Isabelle. Hard to think of her as that, but someone had said something about showing respect and maybe that was the way through this whole thing. 'Let's talk about the knife.'

'Knife?' Isabelle scowled. 'What knife?'

'The one we found in your car.'

'I don't have a knife in my car.'

'We know which car you drive, so don't deny that.'

'Are you sure?'

'Ford Fiesta with '52 plates.' Jolene smiled. 'Surprised it still runs. Took a while, but we've gained access to the interior. We found a knife in the boot. In a tote bag from the Teribus Arms. All covered in blood. Jake's blood.'

Isabelle scowled at her. 'Then you lot planted it.'

'Why was it in your car, Isabelle?'

'Whoever killed him must've taken the knife after they killed him and put it in the boot.'

'So you're saying you didn't put the knife in your car at all?'

'No, I did not put a knife in the boot of my car. Or a bag. Or anything. I couldn't get in the boot because the lock was knackered.'

'You didn't wrap it in a tote bag from the pub you work in?'

'No. I thought they were stupid and I told Mike when he first ordered them. But a few people have bought them. Quite a few. I was surprised. I guess it's the fact people from Hawick call themselves Teries is what attracts them, rather than any particular affiliation with the pub. And let's be honest, the kind of place that would employ someone like me isn't exactly a tourist attraction, is it?'

It was weird seeing another side to her. Maybe Marshall's presence had signalled the shift – maybe she'd attached to him in their previous interview. But whatever the cause, the angry young woman was gone and replaced by someone who could charm the worst of them.

Still, she wasn't charming Jolene. 'But you did proposition young men, didn't you?'

'No. I wasn't working on those nights.'

'I didn't say you were necessarily working then. A lot of people hang out in the bars they work in after hours, especially if they like the other members of staff. Is that what you did, Isabelle?'

'No.'

'You need to tread very carefully here, Isabelle. Part of your licence is you're not allowed to consort with men under the age of eighteen, are you?'

'That's right. And I haven't been. Since I got out, I've only *slept* with adults.'

'Plural?'

'It's all fine. I told Brendan about every single one.'

'Like I believe that...' Marshall stepped forward and rested his knuckles on the table between them. 'Where did you sleep with Brendan?'

Isabelle stared at him. But didn't say anything. She shifted her focus back to Jolene. 'No comment.'

'Was it in his flat?'

'Is that what he said?'

'It is. You know he doesn't really empty his bin, right?'

'What? What the hell are you talking about?'

'It was one of the grimmest finds I've seen.' Marshall grinned at her – whatever it was, it was good. 'Must be over fifteen condoms in there, all used.'

Jolene felt her stomach lurch.

Isabelle looked away from him. 'No comment.'

'Sure about that?' Marshall smiled. 'Even though one of those might be your alibi?'

'No comment.'

'It's pretty gross, I have to say. To be keeping them all. That's a lot of sex. Are you sure you've only been seeing him for a few weeks?'

Isabelle shook her head yet again. 'No comment.'

'It's amazing what we can do forensically these days. We can tell when the semen was ejaculated. Might take us a while, but it could give an alibi.'

Still shaking her head.

'I thought you'd be pleased, Isabelle?'

'No comment.'

She might be saying that, but the repeated examples of frustrated body language showed it was working.

But she wasn't going to break, was she?

'Okay, I've had enough of this.' Jolene stood up and focused on Marshall. 'I'm guessing Sullivan's pretty close to talking, right?'

He nodded. 'Oh, he's not pretty close. He's desperate to spill everything.'

'And you and I both know the courts tend to put a lot of weight on whoever talks first.' Jolene stared at Isabelle. 'Not as much as you do, though.' She left a moment of silence.

But Isabelle didn't say any more.

51

Marshall sat in an interview room like he'd done so many times in his career. Sometimes with witnesses, others with killers. Often with serial killers.

The idiot ratio was far higher than you'd expect, which made them much easier to convict.

But it wasn't often he'd sat with a complete cretin, and yet here he was.

Brendan Sullivan sat across the table from them, head in his hands. 'Can't fucking do this, man.'

It took a lot to blow up your life like that. A huge amount.

'You know that saying, right?' Marshall left a pause, long enough for Sullivan to look up. 'Can't do the time, don't do the crime.'

'And what crime have I committed, eh?'

'Probably something in your terms and conditions of employment about not consorting with parolees.' Jolene flicked through some pages. 'And I think fucking them is on the higher end of consorting.'

'Fucking them? Are you allowed to say that?'

Jolene shrugged. 'If you can do it, surely I can say it?'

'It's not a crime, though. And yet I'm being interviewed by two fucking cops!'

'So it's okay for you to use that word?'

'I don't make the fucking rules here!'

Considering how much experience he had of dealing with people in desperate situations, now he was in the firing line, Sullivan was completely out of his depth.

'This isn't about your sexual relationship with Isabelle.' Marshall left another pause, much longer this time – long enough he hoped it would irritate Sullivan into talking. 'AKA Nicola Ward.'

Sullivan held his gaze. 'If it's not about that, then what the fuck is it about, eh?'

'Despite you being a parole officer, you're not very good at this.' Marshall laughed. 'Are you?'

'What's that supposed to mean?'

'I don't mean you're not good at having sex, because you're clearly experienced at that.' Marshall smiled. 'I'm not sure we can determine the quality, but when it comes to quantity...' He gave a mock clap. 'Well done, sir.'

Rather than irk him, it seemed to make Sullivan proud of his actions. He sat up and seemed to grow in stature. And suck in his belly.

'Just thought you'd be a bit more savvy, Brendan, but you're just getting angry.'

'Of course I'm fucking angry! This is total bullshit!'

Marshall showed him a photo of the tote bag. 'Do you recognise this?'

'Is that... blood?'

'Yes. Do you recognise the bag?'

'Of course I do. Didn't know they did them until the last time I went in for a drink with a mate. The Terie's not the kind of pub that should have merch, but there was a whole line of it. Bags, coasters, T-shirts, ashtrays.'

'So you know the pub, right?'

'The Terie. Aye, I drink in there sometimes. Just told you that. Are you deaf?'

Marshall let him have that. 'Anything else?'

'What do you mean?'

'About there?'

'Eh?'

'Anything else that might connect you to it?'

'The fuck are you…' Sullivan frowned. 'Oh, right. Aye. Issy works there.' He cleared his throat. 'I know the owner. Mike. Mike Teviot. Good guy. He, uh, he's sympathetic to someone in, uh, her situation. Taken on a few parolees over the years for me.'

'Sounds like a good man.' Marshall nodded slowly. 'Okay. Do you recognise this specific bag?'

'Of course not.'

Marshall showed him a photo of the knife. 'What about this?'

Sullivan stood up, hands raised. 'Whoa, whoa, whoa!'

'Is that an admission, Brendan?'

'Of course not!'

'Bit of an extreme reaction to an item you've never seen before, isn't it?'

'It's a fucking knife!' Sullivan started pacing back and forth. 'I've never seen that before in my life.' He stopped. 'Where did you find it?'

'Where do you think?'

'I don't fucking know!'

'It was in the bag.' Marshall tapped on the other photo. 'Which you claim not to have seen.'

'Because I haven't!'

'It was in the boot of Isabelle's car.'

'Well, it's got nothing to do with me!'

'You've never seen it?'

'No!'

Marshall showed him a picture of Jake. 'Describe your relationship with him.'

'I don't have one! Who is he?'

'You know who he is, Brendan. Come on.'

'I don't know him. Never seen him before in my life.'

Marshall sat back and looked over at Jolene. 'Do you believe him?'

'Nope. Not a single word He's lied to us. Lied to his boss.' She sniffed. 'I hope that sex with her was worth it.'

'Me too.' Marshall fixed him with a hard look, shaking his head slightly. 'Destroying your whole life like that for her, eh? Crazy.'

'For a few shags with a convicted murderer.' Jolene laughed. 'I mean, she's a bonny lass, don't get me wrong. But is she pretty enough to explode your whole life over? *Hardly*.'

'He's really gone for it, though. I mean...' Marshall made a face. 'Thing I keep going back to is the bin full of used condoms? That's something you don't see every day.'

Jolene nodded. 'An impressive count, that's for sure.'

'I mean, why would you keep them? To show how young and virile you still are? Or just because you're suffering from undiagnosed depression and can't even empty your overflowing bin once in a fortnight?'

Sullivan leaned back against the wall. He seemed to grin, like this was all some kind of joke.

Marshall pointed at him. 'Sit down, please.'

'No.'

Marshall looked at Jolene. 'See how silly Mr Sullivan is being here? He's giving up his chance to set the record straight.'

Sullivan eyed him suspiciously, then perched back on the chair.

'Thank you.' Marshall licked his lips. 'Let's talk about the men she was propositioning.'

'*What?*'

'Young men. She'd speak to them in the Terie and ask if they wanted to have sex. We don't know how many took her up on that, but you know what drunk young lads are like, eh?' Marshall laughed. 'Wearing a condom was a smart move.'

'Fuck off...' A line of sweat trickled down Sullivan's temple. 'Nothing to do with me.'

Marshall glanced over at Jolene. 'Well, I guess there are two types of stupidity, right? There's your common or garden variety. You know, losing your keys. Lying to the police. But then there's a whole other level. Going to prison for helping someone to kill.'

'I didn't do anything!'

'You've lied to us.'

'No, I didn't.'

Marshall pulled out some more evidence – his files. 'These are yours, right?'

Sullivan squinted. 'Aye. They're mine.'

'Funny. Because they contradict what you've just told us.'

'How?'

Marshall waved the file in the air. 'This says she was propositioning young men in the Terie.'

'What the fuck are you talking about?'

'It's in your report.' Marshall flicked to the page and pointed at it. 'But you removed it from the next draft.'

'That was...' Sullivan wiped the sweat from his face. 'It was a mistake. An honest mistake, before you start. I'd written it in the wrong document and only noticed when I printed it out to review.'

'So who was it for, then?'

'David.' Sullivan wiped more sweat. He cleared his throat. 'David Smith.'

'So David Smith was propositioning men in a bar he worked in, which was in breach of his conditions?'

'Filthy bugger. Not a great idea to do that in a town like Hawick.'

'Why's that?'

'It's not a very woke place, is it? Not saying you'd get the shit kicked out of you for trying it on with a lad, but not far off it.'

'And David Smith would be on the radar of Patrick O'Brien, would he?'

Sullivan frowned. 'Probably not, no.'

'Is that because he doesn't exist?'

'That's...' Sullivan swallowed hard and looked away. He didn't finish the sentence.

'Come on, Brendan. This is just ridiculous. You wrote that about Isabelle, no question. You're not fooling anyone here.'

Sullivan rubbed at his head but he was sweating badly. 'I've done nothing.'

'That's not true. You'd written in a report that Isabelle was caught propositioning young men, which is a contravention of her parole. And you were going to escalate that to your superior.' Marshall weighed up the second file. 'But then you start having sex with her and suddenly she's an angel and the report is very clean.'

'That's...' Sullivan took a deep breath. Then another. 'That's not what...' He looked everywhere but at Marshall. 'Fuck it. Okay. That's what happened.'

'So she *had been* propositioning young men?'

'Yes.' Sullivan wiped more sweat. 'And no.'

'What are you talking about?'

'She did it. I caught her.'

'Do you have proof of it?'

'I did. Statements from people in the pub. The owner too. She promised him she'd never do it again.'

'Can we see it?'

'I destroyed it when we started seeing each other. She can't go back to prison for this, surely? That'd be inhumane.'

'Can we see the video files?'

'Deleted them. Mike's system rolls over every week, so you can't get them from there.'

'If you tell us the names of—'

'I'm not going to do that.'

'Because she's your lover.'

'Listen, pal. I told her how doing that kind of thing in pubs was stupid for someone with her reputation and history. And conditions on her parole record.' Sullivan scratched at his eyebrow. 'So I found lads for her on the internet.'

'I'm glad you're bringing that up now as I was just about to ask you about it.' Marshall felt like he'd run into a brick wall. 'But are you saying she had sex with these men instead of you?'

'No.'

'Come on. Those condoms belong to her lovers rather than you.'

'No.'

'Brendan.' Marshall didn't have the words. 'Go ahead and say it, Brendan, it'll sound better coming from you than from me. We've come this far already, no sense turning back.'

Then he played the silence game, sitting back and crossing his arms.

Next person who speaks, loses.

'The guys weren't for her. They were for us.' Sullivan rubbed at his forehead. 'She wanted to have threesomes.'

'Go on.'

'Right. She was wild for it. All that attention. Two men at the same time.' Sullivan raised a finger. 'And before you ask, they were all over eighteen. We saw ID for them all.'

Marshall sat back and sighed. 'Tell me the rest of it. Don't leave anything out.'

'It's not. And fuck it, you want something else? On Monday night, we were having sex with a man we met on 3sum.'

'What the hell is 3sum?'

'It's an app for couples seeking single people for threesomes. Or the other way round.'

'So you're claiming you had group sex with a man you met on the internet?'

'It's what happened.'

'And you'll be able to provide his name?'

'I think so.'

'Think so? Because it feels like it's Jake Turner.'

'What?'

'That was Isabelle's MO in the past… lure, have sex, murder. Then have sex again.'

'Fuck off.'

'Come on, Bre—'

'It wasn't!'

'You don't think you can just claim it was someone else and we're going to go away? So. Who is it?'

52

Marshall drove them through Elibank Forest, the rough surface making them rock side to side, but it didn't slow him down any. Looked like the place was being prepped for some forestry work. 'This is the one place this stupid truck isn't so stupid.' He pointed to the left, into a thick evergreen wood. 'That's where those bodies were buried. Do you remember?'

Jolene was gripping the handle above the door. 'Hard to forget.'

Marshall rounded a bend and saw a fat man walking two black greyhounds. He slowed to let him move them to the side and got a wave for his troubles, then drove on in silence.

Around another bend, someone was working away in a digger, the giant claws tearing at the surface at the side of the path. It swung around and dumped the overspill down the bank on the other side.

Marshall parked far enough away, then got out into the cool air. At least it wasn't raining – his mantra. He led over, warrant card drawn.

The operator was singing along to some music and it took

him a while to notice them. He stopped and let the claw rest on the ground, then waved at them, like he was letting them walk past.

Marshall stepped forward and raised his warrant card with both hands.

The guy stopped the engine and took his time getting out.

The big guy they'd passed by strode past them with his dogs, glancing over at them like a nosy sod. 'So, he still hasn't replied to my email.'

Marshall thought he was talking to himself then spotted the white earbuds – hard to tell these days if someone was insane or on a phone call.

The man disappeared down a little path to the side, cutting between two similar roads, by the looks of it. 'Aye. I know. I know...'

The guy hopped out of the digger and smiled at them, but didn't speak. He wasn't a buff lumberjack, just a skinny wee guy. Maybe five foot seven and about the same build as Jake Turner – he could easily pass for a teen in the dark. Especially if he wore his hoodie...

Marshall smiled at him. 'Daniel Dunning?'

'Depends who's asking, like?' A thick Geordie accent, all rolling noise. 'You cops?'

'We are, aye. DCI Rob Marshall.' He waved his warrant card again but the guy didn't seem to want to inspect it. 'This is DI Jolene Archer.'

'Right, aye.' Dunning grabbed her ID and took a while to check it. 'Okay. So why are the cops here?'

'It's about Isabelle and Brendan.'

'Who?'

Jolene cleared her throat. 'AKA Bonnie and Clyde?'

'Oh. Right.' Dunning sniffed. 'Can I get you a coffee?' Without a reply, he walked over to a van parked further on, marked with Sutherland Groundworks on the side.

Marshall thought he might make a run for it, but he slid open the side door and reached in for a flask.

Marshall smiled at him. 'Have you got any mugs?'

'Oh, right. Aye.' Dunning poured coffee into the cup lid. 'Sorry. I didn't think.'

Marshall waved around the forest. 'Take it they're flattening this place?'

'That's the plan, aye. I'm just here to harden the logging roads.'

'Right. That's not a local accent.'

'Live in Newcastle, like. Wallsend, really. Born and bred there. Based in Selkirk through the week, like, but I work all over the Borders. Stay here Monday to Thursday in this van, then I head home on a Friday afternoon.' Dunning eyed them nervously. 'But if you're here, then it's because one of those two has told you about what we did together, right?' He took a sip from his steaming mug. 'What we did is perfectly legal, I can assure you. We're all adults. And we all consented to it.'

'So you admit it?'

'Nothing to admit to.' Dunning shrugged. 'I get lonely here. Spend a lot of time on my own. There are a few lads who do this staying here during the week thing. Couple from Glasgow, few from Cumbria too. Most of them take a drink each night and fair play to them, like. I'd rather... do something with my life.'

'And that means...?'

'Sex. I love sex. And I'm good at it. I've got a really strong sex drive. Been meeting up with lasses for ages, you know. All the hook-up apps. But then I heard about... One of the lads told us about these apps where you can meet any number of people. Went to an orgy up in Edinburgh once and that was wild. Judges and doctors there. And you know what? It helps me fill me evenings. This time of year, they're very long.'

'How many times did you meet them?'

'Issy and Brendo? Just the once. Well, twice. We met for a pint in Hawick. Just to see if there was chemistry, you know? And there was. So I had a threesome with them. Right? You happy now?'

'What happened?'

'What do you think? We had a shag.'

'In detail.'

'Wait, was she underage?'

'No, she was twenty-nine.'

'Shite, was he her dad? Knew there was something off about those two.'

'No. They've been arrested for a serious crime and listed you as their alibi. If the stories don't tally, they could be in some serious trouble. It's also possible you would be as well if you obstructed us in our inquiries.'

'Right. I mean... Where to start. All the ins and outs, eh?' Dunning winked as he took a long drink of coffee. 'I turned up at this place in Hawick. Think it was, like, his office, maybe, and the place was pretty rank and not exactly clean, but they'd lit candles and stuff, you know? So it felt nice. But they had a big bed in there. And she was bang up for it. They both were.' He laughed. 'Some guys want you to fuck their wives and they watch. They get off on it, like... If you ask me, it makes them feel powerful because the woman they think they own is desirable to you.' He tipped the coffee out of his mug. 'That's how I see it, anyway.'

'But they weren't like that?'

'Nope. He wanted to fuck her at the same time as me. And we did. For hours. I mean, she was a bit younger than him and she's the same age as me. But he could keep up with us, like. Went on for hours, like. Sheer bliss.' Dunning looked all wistful. 'Not looking to get into a throuple or anything, but aye. I'd be well up for more, to be honest with you. It was a ton of fun.' He shifted his gaze between them. 'What have they done?'

'DI Archer and I are here to confirm their alibi.'

'Alibi.' Dunning looked like he was going to throw his coffee back up. 'Fuck.'

'It's related to the murder of a seventeen-year-old boy down in—'

'Fuck. Fuck, fuck, fuck.' Dunning swallowed something down. 'Listen, there was only the three of us there... Me and them... and if they are saying otherwise, they are fucking liars and I can prove it. Listen. If they killed that lad, then it was *nothing* to do with me, do you hear me? Nothing!'

'Okay, but we need to take a statement from you to confirm this tale.'

'I can prove it.' Dunning held out his phone. 'I've got it on video.'

53

The door opened wide and Marshall looked inside the interview room where Jolene was taking the statement from Daniel Dunning over their threesome.

McIntyre stepped out and raised his eyebrows at Marshall, then shut it behind him. 'Wants another coffee.' He closed the door behind him and charged on along the corridor.

Marshall waited there, holding his phone in his hand, trying to decide what to say to Ravenscroft.

His big case had been burst like a balloon and, in his eyes, Marshall was the prick who pricked it.

Aye, he just had to tell him – and bugger the consequences.

'Rob?'

Marshall swung around and saw Kirsten walking towards him.

'Oh, hey.' He smiled at her. 'It's you.'

'It's me.'

'Are you okay?'

'Why wouldn't I be?' Kirsten frowned at him. 'I've got something for you.' She scratched at her neck. 'But you're not going to like it. That video checks out.'

Marshall winced – aye, that bubble was most definitely burst. 'Definitely?'

'Definitely.' Kirsten nodded. 'We threw every single test we could at it. What's on that video... happened at the time he said it did. Synced to the cloud at the exact same time. The radio was playing in the background too and it matched the schedule.'

'So you watched it?'

'Nobody else offered.' Kirsten handed back the phone. 'All your man there is guilty of is having a kink. Or seventy. I found a few more videos... He's a popular guy. And very flexible.' She raised her eyebrows. 'Because what they were up to certainly wasn't vanilla.'

Marshall laughed. 'That kind of job is going to melt your brain, isn't it?'

'I think it's one of those chicken and egg things. You take a job like that, away from everyone, because you want the loneliness. But the darkness feeds on the loneliness and you start to crave things, I guess.' Kirsten shrugged. 'But he could be into much, much worse things.' She pointed at the phone. 'The stuff on there is between consenting adults. Even if one of them is a convicted murderer.'

'Thanks for doing that so quickly.' Marshall tried to lock eyes with her but she avoided his gaze. 'Any word from Gartcosh?'

'You mean, Jay's futile expedition?' Kirsten folded her arms. 'Not yet. Other than that Jay finally arrived there a couple of hours ago and was starting to get down to it. Shouldn't be much longer, just nowhere near as quick as when the robots do it.' She laughed. 'We're not totally hopeless here, though. The first pass on those condoms just came back.' She grimaced. 'Sorry, but who keeps that many used condoms? What's he planning on doing with them afterwards – make them into spunky soup?'

'Cream of some-young-guy.'

'Rob.' Kirsten covered her mouth as a pair of uniforms walked past. She watched them go, then let herself laugh. 'I know Sullivan's office was supposed to be a bit of a shit tip, but even that description has limits. Place was completely disgusting. I wouldn't go to the toilet there, let alone have sex in that bed. And that bin... That hadn't been emptied in months.'

'It's not often I have sympathy for a buffoon, but Liam Warner had to search through that to find the draft case file, in amongst those condoms.' Just thinking about it made Marshall's stomach swim – and he'd been at hundreds of crime scenes in his career. 'I've been thinking about it, though. Why he'd kept them all. It's like notches on a bedpost. A guy like Brendan Sullivan can't believe he's sleeping with someone like Isabelle. She's, what, fifteen or sixteen years younger than him? And I don't think he would've been a catch back then, let alone now, no matter how you define it. So he wants to know how many times he's had sex with her.'

'Or he's just a lazy bastard who doesn't empty his bin often enough.' She smiled. 'And he'd had sex with her less than you think.'

Marshall frowned. 'Come again?'

Kirsten laughed. 'Rob.' She raised her finger, but couldn't speak for laughing.

'Sorry, I didn't mean it that way.'

'No, I get it. Slip of the tongue.'

'Do you mean he's not well endowed?'

'Based on his performance on that video, he's above average, but nothing to write home about.' She blinked, like she was trying to shake herself free from the joke. 'Based on blood typing, about half of the sample is the semen of one man, presumably Brendan Sullivan. But the rest seem to belong to other men.'

'So there were other men there?'

54

For some reason Marshall couldn't quite fathom, the processing area was always busiest after lunchtime. Probably something to do with conniving sods stretching out the last few minutes of their shift by standing around while Fergus processed their suspects.

Isabelle looked over at Marshall with giant manga eyes. 'You're just letting me go?'

'That's right.'

She looked back into the processing area, where Brendan was still being processed. 'And Brendan?'

'Mr Sullivan is being charged with breach of trust and fraud, for falsifying documents.' He held her gaze. 'There will be a detailed investigation done by people in the parole officer world. They'll be checking to see if you have actually been fraternising with minors and breached your conditions.'

'I haven't.'

'Then you've nothing to worry about.' Marshall smiled. 'But given what you've done, we can't just take your word for anything, can we?'

'Are you judging me?'

'No, I'm just being extremely clear with you, Isabelle. All of the terms of your earlier release still apply. And you're obviously going to get a new parole officer.'

'You are judging me, then, aren't you? Just because I don't lie there and think of Britain?'

'Isabelle, I don't care what you do with consenting adults. But I'd stress both of those things. Consent. Adults. If you're going to keep down this path – and there's nothing wrong with it – just be very careful. Okay?'

'You don't understand.'

'I haven't lived your life, no, but that doesn't mean I can't understand what you've been through. Or empathise with your situation. I met Dominic, like I told you, and he's probably never going to pay the price for what he did, given his sentence. But you've paid your price. Just make sure you don't slip back into old habits.'

Most people would lash out at him, but she just nodded slowly. 'Thank you.'

'For what?'

'For believing me.'

'I don't take anyone on face value. You have to earn my trust.'

'No, but you were prepared to dig into it. A lot of people wouldn't. Most wouldn't. You were prepared to believe me enough to look into it. And that takes a lot. I know I've made mistakes and I'm not proud of the things I've done, but I am a good person. And thank you for seeing that. Or enough of that. It means a lot.'

Heavy footsteps thundered towards them.

Sullivan stood there, hands in pockets, scowling. 'They've finished with me, then.' He looked Marshall up and down. 'Said I'm going to be suspended pending the outcome of my charges. Said you've already spoken with my supervisor?'

Marshall nodded.

'Bloody hell.' Sullivan shook his head. 'This is a joke.'

'No. It's not a joke, Brendan. It's real and these are the consequences of your actions. This is a very, very serious matter. You were put in a position of trust and you abused that. Just to get your rocks off. And I'm not going to kink-shame you, Brendan, but you need to take a long, hard look at yourself because you've blown up your life for pretty much nothing.'

'It's not nothing.' Sullivan pointed between him and Isabelle. '*This* isn't nothing.' He grabbed her hand.

She shook it off.

'What?' Sullivan frowned at her. 'What have I done?'

'Nothing.' Isabelle looked at Marshall. 'Can you give us a lift back?'

Marshall laughed. 'A lift?'

'Aye, to Hawick.'

'I can call you a taxi.'

'But you've got my car, right? Can I have it back?'

'We're still processing it.'

'But it's my car!'

'And we found a murder weapon in it. The whole vehicle is evidence and hasn't been fully processed.'

Isabelle shut her eyes. 'I've lost my car because some fucker planted a knife in it?'

'We're working to determine the course of events that led to that.' Marshall stood up tall. 'I'm warning you now that you may face further questioning over the matter.'

'Seriously? You've brought us all this way and you're not going to drop us back?'

'The transport interchange is that way.' Marshall pointed out of the door. 'The bus to Hawick leaves in about twenty minutes. The custody sergeant gave you a chit in your receipt for the car that's good on the bus.'

Isabelle looked at Sullivan. 'Looks like we're getting the bus back to Hawick, then.'

'I can't afford a taxi, if that's what you mean…'

Isabelle sighed. 'Come on, then.' She took his hand, then led him across to the door. She stopped to look back at Marshall. 'I know you think I'm a monster, but I've paid the price for what I did. I have a darkness in my head, sure, but it's nothing like you seem to think it is.'

'I believe you, Isabelle. I hope you can stay on the straight and narrow.'

'I do too.' Isabelle took one last look at Marshall, then walked through the door.

Marshall watched them weave their way across the car park onto the street, hopefully heading towards the bus station.

A car pulled in next to Marshall's. An Audi.

Marshall winced and clocked the Audi's owner – Ravenscroft.

Well, this would save him that phone call…

Or he could bugger off back to his office and pretend he hadn't seen him.

Aye, better to just lance the boil.

Ravenscroft got out, focusing on Isabelle and Sullivan as they walked past MacArts. He turned and walked towards the station, shaking his head as he stepped inside. Up close, Marshall saw he was still heavily made up for his press conference. 'So they didn't kill him?'

'Pretty much, aye.' Marshall waved out of the door. 'We have evidence of their presence at his address at the time in question. Whatever they were doing, they didn't kill Jake Turner.'

Ravenscroft seemed to consider it. 'Which leaves open the possibility she used someone else to do it?'

'Indeed. It's a possibility. We'll have to go through all the condoms and see if there's a DNA match to Turner but that could take a week.' Marshall frowned. 'But we don't have anyone in the frame.'

'I'm not happy about this, Robert.' Ravenscroft ran a hand across his mouth. 'Really not happy.'

'You say that like you think I'm ecstatic about us not having any suspects now.'

'Don't get fucking cheeky with me, Robert.' Ravenscroft stepped closer to Marshall. 'I've just stood in front of news cameras, where I reassured the community we had two suspects. I look like a complete tit now.'

And not because he'd left his make-up on.

'You'd look worse if we'd tried to charge two innocent people, sir.'

'Robert.' Ravenscroft clamped a hand on both shoulders. 'I expect this to be sorted out and quickly.'

Marshall shook free of his iron grip. 'It's not that easy, sir. This is a complex case with many moving parts and we can't just click our fingers—'

'No, I get all that. But if you're as good as your reputation, Robert, then this should be trivial.' Ravenscroft gave a broad grin. '*If.*'

55

Isabelle was first off the bus in Hawick, her feet hitting the ground and she didn't let up – she needed to put distance between herself and...

This whole thing...

'Wait up!' Brendan jogged after her and caught up with her at the horse statue. 'You haven't spoken to me since we got on the bus in Gala.'

Isabelle looked at him, then nodded. She looked at the statue. 'See that?' She pointed at the plinth. '"Ye Teribus ye Teriodin". It's Old English, apparently. Not Scots, not Gaelic. Old English.' She looked around the town. 'This place has the weirdest accent, and I'm from the arse end of the Highlands... So it explains why. It's not really Scottish, but it's not English either. A sort of living fossil.'

'Do you know what it means?'

'What?'

'"Ye Teribus ye Teriodin".'

'Nope. But the pub took the name from it, right?'

'Do you want to...' Brendan glanced down the side street

leading towards his office and licked his lips. '... do some fun stuff?'

'Fun stuff...' Isabelle stared at her feet. After a night in the cells, the first thing she wanted was to lie down, but the last thing she wanted was him there with her. And while it'd break his heart... 'I don't know, Brendan.'

'What do you mean?'

'I mean, I don't know.' Isabelle grimaced. 'All this shit happening. My past coming... I'm just not sure I'm good for you, Brendan.'

'What? How can you think that?'

'I mean it.' Isabelle pointed at her head. 'What I said to that cop. Marshall. There's a darkness inside here. I don't want to keep inflicting it on people.'

Brendan stared at her like he was a dog who'd not earned a treat. 'You're not *inflicting* anything on me.'

'I am, though. This. This whole thing. Ask yourself, Brendan, is it you? Is this you or is it just because I'm so much younger than you?'

'Of course not!' He looked away, examining the horse statue for a few seconds, then back at her. 'Come on. Let's go back to mine and... We don't even have to do anything. We can just lie there. We can maybe just watch some videos or listen to some music. You said you'd never even heard of Embrace or Sleeper.'

'I don't know.'

'Come on, Issy... We can go back to yours? Get in my car and drive somewhere else?'

'I don't know. Okay?'

'Are you going to make me beg?'

He was even more like a dog. Hell, a little puppy.

Isabelle caught herself. 'Getting you to beg is one kink I don't have.'

Sullivan laughed, but it was snotty like a small boy. 'I love you, Issy...'

'I know you think you do. But I've corrupted you.'

'You haven't.' He pointed at his heart. 'The darkness is in here too. Always has been.'

Isabelle looked away from him. 'Look, I'll call you.'

'That's it?'

'I need to think about everything. More importantly, you do too.'

'Issy...'

'What's happened between us has been great. But I'm toxic. You deserve more. You deserve better.'

'*Issy*, there's nothing bett—'

Isabelle put a finger to his lips. 'I'll call you. Okay? Give me space.'

He looked at her with his big, cute eyes, then nodded.

She walked off along the street and tried to put distance between them.

She could get a bus home and hide in that grotty little cottage where they were watching her. Maybe try to sleep, but no doubt fail.

Everyone was watching her. Whether she was right or wrong before, they all knew now. They knew who she was but probably didn't know what she'd done... but it would start tongues wagging and surely the truth wouldn't be that far behind.

No.

She wasn't just going to hide away from the world. She was going to face it.

She turned around – someone was watching her.

Brendan. Even more like a puppy, but one chained up outside a shop.

Isabelle gave him a final wave then set off again.

She had to end this. It had been great – being wanted like that, desired, hungered for... And by a man who could fulfil her. Who could—

Who…

By a man who didn't need to watch violent porn to climax.

The stuff she'd done with Brendan had been wild, but it had been honest. Nobody was lying.

She stopped outside the Terie and noticed the front window was all boarded up.

And she knew why – because of her. Because of what she'd done.

She should run. Get a cab back to the cottage and flee. Bugger her conditions.

Or maybe she should call Patrick O'Brien and try to force the issue, get a move elsewhere.

No.

She needed to just grasp the nettle and pull on her big girl's knickers. She entered the pub, bold as brass, and walked through the place. Knowing they were watching her but not caring.

Mike was behind the counter, wiping the surface. He looked over at her, then did a double take. Eyes wide. 'Wow. She has risen.'

'And it's not even Easter yet.' Isabelle joined him behind the bar. 'Surprised to see me or something?'

'Just a bit.'

'Why?'

'Well. All that stuff with… With the cops.'

'It was nothing. A misunderstanding.' Isabelle smiled at a punter, itching for a drink. 'What can I get you?'

'Eh, just a pint of lager, love.'

'Just a sec, Darren.' Mike grabbed Isabelle by the arm, then took her aside. 'What's going on?'

'I was going to ask you.' Isabelle pointed at the window. 'Who did that?'

'No idea. Happened overnight. Insurance better pay up.'

Mike looked her up and down. 'I meant, what happened to you?'

'What do you mean?'

'I've had cops in here, asking all sorts of questions about you.' Mike gave her a hard stare. 'What did you do?'

'Nothing. Hence me being back here.'

'You don't get hassle like that for nothing. This is to do with what happened to Paul Turner's lad at the museum.'

After all he'd done for her, Mike was the one person who deserved the truth more than anyone.

She tried to hold his gaze, but she couldn't so she looked away and focused on the brewery calendar pinned to the wall. 'I had sex with two men at the same time. That's it. That's what happened.'

Mike scowled at her. 'What are you talking about?'

'My boyfriend and a lad. I think he was a forestry worker.'

'Issy...' Mike looked at her like she'd cracked. 'Why the hell are they interviewing you because you've had a threesome? Sounds like shit. It's because of that lad, isn't it? Jake, right?'

She nodded. 'They thought I'd killed him, Mike.' Now she was out of the police station and away from Galashiels, the magnitude of it hit her. She let herself feel the emotions for once. And they were going to hit her like a tidal wave. 'But I didn't, Mike. Of course I didn't. I gave them an alibi. They didn't believe it... But they... This cop, the guy who's in charge, he checked it and they've let us go.'

'Us?'

'Me and my boyfriend. We were having—'

'Bloody hell.' Mike shut his eyes. 'It's Brendan fucking Sullivan, right?'

'Don't say it like that.'

'What other way is there to say it?' Mike shook his head. 'He's a daft bastard.'

'Why, because he hooked up with me?'

'No, Issy. I've known Brendan since school. He's always had the capacity to self-destruct. Number of times I've had to clear him out of here and stick him in a cab. I just didn't expect the implosion to be so spectacular when it finally happened.'

'People talk about this whole thing like I'm just some object.'

'That's probably how he sees you.'

'It's not.'

'Issy. Think about it. You're a lot younger than him and, let's be honest, he was punching above his weight. As hard as this is for you to hear, this is a mid-life crisis for him.'

'It's not. It's love.'

'Love. Right. Sure. More like lust.'

'I mean it. We talked a lot. We listened to each other. Believe me, this isn't anything other than love. He loves me, Mike. He loves me.'

'Right. Sure. He can't believe his luck. And you? Do you love him?'

She shrugged. 'I like him.'

'Like, not love.'

'Okay, I maybe love him.'

'Do you? Do you, really?'

'I do.' Isabelle nibbled at her thumbnail. 'I just don't think I'm good for him.'

'Of course you're not. Daft sod left his wife and kids for you, didn't he?'

'It's not like I told him to do that. He just did it.'

'See what I mean? That capacity for self-destruction… Would you want to be with someone who could do that to you?'

'Eh?'

'Imagine you shack up together. A few years down the line, maybe you've got a kid or two. I'm not saying you wouldn't want to or whatever. But let's just say he gets in a sexy new parolee. Would you trust him with her?'

She bit right through the nail, then started chewing it.

'See?' Mike sighed at her. 'Level with me here, Issy. I want the whole truth.'

'What do you mean?'

'The cops were in here, Issy. Asking me tons of questions.' Mike laughed. 'I backed you up, but I want to know if you've sold me a pup and lied about what you've done.'

'So you're just going to judge me?' Isabelle gave him a sour look. 'I thought you were different. All that talk about being inside... It's just talk.'

'I am different. I spent time inside when I was your age, like I've told you many times. I know what it's like.' Mike sighed. 'The code inside was, you don't ask what anyone else is in for or what they did. You do that, you almost always get a punch in the mouth. But worse, you get labelled as a grass. And grasses always want to know what you are charged with, so they lead their way up to asking if you did it and how. And later on, grasses end up in court testifying against you so they can work time off their own sentence.' He left a long pause, like he wanted the words to settle in. 'If you want to talk about what you did, that's okay. I'll listen. But I won't ask and I won't back you up anymore.'

'I've only told you the truth.'

'Whatever you did, Issy, is in the past. If you're out, then you've paid your price to society.' He gave her a hard stare. 'Unless you've done something since.'

'I haven't.'

'And that's the truth?'

'Do you have any reason to doubt me?'

'No. But when cops come sniffing around, I start to worry I'm being lied to.'

'I haven't lied, Mike. I'm not lying to you.'

'Then it's all cool with me. There's nothing to worry about.' But that stare got even harder. 'I totally get it, Issy. Whatever you did, as long as you behave and tell me the truth, then I'm pretty liberal about it.'

'So, back to work, then?'

Mike looked at her for a long time, then gave her a nod. He grabbed a swag T-shirt and held it out. 'Now, put this on. That top is *humming*.'

56

Marshall sat in the canteen, puzzling through what to do next on a bit of paper.

Drawing blanks everywhere.

And feeling pretty useless.

All that training and experience... But this case was getting away from him. Only three days, but still... He could tell it wasn't heading to a nice, safe place.

His phone buzzed with a text.

He picked it up and checked it.

> RAVENSCROFT:
>
> Been with the parents. Promised them we'd solve it. And I expect you to. Let's pick up at five and see where we are. John

Arsehole.

Marshall dropped his phone on the table and sat back. He checked his watch – two hours. Brilliant.

What a total arsehole.

'Has your phone just called you a dick or something?'

Kirsten sat opposite with a steaming mug of tea and handed him one. 'Here you go.'

'Might as well have done.' Marshall sighed, then looked around to check they weren't going to be overheard. 'Ravenscroft.' He raised his mug. 'Cheers.'

'Don't mention it. But this isn't much of a lunch, is it?'

'No. Sorry. Day's kind of getting away from me here.'

'Heard you've let them go?'

'Aye.'

'After all that work on the car and the knife?'

'Your analysis of the video was the clincher.'

'Oh. Whoops.'

'The only two real suspects we had are now back in Hawick. They seemed perfect, Kirst. Her desire to control, his desire to be wanted and do everything she asked.'

'Too perfect?'

'Exactly.'

'And is that related to why you're annoyed with Ravenscroft?'

Marshall looked around again, but still nobody who could listen in. 'He's made promises I have to keep. Promises he shouldn't have made.' He took a sip from his coffee mug. 'Thought I was doing a good thing coming back here. But then I didn't know I was going to have to work for him.'

'I'm sure you've dealt with worse.'

'Aye, but there's just something about him I can't quite put my finger on, Kirst. It's not that he's an arsehole. He is. It's just...'

'He's a dickhead too.'

Marshall laughed.

Kirsten leaned forward, concern etched on her forehead. 'Are you okay?'

'I'm fine.'

'I believe you, thousands wouldn't.' Kirsten passed him a bit of paper. 'This might give you some hope.'

Marshall looked at it, but had no idea what it meant. 'What is it?'

'My credit has been used for the hair we found on that knife.'

'So you've got the results back?'

'No, but it's next in the queue. It's being processed right now.'

Marshall puffed out his cheeks. 'So much for it being in time for his eleven o'clock, right?'

'That was never going to happen. But that might save your bacon. The DNA from the blood on the knife matches Jake Turner's.'

'Wait. The blood type matches?'

'No. The DNA does.'

'Is that what Jay's been doing?'

'No. He's sitting there, waiting. We can do some stuff here. And it's much easier to extract DNA from blood. Analysing a hair takes some time.'

'Obvious question I'll get asked by him is when it'll be processed?'

'Could be any time, Rob. A big gang thing happened in Glasgow at the weekend. Hundreds of items to run.'

'And they didn't let us skip ahead of the queue at the tills with our loaf of bread and pint of milk?'

'Nope. That's Glasgow South for you – processing their full trolley first.' Kirsten smiled but it soon turned to a wince. 'Sorry. Thought you'd like to know it's in the sausage machine for when Ravenscroft comes knocking again.'

'Thank you. That it's definitely Jake's blood gives me some hope. Keep me posted on it.'

'Will do.' Kirsten nodded slowly, then frowned. 'Oh. Cath was lurking around when you were in those interviews.'

'What was she up to?'

'Just waiting in the car park. She said to tell you she's been here.'

'Weird.'

'What's going on with her?'

'I don't know.' Marshall took a long drink of coffee, at that perfect temperature. 'She turned up at Mum's last night. We went for a drink and she acted all weird. Then she buggered off pretty quickly.'

'Is she after something?'

'Money.'

Kirsten sighed. 'How much?'

'Didn't say. Like I said, she just buggered off.'

'Watch yourself, Rob – you can be a right soft bastard at times.'

'You say that like it's a bad thing.'

'I'm serious. If you...'

'If I what?'

Kirsten looked away. 'Nothing.'

'No, out with it. If I give her some money, then what?'

'You'll never see it again.'

'Right. But that's my problem.'

'Not if it's money for *our* house.'

'So that's back on, is it?'

'I need to actually get my flat sale over the line, but that's the plan. Isn't it?'

'So what was all that stuff earlier about?'

'Just... Working things out. It's been hard, Rob. I'm sorry. It was out of order. We need to move on and I shouldn't let my nonsense affect us.'

'You don't have nonsense.'

'I do. We all do. It's just...'

Marshall reached for a cuddle. And she let him. It felt good. It felt right.

She broke off with a deep sigh. 'Need to get back to it…'

'So do I… Time to find another suspect…'

57

Isabelle just couldn't get this bloody glass clean. It'd been through the dishwasher twice now and she was driving the brush deep in, but that little black mark still wouldn't shift.

She peered at it again.

Bloody hell – it was a crack.

She sighed, then dumped it into the recycling.

Would've spotted that if she wasn't so tired. And she was so bloody tired. Spent a night in the cells, after all. Barely slept a wink. But coping on no sleep was something she was good at. All those nights in HMP Grampian's Banff Hall.

She couldn't face going back there.

She'd rather die.

A nine-year sentence. Should've been out in five at the very most, especially with the pre-trial sentence, but those witches knew and they'd targeted her. Guards and inmates alike. Every day had been a battle, some literally.

Still, it was simple. Once she'd established herself, it was easier to navigate. And she could've become institutionalised –

she might not belong outside. Mind you, the sex was better as a free woman.

She looked across the pub but nobody wanted to be served. The glazier was working away at the window, rubbing putty into the casements...

That window... It had to be because of her.

Had to be.

She couldn't stay here in Hawick, could she?

Another look around the pub, at Auld Alec and Auld Eric and all the rest of them...

Did they knew what she'd done? Who she was?

No. If they did, O'Brien would be here, ready to relocate her. And he wasn't. So they didn't.

And the police... They'd keep hounding her forever, wouldn't they? The next time something happened in the area, they'd haul her in.

And she'd already cost Brendan enough – he'd left his wife for her. And now he was going to lose his job.

That wasn't solely her fault, she knew. But still...

The door opened and Brendan staggered in.

Speak of the sodding devil...

Seemed like all she had to do was think about him and he'd appear.

He staggered up to the bar, almost knocking over Auld Alec.

Jesus – she could practically smell the drink off him. He looked around, swaying.

Drunk.

Shitfaced.

How could he get so pissed so quickly?

How?

She hung up her apron and left the bar area.

Sullivan got down on his knees. 'Please don't do this.'

'Do what?'

'Dump me.'

'Haven't said anything about that, Brendan.' She tugged at his arm until he stood up. 'Get up, you daft bastard.'

'But you've thought it.'

Isabelle shook her head. 'You're drunk.'

'M'not.' Brendan burped. 'Issy, I love you.'

'This isn't endearing you to me.'

'See? You want to end things.'

'I don't know what I want, Brendan, you're right. But you coming in here steaming isn't helping your case any.'

'I love you.' Another burp. 'I love you, I love you, I love you.'

'We've only been back here, what, two hours?' Isabelle scowled at him. 'How are you this pissed already?'

'White fucking wine for the win.' Brendan went down on his knees again and pumped the air. 'I love you! Please! Don't do this to me!'

The side door clattered open and Mike rushed over. 'Right, you!' He grabbed Brendan and hauled him up to his feet, then away from the bar. 'You're drunk and hassling my staff, so I'm asking you to leave, *sir*.'

Brendan pushed him away. 'Not drunk!'

'You are. Brendan. Fuck's sake, mate. And you're not even denying the fact you're hassling her, are you?'

'I love you, Issy!' He tried to go down on his knees again.

But Mike pulled him away and dragged him out through the front door.

'I love *youuuuu!*'

Auld Alec stood at the bar, staring at the door, then over at Auld Eric, then back at her. 'Seen it all, hen.' He idly chapped his card against the wood, but the news playing on the TV took his attention.

The case in Hawick was taking centre stage nationally, putting the wee town on the map for the grimmest of reasons.

A senior cop talked to camera, looking flustered and orange, like he'd put on way too much spray tan. Quite handsome, though.

Det. Superintendent John Ravenscroft

Isabelle didn't know police ranks off by heart, but she figured he must be Marshall's boss, or his boss's boss. Then again, he was a *chief* inspector…

'Hell of a story, that.' Auld Alec shook his head at her. 'Hanging's too good for some. Should give them the fucking guillotine! Those boys in France know what they're doing!' He laughed and stared right at her, like he was expecting her to cackle. 'Here, did you know the last boy in France to get the guillotine could've watched *Star Wars*? I know! Sounds mental, but it happened in, eh, 1977 or 1978 or something. Heard it on this podcast the wife listens to when she's cleaning. Mental. Absolutely mental. I mind 1977, too. Hell of a year. Had to drive up to Gala to see that at the pictures. Braw film, though.'

Isabelle gave him a tight smile. 'What can I get you there, Alec?'

'Smashing pint you poured us last night, hen. What was it again?'

Isabelle looked around but didn't see the guy who'd confronted her. Whoever the hell he was. 'Just a half of lager. Cowshed, I think it's called.'

'Cowshed it is. Must be the way you pour it, doll. Get us the same again.'

'A wee hauf with that?'

Auld Alec winked at her. 'Why not, eh? It's Christmas, after all.'

'It's February.'

'Aye, but it's Christmas somewhere!' He cackled. 'Get it?'

She didn't.

'Sit yourself down and I'll bring them over.' Isabelle smiled. 'Anything else?'

'Wee bag of nuts, aye.'

'Smashing. Take a seat.'

'Champion, doll.' Auld Alec shuffled over to his table, where Auld Eric was waiting with his domino set.

She poured out his half of lager and couldn't help but think about spitting in it again. The old reactionary prick deserved it.

But that was Nicola's actions, not Isabelle's.

She'd let the demon out. Careless, so careless.

The door opened and a man walked in, stamping his feet on the floor. He looked around the place and seemed a bit familiar. One of those people who wasn't quite a regular. He sidled up to the bar like he knew a few people in there.

Isabelle smiled at him. 'Be with you in a second, sir.' She turned and pressed the whisky glass up to the Grouse optic.

Sod it.

She poured Auld Eric a second measure on account of her gobbing into his pint the previous night. She'd have to remember to pay for it...

'Killer!'

Isabelle turned back round.

The man stood there. 'Killer.'

'Excuse me?'

'Don't fucking deny it.' He leaned across the bar, hissing his breath at her. 'You. You're a fucking killer.'

Isabelle panicked, her eyes scanning everywhere. 'What the hell are you talking about?'

The door opened and Mike walked back in, shaking his head.

The man jabbed a finger at her. 'I fucking know!' He reached over and grabbed her arm. 'You fucking witch! You killed all those lads in the Highlands and now you've killed my son!'

Isabelle tried to tug herself free. 'Let go of me!'

Mike surged into action, charging over and taking down her attacker and pinning him to the floor. 'Jesus Christ, Paul, what the hell are you playing at?'

'You killed my son! You fucking killed my son!'

58

Marshall cast his gaze across the whiteboard in his office, trying to connect dots that just wouldn't go together.

Bloody hell...

He wiped down the whiteboard and started again from scratch.

Jake Turner. Victim.
Paul Turner. Alibi.
Isabelle Ward. Alibi.
Brendan Sullivan. Alibi.
Goodwillie, C. Incapable.
Goodwillie, H. Alibi.
Some Other Guy.
Applecross.
Shearer.
Dominic Hayes. In prison.

Marshall focused on "Some Other Guy" again, but he didn't have anyone. He had to face it – he was getting nowhere. Time to rub it down again and see what he could shake loose...

But he was mindful of what they said – madness was doing

the same thing over and over again, but expecting a different result.

Meaning he needed to do something different.

Maybe he could go back down to the museum and walk across the lawn. Put himself in Jake's shoes, or those of the killer.

So he wiped it all down and started writing all the names again.

O'Brien stood in his office doorway. 'Careful, you'll create sparks if you write that quickly.'

Marshall put the cap back on the pen. 'Getting bloody nowhere here.'

'And meantime, the boss is piling on the pressure, right?'

Marshall grinned. 'Oh, I see you've met a senior officer before?'

'Just a few.' O'Brien joined him and scanned across the board. He tapped on Isabelle's name. 'On a scale of one to "fuck right off", how pissed off is your boss that we let her go?'

'Put it this way, I think there's a dartboard in Tulliallan with a voodoo doll of me pinned to it.'

O'Brien laughed. 'That'll be "fuck right off", then.'

'Right, exactly.'

'Okay. We need to talk about what happened to Isabelle at her work. Is she here?'

'She was badly shaken up. Took a quick statement and she knows she's probably going to have to move. Not happy about that.' Marshall focused on Isabelle's name.

Why the hell had Paul Turner attacked her? Was it connected to the case? Or just something unrelated?

Marshall had plenty of theories, but nothing concrete. Or certainly no actual answers.

'Where's her attacker?'

'Got him in Hawick. We're going to interview him soon.'

'And he's the victim's father?'

Marshall let out a slow breath. 'Aye.' He tapped his name on the board.

'I know this is looking pretty shitty for you, but this is a complete disaster for us.' O'Brien folded his arms and glowered. 'While Isabelle's abided by the conditions of her release, subject to us checking whether she did chat up those lads or not, she appears to have been a model citizen. Or just someone who hid away in her cottage. But remember what I was saying about the metrics we assess things by?'

'Threat *from* her, threat *to* her, risk to Police Scotland?'

'Right. Well remembered. Well, there's clearly a threat to her.'

'And a risk to Police Scotland...' Marshall frowned. 'What are the conditions?'

'I told you.'

'All of them. It might help.'

'Aye, it probably won't, though.' O'Brien looked up at the ceiling. 'Off the top of my head... No weapons, ammunition or explosives. Curfew of ten o'clock unless gainfully employed like she was in the Terie. Staying only in her cottage, unless approved by her parole officer.'

'That didn't end up well, did it?'

'Nope.' O'Brien scratched his head. 'Oh, and no unsupervised solitary contact with anyone under the age of eighteen.'

'And she might have been propositioning young guys in the pub, right?'

'Emphasis on might.' O'Brien sniffed. 'Spoke to a few of the more disgruntled punters in the Terie. Some suggestion that Mike Teviot turns a blind eye to identification after ten, but nothing concrete. They were mostly just annoyed the place turns into a nightclub for a few hours.'

'Isabelle said she never worked a weekend night.'

'Aye, trouble is, it's not like she's working in an office with a swipe system, is it? She's working in a rough pub in Hawick. And I don't fully trust Mike Teviot.'

'Any reason why?'

'Just don't like the bloke. I think he exploits the desperation of people like Isabelle to keep their pay low. Either way, whether Isabelle did or didn't work there, it does sound like Brendan Sullivan started doing that propositioning side of things after they got together.' O'Brien shook his head. 'What an absolute idiot.'

'Wouldn't be the first or last man to not heed the age-old adage – when the dick is hard, the mind is soft.'

O'Brien laughed. 'Thing is, she can have all the kinky sex with adults she wants, but we need to check they were all over eighteen. We'll have a hard enough time tracking them down, but then we'll have to prove she knew they were underage.'

'Right. And that'll be pretty much impossible.'

'Exactly. It's not like she was asking them if they wanted to see some puppies. Just her tits. Add in the fact this was probably for group sex, and we're the last people they'll speak to about it. Well, maybe their parents, but you know what I mean.'

Marshall couldn't argue with the logic, but maybe wouldn't have put it so coarsely. 'So, what are you going to do with her?'

'We're going to have to move her.'

'Expected as much.'

'I mean... Bottom line, we don't have her in violation so we don't have the grounds to breach her, much less sit on her twenty-four-seven. But the word is out about her, making this a protection job. We need to keep her safe from the numpties.' O'Brien ran a hand through his hair. 'Hence us having to relocate her.'

'Even though they all think she lives in Burnfoot?'

'Just because they haven't got her real address doesn't mean anything. The threat is there and pretty severe. They know where she works. It'll be pretty easy to get to her address. And right now, we need to protect her.'

'Where are you going to move her to?'

'We've got some free places in Eyemouth and West Linton. At least to start with. Pretty much as far away as we can get her and still be in the Borders area. Obviously, we need to do an environmental scan before we can get her shifted.'

'Not East Lothian? Or say, the western end of West Lothian?'

'Nope. Not without another MAPPA. Borders it is.' O'Brien stared at the board, like that would help him any. 'You spoken to Paul Turner yet?'

'Letting him stew.'

'As in sober up?'

'Stone cold when he did it, apparently.'

'And he went tonto on her?'

'Tend not to use that term.'

O'Brien frowned. 'How not?'

'Think about it. When you say someone's going "tonto" you mean a Native American... Same with "going off the reservation".'

'Never thought about that.' O'Brien scratched at his temple. 'Bloody hell. Language is a minefield, isn't it?'

'Tell me about it.'

'But you're planning on going tonto on him?'

Marshall rolled his eyes at him. 'We're going to interview him, yes. Trouble is, he's a grieving father, so what can we do?'

Someone knocked on the door.

Jolene had Isabelle with her.

'Hi, Isabelle.' O'Brien smiled at her. 'How are you doing?'

'How do you think? I'm pretty fucking rattled.'

'It's okay. You're safe. We've got Mr Turner in custody.'

'Good. Are you going to charge him?'

'He's been detained.'

'Right. But does the mean he's going to jail?'

'Not for that, no. I doubt he will.'

'But he attacked me!'

'Trouble is, he made no threats of violence, no physical contact. He just confronted you.'

'He grabbed my arm!'

'And nobody at the bar could confirm or deny that.'

Isabelle glowered at him. 'What about verbal assault?'

'That's not a thing, aside from in a domestic abuse situation.' O'Brien sighed, then pointed at Marshall. 'But Rob here is going to give him a stern warning and make sure he doesn't do it again.'

'Thank you.' Isabelle nodded at him. 'That'll make it easier on my next shift. I won't be looking for him all the time.'

'Em, sorry but I need to explain to you what's going to happen.' O'Brien stuffed his hands deep in his pockets. 'Now your story's out there, Isabelle, you're in jeopardy.'

'But I've done nothing!'

'I know.' O'Brien raised his hands. 'But that's the way it goes sometimes. We're going to have to move you.'

'Move me?' Isabelle looked around the room, eyes misting over. 'I like it there. That cottage feels like home.'

'Sorry. I know this sucks, Isabelle, but that's what we've got to do. Part of my job is to keep you safe, okay? And you'll have protection for the next twenty-four hours, while we sort out your new address.'

Isabelle shook her head. '*He* fucking shouted at me and I've got to move?'

'I know. Believe me, I'm as pissed off as you are, okay?' O'Brien patted her on the arm. 'How about we get you all packed up, ready for the big move tomorrow?'

59

Jolene hated Hawick as much as it hated her.

The police station might've been more recently built than her local in Gala, but it stank of those noodles, the ones her husband ate when he was hungover. Absolutely reeked of them. Felt like at some point at every time of the day, someone was making them. Or there was a fungus problem that spread the mushroomy tang everywhere in the station.

Not that Paul Turner seemed to have noticed, sitting there all bored like he was waiting at the doctor's for a minor appointment. Apparently, he'd been a monster when he was arrested in the Terie, but right now he was the epitome of calmness and restraint.

And Jolene much preferred being in here with someone like him than a serial killer.

Paul looked up at her. 'You should be out trying to find out who killed my boy.'

'We're doing that, sir. But we're not here to discuss your son's murder, are we?' Jolene tapped the table. 'The reason we're here is for you to explain why you decided to approach

Isabelle Ward at her place of work. Why you decided to accuse her of killing your son.'

'Right.' Paul burped. The disgusting tang lashed across them. 'Guess I've given up any hope of you shower of twats ever finding out who did that to my son.'

'It's only been three days, sir. Most cases take a lot longer to solve than that.'

'You're in charge here, right?' Paul jabbed a finger at Jolene. 'You should be prosecuting her, not fucking questioning me! Instead, you let her go for killing my lad.'

Jolene folded her arms. 'Letting her go?'

'Don't fucking lie to me. You had her in here, didn't you? Your boy on the telly. Ravenscroft. He was saying on the news about how you released two people from custody.'

'That's true.'

'It was her, wasn't it?'

'I can neither—'

'Aye, aye. What a joke this is. She was one of them, wasn't she? Isabelle Ward. Fucking Nicola fucking Grant! Heard what she did up in that wee teuchter town up north. Applecross, right? Killed three laddies just like my boy. If you twats let her go, she must still know who the killer is, why don't you interrogate her instead of me?'

'That's not a very helpful attitude. I'd advise you to assist us with this, otherwise we'll be forced to caution you with a breach of the peace.'

'A what?'

'Think of it as a warning.'

'So you're saying if I play ball and act like a good boy by answering your questions, then you won't do me with something else. Is that it?'

'I'm saying we *might* not.'

'Isn't that blackmail?'

'No. It's not. You've committed a crime. We have discretion

over whether we charge you or not. Right now, we're taking into account the circumstances surrounding your son's unfortunate passing.'

He didn't say anything, but he seemed to accept that. He drummed his fingers on the table, thinking it all through. 'People have been talking, alright? Someone was saying she'd been arrested over... Over what happened to Jake.'

'And this mate named her?'

'Isabelle Ward, aye. She works in the Terie.' Paul screwed up his eyes.

'Let me get this straight...' Ash cleared her throat. 'You decided to visit the Teribus Arms and approach her?'

'Fucking right, I did.'

Ash frowned. 'Why?'

'Why do you think, pal? Because she killed my boy.' Paul gave her a hard stare. 'I was seeking justice for what happened to my boy.'

'This doesn't stack up for me.' Jolene sighed. 'Hearing someone had been arrested is one thing. But you went to the Teribus because you'd heard it was Isabelle, didn't you?'

'I told you. It said she worked in a pub. There aren't a lot of boozers left. Listen, I drink in that pub. I recognise her. And you had her in for his murder? I thought, fine. That's that. I can get on with things. But then you let her go. Why?'

'Because she didn't kill him.'

'It wasn't her?'

'Definitely. She's got a cast-iron alibi. And then there's a threat to her life from you.'

'Her life? *Her* life?' He slammed the table. 'Fuck this. You lot make me sick. You fucking let her go! After what she did up north? After what you let her do to my boy. You let her go...'

'She served her sentence and has been deemed to have paid her debt to society. As such, we have to look after her safety. Okay?'

'Why is she more important than Jake?'

'She's not. And she didn't kill your son. Her life is important. And we need to protect it. Now, it'll really help us get on with our day if you can tell us who told you about her.'

'Fuck you.'

'Where were you on Sunday night?'

'Fuck off.'

'Does that mean you won't give us an alibi?'

'I loved my son. He wasn't easy. We butted heads. All of that. But I loved him. He was going to inherit the business. There's *no fucking way* I'd murder him. Do you hear me?'

'I do.'

'You think I killed him?'

'Did you?'

'No. So fucking drop it.'

'Did you pay someone to kill Jake?'

'What? Why?'

'Because you found out he was gay or bisexual?'

'My son wasn't a fucking poof.'

Ash scowled at him. 'Poof?'

'Aye. He wasn't gay. Or bent. Or an uphill gardener. Whatever. He was straight.'

'Let me ask you a question.' Jolene left a long pause. 'It seems to me like you're trying to make it look like Isabelle killed your son. The way I see it, it's entirely possible you discovered he was having sex with a man and you—'

'Shut the fuck up!' Paul's mouth hung open. 'Fuck off!' He shot to his feet, clenching his fists. 'Whatever my lad was, he wasn't fucking gay… I don't have a gay son! He shagged lassies!'

Ash shrugged her shoulder. 'People can be bisexual.'

'Bisexual?' Paul sat back and cleared his throat. 'Listen, mate, just because you're bisexual doesn't mean everyone else is.'

'What are you talking about?' She scowled at him. 'I'm a straight woman.'

'Eh?' Paul looked at her like she'd gone mad. 'Whatever. My Jake wasn't gay.'

'Okay, but was Jake involved with anyone as part of a threesome?'

'A *what*?'

'Did he have sex with a couple?'

'What the fuck are you talking about?'

'Well, it could've happened on an earlier occasion and that's why there's all this aggro towards Isabelle now?'

'From me?'

'Yes.'

'I don't know what you're talking about. You're saying this… This Isabelle was into group sex? Fuck me.'

'I'm prepared to accept that, for now.' Jolene sat there, nodding. 'But that doesn't connect the dots about how you found out about what Isabelle did in Applecross.'

'I don't remember.'

'And that's fine. But the trouble is, you told two of our colleagues when they arrested you… What did you say again?' Jolene got out her notebook and sifted through it. 'Oh aye. "Nicola, you killed my son! I hope you fucking burn in hell for this!" That doesn't look good for you.'

'Why is it important I tell you who told me?'

'Because if we've got someone leaking information, that can cause an issue with public order. Additionally, it can muddy the waters with us trying to find out who killed your son. So who told you?'

'Someone Ravenscroft.' Paul frowned, then looked at each of them in turn. 'Your boss's boss, right?'

60

Marshall waited outside the station, arms folded. The rain teemed down and thrummed off his jacket, a soft whisper. So dark now, even though the sun hadn't set that long ago. He longed for the summer, not that it would be that much better. Just stayed daylight for a lot longer.

An Audi pulled through the gate.

Marshall flicked his phone to silent, then walked over. He opened the passenger door and got in.

'Steady on, cowboy.' Ravenscroft looked over. 'You don't just jump in my car like I'm a kerb crawler.'

'I'm not in the mood for this, sir.'

'O-kay.' Ravenscroft drummed at the wheel. 'Aha, I get it. Listen, Robert, I got your voicemail and tried to return the call but you didn't pick up. I've had to postpone your annual appraisal because of this... this whole business. Don't worry, we'll get time in the diary to do it properly.'

'It's not about that, sir.'

'Listen, you're lucky I was in Hawick and that this is on my way home. What's got you so upset?'

'Shut up and listen.'

'I'll do nothing of the—'

'Someone leaked Isabelle's identity.'

'What?'

'Somehow it went from some murderer living in Burnfoot to it being her. Isabelle Ward being Nicola Grant. They know both her real name and her assumed name. O'Brien's in the process of moving her to a new home. The risk to her from the public is now high. PPU dropped her off to pack up. Not that she's got much stuff.'

'I mean, talk about having sympathy for the devil…' Ravenscroft's finger twitched. 'Do you know who leaked?'

'We do. I informed DCS Potter about it.'

'Oh? Why did you do that?'

'Because it was you, sir.'

'What the fuck are you talking about?'

'When you visited the Turner home, you were so happy you were about to clear the case, you told them the name of who we'd arrested and were about to charge. And you told them Isabelle had priors for the same thing. How she used to be Nicola Grant. This is on you, sir. You daft bastard.'

Ravenscroft's forehead creased and un-creased. 'You've honestly told Potter?'

'*That's* what you're worried about?' Marshall laughed. 'You're not worried about us having a town full of angry people armed with pitchforks and flaming torches hunting for Isabelle Ward?'

'She's *hardly* innocent.'

'I hate to repeat myself, but she's paid her debt to society so she's free to get on with her life.'

'Robert. It was an honest mistake.'

'No. It was arrogant. And inept.'

'Inept? Fuck you. I'm not the inept one here. You've not got a single viable suspect, have you?'

'I get it, sir. You're good at cutting costs and maintaining operational efficiency. I'm not.' Marshall smiled. 'But you're not a copper anymore. Enough think I'm not, but I've got way more arrests to my name than you've got spreadsheets.'

'Listen, you prick. If anyone's inept here, it's you. I told the Turners after *you* assured me it was the right thing to do. And you're the SIO on the case. Don't forget that *you* failed to appoint an FLO for them. I was quite shocked to learn the family had been abandoned and had to earn their trust back.'

Marshall stared him out. 'Listen to me – I offered them an FLO and they refused. And besides, my actions were filed contemporaneously with the events.'

'What do you mean?'

'When I got back here, I documented it on the system.' Marshall gave him a hard look. 'And you, as my line manager, are required to sign off on my actions, which you did.' He gave a cold smile. 'Well done for being so efficient. You didn't read the actions, which makes *you* the inept one.' He prodded his arm. 'Trouble is, you overstepped the mark when you blabbed to the family. Isabelle was attacked. And you need to make this right.'

'Fuck.' Ravenscroft's left eye was twitching. Flickering like a broken light. 'You're covering your own arse, aren't you?'

'Damn right I am. And before you hang mine out to dry. You say I don't do politics well, well here's me doing politics very fucking well. I did the right thing. All by the book. And I'm thinking about the victims here. The Turners. Isabelle Ward. You fucked this up, so you need to fix this. And I suggest you start by calling Miranda.'

'But you already called her?'

'I did, but I didn't name you, sir. That's on you.'

'Right. Thank you.'

Marshall got out, then stormed through the rain, back into the warmth of the station. He kept feeling the urge to look back at Ravenscroft, but he didn't deserve that much.

Arsehole.

Jolene was waiting in reception, sipping on a can of Wakey-Wakey. 'Well?'

'Drinking a can of that stuff is a bad idea. Drinking two in one day is a terrible one.'

'Sure, I'll stop soon.' She tilted her head to gesture behind him. 'But how did it go with Ravenscroft?'

'He admitted it.' Marshall glowered at the door, then clicked the stop button on the recorder in his pocket. 'Daft sod is more concerned about his career than Isabelle's safety.'

Outside, Ravenscroft's Audi eased through the car park, the indicator glowing as it throbbed right to left.

'Figures.' Jolene crumpled her can and dropped it into the recycling bin. 'Listen, I really want to charge Paul Turner with that breach of the peace.'

Marshall shook his head. 'We can't do that.'

'Let me guess.' Jolene rolled her eyes. 'Because of the optics?'

'It's not that. On a human level, it's just pretty callous to charge a grieving parent. If he'd punched her or worse, then it'd be a very different story. But grabbing her arm and swearing at her wasn't exactly fun for her, but... He's promised not to approach her again. Let's leave it at that.'

'I get it...' Jolene exhaled slowly. 'Fine.'

Marshall could only offer her a shrug in return.

His mobile rang.

Perfect timing...

He checked the screen:

Cath calling...

He answered. 'Hi, you okay?'

Music blasted down the line, really loud and distorting.

Someone was shouting.

Sounded like Cath, but he couldn't make out the words.

'Cath, are you okay?'

She was frantic but her words were drowned out by the din in the background.

'Cath, I can't hear you. Can you turn the music down?'

'I need help!'

'What's going on? Turn it down!'

'There's someone at the door! I'm scared, Rob!'

'Open the fucking door or I'll kick it down!'

Then the line went dead…

61

Marshall powered through Galashiels, past MacArts then up to the confluence of roads, where Bank Street merged at the High Street with Channel Street's pedestrianised extension. He shot off, but his stupid American truck struggled to accelerate away and a knackered old Corsa was right up his arse.

Panic was coursing through his veins.

'Open the fucking door or I'll kick it down!'

Hard to shake that free – Cath was under threat here...

The other night, when she'd showed up desperate for money... He'd thought it was for a stupid reason... But what if it was because of the dodgy circles she moved in?

And Kirsten said she'd been lurking around the station, meaning she was desperate.

And he couldn't remember which number was Cath's – he'd remember it when he got there. Given the din in the background, he'd probably hear it from the street. And he'd see an open front door...

Christ. Who was it?

Shite.

She wasn't even in his fucking life and he was the only one she'd come to…

Back-up.

Bloody hell.

Think like a cop instead of a brother…

He reached over for his radio and called Control. 'This is DCI Rob Marshall. Need urgent back up to an address on Rosebank Place in Galashiels. Over.'

'Receiving. Hi, Rob. Do you have a house number there? Over.'

'Sorry.' Marshall drove on, knowing it was going to take him some time to get there but he'd be there way before any backup. 'Over.'

'Okay. We've got officers already on the scene at number 18. Over.'

Marshall felt a flush of relief as he pulled up at the lights. At least he was first in the queue to head straight on, so he could blast away. The curry house was doing good business and it made him feel that bit hungrier. He could practically see her house from here, stuck away up the hill but hidden behind the thick trees. And if it wasn't so dark…

At least Cath'd had the presence of mind to call 999 as well as her estranged half-brother she hadn't spoken to in ages. Couldn't be that bad.

Right?

'Can you give me their status, please? Over.'

'Officers were dispatched for a noise complaint. PC Taylor and PC Warner.'

Bloody hell. The last person you want in a situation like that…

'Last update is they now have one in custody for prostitution and assaulting an officer.'

Marshall set off from the lights, finally getting a kick of acceleration. '*Prostitution?*'

'The sergeant is on her way as well. Over.'

'Okay, thanks for the update. Over and out.' Marshall took the left and powered on up Kirk Brae, then took the left along Scott Street. He slowed to enter her street, just as a patrol car was pulling up.

There was barely anywhere to park, so Marshall did the second-worst thing he could – double-parking across an empty drive. The only thing worse would've been if there was a car there...

He got out into the heavy wind, just as the patrol car's door opened.

PS Isla Routledge stepped out, scowling at everything and everyone. Those narrow eyes searching everywhere. Dark hair tied up in a functional bun, which she covered over with her cap. She was hardcore, though, just a fleece on in these conditions.

Marshall raced over to join her. 'Hi, Isla.'

She looked him up and down, assessing him as though he was a member of the public – and a threat. Then she seemed to clock him as a cop and her scowl softened. 'Rob.' She coughed. 'I mean, sir. Why are you here?'

'Because Catherine Sutherland is my sister.'

'Your sister? Isn't that Jen Marshall?'

'It's a long story. Cath called me so—'

A scream cut him off.

Marshall looked over at the house. Missing the front door, presumably kicked in by someone.

Then a slammed car door.

Marshall raced over towards the other patrol car.

As he neared, music blared out of the house – that Lola Young song Kirsten loved. He couldn't remember the name – 'Messy', maybe? Something like that.

Cath was in the back of the patrol car, handcuffed and

kicking at the windows with her pink socks, leaving marks on the glass.

PC Steven Taylor – AKA Stish – opened the driver door and noticed Marshall, but his focus was mostly on Isla. Typical Geordie lad, standing there in his T-shirt despite the wind and the rain. 'Just taking her to the station now, Sarge.'

'Hopefully she won't break free before then.'

'No, Sarge. Stish opened his door.

Isla pointed at the house, just as the song finished. Then started up again. 'Can you turn off that bloody song!'

Stish followed her instructions and entered. Seconds later, the music cut out.

Marshall could hear himself think again. 'Thank God for that.'

Stish reappeared then got in the car and reversed out, shooting off away from the house.

Cath stared at him as she was driven past.

Warner was sitting on her front doorstep.

Marshall had no idea what was going on, but two things were clear.

First, that Warner's voice had been the one at the door, so it hadn't been anything more sinister than him trying to gain entry.

Second, he'd clearly lost the fight – his face was a patchwork of scratches and cuts, like a wild cat had attacked him with its claws. Or Cath with her fancy nails.

Isla shifted her scowl towards Marshall. 'You might be a chief inspector, but this is my operation and I don't want any detectives trying to get in the way of proper police work.'

Marshall hadn't dealt with her that often, but he knew her to be one of the better uniformed cops. Honest and driven – and with no desire to become a detective. Even viewed them as wankers.

'Totally get that.' Marshall raised his hands. 'I'm just here to listen, okay?'

'Glad we're clear on that.' Isla shot him another look, then crouched next to Warner. 'You okay there, Liam?'

'How do you think I feel? She's like a fucking banshee, Sarge! Scratching and cutting and everything. I was lucky Stish was with me!'

'This is all just from her fingernails?'

'Right.'

'We'll get you sorted out once you're back at the station, okay, but how about you tell us what happened here.'

'What's there to say? You know we were called out, Sarge, because you told us to attend.'

'I do. But when an officer of mine gets assaulted like this, I want to know the full facts. Okay?'

'Sure thing.' Warner stopped patting his face for a few seconds, then sighed. 'Okay. So you'll remember how this was a noise complaint?'

'Aye, and I heard the noise myself.'

'Well, we got here and Stish knocked on the door, but there was no answer.' Warner pointed at the next door along. 'So we knocked on that door, right, and she answered it. The old lady who reported it. Margaret Turnbull. She's one of those curtain twitchers, you know? Has a little book that documents when everyone comes around. Who's there. All of that. And she thinks your woman there—' He thumbed behind him as though Cath was still in the house. '—has been dealing drugs and selling her body.'

Isla narrowed her eyes. 'Drugs and prostitution.'

'Right.'

'Has she got any proof of this?'

'She's got photos of about twenty different men and women going in and out of the flat. What else could it be but drugs or prostitution?'

Marshall stifled a sigh, but he felt the frustration deep in his soul. His sister was deep in the shit and she'd tried to reach out to him. He'd been too distracted by the bloody case and his hunger to offer her the help she desperately needed.

'Okay. So what did you do next?'

'What do you think, Sarge?' Warner dabbed at the cut on his cheek and searched his fingertips for blood. 'We went next door to tell her to turn the music down. Your woman, Catherine, was very rude to me.'

'Straight off the bat?'

'What do you mean?'

'I mean, Liam, did you ask her about the drugs and prostitution allegations?'

'Well, it might've slipped out, yeah.' Warner traced a finger along a cut on his forehead. 'She slammed the door and turned the music up. And I might've booted the door in. And the fight was on.'

'Liam...' Isla pinched her nose. 'Did you have your body-worn video running?'

'Of course. I'm not an idiot.'

Marshall had to look away.

Isla nodded. 'Okay, how about you stay there and guard the entrance until Kate and Sarah come back out, then get one of them to take you to the station?'

'Sure thing. Feels like it's an A&E job, though, Sarge.'

'Okay.' Isla gave him a smile then walked away, beckoning for Marshall to follow her. 'Useless sod...'

'No comment.' Marshall gave her a conspiratorial nod. 'What are you thinking there?'

'I'm thinking this is a bad arrest. He broke down the door and attacked her. She defended herself. And of course he had to record it all. He couldn't have just accidentally switched it off, could he?' Isla held out a hand. 'Forget I said that.'

'Mum's the word.'

'Bloody hell.' Isla sighed. 'This is a total mess.'

'It's what happens when you keep incompetent officers in a job, right?'

'Ach, Liam's not that bad.'

'No. He is. I've had him on a few cases. And he's terrible.'

'You've had him because he wants to be a detective.'

Marshall laughed.

'Rob, I'm serious. It's in his development plan.'

'You can't palm him off onto me, Isla. There's no way he's going to be a detective. No way at all.'

'I had a chat with your predecessor last year and he was keen.'

'Jim Pringle?'

'No. Ryan Gashkori.'

'Aye, well, the less said about him, the better.' Marshall smiled at her. 'Do you need me to help here?'

'I can fight my own battles, sir. You detectives all think you're superheroes, right? Well, we're doing the real job here. So thanks for the offer, but no thanks.'

'No, it's... Not professionally. I mean, I can speak with Cath. She's my sister. Half-sister. And maybe we can all come to an understanding. Get her to drop any complaints against your team. And maybe I can get the truth out of her, then we can all be on our merry ways.'

'I might take you up on that.' She looked at the door. 'But first, let's speak to this neighbour and see how we've leapt from photos to drugs and prostitution, for fuck's sake.' She looked him up and down again, like she was appraising some prize cattle. 'But you're just here to stand there looking pretty, okay?'

'Certainly.' Marshall raised his hands again. 'Well, I can do the standing there bit.'

'Aye, aye.' Isla gave a flick of her thin eyebrows, then walked over to knock on the neighbour's door.

She didn't have to wait.

The door cracked open and an old woman peered out over the chain, all lined and puffy, her eyes bloodshot. 'Can I help you?'

'Police.' Isla smiled at her, even though the uniform was more than enough of a clue. She tilted her head towards Cath's door. 'Need a word about your neighbour, if it's a convenient time?'

'Of course it is.' She disappeared, then the door opened wide. 'In you come.'

Isla entered first, stamping her feet on the mat, then following her through.

Marshall flashed a one-minute gesture to Cath in the back of the patrol car, then slipped inside.

Three cats swirled around his feet. The place stank of cigarette smoke, a blue haze filling the place.

'I'm Margaret, by the way. Come on through.' The way she shuffled through the living room, it looked like she needed a new hip. 'Can I get you a tea or a coffee?'

'We're fine, thanks.'

'Well.' Margaret collapsed onto the sofa with a crunch. 'How can I help?'

Marshall stayed standing and stayed silent, even though she was looking at him.

Isla joined her, sitting at the other end of the sofa and taking her time to sift through her notebook. She looked up, pen in hand. 'I gather you made a complaint regarding your neighbour, a Miss Catherine Sutherland.'

'Is that her surname? Used to know a Sutherland laddie who lived nearby.'

'I gather it's not the first time you've had cause to call us regarding her?'

'No. Far from it. It's her music, you see? Can't hear myself think when she plays it. Thumps through the wall at all hours.'

'That must be very frustrating.' Isla nodded and gave a kind smile. Then it hardened, along with her eyes. 'But I gather you made some serious allegations too.'

'That lassie's up to all sorts.' Margaret shuffled forward. 'I'm sure she's on the game. And she's dealing drugs too. It's awful. *Awful.* I lost my nephew to heroin. He lived in Edinburgh, but got in with the wrong crowd. Awful business. A good wee laddie who just...'

'That must've been tough.'

'It broke my sister's heart. She was never the same after it.' Margaret was still focused on Marshall, like she couldn't understand why he was there or why he wasn't speaking. 'There are people coming and going at all hours.'

'Like, during the night?'

'No, no. Just during the day. But the music's loudest at night. And she shouts and bawls at me too, when I go in to complain.' She shook her head. 'It's really not right.'

Isla nodded along with it. 'My colleagues who were here earlier mentioned you had some photographs?'

'Right, right...' Margaret got up and shuffled over to a side table. She looked through a set of photos. She shuffled back, then showed two photos of the same man. 'See? They turn up, have S-E-X with her, then they have a shower. Or they're just buying drugs from her, like the women. Or both.'

'It's not a good idea to photograph your neighbours like that. It's a breach of privacy.'

'I'm sorry. I won't do it again.'

'It's understandable and it'll just be our little secret, eh?' Isla winked at her, then reached over and handed her a business card. 'Next time you have any concerns about her, anything whatsoever, I want you to call me. Okay?'

'Okay. Listen, I didn't think about the photos. I'm sorry.'

'It's fine. We rely on people like you to keep things safe.' Isla got up and put her cap back on. 'Thanks for your time.' She nodded at Marshall, then led him back outside. She shut the door, then looked at him. 'What do you make of that?'

'It doesn't look good, does—'

Locks started clicking behind the door.

Marshall stepped away from it, back over to Cath's.

Warner still sat there, eating something out of a plastic tub.

Isla shut her eyes, let out a sigh, then smiled at Marshall. 'You were saying?'

'It doesn't look good.'

'No, it really doesn't. I might need to take you up on your offer to speak to your sister.'

'Happy to.' Marshall frowned at her. 'Mind if I take a look at those photos?'

'Why?'

'Because I work across a range of different cases. I might recognise someone. If there's a known dealer supplying her, then we've got the start of a case, right?'

'Fill your boots, sir.' Isla handed them over.

Marshall started flicking through them. Sure enough, it was hard to disagree with the neighbour's assessment. Men and women, all taken during the day. The fact both genders featured meant drugs were probably in play, but the men did all look like they'd had a shower – or most of them did, anyway – so prostitution was an option too.

He flicked to the last one and stopped dead. 'Oh, bloody hell.'

62

Marshall charged through the custody suite and into the cells. Pretty quiet in there, for once, but it was Wednesday evening. Hard to imagine a quieter time.

He opened the door to cell three.

Cath Sutherland sat there on the bench. Head in her hands. She looked over at him. He could smell the booze wafting off her even from this distance. 'Can you get me out of here?'

Marshall just stood there, hands in his pockets. 'Do you actually want me to?'

'What's that supposed to mean?'

'It means I want to hear your side of this.'

'My side?' Cath flicked him the Vs. 'Piss off, then.'

'Sure.' Marshall made to leave, but she didn't even look at him so it didn't have the required effect. Bloody hell... 'We all like a tipple, don't we? Good to let your hair down, as they say. Every now and then.'

Cath didn't say anything.

'But my colleagues were called to your property because of a noise complaint. And it's not the first time, is it?'

'Never charged me with *anything*.'

'No, I noticed that. Does Dad get the charges dropped for you?'

'No.' She looked at him again. 'Why would you think that?'

'Come on. I can see how it happens. Big, bad superintendent in the Complaints comes down here and puts the fear of death into Fergus through there. Or someone in Isla's team.'

'That's not what happens.'

'So what does happen, then?'

'Nothing.'

'You just get let out?'

'Yes. Because I haven't done anything other than get pissed! And...' Cath tugged at her hair. 'I might play my music a bit louder when I'm pissed, but... They come around and they start shouting at me and I might get a bit lippy. Then they bring me in here. Then they sit me in a cell and they let me go with a warning.'

'So you're telling me every time you've been picked up, it's because you're drunk?'

'Yes. I... They let me sleep it off, then they let me go.'

'You're stinking just now.' Marshall shook his head. 'But this time, you attacked an officer. Didn't think you were the violent kind, Cath.'

'I'm not. That's not what happened. He grabbed my arm. I fell. Accidentally took him down with me.'

'Sounds like bollocks to me.'

'It's the truth, I swear.'

Marshall laughed. 'If it's true, then how did he accidentally scratch his face open?'

She looked away from him again.

'Guessing if we scrape away under your nails, Cath, we'll find some of his DNA there, right?'

'It's all bullshit, Rob. Why don't you believe me?'

'I don't believe anyone without them first earning my trust.

Since I've known you, Cath, you've done a few things which make me think not just twice but a hundred times.'

Cath took a halting breath. 'I'm telling you the truth, Rob.'

'Cath, you've been picked up four times.'

'And the reason they pick me up is because I drink too much.' Cath looked over at the wall. 'And when I drink, I can be a bit loud. I'm not proud of it.'

'Okay. How about you talk me through these times you've been picked up.'

'What's there to say? The first one, I was at a gig with a few mates. Got into an argument with this guy at the bar. He was very touchy-feely so I pushed him over. His mates stepped in. I pushed one of them over too. Bouncers grabbed me and they called the cops.'

'Okay. That sounds like it has the semblance of truth to it.'

'It's the whole truth, Rob.'

'And the rest?'

'They're all the same thing. I live alone, Rob. When I'm not working, I get *bored*. Open a bottle of wine or have some gin or vodka. And next thing I know...' Cath swallowed. 'There are cops asking me to turn the music down.'

'That doesn't quite ring true, though.'

'My neighbour is this old battle-axe who has no joy in her life. She hates me. And I totally get why she'd be annoyed. I'd be annoyed having to live next door to me. But her TV is on so loud too. But she keeps on reporting me. And I...' Cath shrugged. 'I know I've got a drink problem. I know it. But I don't want to stop. And when the cops come out, they get in my face and I get all aggy. And it doesn't end well, does it? I get all lippy.' She looked away, shaking her head. 'Like today, she knocked on the door, asking me to turn the music down. And I didn't. Then two cops came out and shit happened.'

'Shit happened, eh?'

'I slapped a cop. They brought me in here.'

'Lippy's one thing and slapping's another, but you assaulted a cop. You cut his face open.'

Just then, Isla appeared and gave her a hard look. 'His name is PC Liam Warner. He's going to A&E now to get those cuts seen to. He'll need a tetanus shot because of what you did.'

'That's bullshit.'

'It's recorded on video. We've got proof of what happened. I've just seen the video from both of my officers. And it didn't look like anybody touched you until you started scratching him.'

'Still had no business caving in my door.' Cath curled up into a ball. 'Who's going to pay for that, not me, I'm skint. Are they even allowed to do that?'

Marshall squatted next to her, raising his eyebrows towards Isla. 'Thing is, Cath, you've been picked up three times at your home for being drunk. And now you're assaulting police officers.'

'Fuck off.'

'Fine. I'm fucking off now. Come on, Sergeant.'

'Don't go.'

'Why should I stay? You're just lying to us.'

Cath sat still.

'Listen, I don't need to do this. I've been up since five this morning. I've been working a murder case all week. I was up in Inverness yesterday and the only thing keeping me upright just now is way too much caffeine and that's really not good for my health. So I'd rather just go to bed or tackle some paperwork or, you know, catch a murderer... But instead I'm here. So why should I help you?'

Cath looked up at him for a few seconds. 'Because I'm your sister.'

'Right. So it seems to me that Dad, being who he is, gets you off. And that gives you a sense of entitlement.'

'Fuck right off.'

'Hope he's got reception when you call him, Cath, because he doesn't seem to when I try.'

'Rob. I need your help here. Just get me out and I promise I'll keep the music down.'

'That's not really going to cut it, I'm afraid. Your neighbour thinks you've been selling drugs or being a prostitute.'

'That's bullshit!'

'Right. Sure.'

'What's that supposed to mean?'

'Just that it tallies with what I've heard.'

'You don't believe me, so why should I bother?'

'Fine.' Marshall shrugged. 'I'll give Dad a call and see if this checks out with him.'

'Don't.'

'Does that mean it doesn't?' Marshall smiled at her. 'Why does she think you're selling drugs or—'

'Or selling myself?' Cath shrugged. 'I don't know. But I'm not.'

Marshall gave her his police officer's look. 'Cath, I don't believe you.'

'You honestly think I'm dealing drugs?'

'We do.'

'Plural?'

'Myself and another cop spoke to your neighbour.' Marshall reached into his pocket and got out his phone. 'And she gave us these.' He'd snapped all of the photos and he sifted through them for her benefit. 'Men turning up at all hours. Coming out looking like they've had a shower. Women too, but they don't look like they've had a shower.' He stopped on a particular photo. 'See what I mean?'

Cath looked at them, then shut her eyes.

'This is what we call evidence, Cath. We can combine it with a lot of other stuff and we can then build a case against you.'

'You mean I'm going to jail for this?'

'Not my call, but I'd say it's likely.'

'This is bullshit!'

'Cath, I'll ask you straight. Is this the truth?'

'It's not! She's lying.'

'Let's start with this guy.' Marshall held out the phone again. 'Do you know him?'

'Of course. That's Bongo.'

'Bongo?'

'Brian Wilkie, I think.'

'How do you know him?'

'Used to work together.'

'And now we're getting somewhere.' Marshall smiled, but it wasn't full of anything like warmth. 'See, I really don't like it when people lie to my face.'

'What are you talking about?'

'I know Brian Wilkie, Cath. He works for Gary Hislop.'

Cath shrugged. 'So?'

'And you're saying he's not a drug dealer?'

'Of course not.'

'He's not the one supplying you?'

'Bongo?' Cath laughed. 'He works at Scott Street Hardware, Rob. Drives the van between the shops. Berwick to Peebles and up to Dalkeith.'

'Sounds a lot to me like someone who deals drugs.'

'Rob. He's just a mate. We worked together in the shop for a bit. Remember all that stuff in Kelso?'

'When someone tried to kill the shop owner?'

'When you got me sacked, Rob.'

'Aye, but you were sacked by Gary Hislop, renowned drug dealer. Owner of Scott Street Hardware. Where Wilkie works. Where he drives the van between locations. For crying out loud, Cath…'

'He's not like that.'

'Hislop? Of course he is. Trust me.'

'No. I meant Bongo. He's a good guy.'

'Okay, so if he's not buying drugs, are you having sex with him?'

'Fuck off.'

'I don't think you realise how serious this is, Cath. We've got evidence here. This is stacking up into a case against you. We're talking jail time here.'

'Rob, that's not the truth.'

'So what is? Does this Bongo come to your flat and you just sit there talking about films?'

'I cut his hair.'

Marshall laughed. 'You cut his hair?'

'Exactly. I've been doing haircuts at home.'

'Haircuts. Right. Okay. I've heard it all now.'

'I mean it, Rob.' She scowled at him. 'I was a hairdresser in Aberdeen. Worked in a few salons.'

'You expect me to believe this?'

'It's the truth. I've got people coming around most days now. They pay cash.' Cath raises both hands. 'I put it all through my books. It's all legit. And when Bongo comes, I cut his hair and he plays *Fortnite*.'

'*Fortnite*?'

'You know, the game?' Cath put her cup back down again. 'Bongo's a massive gamer. So am I. He plays it while I cut his hair.'

'I don't believe you.'

'Fine, I'd fucking show you my PlayStation but you've got me stuck in here.'

Trouble was, Marshall could see some truth in it. 'And you can give me contacts for all these supposed customers, right?'

'They're real, Rob. She thinks I'm a hooker or a drug dealer! And I'm not! I'm just cutting their fucking hair!'

Isla beckoned him away. 'We both know Warner is an idiot.

Well meaning, but an idiot. I'll give him and Stish to pitch in for the joiner. That, or you can get them written up. Your choice.'

'I'll get you an invoice.'

'So you're going to help her, Rob?'

'Got no choice, do I? She's my sister.'

'Wish I had a brother like you.' Isla held out her handcuff key, then walked off.

Marshall walked over and started un-cuffing her. 'Jesus Christ, no wonder people think you're dealing drugs. You need to clean up your act.'

'Do you think I like being this way? Getting into these fights?' Cath scowled at him. 'Look. I'll change. I'll stop drinking. Is that what you want to hear?'

'It's a start.'

63

Cath stood at the processing desk and looked away from Fergus to glance over at Marshall. She knew enough to not talk.

'This is your grave, Rob.' Isla shook her head. 'This Wilkie guy? He works for Gary Hislop, right?'

'Apparently.'

'So he could be a dealer?'

'Could be. We'll keep an eye on him.'

Isla looked away, shaking her head, then did the old up and down yet again. Becoming a habit... 'Anyway, I need to head to hospital and give Mr Warner a crash course in that whole bit about probable cause. Rather have overly ambitious than clinically dead on my shift...' She smiled at him. 'Thank you, Rob.'

'What for?'

'Treating me with respect. You're a chief inspector but I'm just a sergeant. You didn't strong-arm me.'

'No. I don't work in frontline crime, Isla. That's your remit. I shouldn't be doing this. I'm only sorting this out because she's my sister and because she promised me it's the truth.'

'Do you believe her?'

'As fucked up as it sounds, I do.'

'Okay, I'll get Stish to drop a report that says, while investigating a noise complaint, he discovered that Ms Sutherland was operating a hair-cutting business out of her residence. All involved were cautioned for their actions.'

'Good stuff. And thank you.'

'Don't mention it.' Isla crossed over to the desk and nodded at Fergus. 'Let her go.'

Marshall followed her over, but kept his distance from them – another way he could show Isla respect.

Fergus handed Cath her things back. 'Sign here.'

'But how do I—'

'Just do it, please.' Marshall fixed her with a hard stare – he needed to be strong with her, especially if she was going to be his fault now.

'Sake...' Cath signed it and handed it over to Fergus. 'There.'

'Cheers.' Fergus lifted up a tray and rested it on the edge of the desk. 'There's your belongings.'

Cath took her rings, purse and watch. 'Where's my phone?'

'Rob's got it.'

She looked over at him. But his police officer's stare actually worked this time and made her shut up.

Marshall gestured at Isla. 'You can thank Sergeant Routledge here.'

A flicker of anger creased Cath's forehead, then she just did as she was told and smiled at Isla. 'Thank you for letting me go.'

'It's okay. I mean, it's obviously not. Not what you do. But it is what is. Just behave yourself, okay?'

'I'll try to. And I'll send a note to your colleague.'

'Come on.' Marshall tugged at her sleeve then set off through the station. 'I'll give you a lift home.'

'I can walk, you know?'

'I don't doubt it, but I want to keep my eyes on you.'

'You can be such a dick.'

'I can. But I'm also the dick who's helping you.' Marshall led her out of the custody suite, into reception. The front door was open and it was freezing in there.

Cath stopped just outside. 'Freezing out there. Could do with a coat.'

'You can have mine.' Marshall sighed, then shrugged off his jacket. 'And I want it back.'

'I'm not some thieving git, you know?'

'Didn't say you were.'

'The implication's there, though.' She shut her eyes. 'Look, I'm struggling. Hairdressing at home and working in the Gala Tap and at BGH aren't exactly paying the bills. Dad helps, but he's... I can't keep asking him. I'm constantly on a knife edge here.'

'Okay. Last night, you were after money, right?'

'A loan.'

'Right. How much?'

'Forget it. I don't need your help.'

'Fine.' Marshall shrugged. 'But you need somebody's help, right?'

'Right.'

'Cath, if you need money, I might be able to give you it.'

Her eyes lit up with hunger.

'This can't just be a loan to cover a shortfall in your living expenses, okay, because that'll just get eaten up.'

'It's not for that.'

'Okay. Cards on the table. How much do you need and what's it for?'

'Ten grand.'

'Ten *grand*?' Marshall exhaled slowly. He looked around the car park and felt like everything was in black and white. 'What the hell do you need ten grand for?'

'A mate of mine is selling her salon.'

'You can't buy a salon for ten grand, Cath.'

'I know. But... You know how they rent out the chairs, right? Well, she's kind of doing that, but sort of selling them. There's eight chairs there. Ten grand and it's mine.'

'And you'll own it?'

'Right. That chair will be mine forever. Or until I sell it. There's a, like, contract. They can buy me out, but it's more than the ten grand. And if we decide to sell the whole... All that kind of stuff.'

Marshall looked back through into the reception area. This was a big ask. She might be his flesh and blood, but he barely knew her.

Still, she was in trouble. And this might be the chance to turn her life around.

He looked at her and saw the desperation in her eyes. She needed it. Desperately. 'Okay.'

'You'll give me it?'

'Yes, but it—'

Cath wrapped him in a hug. 'Thank you!'

Marshall shook her off. 'But it comes with conditions, Cath. Like you need to stop drinking.'

'So you're threatening me?'

'No. That has to come from you, okay? You have to want to change. But if you want my help, you need to stop causing trouble like this.'

'Fine. I can stop. I *will* stop.'

'And it'll be a business partnership, okay? I need to be party to the agreement. And we need a legal agreement between us.'

'So you're going to take half the money? There's no point in—'

'Cath, of course I'm taking half the money. But we'll use it to repay my share. If this works – and I see that you think it will – then you'll own that chair outright in a few years. But I need to protect my investment and I also want to make sure you're doing the best you can.'

'Okay.'

'So you agree?'

'I agree.' She smiled at him. 'Thank you.'

Marshall took a deep breath. This might be fucking stupid, but he wanted to help her. He reached into his pocket and pulled out her phone. 'I'm trusting you, okay?'

She nodded. 'Okay.'

He handed it back to her.

'Rob?' Steve from the front desk was standing in the doorway. 'You got a minute?'

Marshall glanced at Cath. 'Two seconds, okay? Wait right here.'

She nodded. 'Not going anywhere.'

Good.

Marshall followed him over to the front desk. 'What's up?'

'Woman here to see Catherine Sutherland.'

Jen spun around.

Marshall's twin sister.

And Kirsten was next to her.

64

The rain slammed against the windscreen, faster than Marshall's wipers could cope with.

He parked outside Cath's flat on the top side of Gala and let the engine die. 'I agreed to help you on the grounds you were trustworthy.'

'And I am.'

'Well, here's what's going through my head. I'm only hearing about your issues now, Cath, but not because Dad sorted it out – because Jen did.'

Jen's Volvo pulled up behind them.

'Don't need this.' Cath got out of the car and walked over to her flat.

If anyone didn't need this, it was Marshall.

Jesus Christ. He should be at work, trying to solve this case, but here he was, trying to help his half-sister.

Marshall got out into the rain and followed Cath across the street to the flat, getting soaked.

She stood there, scowling at the toppled-over door, then went inside, hopefully to call a joiner.

Marshall waited for Jen, so he could have a stern word with her.

The curtains twitched next door, so Marshall raised his hand to wave. They stopped twitching.

Jen charged up to him, fists clenched.

Marshall blocked the door.

Jen glowered at him. 'Really?'

'Really.' Marshall folded his arms. 'I asked her, but she didn't really answer, so I'm asking you – why am I only hearing about you helping her now?'

'Why do you think, Rob? Because you're a nightmare. You'd pry deep into her life.'

'And that's a bad thing?'

'You pried into mine and it was a complete nightmare.'

'You should've come clean about what happened with Ryan.'

'That wasn't my fault.'

'No. Him having a coke problem wasn't your fault. Him being in hock to Gary Hislop wasn't your fault. But you knowing about it and not telling me or Dad, *that* is your fault.'

'Fuck off, Rob.'

Marshall shrugged. 'I can just leave, you know?'

'So go.'

'Fine, but I won't be able help Cath the fifth time she gets arrested. And I'll make sure she gets charged. I can't believe she's got away without a breach of the peace so far.' Marshall glared at her. 'Did Dad do that for her?'

Jen looked away. 'No. Just me.'

'You don't have any authority.'

'No, but I've got a heart.'

'We both know that's not true. But I guess you're due a favour or two back from some cops who needed to speak to someone in A&E, right? Victims or suspects, they often end up under the care of the senior charge nurse, right?'

'Not saying anything.'

'Okay, Jen. I get it. But you're not helping her if she doesn't change.'

'What would you know about help?' Jen pushed past him. He stood tall and didn't let her past.

She twisted his nipple and he yelped.

She squeezed past him.

'Christ's sake.' Marshall followed her inside.

Cath was in the kitchen, standing by the kettle, spooning coffee into a cafetière. Not a bad room, tastefully decorated in cream and beige with the splash of vivid purple on the units. The wall-mounted TV looked old and was way too high – he'd be surprised if it even turned on. 'Thought we could do with some coffee.' She looked around at them. 'I mean, you both look tired and I'm... Not exactly sober.'

Marshall rested against the counter opposite her. 'Next you're going to tell me you're a barista.'

'Funnily enough, I did work as one for a bit...' Cath cast a hand around the tiny kitchen. 'But you don't see a bean-to-cup machine here, do you?' She shoogled the cafetière. 'Have to make do with this bad boy.'

'I'm sure it'll be good.' Jen thumbed at Marshall. 'Rob takes it the exact same way I do.'

Marshall frowned at her. 'So you two have been having coffee together?'

They stood in silence while the kettle rumbled to a boil.

Cath waited for the water to cool. 'Joiner's on his way over, by the way. He'll get the door fixed soon.'

'That's not the first time that's happened, is it?'

'Nope...' Cath reached into the cupboard and got out three chipped mugs. She dropped one onto the floor. Then bent over to pick it up. And stood up tall, her eyes wobbling around in her head.

Aye, she definitely wasn't sober.

She poured the hot water into the cafetière, making it all bubble and thicken, then pulled a carton of milk out of the fridge.

Marshall waited for her to look at him. 'Did you call Jen every time?'

'Every single one. And *she's* helped me every single time.' Cath tapped her long nails off the top of the cafetière, rhythmically. 'Couldn't get hold of her this time.'

'Sorry I couldn't be there today, Cath.' Jen ran a hand through her hair. 'I was busy and got the voicemail when I was at the tills in Tesco.'

'It's okay. Rob picked up.' She looked over at Jen. 'Thank you for coming the other times.' She pressed play on a speaker and the music exploded out, ridiculously loudly.

Marshall raced over and stabbed the button.

Took three goes to get it to behave itself.

'Cath, that's way too loud.' Marshall scowled at her. 'No wonder the police are coming around!'

'Sorry.' Cath looked away. 'Just thought we could have some tunes, you know?'

Marshall tapped the volume button down several times, then played it at a sensible level. 'There.'

Cath plunged the cafetière, then started pouring. 'Oh. Before I forget.' She opened a low drawer, one of those extra-wide ones you got in fancy new kitchens. 'See? All my stuff for cutting hair.'

Marshall checked it out – clippers, combs and scissors. Even one of those hand mirrors. A gown. Stuff for cleaning. It did seem legit.

Cath looked at his hair. 'I could do yours, if you want. Especially as you'll own half of me.'

'Maybe.' Marshall ran his hand through it, then let out a deep breath. 'That might be good, actually.'

'I need to pee.' Cath burst past them and thundered up the stairs.

Marshall sipped his coffee, keeping his eyes locked with Jen.

Jen glowered at him. 'Don't look at me like that.'

'Like what?'

'Like I've done something wrong.'

'I'm not.' Marshall gave her his best police officer stare. 'But you're always acting so guilty...'

'I just tried to help her. That's all.'

'So you've done this a few times for her?'

'Right. The first time I got called was after she got chucked out of MacArts for being too drunk at a Killers tribute act. She started a fight with a lad from Lauder. Well, he was a bit full-on but she... She's a bit crazy. And the second... Got called at, like, half ten at night. Absolute state. Total nightmare.'

'You bailing her out isn't helping that. Meanwhile, she's attacking police officers. Warner's in A&E for that.'

'Shit. He's a good guy.'

'Maybe. But he's a terrible cop. She's lucky he kicked that door down.'

'Why?'

'Because it means it was a dodgy arrest. He shouldn't have done it. He'll get his knuckles rapped for it.'

'Okay.'

'Jen, I don't think you're taking this seriously enough. Cath's got a drink problem.'

'A drink problem. You sound so old-fashioned.' She smirked at him. Then it faded. 'I know. She admits it, but she doesn't change. But what do you want me to do?'

'*Help* her. Don't *enable* her.'

'Fine.'

'I mean it. She causes chaos when she drinks. You heard the

volume she had the music at. She's promised me she'll get sober. I'm going to help her. We both need to help her.'

'Okay.' Jen nodded.

Then they stood in silence, save for the TV booming through the wall. Aye, it wasn't just one-way, was it?

Marshall sipped his coffee. 'Why didn't you tell me about this, Jen?'

'Things have been weird between us, Rob... Otherwise I'd have told you.'

'Have you spoken to Dad about it?'

'Still feels weird calling him that, doesn't it?'

'Very much so. Have you?'

'Tried to once, aye. Said he wanted nothing to do with that stuff.'

'Weird. I thought it was him fixing it for her. But it was you.'

'There's nothing to fix, Rob. She's just being stuck in the drunk tank.' Jen finished her coffee. 'But if there's something dodgy going on, Dad would've known. Right?'

'I've no doubt the father we share will have put his feelers out. Then again, someone in his line of work isn't going to be that popular with the drug squad. They're all bent and he was in charge of finding bent cops.'

'Bent like Ryan was?'

'Precisely. But I can't quite square Cath cutting the hair of someone who works for a drug dealer.'

'This Bongo guy?'

'Right.'

'Is that who Ryan worked for?'

'It is. I asked around with some contacts and he seems to be the only person in that organisation who is actually legit.'

'Did Cath ask you for money, Rob?'

Marshall looked back at his sister. 'Has she asked you?'

Jen nodded. 'But I've got nothing. It's all tied up in the

house. To say nothing of my darling daughter at university. Living expenses are mental nowadays. How much did she ask for?'

'Ten grand.'

'Fuck!'

'I know.' Marshall sighed. 'Wants to buy a share in a salon.'

'Wow. And what do you think of that?'

'I'm going to dig into it, but I'm minded to loan her the cash.'

'To a barely functional alcoholic?'

'That's the problem, right? She's promised to stop drinking, but... Thing is, the money's just sitting in my bank account.'

'Thought you and Kirsten were buying someplace?'

'Long story.'

'Rob... you need to stop using that line.'

'Look, I want to buy a house. We've had an offer accepted on a place in Melrose. I hate having the money just sitting there. I'm off the property ladder and I hate the feeling everything's just getting more and more expensive.'

Jen glanced over to the window. 'Are you and Kirsten having a difficult time?'

'Surprised you haven't heard.'

'We don't really talk about you.'

'Just like you don't talk *to* me.'

'I'm talking to you now.'

'And how am I doing?'

'You'll keep.' Jen laughed. 'Do you think you should help Cath?'

'I want to, but I'm worried about not seeing the money again.'

'Rob, it's very noble but just don't expect to ever see that cash again.'

'I know. Thing is, Jen, if you needed the money, I'd do the same for you.'

'But we've known each other all our lives, Rob.'
'I'm trying to think better of people.'
'Even with your job?'
'Even with it. I think I should give her it.'
Jen shook her head. 'Well, I think you're a bloody idiot.'

65

Marshall stepped out of Cath's house and shut his eyes, letting the cold wind blast over him. No wonder Cath was short of money if she was going to insist on keeping her heating on. He slipped his jacket back on.

'Rob?' Kirsten frowned at him. 'What are you doing here?'

Marshall hadn't seen her. He walked over to Jen's car and crouched by the open window. 'Have you been here all that time?'

'Aye. Feel like I'm seven years old and my dad's left me in the car so he can go into the bookies again.' She tried to laugh it off. 'Are you okay?'

He smiled. 'I'm fine.'

'Right.' Kirsten got out into the cold too. 'I was supposed to be meeting your sister for a drink, but she had to go to Tesco first and she got a call from Cath.'

'Well, I'm sorry you've had to wait here all that time.'

'It's fine. Is everything okay?'

'I think so. I mean, it's a total mess, but I think we're getting there.'

'So, what did she want?'

'What do you mean?'

'Cath. She was lurking around the other day.'

'Right. Well, she wanted money, like you thought.'

'I did warn you.'

'You did.'

'How much?'

'Ten grand.'

'*Ten grand*?' She laughed. 'I take it you told her to piss off.'

'I'm going to lend it to her.'

'Rob... Are you fucking insane?'

'It's an investment.'

'It was supposed to be an investment in our house! Seriously, Rob. Lending money to *Cath*? She's a train wreck. Drunk, violent, irresponsible. Not to mention associated with Gary Hislop.'

'This isn't about policing, Kirst. I'm just trying to be a good brother.'

'You should've asked me first.'

'I... Look, I can still back out of it.'

'And how's that being a good brother? And this is supposed to be fifty-fifty. Doesn't that include discussing things with me?'

'It's my money.'

'Not *our* money?'

Marshall didn't have an answer for that. He knew he could be cowardly and just let things drift. And he could let their father pick up the slack.

But Cath hadn't exactly had the best of times and nor had he – maybe helping her would help them both.

'Okay, so I should—'

A van drove up, going way too fast for the cul-de-sac.

Broadfoot & Farrell
Joiners of distinction

Two men got out and Marshall wondered if they were a couple – they were arguing like they were. They walked over to Cath's and stood by the broken door.

Just as Jen hurried out through the hole where a door should be. She walked over to them. 'Sorry about that, Kirst. She's not in a great way.'

'No, I heard.' Kirsten rolled her eyes. 'But she's about to be in a very good one, right?'

'Aye, well, the less said about that the better...'

Kirsten's phone rang. She got it out and checked the display. 'Bollocks. I better take this.' She walked off, phone to her ear. 'Hi, Jay. What's up?'

Leaving Marshall with Jen in a very uncomfortable silence.

She shifted her focus between Marshall and Kirsten, on the other side of her car. 'Something I said?'

'No.'

'Were you talking about me?'

'No, Jen.'

'Take it Kirsten's not happy?'

'Right, exactly.'

'Rob!' Kirsten rushed back over. 'We've just got a fresh ping on Jake's mobile.'

66

Jolene drove them along what the pool car's buggered satnav told her was the A6088, though it no doubt had a more ancient name. Heading away from Hawick and towards Cavers, wherever that was. 'This is where the ping from phone came from the other day. When you were up in the Highlands.'

Marshall had never heard of the place and he'd grown up in the Borders. He pointed at a gatehouse. 'Her cottage is just down that lane.'

'Seriously?' She frowned. 'Has Isabelle brought it here with her?'

'Maybe.'

'Why would she turn it on again, though? Why now?'

Marshall didn't have answers for that.

'Where did you go, by the way?'

'My sister's... Long story.'

His phone chimed – saved by the bell. He checked the display.

A new message from Kirsten:

> Phone off now x

'Shite.' Marshall glanced over at her. 'Kirsten says it's not on anymore.' He let out a deep breath.

'Okay, but we've narrowed the radius.' Jolene pulled through the gap then drove along the lane and stopped next to the cottage.

It was a dark night, but the building was even darker. A faint light on in the front room, though.

Marshall got out first and didn't have to exactly walk far to knock on the door.

No answer.

'Did Ash visit here?'

'I think so. No answer.'

'Figures.'

'I'll do a sweep of the perimeter.' Jolene disappeared around the side.

Marshall stayed there and peered in through the front windows, casting his phone's torch across bare wooden floorboards. Dark, but a glow came from the side. The net curtains didn't help any.

Like Crawford had described it that morning, though, the place was spartan. Like Isabelle owned nothing.

'She's not in.' Jolene reappeared at the other side. 'Shouldn't O'Brien be here?'

'Spoke to him. He took Isabelle home. Then he had a phone call with her, to let her know about the relocation. O'Brien gave her until tomorrow to pack up and said for her to call 999 if there were any problems.'

'And this is a problem.'

'Agreed.' Marshall turned his torch off again, then called O'Brien.

It just rang and rang.

'We're sorry but—'

'Not answering.' Marshall sighed, then sorted through their options in his head. They'd got a ping from his mobile, leading them to her home. It was a case of two plus two and they needed to know if it summed to four or five. 'We need to get in there.'

'We don't have a warrant.'

'No.'

'We should call Captain Manboobs and see if he has an idea where she is.'

'Captain Manboobs?'

'The parole officer. Sullivan?'

Marshall looked around. 'Sod it.' He locked eyes with Jolene. 'Look, we have exigent circumstances... The time it'd take to obtain a warrant would result in loss of life, or the destruction of evidence.'

'What do you mean?'

'I think the fire's on. Could be burning anything in there.'

Jolene stopped. 'Are you telling me to break down the door?'

'I'll justify our actions after the fact.'

Jolene rolled her eyes. 'Isn't this a man's job?'

'Bit sexist. But you're right.' Marshall sucked in a deep breath, then launched his foot at the door.

It caved in like it hadn't even been locked. Probably should've checked...

Marshall followed her inside, into a living room. It looked even more empty from the inside, if that was possible – the only sign of humanity was the fire burning away.

That explained the glow...

His white lie hadn't been completely false, then.

Jolene walked through to the back room.

Leaving Marshall to check the kitchen at the side. Battered old units and scored worktop. The whole thing needed replacing. The appliances were new – the exact same air fryer his mum got him for Christmas. And a shiny new kettle and toaster.

A cupboard to the side, just with a washing machine and a mop.

He went back into the living room.

'Nobody's here.' Jolene's voice echoed around from up the staircase, sounding like she was in the bathroom.

Marshall stared at the log burner. 'Shite.' He opened the door and looked inside.

Bits of paper, half turned to ash but half showing the handwriting.

Some clothes.

Fuck.

He yanked them out.

Navy 501s.

A Sugarman T-shirt.

Bawbag trunks.

Lacoste socks.

Marshall got out his phone and logged into the system. There it was, in his inbox – a description of what he'd been wearing the last time his parents had seen him.

These were Jake's clothes, missing from the crime scene.

Marshall grabbed the tongs from the set of tools beside the fire and started pulling the rest of the contents out onto the floor.

Two half-burnt logs, but nothing useful in there. The notebooks were burned beyond recovery, their words lost to the flames.

A lump of metal lay at the bottom.

The exact shape of a smartphone.

Marshall gripped it with the tongs and pulled it out.

Jolene came over and looked at it. 'That's his mobile, isn't it?'

'Or was.'

No matter how he looked at it, the phone was absolutely destroyed.

'Fuck.' Jolene looked around the room. 'She's run away, hasn't she?'

67

Marshall stepped outside the cottage. The rain was a thin mist now. Lights danced in the farmhouse window up on the hill, like they still had their Xmas lights on, this deep into February.

Hard to escape the feeling Jolene was right – and Isabelle had run.

But he needed to keep calm and keep everything completely under control. No making assumptions or jumping to conclusions.

Still, it was pretty hard not to do either when you found the victim's phone and clothes in a burner.

It looked a lot like Isabelle had actually been the killer...

But how? Was there another man doing her bidding? Was she with Sullivan and Dunning while another disciple killed Jake?

Did *he* video it for her? The sex, the torture, the murder?

The lane was filled with three pool cars now, but none of them belonged to O'Brien's team.

Marshall called O'Brien again, trying to keep calm.

'Hey, Rob.'

'Hey yourself.' Marshall turned back to look inside the cottage. A few people in every room, but nobody seemed to have anything – certainly nothing useful. 'Do you know where she is?'

'Who? Isabelle?'

'No, Mary Queen of Scots.' Marshall sighed. 'Yes, Isabelle.'

'No need for that kind of sarcasm, Rob.' Sounded like O'Brien was driving. 'What's happened?'

'She's not at her cottage.' Marshall left a pause. 'This is where you tell me you've still got her in the car.'

'We dropped her off... A few hours ago. Told her she's got a day to get packed.'

'And you just left her?'

'Rob, she didn't want us there. And she's not under arrest. Besides, I needed to brief the super. Like I told you, we're moving her – West Linton is nice this time of year.'

'Doesn't look like you've got anybody watching her.'

'Are you there?'

'Standing right outside.'

'Right.' A long sigh. 'No resources, mate. Our response plan for a circumstance like hers is to harden her as a target. Basically, if there's a danger from the public, we encourage her to stay indoors and call 999 if something seems amiss.'

'Response plan, my arse.' Marshall laughed. 'Have you got any idea where she might be?'

'Don't get arsey with me, Rob. You don't have the staff to watch everyone all the time either, do you?' O'Brien sighed. 'Think about it, mate. She's not under arrest. My job is to protect her from society and society from her.'

'Right. But your reputation will be in tatters after letting her bust and run.'

'You say that like you've got something that's going to make me look stupid.'

'We found Jake Turner's clothes and her notebooks in the log burner.'

'So you think she's run away? Listen, I told Isabelle she couldn't stay in Hawick anymore and we were going to relocate her. But she's clearly decided she doesn't like that idea and run off herself.'

'She's in the wind. That's a breach of her conditions, isn't it?'

'What, because she was to only reside at the cottage and nowhere else?'

'Right.'

'Guess you're right.' O'Brien left a long gap, filled with revving and braking. 'Well, with all the unwanted attention and a link from her past to her new identity, she's clearly a little unsettled. Do you blame her?'

'Of course I don't. But that doesn't make it feel any better.'

A car pulled along the lane and parked behind the other three pool cars.

Not O'Brien, though – Kirsten got out and walked up to the door. She frowned as she passed him.

Marshall turned away from the house. 'Reason we're here is we got a ping on the phone belonging to the victim. We've found it, Patrick. It's in her fire too. Thing's buggered beyond belief.'

'Shite. So you think she's involved?'

'Looks that way, doesn't it? She has a third man. Some Other Guy did the deed while she established an alibi with two others. She can't face prison, so she's cutting and running.' Marshall felt everything spinning out of control. He tried to focus on the here and now – and on the things he could control. 'Can you go through the surveillance logs and pass everyone on to me?'

'Known associates?'

'Everyone. Every single contact you know about and have

her speaking to. People from the past. Flatmates, co-workers, friends, family. I need to know them all.'

'Okay. I'll send the logs on to you, Jolene and Crawford. But I'm warning you now, Rob – there's a lot of it.'

'Thanks. We've got people to go through all of that.' Marshall took a deep breath. 'Biggest priority right now is finding her. Have you got any ideas?'

'Let me think… Car's still impounded. You've got her phone, right?'

'Forensics do, aye.'

'Okay, so let's wind back to the arrest. You held her overnight. Then after you let her go from the station, they got the bus back to Hawick, right?'

'Right. Then she went to work. Where Paul Turner confronted her. After that, you dropped her at her cottage.'

'And that's where the trail dies. Trouble is, Rob, if someone's determined to escape, they will. This isn't my first time – we need to unpick her last movements.'

The line went silent.

Marshall checked his phone – he'd lost him. Either he'd hung up or he was driving somewhere with patchy reception. Down here, when you were away from the towns, it was much more common to not have a signal than to have one. Even in 2025.

Jolene was in the doorway. 'O'Brien got any ideas?'

'Nope.' Marshall shook his head. 'Drawn a blank.'

'If you ask me, we should be speaking to Captain Manboobs.'

'Sullivan?'

'Hard to think of anyone else. They were bumping uglies, so it stands to reason he'd help her destroy all this evidence for her, doesn't it? And he did lie for her to give that alibi.'

68

Marshall walked up the steps to Brendan Sullivan's office and knocked on the door.

'There you are.' Crawford rushed over from the side and joined him. 'Didn't see you arrive.'

'Thanks for meeting me here.'

'No worries.' Crawford yawned into his fist. 'O'Brien sent us the surveillance logs.'

'Good stuff.' Marshall glanced over at him. 'Have you got someone looking through it?'

'Three DCs, aye.' Crawford nudged the door and it opened.

Marshall let Crawford go first.

The office was an even worse state than earlier. The files were everywhere with not even the semblance of order. Like they'd all been thrown around. And the contents of the bin were spread over the floor – minus the used condoms.

Still, Brendan Sullivan wasn't behind his desk.

The throb of music came from the back, the slow pulse of Barry White. Or something similar.

Could she have just come here?

Marshall stepped through to the back room, hope bubbling in his guts.

Sullivan lay on the bed, spread out. He farted and woke himself up, jerking up into a sitting position. He absolutely reeked of booze. He looked at them and struggled to focus, then rubbed at his nose. He stood up and slammed the door.

It bounced off Crawford's toes.

'Fug off away from me.' Sullivan tried to slam it again, but it caught on Crawford's toes again.

'Stob fuggen doon that!' Sullivan reached for the door again, but he missed it and stumbled forward, then fell face first.

Marshall took a second to look around the room – Isabelle wasn't here – then he grabbed Sullivan and hauled him up to sit him on the edge of the bed.

Sullivan sat there, drunk, depressed and angry. 'Fugging mess.' He looked up at Marshall. 'I left my wife for Isabelle. Stupid. So fucking stupid. All those years and for what? A few shags of a tight snatch?' He reached over for a bottle of cheap whisky.

Crawford patted his hand away. 'You've had enough, mate.' He grabbed a pint glass, milky white, and filled it up from the tap. 'Here. Drink this instead.'

Sullivan drank it all in one go, but his focus was on the cheap whisky. 'So tight. So fuggen tight.' He looked up at them. 'You've no idea. I could fuck her for hours too. I felt like a teenager again. I haven't had to pop a blue pill any time I'm with her.'

'This sign of true love, eh?' Crawford crouched in front of him. 'When was the last time you saw her, Brendan?'

'Eh... I haven't seen her since we got back to Hawick. By bus. She went to work.' His eyes bulged. 'Oh, fuck me hard and fast. I... went in. But she told me to go.' He looked away from them, staring at the whisky. 'I might've been kicked out of there.'

'Might've been?'

'I was. That wanker... Mike. Mike Teviot. He shoved us through the front door and gave me an earful. Fuck. What a dickhead I am...' Sullivan started hammering his forehead with his fists.

'Stop that!' Crawford did it for him. 'Did Isabelle say anything to you?'

'I can't remember.' Sullivan pointed at the bottle. 'I'd been drinking.' He shook his head. 'Fuck. I've really screwed this up. I loved her. *Loved* her! Still do. And she's breaking up with me!'

Crawford frowned. 'She said that?'

'I... I don't know. Maybe.'

'But you think she did?'

'Probably.' Sullivan sank back on the bed. 'I'm a fat old waster. Why would she want to be with me?'

'Do you have any idea where she would go?'

'She's run away?'

'We think so.'

'Fuck.' Sullivan shook his head. 'I don't, sorry. I don't know any friends of hers. Never met them, if she even has any.'

'What about her folks?'

'She never talked about them. I think they disowned her after... After what happened. So she wouldn't have gone there.'

Marshall smiled at him. 'We've got people heading there to speak to them.'

'Right.' Sullivan got up and tottered over to the side. He grabbed the whisky and sank a good few measures, then ran the back of his hand across his lips. 'I'm a fucking bad man. So stupid. And rotten to the core.'

'You're not bad. You've just made a mistake.' Marshall fixed him with a hard stare. 'Go back to your wife and apologise.' He jabbed a finger towards him. 'Once you've sobered up.'

'Fuck off.'

'I'll take this.' Crawford grabbed the whisky out of his hands. 'I'll give you it back if you track her down.'

69

Marshall charged through the station, leaving Crawford in his wake. He found Jolene in the incident room.

Callum Taylor was still there too, sitting in the corner.

Marshall stood over him. 'What are you still doing here, Cal?'

'I'm fine, Rob.' Taylor shrugged, then grinned. 'Just don't ask me to run. Or walk.'

'Come with me.' Marshall walked over to his office. His AeroPress was sitting in the middle of the meeting table. 'Who put this here?'

'Not me.' Taylor shrugged as he hobbled in. 'Ravenscroft was in here earlier.'

Wanker...

Marshall chucked it onto his desk then walked over to the whiteboard. He waited for the other three to join him, then looked at them one by one. 'Okay. We're in a weird situation here. Isabelle Ward has disappeared. She's left the cottage, but it appears she tried to destroy evidence.'

Taylor raised a hand. 'Thought we'd excluded her as a suspect?'

'We had. Which is why this is weird.' Marshall circled Some Other Guy on the whiteboard.

'Okay, the obvious thing is...' Jolene was frowning at the whiteboard, like that could solve anything other than Marshall's morning Wordle. 'She was approached by Paul Turner, who seems to think she killed his son.' She looked at Taylor. 'And like you said, Cal, she had an alibi. We'd cleared her.'

They all stared into space.

'Exactly. This doesn't make sense.' Marshall picked up the whiteboard marker from the lip below it and uncapped it. 'So let's go back to first principles with this.' He looked around them. 'Assuming you can all stay on for a bit?'

He got three shrugs, the most enthusiastic being from Taylor, which made sense.

'Good.' Marshall nodded at Crawford. 'Douglas, you found Isabelle through ViCLAS.'

'Right.' Crawford sat at the table and was somehow fiddling with the AeroPress, but it was like he was trying to figure out how to dismantle a nuclear reactor. 'But this isn't my fault. Is it?'

'It's nobody's fault, okay? That's not what this is about. It's not how I run things. I want results. And I want us to start by retracing our steps and seeing where it leads us.'

Another three nods, but Crawford was obsessing over the AeroPress, trying to slot the two pipes together in completely the wrong way.

'The reason I asked, Douglas, is just so we can understand why she's important. The reason we were interested in Isabelle in the first place is Jake's murder bears all the hallmarks of the three murders she collaborated with up in Applecross.' Marshall tapped on her name, then on Dominic's. 'Now, he's cleared because he's inside. But Isabelle has been out since

August and living near Hawick. She works in the Teribus Arms in the town. And for the time of Jake's murder, she gave us an alibi, which checked out. Right?'

'Supposedly.' Taylor looked at the other two. 'That stuff about threesomes... is it true?'

'Very true.' Jolene nodded. 'We've got it on video.'

'Holy shit.' Taylor laughed. 'Who films themselves having sex?'

Crawford dropped the AeroPress onto the table, blushing. 'So, given Dominic is safely ensconced in Barlinnie, like you say, Rob, it's safe to say this is a copycat. Right?'

'Is it?' Jolene shook her head. 'Or is it possible Dominic and Isabelle didn't kill the guys in Applecross?'

'No.' Marshall shook his. 'They definitely did it.'

Taylor frowned at him. 'You're sure?'

'I'm sure.' Marshall nodded, but looked over to Crawford for validation. 'You were up in Inverness with me, Douglas. It's them. Right?'

'I'm sure, aye.' Crawford scratched at his neck. 'As far as I can tell, anyway. He admitted it. They both did. And their forensics were all over the victims.'

'Okay.' Taylor sat back and started stretching out his foot, making it crunch like a mistimed gear change. 'The thing is, we need to be careful when we just assume it's a copycat. Right? We can't just assume it is. How close are the two murders?'

'Really close.' Marshall looked over the board and noticed he hadn't even added that information under Applecross. 'Our hold-back stuff checks out fully.'

'How can it, though?' Taylor frowned. 'Hold-back information on the original murder expires during the trial or the plea, so it then becomes part of the public domain.'

'Aye, but our case is still locked down. And nobody knows the two cases are connected.'

Crawford nodded. 'It's a very good match on ViCLAS.'

'Okay...' Taylor hauled himself up to standing and hobbled over to the board. 'My point is, the common elements of this case and Applecross are on ViCLAS. So conceivably someone with access could mine the old case and duplicate it here. Right?'

Marshall could follow the logic. To a point. Something in it made his head throb, though. 'I know what you're saying, but...'

'I don't.' Jolene joined him by the board. 'I don't buy this at all.'

'I mean, it could be.' Marshall scribbled it down as a possibility. 'We should go through the original team and eliminate.' He looked over at Jolene. 'We can go through anyone who's accessed the ViCLAS record from then until Douglas.'

She rolled her eyes. 'Fine, I'll do it.' She grabbed the pen, then jotted down an action at the side. She tapped on Applecross. 'Where else could someone get that level of detail?'

'Court.' Crawford smiled. 'Think about it. All evidence is presented there. While we can be smart and hold back evidence from our murder because it's not been tried, those old murders *were* tried in a court. And for weeks too. Every single exhibit was examined and cross-examined. The knife alone took two days of testimony, including three experts.'

'So we could be looking at a lawyer.' Taylor uncapped a pen and wrote it all up on the board. 'Or a judge.'

'Or a guard.' Jolene nodded. 'Or a stenographer who transcribed the case. Or a journalist who covered the trial. Or even a spectator.'

'Maybe.' Crawford tapped his finger off each name. 'But have we any idea who?'

Jolene frowned at him. 'We can get a list of who attended, surely?'

'Right.' Marshall scribbled the action down below her other one. 'Do that.'

'I'm getting all the actions here.'

Marshall smiled at her. 'We'll divvy them up later, once we've gone through this.'

'Just thinking...' Taylor pointed at Applecross, then grabbed the pen from Marshall and drew two branches from Applecross, one he marked Nic/Issy and the other Dominic. He drew a third with a question mark. 'Could there have been a third accomplice back then?'

'I've been through the case files.' Crawford shook his head. 'Dominic was asked and he said no.'

'But Isabelle's been into threesomes.' Taylor circled "Nic/Issy". 'Think about it – the violent homosexual fantasies that got Dominic off back then. What if there was someone working with them? Someone they've both protected?' He circled Some Other Guy on the whiteboard. 'Some Other Guy who is back in Hawick helping Isabelle out now.'

'I see what you're saying, Cal, but we don't have any evidence for it.' Crawford grabbed the pen and circled the question mark. 'When me and Rob spoke to him, Dominic seemed to be very open about everything. He said it was just the two of them.'

'And you believe him?'

'I do.' Crawford circled "Nic/Issy" again, even tighter than Taylor's. 'So did she. Right?'

'I wouldn't trust her.' Taylor looked over at Marshall. 'Rob?'

Marshall thought it all through. 'I agree with Douglas, but I also see Cal's point. This whole case is making my head feel like it's going to burst open. We're missing something. And I worry we're falling into the trap of tunnel vision here, so we need to open up the old case file and go through every single known associate of both of them from back in the day. Locate them. Speak to them. See if anything fires off about Hawick or Jake Turner or just seeing both of them in prison in the last ten years.'

'Okay.' Taylor was nodding. 'But won't that piss off the Inverness lot?'

'I don't really care. If it opens up their case, then they've basically executed a miscarriage of justice and we shouldn't shy away from that.'

Crawford jotted down a few more items in the actions section. 'I'll pull together a list of all the people who worked the original case and who attended the court case. Cal, you get the original known associates. Jolene, you assemble those surveillance logs. Then we'll have a population to cross-reference with each other.'

They stood there in silence, broken by the crunch of Taylor stretching out his ankle.

Marshall nodded at Jolene. 'How are you doing with the review of the surveillance logs?'

'There's a lot of it. I've got three DCs on it. We're going to divvy up anyone who stands out and speak to them tonight or tomorrow.' She checked her watch. 'Which means tomorrow.'

'But this is probably the right end of the telescope. If we speak to everyone on there, then we can look back at the old stuff. Drive it that way.'

'Will do...' Jolene frowned. 'But you do think Isabelle is connected to Jake's murder, don't you?'

Marshall hadn't thought about it concretely before. 'I think she's got to be. And his phone is the key. The way I see it, he was lured to Hawick Museum, where someone attacked him, then drugged him and stabbed him through the heart.' He tapped the board. 'Isabelle's the elephant in the room here. Forget stenographers, journalists and cops, or mysterious third parties. She's the one who knew everything about the case. She was a co-defendant turned star witness.'

Taylor frowned. 'Thought you said she couldn't have done it? Those threesome videos?'

'That's right. But it doesn't mean she didn't influence someone else into doing it for her.'

'So we need to speak to Brendan Sullivan again? And this swinging lumberjack?'

'We do. Sullivan is proof positive how easy that was for her to influence someone. We need to go through the 3sum app to see who else they matched with. And make sure it happens tonight. Okay?'

70

Marshall looked across the car park, kind of wishing he smoked. That moment to yourself where you just stare into space and let the world dissolve. Sure, it might decimate your lungs – and those of your loved ones – but that mindful time... He needed that and drinking a coffee didn't give the same effect, even though his AeroPress had turned up and he could make his own stuff again.

But he couldn't get close to a mindful state, so drinking more coffee was the only solution he had. And he was hiding from that whiteboard while the team beavered away...

Drinking coffee at eight o'clock at night... What was he playing at? He'd be up all night *again*, either too wired to avoid sleep – like yesterday – or needing to get up to pee every five minutes.

And his mind would be racing because this case was in the shit.

Truly.

Marshall was having to pretend to the team that he was in command of this. Talk about clutching at straws... Some notion that Isabelle had persuaded *someone else* to do her bidding, when she had Brendan Sullivan there, desperate and ready to do her bidding...

Aye, the case was shite.

And he was freezing – maybe he didn't want to smoke after all. *Having* to spend time outside in all weathers just to feed your addiction wasn't great. So he just finished his cup and tipped out the dregs on the slabs, then went back inside to the warmth.

Sound rattled through from the incident room – the team, bless them, sticking to their tasks and just getting on with it.

Marshall took the other door, though, and found Kirsten in the lab, packing up her stuff. 'You running away?'

Kirsten looked around at him and let out a breath. 'Rob.'

'Leaving without saying goodbye?'

'Bone tired, Rob.' Kirsten shrugged. 'And tonight's viewing cancelled.'

'Didn't know there was one.'

'Sorry. Thought I'd told you?'

Marshall didn't know what to say. He just felt that difficulty between them, floating in the air like a toxic gas or something solid. 'Have the offers come through?'

'Not even a note of interest.'

'But you were hopeful, right?'

'Right. Aye, they didn't get in touch. Or their solicitor didn't.'

'Happens a lot. Guess they could still?'

'Guess so.' Kirsten shrugged again. 'Well, I'm back to square one.'

'We are.'

'Doesn't feel that way. Feels like you're looking down on me.'

'What have I done to make you feel like that?'

She wouldn't look at him.

'Kirst, we've got tons of options. For instance, I could buy out your mortgage, then we could stay at yours while things get sorted. Takes away the time crunch and puts us both on an even footing.'

Kirsten frowned. 'I hadn't thought about that.'

'How about we get something to eat and talk about it?'

'Not really.'

Marshall felt a wave of nausea crawl up from his stomach. Took everything he had not to be sick. 'What's going on?'

'The phone's not looked great, Rob. Suffered severe damage in that fire. We got the IMEI number off it, so we can at least prove it was his. This is like that bit in a film where they stamp on a phone to destroy it, but except we'd be able to recover stuff in that case. With this? No chance.'

Marshall smiled at her, but the wave of nausea was threatening to become a tsunami. 'I meant with us.'

'And those results just came back from Gartcosh. I've just emailed them to you.' Kirsten twisted up her lips. 'That hair wedged in the hilt...' She clenched her jaw. 'It belongs to a fucking *cat*.'

'What?'

'It's not human, Rob. A domestic short-haired cat. Marmalade coloured, if that helps.' Kirsten shook her head, then pecked him on the cheek. 'See you tomorrow.' She barged past, then left the room.

Leaving Marshall alone in her domain.

Felt like she was running away from him.

And maybe he should just let her go and live *her* life, because it really didn't feel like she wanted *their* life anymore.

Or maybe he should fight for this...

Maybe.

He got up and walked through the station into the reception area.

Outside the station, Kirsten's car whizzed out through the gate.

Too late…

Too bloody late…

Crawford jogged past with a determined look on his face, heading through to the incident room.

'Where's the fire?'

'No fire, Rob.' Crawford glanced around at him. 'Just trying to co-ordinate three teams of very tired people.'

'Okay, good luck with it.' Marshall watched the door to the incident room slide shut. He realised he was still clutching his coffee mug.

BEST MAN

He didn't know whose mug it was, but right now he felt like the worst one.

He needed to snap out of that funk. He was—

'It's Marshall, isn't it?'

He swung around in the direction of the voice.

Emily Borthwick stood to the side, hiding in the shadows and soaked through. 'Can we speak?'

71

Marshall sat with Emily in an interview room. The nicer one – the one that had been painted in the last decade.

Emily pushed her teacup over the table. 'Not enough milk.'

'Okay...' Marshall sat back in his chair. 'Do you want me to get you some more?'

'I'm fine.'

'It's no big deal.'

'Said I'm fine.'

'Right. Well, here we are, Emily. Having that word.'

But she seemed to shrink in on herself. The last thing she looked like she wanted to do was talk.

'Whatever it is, Emily, you can talk to me. Okay?'

The door opened and Jolene walked in.

Emily eyed her nervously, then scowled at Marshall. 'Why is *she* here?'

'We need to have two officers for all interviews.'

'Do you think I've done something?' Emily frowned. 'Is that what this is about?'

'No. You're the one you turned up here, desperate to speak

to me. But then you clammed up, so what am I supposed to think?'

Emily pulled her mug closer and wrapped her fingers around it.

'We need to get these things on the record.' Marshall smiled at her. 'So. What is it you want to talk about?'

'It's...' Emily sighed. 'I can't...'

'You show up to talk and now you don't want to?' Marshall leaned forward and made eye contact with her. 'It looked to me like you had something on your mind the last time you were here too, Emily. What's going on?'

Emily hugged her shoulders tight.

Whatever it was, she wasn't happy about sharing it with more than one of them...

Marshall looked over to Jolene. 'Can you fetch the milk?'

'The milk?'

'Aye.' Marshall pointed at the mug. 'I made her tea too strong.'

'He always does that.' Jolene smiled at Emily. 'Never get a coffee man to make tea.'

But the joke just bounced off Emily.

'Back in a sec.' Jolene got up with a sigh, then left the room.

Emily looked over at the door, then back at Marshall. 'Thought you need two of you?'

'Well, we do. But you'll get a better cup of tea. You like it really milky, right?'

Emily smiled. 'Mum says I like "baby tea".'

'I like that. How does she take hers?'

'Black with barely a splash of milk.' Emily frowned. 'Like, the amount of milk left in the bottle when you'd just rinse it out. That much.'

'I know people like that. My mum's the same.'

'My dad... He was like me. He liked it all milky.'

'Right. I get it.' Marshall waited for a few seconds to see if the girl would start talking now it was just the two of them – and now he'd got her talking about something trivial. 'Is this about your mum, Emily?'

'Eh? Why would you think that?'

'It's just, she's not here. She's usually with you, right?'

'Right.'

'So, where is your mum, Emily?'

'We... We had an argument. I told her to fuck off. And... I came here.'

'Hawick to Gala is a decent distance.'

'Got the bus.'

'Right. Must've been a big argument for a Terie like yourself to come up here to the land of the pail merks.'

She laughed. 'You know why we call you lot that?'

Marshall did, but he gave her a frown. 'I don't.'

'Gala was the last one to get on the mains water, so you lot had to crap in buckets, while we all had toilets.'

'Didn't know that.' Marshall laughed. 'That true?'

'It's what my dad told me.'

'You miss him, right?'

'I do. I mean, Mum tries, but she's really hard on me.'

'I get it. But sometimes that comes from a position of love and care. She wants you to do well.'

'Funny way of showing it.'

'What did you argue about?'

'This.'

'This? What do you mean by this?'

'Thing is... When you came to the house the other day... You asked me all those questions and it was the first time anyone's ever treated me like that. You were patient but you were firm and... You were interested in me, right?'

'What do you mean by interested in you?'

Shit.

This was nothing to do with the case.

He'd been the first person to show her kindness and she was latching on to that.

Marshall watched her, sitting there like an adult. Acting all sophisticated and grown up, but huge parts of her were still a child. And she'd suffered the loss of a parent at a young age. And had her own health risk hanging over her head. No wonder she was all messed up – she just wanted to be a normal kid.

The door opened and Jolene slouched in with the carton of milk. She sploshed some into Emily's mug, but it ran out. 'That do you?'

'It'll have to.' Emily laughed. 'Actually, that's perfect.' She took a big sip of tea. 'Okay. Thank you.' She wouldn't look at Jolene. 'You were nasty the other day.'

Jolene's forehead tensed up. 'Nasty?'

'Aye. Kept asking me all these difficult questions.'

'It's part of the job, Emily. We ask those questions to check that we're getting to the real truth, not lies.'

'You think I've been lying?'

'I don't know. Have you?'

'I've... I've felt so guilty.'

Jolene frowned at her. 'Guilty about what?'

'Things went too far with that teacher.'

There it was... Out in the open now.

Marshall locked eyes with her. 'Mr Goodwillie?'

'Right. When he... hurt himself.' Emily snorted, snot bubbling in her nose. Tears moistened her eyes. 'Now Jake's dead, there's no point pretending anymore. It was his idea. I'd have done anything Jake said. And I did. But when he dumped me I felt used and stupid.'

Marshall felt the silence swell up around them until it felt like a scream. 'What was his idea, Emily?'

'Jake wanted to frame Mr Goodwillie. Got me to say he raped me. He just wanted to cause him some hassle, you know?

Get him into shit. Jake was always up to stuff. Sometimes it was daft, but sometimes...'

Marshall had expected as much, but hearing the words said aloud made him start to doubt it now.

Emily sipped her tea. 'Sometimes it went too far. What he did... It wasn't cool. He tried to kill himself. That's what they told us. He hung himself. His dad saved him, but I heard he's not in a good way. And that's my fault.'

'What happened to him isn't your fault, Emily.' Jolene reached a hand halfway across the table. 'Okay?'

Emily took it. 'But I did it?'

'He put you up to it.'

'I didn't have to do it, did I?'

'No, but he manipulated you. I know what that feels like. It's crap.'

'He did. You're right. My therapist said that's what he did. He used me. And.... I spoke to this other girl he used to go out with. Casey. She works at Aldi too. She's... She tried to warn me about him, but I didn't listen. Thought she was just jealous. But nobody's "just" anything, are they? Everything's always so complicated.'

'Those are pretty wise words, Emily.' Jolene squeezed her hand. 'Why did Jake do it, Emily? Why did he make you do that?'

'He wanted to settle a personal grudge against Mr Goodwillie. One day, Mr Goodwillie caught him sleeping in class.' Emily finished her tea in one gulp. 'He grabbed him and woke him up. Literally scared the shit out of him.' She pushed the cup away then wiped her lips. 'Jake crapped himself. Literally.' She shook her head. 'It was really messed up. And Jake... He hated him for it.'

'I take it the whole class knew?'

'No. Just me. I sat next to him. Could smell it. He covered it up, saying he'd done a really stinking fart, but I knew.'

'Did you talk to anyone?'

'Just Mum...'

'And about this big lie?'

Emily nodded. 'I wanted to come clean. She said no. Said we need the money. And I couldn't tell anyone. Well, fuck that. The truth needs to come out.'

72

Christopher Goodwillie lay there, so quiet and still it looked like he was dead.

Then he looked over at his parents and smiled. 'Mummy.' He made a loud moaning sound, but it seemed to be a happy one.

Marshall stood by the window, looking at Hugh, Muriel and Jolene.

'I caught this earlier.' Hugh pointed at the TV, playing the news – Ravenscroft's latest news conference from the afternoon. He focused on Marshall. 'He said you've had to let the suspects go?'

'That's right, aye.'

'Why are you here, then? Shouldn't you be trying to rustle up some new suspects?'

Marshall could've tried to tease him, pretend he was still a suspect, despite Pam Campbell giving him an alibi even he didn't want to give. But he didn't. 'Got some news for you.'

'Oh?'

'Not sure if it's good or bad, sir. But it'll maybe help.' Marshall sat in the armchair next to the bed. 'Emily Borthwick visited me this evening at the station. She came clean about them fabricating the story.'

'What story?' Muriel gasped. 'The allegations?'

'Right.'

'Them being her and Jake, right?' Hugh ground his teeth together. 'Well. That doesn't surprise me.'

'We gather there was an incident at the school involving Christopher and Jake.' Marshall sat forward. 'Christopher shook him awake. Made him... have an accident.'

Muriel shook her head. 'That didn't happen!'

'We're going to speak to people at the school tomorrow. But we spoke to someone who was there and I believe it happened, unless a whole class is lying to the police.'

'Heavens.' Muriel looked over at her son. 'I had no idea. I mean, I was worried she'd made it up.' She tilted her head towards Christopher. 'Christopher raping her seemed... Out of character, shall we say. But...' Tears flooded her cheeks. 'I... I can't believe it.'

'Come here...' Hugh wrapped an arm around his wife and they both looked at their son for a few seconds. 'Have you told Pam?'

'No. I tried calling but she didn't answer. Thought she'd be here with you.'

'We try to give her some time off. She'd be here all the time, if it was up to her. But she needs her own life, doesn't she? That book group's good for her. Gets her speaking to people.'

'It took a tragedy to bring Pam to us.' Muriel gave Marshall a polite smile. 'It's been really hard for her.' She got up to help Christopher lie back in his bed. 'Christopher had always been a bit of a lad. Never one to bring his girlfriends home to meet us.'

'And let's be honest, they were mostly just random shags.' Hugh pointed at the window. 'We would see a cab pulling up and know what he was up to. Gets it from his mother.'

'*Hugh.* For heaven's sake...'

'It's a joke.'

'Well, it's not a funny one, is it?'

'Can I get a little doggy?'

Muriel walked over to her son and tended to him.

Marshall stood up and walked away to give them space.

Hugh was brushing a hand over the stubble on his chin. 'Emily fucking lied... I knew it. I fucking *knew it*.' Rage flashed across his face, twisting his lips. 'Because of... Because of *Jake Turner*?' He collapsed onto the bed next to Christopher and grabbed his son's hand. 'He put her up to it? Fuck sake. That wee prick. He...' He shut his eyes. 'Jake fucking Turner did this to him. To us. To all of us.' He reopened them, with an icy steel. 'At least he's dead.'

'Hugh! Don't speak like that!'

'Why not? Whoever killed him is a hero. That wee shite can't do this to anyone else.'

'Hugh, I mean it. Think about his poor parents.' She waved at Christopher. 'Doesn't this give you a sense of what they're going through?'

'Poor parents, nothing.' Hugh laughed. 'Paul Turner's a fucking arsehole. Where do you think Jake got it from?'

'How the hell do you know that?'

'Shagged my wee sister years ago... When they were at school. Acorn doesn't fall far from the oak, does it?'

'Anyway.' Marshall smiled at them. 'I thought you should know. It will help with your lawsuit. Hopefully you can come to an agreement with them and get some money to help with Christopher's care.'

'Money...' Hugh brushed tears from his eyes. 'I'd rather have my boy.'

'I understand that.'

'Do you?' Hugh laughed. 'Do you really?'

'Believe me, I do.' Marshall held his stare until he looked away. 'We'll visit the school tomorrow to discuss the matter with Maria Ferguson and further validate the story as much as we can.'

'Do you think... Are you saying there's still some doubt?'

'No. But we just like to do things by the book, you know?'

Hugh squeezed Christopher's hand, then smiled at Marshall. 'Thank you.'

73

THURSDAY

Marshall waited in the new Starbucks in Gala, an incongruous new building in amongst a church and some old buildings. He'd driven past it hundreds of times in his life, but he couldn't remember what this had replaced. Getting to that age, eh?

Way too early for this shit, but the place was thriving. The joys of early opening.

Marshall sipped at his coffee, but it was still way too hot to drink. And already the second of the day and it was only seven. He regretted his cup last night – he'd slept like a log. With a chainsaw in it.

The door opened and Ferguson stepped in, searching the place. She came over to his table and looked him up and down. 'There you are. Have to say, Mr Marshall, you're a bit keen.'

'Know what they say.' Marshall smiled at her. 'Early bird gets the worm.'

Ferguson bit her lip. 'And the early worm gets to be breakfast.'

'Thanks for meeting here, saves me a journey.'

'It's on my way. I live at Melrose Gait.'

'Ah, the posh end of Langlee.'

'Don't.' She laughed, then looked over to the counter. 'Can I get you something?'

'Let me.' Marshall got to his feet. 'What can I get you?'

'Just a latte, thanks. No sprinkles or syrups or any of that shit. Full-fat milk. Two shots.'

'I love a precise order.'

'I know my coffee.'

'Back in a sec.' Marshall walked over to the counter and repeated the order, but without the swearword.

The barista nodded at him. 'What's the name?'

Marshall was tempted to say Costa, but just settled for, 'Rob.'

'It'll be a few minutes.' She turned around and started working away at the coffee machine.

Marshall went back to the table and took his seat again. His coffee was at the upper limit for drinkability.

'You, uh, wanted to see me?'

'I do.' Marshall took another sip. 'Sorry for the late text message last night, but I thought you'd like to know.'

'Obviously you were quite subtle in what you were after...' Ferguson gave a flash of her eyebrows. 'What matter do you urgently need to discuss with me at this time?'

'It relates to one of your students.' Marshall lowered his voice: 'Emily Borthwick.'

Ferguson leaned forward. 'What's she done?'

'You're assuming she's done something?'

'There's always someone doing something at a school like mine.' Ferguson gave a deep sigh. 'This job is killing me, Rob. Been doing this four years. Fifteen as a teacher. And it doesn't get any easier. Still, it's Friday.'

'It's only Thursday.'

'Jesus.' She shut her eyes. 'See what I mean?' She snarled. 'I remember getting hit on the hand with a ruler when I was at primary school and now you can't do anything to them. At *all*. Can't expel the little shits anymore, just have to exclude them for a period of time. Did that with Jake. He was *clever*. Never got caught doing anything *too* bad, just disruptive.' She frowned. 'Emily, though... She was a sweet girl. Only mistake was being with Jake, but that ended soon enough.' She swallowed hard. 'What happened to her father was... I didn't know the half of it, to be honest with you. With something like cancer, like with my dad, you get to say goodbye over a period of time. It might not be long, but *you* choose whether you leave anything unsaid. With a car crash... You don't get to choose. It's brutal.'

The barista appeared with her coffee. 'Here you go.'

'Thanks, very much.' Ferguson watched her retreat, then leaned over her coffee. 'Plus, if you're raped like that, it can do dark things to your mind.'

Marshall held her gaze. 'Emily wasn't raped.'

'Based on what?'

'Emily came to the station herself last night. Told us the allegations made against Christopher Goodwillie were false. Jake had put her up to it.'

'Fuck.' Ferguson collapsed back in her chair. 'Her mother wasn't there?'

'No. I gather they might've had a bit of a bust up.'

'Oh?'

'I'm debating whether to charge Emily with making a false allegation or accusation. Technically, because the school was handling it, there was no report to the police and that's a pivotal element of the offence.'

'Fuck.' Ferguson snarled. 'Christopher Goodwillie went to hell because of that... that...' She shook her head. 'You're sure?'

'We spoke to Emily, then we had a word with a friend of hers. Kid named Josh.'

'Josh Scott. He lives in Gala. Parents split up and he lives with his dad but still goes to my school.'

'Well, Josh backed up her story.' Marshall took another sip of coffee and it was nearing the lower limit of temperature. 'So, the reason I asked to meet rather than do it over the phone, is we need to speak to the rest of the class and validate the story.'

'This isn't anything to do with your murder, is it?'

Marshall didn't know how much he could trust her, but she was due the truth. 'It might be.'

'How?'

'Think about it. Jake puts her up to that, then that happens, then he's killed.'

'So you think Hugh did it?'

'He has an alibi, but alibis can be fudged by good intentions.'

'I can see it. He's an angry man. They're suing us because of what happened. Normally, like with Emily's mother, you could see the glint of gold in their eyes, right? But with Hugh Goodwillie, there was none of that. He just wanted justice for what happened to his son. And who could blame him? Chris is permanently in purgatory now. His poor parents… I can't imagine what they're going through.'

'I know. I've seen it. It's awful what they have to do.'

'When?'

'We visited them after your secretary passed on the address.' Marshall tapped his nose, then finished his coffee. 'Sometimes the worst stuff happens to the best people.'

'Christopher wasn't a good guy, though. But he didn't deserve this.'

'Oh?'

'Had a few issues with him overstepping the mark.'

'Sexually?'

'No. Well, not at school. We only ever had that one report from Emily.' Ferguson shook her head. 'No. In this job, you're shot from all sides. Sometimes I think us heads only get that job because we've survived long enough without being caught.

As well as the kids constantly trying to destroy the school, we see all sorts with the teachers. Drunks, gamblers, shaggers. Chris was a shagger.'

Marshall felt a jolt of worry there. A man who was deemed a shagger… Working in a school… 'What do you mean by that?'

'I'm as sex positive as anyone but Chris Goodwillie was constantly looking for his next conquest. And there were a lot of previous ones. He was on all the hook-up apps. Not dating, just looking for sex.' She laughed. 'I ended up getting paired with him once, which was bloody embarrassing. I obviously won't judge anyone for that, as long as it's private and between consenting adults, but he took it too far.'

'How do you mean?'

'Had to warn him to take a few things off Facebook. The kind of thing you really can't post while you're employed as a teacher. You know what I'm talking about. A few suggestive photos at the gym. A few drunken messages where he was flirting with school mums a bit too overtly.'

'Thought he wasn't a drinker?'

'Oh, he was. It was just secondary to his sex addiction.'

'Addiction?'

'Not that bad, where he's masturbating in the cupboard while the class are doing their exercises. Just the thrill of the chase, you know? Hunting for that next conquest, like I say.'

'Even so. It's good how Pam looks after him.'

Ferguson scowled at him. 'Pam who?'

'Pam Campbell. Not many women would stand by their man through an allegation like Emily's and certainly not take care of them after an injury like that.'

'What are you talking about?'

'Chris Goodwillie is her boyfriend. They're still a couple, despite what happened. She looks after him every night.'

'No, he wasn't.' Ferguson laughed. 'There was nothing between them.'

'I mean, I know they wanted to keep it a secret from the other teachers, but Pam Campbell is his caregiver, along with his parents.'

'I don't know who told you that, but they're obviously winding you up. There was *nothing* between them.'

'I'm sorry, but that's not our understanding.'

'Then understand this, Marshall. Chris once gave Pam a lift home after a night out. And she latched on to him. Nothing *too* stalker-y, but pretty stalker-y. And he just couldn't shake her off. And you can see why. Pam Campbell doesn't have much in her life. Just her cats, her true crime and her writing. Before all this happened, Chris asked me to have a quiet word with her... Get her to back off.' Ferguson fixed him with a hard stare. 'I can categorically state there was *nothing* between them.'

74

Marshall pulled up on Back Row in Selkirk. A wide street that felt ancient but was filled with post-war houses. Ahead, the church spire in the distance seemed to prick the low clouds. Four squad cars and a meat wagon rumbled, engines still running in case they needed to drive.

Marshall got out and walked over to them.

Jolene was leading the operation – and it looked like Marshall had just missed the action.

A squad surrounded the address they had for Pam Campbell, a two-up two-down in the middle of a long terrace. Freshly harled with a pink stone. A dormer poked out of the upstairs floor.

The entrance was a gaping, toothless mouth, with no sign of the front door. The bulk of the team were presumably inside.

Jolene spotted him, then cleared her throat. 'The warrant was pretty quick. Ravenscroft caught the judge at the right time.'

'Good.' Marshall clenched his teeth. The mauling he'd endured from him over the phone had been worth it, then. He watched the operation for any signs of life, but it was all quiet. Too quiet, maybe. 'All I could think about on the way here was when I spoke to Pam Campbell on Tuesday night.'

'When she brought Emily to the station?'

'Right. Thought that was weird, but she was using the girl to get close to the investigation.' Marshall stared at her. 'But she knew Nicola was Isabelle's real name. Even used it. Said something like, "Nicola and her probation officer, right?" So stupid.' He shook his head. 'I should've spotted it.'

'So you're going to blame yourself for what's happened?'

'No, but…' Marshall looked away. 'She wasn't even in a relationship with Goodwillie. Just lived this weird fantasy life where she pretended she was.'

'Jesus.'

They stood in silence.

A burly uniform stepped out, shaking his head.

Ash Paton followed him out and waved over, shaking her head. 'She's not here.'

Marshall had expected as much. 'She killed Jake, didn't she?'

'I…' Jolene swallowed. 'I think so… Dumped his clothes and phone in the burner in Isabelle's cottage. Either that, or she's covered for Hugh Goodwillie and he's done the deed. Need to check her name against the attendees at the trial.'

'Where is Isabelle, though? Does she have her?'

'Maybe.' Jolene shrugged. 'Okay, let's see what she's left behind.'

Marshall sucked in a deep breath, then followed her into the house and looked around. Tastefully decorated, but soulless. Like she'd copied something from a magazine and forgot to make it look like someone with a soul lived there.

Downstairs was a hallway with exposed stairs leading up. Two doors, both open – living room and kitchen.

Marshall took in the lounge.

Thumping came from upstairs – an aggressive search was underway.

Down here, though, there were books everywhere. All the crime novels, mostly in hardback: Rankin, Kirk, MacBride, Lancaster, McDermid, Gray, Anderson and Billingham among many, many others. But even more of her collection was true crime.

Ash walked out of a side door carrying a cat. 'Think she's a rag doll. They go limp when you pick them up. It's pretty cruel.'

Marshall shut his eyes. 'The knife…'

Ash scowled at him. 'What?'

'The murder weapon had a cat hair in the hilt.' Marshall focused on Ash. 'Can you secure her somewhere then get Kirsten to process its DNA?'

'A cat's DNA?' Ash scowled at him. 'You're serious?'

'Highest priority.'

'Your bill, sir.' Ash walked off with the moggy, which was way too placid – Zlatan would've cut Marshall's arm wide open after two seconds of that.

Marshall looked around the room, his blood thudding in his ear.

Campbell had run off. Fled. Had she known they were onto her?

But why did she leave her cat behind?

McIntyre popped his head around a door. 'Sir?' He beckoned Marshall through.

Marshall followed him into the room he'd assumed was a kitchen – Ash was shoving the cat into a pink pet carrier in the corner.

An office led off it. A small room, just a desk bearing a sleeping laptop, with cupboards and filing cabinets covering all of the walls. Not even a window.

Warner and his mate, Stish, were in the corner. His face was a latticework of scratches and scars. He spotted Marshall.

'C'mere.' He held up a box containing some trinkets. 'Have a look at that, sir.'

Two sovereign rings.

A fancy wristband with letters.

Marshall felt a jolt in his gut. 'Those are Jake's.'

'We found these too.' Warner held up some pages. 'They're from someone called Goodwillie.' He let out a high-pitched giggle. 'That can't be a real name!'

'Of course it's real.' Marshall pulled on his gloves then snatched them from him and checked through the pages.

Emails from Goodwillie, all printed out and looking pretty authentic.

Not declarations of love, though, or future plans.

> Leave me the fuck alone, Pam. I mean it. You can't stalk my house like that.

> That's it. I'm calling the cops.

Fuck.

It was all slotting into place.

Pam Campbell was completely delusional. She'd killed Jake Turner to enact revenge against him for what he did to her lover. But they never were. She'd built up this rich fantasy life where she and Chris Goodwillie were an item.

'And this, sir.' Crawford held out a manuscript. 'Looks like she was writing a book.'

Marshall took it and had a flick through. His blood ran cold. 'This is about the Applecross case.'

Like a giant Rubik's cube, the case slotted together. At the heart of everything was Pam Campbell, her obsession turning malignant.

Warner laughed. 'Oh, cool, a screenplay.'

Marshall snatched it off him and flicked through it. Pages of dialogue, action and voiceover, all in the voice of the intrepid amateur sleuth, Pauline Cartwright – no prizes for guessing who she was... 'Jesus Christ, she's written down everything she intended to do.'

'Jesus.' Crawford was reading over his shoulder. 'So Pam was the hero investigating the heinous crime of a fake rape. A lonely cat lady with a boyfriend in a coma.'

Marshall winced. 'I know it's serious.'

'Eh?' Warner scowled at them. 'What are you talking about?'

Crawford laughed. 'Not a Smiths fan, then?'

'Can't stand your man Morrissey.'

'Yeah, I can understand why these days.'

'Eh?'

'All the alleged racism and stuff. Falling out with Johnny Marr.'

'No. I hate that song of his. "Happy Hour".'

'That was the bloody Housemartins. I *hate* them.'

'There's no sign of her, is there?' Marshall scowled at them. 'Fuck, she's in the wind.'

75

Like the previous evening, Marshall was stuck in his office with Jolene, Taylor and Crawford.

This time, though, he didn't feel any hope or excitement – or even just the forward momentum. All he had was the dread of another escaped killer.

'Bloody hell, Rob.' Crawford was at the desk, flipping through the screenplay. 'There are definitely parallels with what happened in Hawick, without hitting the nail squarely on the head.'

Marshall walked over and tried to peer over his shoulder, but Crawford was an expert at blocking.

'Not just that...' Crawford flipped back to the start. 'See this, where the killer is murdering Jake? She carved those hold-back phrases onto Jake.'

'Jesus.' Marshall blew out a breath. 'Does it give any clues as to where she'd go?'

'Nope.' Crawford started from the end. 'Does have her living a peaceful life with cats and little babies. Presumably the babies are Chris Goodwillie's. But in this, the blame lies with Isabelle. There's a big confrontation between Nicola and the police. This must've been written before she'd met any of us, because the cops are all named like John Thomson and Fred Bloggs.'

Marshall looked across the whiteboard, focusing on the blank space around Isabelle/Nicola. 'Where the hell is she?'

'We don't know, sir.' Taylor was next to Crawford, the only one working at any of the three laptops. 'Just going through the lists of prison visitors. She just seems to have had her lawyer once a year, plus the occasional well-meaning sort from a charity.'

'Nobody obvious?'

'Nope. And no crossover with his list.'

'Okay...' Jolene took the seat next to him. 'So, do we think she's run away? Or do we think Pam's got her?'

'Hard to say.' Taylor shrugged. 'Could be either. But it's clear she was trying to make us think Isabelle was up to her old tricks again.'

Hard to argue with that...

'Let's focus on Pam, then.' Marshall wiped down the whiteboard and started scribbling names. Pam Campbell. Chris Goodwillie. 'Okay. So she's in love with Chris, but it seems like it was unrequited during his... Not his life, but you know what I mean.'

'I do.' Jolene nodded. 'Let's say his prior existence.'

'Right. During his prior existence. Why's she doing that?'

'Is she getting some kind of kick out of looking after him?' Taylor looked up from the laptop again. 'Like Munchhausen by proxy?'

'Maybe. She did talk about extracting his sperm. Taking something from him that he would've denied her in his previous state. Power, domination, control. She wanted babies by him.'

Taylor smiled at him. 'As our resident psychologist, is that a formal diagnosis?'

'No, but… It's not a bad idea. They call it factitious disorder imposed on another. FDIA. His parents have put her on a pedestal. She's like an angel to them, helping their ailing son. It's all the hallmarks of FDIA.' Marshall scribbled down their names, but didn't know where to take it. So he wrote down Jake, who had two connections to Campbell – one direct, the other via her supposed boyfriend. 'But the reason Jake got Emily to lie was because he was embarrassed by Goodwillie in class one day, right? Woke him up in class and he crapped himself. That fucked him off, made the school bully feel tiny. And you don't lightly make an enemy of someone like Jake Turner. He's vicious and vindictive. He made Emily make a false allegation against him, seemingly in revenge.'

'McIntyre's down at the school now. We've got six kids confirming Emily's story, not just that Josh kid. It wasn't blatant that he'd crapped himself. He did it, they smelled a big stink, then he waddled to the toilets. Last class of the day, so it wasn't like he had to spend the rest of the day in shitty trousers, just probably binned his pants and went commando.' Jolene tapped on Campbell's name. 'Let's focus on what we know about her. How long has she been a teacher?'

'Years.' Marshall grabbed his notebook from the table and flicked through it. 'Seven years. Lived in Edinburgh before she moved to Selkirk. Told us she had a monster commute, remember?'

'I do, aye.'

'Hang on a sec…' Crawford sat down again and opened his laptop. 'I made some notes on her last night. She went to Edinburgh uni. Studied English lit. Then converted to get a postgraduate qualification in teaching from Moray House, which is part of Edinburgh, right?'

'Been a fair few years now.' Marshall nodded. 'When was she there?'

'2012 to 2016 for her undergraduate. Then another year for

her PGDE. Eh, that's Professional Graduate Diploma in Education.'

Marshall smiled his thanks. 'Is she from Edinburgh?'

'Don't think so... Hang on.' Crawford tapped away at the keyboard. 'Here we go. Portree.'

'Eh?' Marshall jerked away from the board to hover behind him. 'On *Skye*?'

Crawford looked over at Marshall. 'Right.'

'As in, near Applecross?'

'I mean it's a couple of hours away, but aye.'

'But the case would've been all over the news back home.' Marshall looked over at Taylor. 'Cal, have you got the sign-in list for the trial?'

Taylor looked up. 'Aye. Give me a second.' His fingers danced across his laptop keyboard. 'There it is... Pamela Campbell...'

Crawford looked over his shoulder. 'She was at the trial the whole month!'

'Bloody hell.' Jolene scowled. 'So she knew?'

'She knew.' Marshall tried to calm down. 'But how would she find out Nicola was Isabelle?'

'I mean, going from Isabelle back to Nicola is next to impossible.' Crawford ran a hand across his head. 'But it's plausible she traced Nicola to Isabelle.'

'*How*?' Jolene coughed a laugh. 'This isn't like what happened with Andrea's husband.'

Crawford frowned. 'Who's Andrea?'

'Never mind. I'm just saying... It feels like a bit of a stretch.' Jolene shook her head. 'There's no organised crime angle with this.'

'Right. But it's not impossible, is it? Pam Campbell's on all these online forums. Weird shit goes on there. And a lot of them are hidden away. Had a case last year about a guy who was in HMP Polmont. Got let out and three days later, he's found dead in his flat in Glasgow. This group of weirdos track who's been released from prison. They name them, saying they're doing it to make sure communities are safe. All they're doing is painting a target on the heads of ex-cons. We shut it down but this was after her release. And it stands to reason Nicola Grant's going to be one of the most monitored.'

'Okay. I see that.' Jolene was still frowning. 'But what I don't get is the connection from Nicola to Isabelle.'

'That Glasgow guy, David Armstrong, was still living under that name. She's changed hers but that's not hard, is it? Just needs someone to leak from the PPU.' Crawford raised his shoulders. 'Could even just be a coincidence. She's pretty distinctive after all. Standing at the tills in Morrisons and she recognised the woman with the massive tattoo on her neck paying for her shopping at the next till. Oh, it's someone convicted of assisting serial murder.'

'Or popping into the Terie for a drink one day…' Marshall raised an eyebrow. 'Or just seeing her walking to work through Hawick.'

'Okay…' Jolene stared into space, then nodded. 'See, that I can buy.'

'I don't know how it's happened, but Pam Campbell's clearly done it, so we shouldn't really focus too hard on that.' Taylor stretched out his ankle with a sickening crunch. 'But one thing is for sure – all the stuff at the cottage. The phone. The clothes. She was waiting for Isabelle to get back so she could cover her tracks and then she's taken her, hasn't she?'

Jolene nodded. 'But where?'

And nobody had any idea.

76

'Just pinched it right out of my hands!'

Thursday day shifts were always mad, for some reason. Steve thought it was something to do with proximity to the weekend that did it – the numpties could taste the freedom, so they ratcheted up their insanity.

He tried not to think of his noodles sitting in the fridge in the canteen. Those delicious noodles in plum sauce.

Steve let out a deep breath. 'Okay, so you're alleging Mr Jameson stole a scratch card from you. Is that right.'

'Aye, pal! And not just an allegation! He fucking did it! In Smith's, about twenty minutes ago.'

'You mean WH Smith?'

'Eh?'

'And not the toy shop.'

'That's Smyths. And it's up at the Fort in Edinburgh.'

'Still, that's just a few stops up on the train.'

'What does it matter?'

'Well, if it happened there, then it's not my fau— responsibility. You'd need to take this matter up with Craigmillar police station. Not here in Galashiels.'

'Well, it happened in WH fucking Smith on Channel Street. I was just about to scratch the bastard thing off and the son of a bitch grabbed it right out of my hands!'

'Do you have any way of proving this?'

'I bought it!'

'But...' Steve sighed again – Christ, it was as much of a habit as these lot being mad. And he needed his lunch. Those delicious noodles and the crispy toasted cashew nuts. And it wasn't even ten. 'Is there any value to it?'

'I don't know! He hasn't scratched it.'

A woman walked through the front door and looked around.

Pretty. Late twenties, maybe. A few too many tattoos for Steve's taste, especially that one on her neck. Who the hell thought that was a good idea? Sod it – Steve knew he was a beggar in those stakes and he knew he couldn't be a chooser, so he'd take a chance.

'You listening to me?'

'Sorry, sir. What were you saying?'

Tattoo-neck cut to the front of the queue, bold as brass.

There were rules in here.

Steve gave her a stern look. 'Just be a minute, madam.'

'This can't wait.'

Steve smiled – some people could be so fucking cheeky, couldn't they? He pointed to the side. 'I'm dealing with this matter now. I'll be a few—'

'And I told you, this can't wait.'

Cheeky sod...

No matter how good-looking someone was, it didn't mean they could get away with this kind of nonsense.

'Excuse me.' Steve leaned forward to rest on the edge of the desk. 'This station, and many like it all across this fair land, operate on the same basis – first come, first served. Now, this gentleman here arrived before, then he patiently waited in the queue for five minutes while I dealt with another matter. Now, if you can afford him the same courtesy then, once I've passed this matter on or successfully resolved it, I will have sufficient time deal with your concern.' He looked her up and down. Holy crap, she was *gorgeous*. 'Is that okay?'

She shook her head. 'I need to talk to DCI Marshall about a murder.'

77

Marshall sat on one side of the table with Isabelle the other.

Jolene sat next to him, reading the bumf into the microphone, while the video cameras recorded.

Isabelle stared at Marshall with those intense eyes of hers.

Marshall couldn't believe she was here. He'd thought she was dead. Or he'd allowed himself to hope she'd just fled.

But she'd just walked through the door and asked to speak to him.

He got a nudge to the thigh from Jolene, so he leaned forward to smile at her. 'I have to say, I'm glad you asked for me.'

'Glad?' She held his gaze, like staring at a train rushing through a tunnel towards you. 'What are you talking about?'

'Usually when I speak to people, they don't want to be there, but you asked for me. Why is that?'

'Because I trust you.'

'What did I do to earn your trust, Isabelle?'

'I owed you the same consideration you gave me. When we spoke the other day, you *looked* at me. You pushed me hard, sure, but you looked at *me*. I wasn't some... I don't know. Suspect. Or ex-convict. You treated me with respect. And you knew what I'd done back then, but you still treated me like a human being. Not an inmate or a former murderer or cheap labour or someone you could fuck. And nobody's done that in a very long time. So that's why I trust you.'

'That's good to hear, Isabelle.' Marshall smiled at her, trying to encourage her to keep trusting him. And using her new name too... 'I gather there's something you want to talk to us about?'

'I killed Pam Campbell.'

That chilled Marshall right to the marrow. 'Thank you for telling me that.'

'I killed her. Stabbed her with a knife.'

'Where?'

'I'm not going to show you where she is. And I'm not going to give you any evidence. But she's dead. And I killed her.'

Jolene shot to her feet and left the room – Marshall knew she'd be getting someone to check that out, but they had no idea where Pam Campbell was, so it was going to be impossible...

He sat back and tried to act calm – he'd been in a room with murderers before. That was his mantra. So why did this one feel so different? 'So you're just saying you've murdered Pam Campbell, without us being able to prove it?'

'It's still a solved case for you, right?'

'No. If we don't have a body, we don't have a murder.'

'Come on. I've told you I've killed her.'

'That's not enough.'

The door opened and Jolene slipped back in. She made eye contact with Marshall as she sat, but didn't say anything.

'I'm actually the victim here.' Isabelle stabbed a finger into her own chest. 'Okay? She tried to frame me. Don't you see that?'

Marshall nodded. 'I do.'

'Eh?'

'I see the real you. Isabelle, rather than Nicola. Because when you change your name, you can shed all the baggage and become the real you. The one you always wanted to be. The one I saw when I spoke to you. And you're saying Pam Campbell tried to bring you back to that.'

'Right. Exactly.' Isabelle shook her head, then fixed those icy eyes on him. 'You know what? She deserved it. She fucking ruined my life. I liked being Isabelle. She's a good person. But she tried to frame me *for no reason*. And that got you looking at me. And that means people found out who I was. All of them. All those people in the pub. They'll talk to other people in Hawick. Everyone will know what I did. And you can't escape your past, can you? I tried to think I could, and O'Brien reassured me I'd be safe down here, hundreds of miles from home... He's a good man, but he told me I'd need to get another identity and move somewhere else. Forfar, Falkirk or Stranraer. God knows where. West Linton to start with. I... Why should I have to do that? Eh?'

'If you'd brought Pam Campbell to us, we could've seen what we could do about that.'

'How? I'd killed her.'

'So show us where her body is.'

'I won't. I won't offer you any proof, but I'll tell you what happened.' Isabelle leaned across the table. 'She abducted me.'

Marshall sat back and folded his arms. '*She* abducted *you*?'

'Right. That's what I said.'

'But you're the one sitting here.'

'Because I turned the tables on her. I tortured her and she told me her story. Then she bled out and died.'

Marshall didn't know what the hell to think here. She could be as much of a fantasist as Pam Campbell. This could all be a figment of her imagination.

But it could also be the truth. So he let it play out.

'O'Brien left me at my cottage and I felt the walls closing in on me. It happens a lot, so I went for a walk to clear my head and think things through. Being stuck somewhere else and having to start again. But when I came back, I saw a strange car. I know everything about where I live, so I knew something was up. So I took my time going around the area. She was hiding in the woods. She didn't see me, but I saw her. And she was casing out my place.'

'Did you recognise her?'

'Nope. Never seen her before in my life, or so I thought.'

'What do you mean by that?'

'I thought she might've been a cop. Someone working for O'Brien, maybe. He had me under surveillance, you know? When I got here first. They watched me all the time.'

'It's standard procedure for cases like yours. It's as much protecting you as anyone else.'

'Right.'

'What happened next? Did you attack her?'

'God no. She... She was watching the cottage. Like she was waiting for me. But then she... It's weird, but she switched on a phone. Thought she was going to call someone, but she left it by my cottage on the windowsill. I was going to put flowerboxes there for the summer, you know? I had plans to make that place look nice, but I'll never get to do it.'

'And then?'

'Then? Then she broke into my fucking cottage. My *home*. I left the cottage unlocked. I just went for a walk and I live in the arse end of nowhere. And I watched her go inside. Then I followed her in. She was putting the phone into the fire, along with some clothes. She didn't know what she was doing with that, though, so she couldn't get it lit. But I soon figured out what she was doing. She wanted you to think I'd stolen the phone and the clothes, then look like I'd destroyed the evidence.'

'Did she say whose it was?'

'Jake Turner's.'

'Do you know him?'

'Nope. Only other time I've heard that name was when you spoke to me. She was trying to make it look like I'd killed him. But I only found that out later... At the time... I just saw red. Someone was in my house. I ran towards her. But... She had a knife with her. A massive one. And I hadn't seen it. She thought she'd got away with it.'

'But she didn't.'

'No. She didn't expect to get caught by me. So she made me light the fire then she walked me out to her car and took me to this place.'

'Did she plan to kill you?'

'She did, I think. At least initially. But she changed her mind. Not out of some sudden need to preserve my life. No, she'd found another way to make her perfect crime that little bit more perfect. She tied me to a chair and started filming me on her phone. I was supposed to confess to the crime. But I knew that would only be the start of it. I thought she'd then make it look like I'd killed myself. Chuck me off a bridge somewhere. Give me all the pills she had. Enough to make me overdose on it. When she started recording, I knew as soon as it finished, I'd probably be killed.'

'So how did you manage to turn the tables?'

'By accident. I fucked up a line and she shouted at me. So I went quiet and she hated that. She came over and slapped me. It hurt like hell, but I did it again. And she did it again. So I knew what she'd do. The third time I went quiet, I rocked the chair forward. It threw her enough to let me trip her. I managed to overpower her.'

'How?'

'She was arrogant. Got too confident. Got too close. I bit her ear. Tore right through it. She screamed and panicked. I managed to get free. Then I used the knife to cut myself free. I only intended to scare her. I need to torture her a bit to get the truth from her, like why the fuck she'd done this to me. I needed to clear myself. And she talked. Quickly. She had no resistance to it. She told me it all. How she copied what he did so she could frame me.'

'He being Dominic?'

'Right. She thought she'd framed me. And I've got to admit, it looked good. You know, when I was in the cells here, I thought... I thought some pretty dark thoughts. But then you lot released me. And that's when she got desperate. So she decided to plant some more evidence against me. The phone. The clothes. And it made me so angry. I... I started scratching words into her arm. And I loved it. I loved causing the pain. Turns out, I enjoyed executing the torture myself and... She tried to fight me off. And... I just went for it. Stabbed the knife through her heart.'

'You've seen Dominic do it, but never did it yourself.'

'No. Exactly. I killed her and I felt powerful. So fucking powerful.'

The room went silent.

'Here's a thing. Pam told me how, in her true-crime world online, they all think I devised the murders. Me?' Isabelle shook her head. 'In their eyes, Dominic was "only" a prolific rapist of young men before I came along... But I was the one who planned the murders. Women are always the brains behind it. It's so sexist. It's that or we're coerced.'

'I understand what you went through, Isabelle. You didn't want to meet Dominic, did you? Didn't want to fall in love with him. Didn't want to put up with his issues. Didn't want to kill those men.'

'Exactly.' She scowled. 'It was all him. That's why I got a

lighter sentence while he's going to be locked up forever. Sure, he killed Kieron, but *he* hated Kier. He totally despised him and he knew precisely who he was killing. And it was nothing to do with me – I didn't put him up to it. Dom just killed him. All I ever did was video him, just so he would have sex with me. So he *could* have sex with me.'

'That's accessory to murder.'

'I know. And I've paid for it. I served my time.'

'Pam Campbell won't pay for what she did.'

'Not in this life.' Another blast of those icy eyes. 'I'm not going to tell you where she is, but seeing as how you've been so kind to me, I'll tell you what she told me about her killing Jake Turner. At least you can solve *that* one. She made it look like I'd done it but the most fucked-up thing about it is she didn't pick on me. Or rather, Nicola. She just got lucky.'

'How do you mean? You were moved here and we understand she was an expert on your case.'

'Right. That's all true. She said she'd attended the trial. It's pretty ghoulish, right? She was a student in Edinburgh at the time, so she had plenty of time on her hands. She'd seen the knife in person, so she could buy two exact replicas. But my point is, she knew hundreds of other murders to the same level of detail. She went to court a *lot* to watch cases unfold. She'd become fixated. It could've been Sharon Buckeridge or Caroline Naughton or Erica Black or any number of male killers. But she found me.'

'How?'

'How what?'

'How did she find you, Isabelle? How did she know you'd served your time as Nicola Grant but were now Isabelle Ward? She shouldn't have known that. It was hard enough for us to find it.'

'How do you think?'

'Well. When you got out, Nicola fell off the radar. She

checked obituaries and... Eventually she must've concluded it was a name change. Some digging around online revealed your new name and address.'

'Sure. I'd love it to be that complicated.' She stared at Marshall. 'She saw me working in the Terie. Even asked to use the toilet and I let her. I fucking let her in. She knew it was me. Nicola. And she knew she could frame me and get away with it. That's it. Nothing more complicated than that. She got lucky... I just happened to step into her crosshairs at the right time. And then she started following me. Thing is, I'd spotted all the officers running surveillance on me. When you spend time in prison, you get to be hyper-vigilant. You learn to spot threats from not a mile off, but so close. Your immediate environment is something you learn to control. She spotted I was being watched too. She followed them and learned where I lived. And she knew my car. And once they stopped following me, she started to. Weirdest thing, I had this feeling someone was watching me. Made me think I was going mad. I couldn't sleep because of it. But it was her all along. And I had no idea who she was. But she targeted me because of what she could use me for.'

'Did she tell you why she killed Jake Turner?'

'Because of what he did to Christopher. Her boyfriend. He was a teacher, like her. Said he's the kindest, most gentle man you'd ever meet. I've met a lot of men, so that's not a high bar. She said Jake had framed Christopher. He'd got his girlfriend – Emily or Emma or Erica or something – to lie to them and tell everyone Christopher raped her.'

'So she lured him to the museum to take revenge.'

'No.'

'No?'

'That's not what she said. She'd been following Jake for a while, just like she did to me. She learned his routine. Every couple of weeks he went to Hawick Museum, where he'd masturbate into the fountain.'

'She said that?'

'Right. It wasn't regularly, like every Friday at eight o'clock, but it was often enough. He was a twisted little shit, she said. And when she saw him heading off towards the museum on Sunday night, she knew where he was going. She got there first by car, then waited. In the rain. She saw him walking over the grass, heading for the fountain. And that's when she attacked him. She was pretty strong. I've been in fights with women in prison, but none are as strong as her. She fed him temazepam, which Christopher used to control his... I don't know the term but it's something to do with muscle twitching during his sleep. Something to do with his brain damage.'

Marshall frowned at something, a tiny little detail. 'Pam didn't have a car.'

'No.'

'So how could she drive there?'

'She stole Brendan's car. Stupid sod left the keys on the desk in that office. She just grabbed them while we were fucking in the other room... And she drove there, trying to frame us.'

'And meanwhile you were with Brendan.'

'Right. Brendan and... I can't even remember his name.'

'Daniel. Daniel Dunning.'

'Right. Him. Brendan...' She shook her head and wrapped her arms around herself. 'He was like you, Marshall. He saw *me*. He loved *me*. And I've ruined his life. I ruined what was good about him. I caused his kids all that pain. Because of me.' She shivered, goosebumps rising up the dragon tattoo. 'But we didn't kill Jake. She did. You know what she told me? She said she raped Jake with a dildo. Shoved a condom on it, then stuck it up his arse. To make it look like I'd been involved. To make it look like I'd found another Dominic.'

'Brendan.'

'Right. Brendan. And why? Because Jake had ruined her boyfriend's life. Christopher's. He tried to kill himself because of it.'

'They were never an item.'

Her mouth hung open. 'What?'

'Pam and Christopher. It was a fantasy.'

'No...'

'We've spoken to his parents and people at the school. We've found emails from her. There was no *them*.'

'Jesus Christ... All *this* was over *nothing*?'

'I'm sorry.'

'Fuck it, she deserves what happened to her. She deserves to die where nobody will find her. She's... These idiots who obsess about true crime and conspiracies... They think they can design the perfect crime, but I know from bitter experience that executing it is something else entirely. And then living with yourself afterwards? It's a whole other affair. It's not a jigsaw puzzle. Pam Campbell died because she fucked with the wrong person.'

'You think *you* can live with killing her?'

'I can. I will. And you know what? I did design the perfect crime. And I executed it. You have no body and only my admission that she's gone.'

'You're going back to prison, Isabelle. You know that, right?'

'I know. And do you know, after what's happened today, it's probably the only place I should be. I don't want to be on the run forever, constantly looking over my shoulder. I can sleep in my own bed. Serve my sentence. It'll be mitigated by the fact Pam abducted and framed me and was going to kill me... Might even get off with self-defence or at least it'll reduce the sentence. I could even further reduce it in exchange for the body. Could be looking at ten to fifteen... Not life. And I can spend the time in there helping other women who've been in situations like mine. I can finally do some good in my life.'

78

Marshall stood in the middle of his office and looked around it. Felt like it was spinning around and he might collapse at any second.

Isabelle's words still rattled around his head.

And the worst thing was, he believed every single word of it.

She'd done what she'd done, but he knew why.

Marshall focused on Ravenscroft.

'I've briefed Potter on it.' Ravenscroft sat back and sipped coffee. 'Thank you, Robert.' He took another drink, taking time to chew things over. 'Sounds like Pam Campbell was a ticking bomb. She murdered in cold blood and almost got away with it. But she grew desperate and we were lucky. Like Isabelle was unlucky.' He blew across the surface of his coffee. 'There's no chance we'll find the body, is there?'

'We'll find it eventually, sir. There's no such thing as the perfect crime.'

'Glad to hear it. Well done.'

'I didn't do anything. She confessed.'

'But you gained her trust, Robert.' Ravenscroft got up. 'Okay. Well, I've got places to go. People to see.'

'Your loose lips with Paul Turner almost jeopardised the case, *sir*.' Marshall shrugged. Not to mention half-inching his AeroPress. 'But we're willing to not underline that in the report.'

'You won't underline it?'

'As in, DCS Potter won't draw any undue attention to it.'

'Is this...' Ravenscroft laughed. 'Are you blackmailing me?'

'I'm helping you, sir. You fucked up. I'm making sure it's documented but also making it clear that nothing too bad happened as a result.'

'What do you want in return?'

'Nothing.'

'Bullshit. Everybody wants something.'

'The only reason I do this job, sir, is to get results. We got one here. One way or another. And no thanks to you.'

'Yes, well. It's a shame.' Ravenscroft gave him a long, hard look. 'But I get it. How about you and I work on that second round of whether to keep the Borders MIT, eh? I'll ask my secretary to schedule some time tomorrow morning to review your slides.'

'I doubt I'll get the time to revise them today.'

'Oh, you don't need to dust anything off, Robert. This case has illustrated the need for an on-site MIT down here. Sometimes you might be underutilised, sure, but I guess we can bring you north as needed. Could even divide up Edinburgh, so that any cases south of the Bypass, say, or east of the A1 might just fall your way. Maybe even put the whole Gary Hislop operation under you. And cases where Livingston or Dunfermline would normally take precedence, we can give you preferred substitute status.'

'You mean, we're a substitute?'

'Are you a rugby man?' Ravenscroft frowned. 'Or football?'

'Neither.'

'Suggest you get into sport, Robert. Helps keep you sane.'

Ravenscroft cleared his throat. 'Anyway, there's a term in rugby, which came into play a few years ago. They talk about starters and finishers. It's become commonplace in football now, though as an Everton fan I'd rather not talk about it. Substitutes were introduced for injuries, right, but then it evolved to become a remedy for tactical disasters. You started to see things like two substitutes at half-time, for example, if things were going really badly. Now, there are so many subs in a game of football. Five players, plus concussion subs as needed. It's given rise to this concept of, rather than starting with your best eleven players, you can bring on a few fast lads after seventy minutes to stretch an exhausted defence.'

'Starters and finishers. And that's what you want for us?'

'Exactly. I can see why you lot need to be here. But let's get you elsewhere too, eh?'

'I'm fine with that.'

'But I need to be clear, that whole Centre of Excellence part isn't happening, okay? You can relay evidence far cheaper than building a new lab. We just need to have a secure courier. In fact, you just proved that through Jay's jaunt to Gartcosh. It was Jay, wasn't it?'

'It was, sir. But that's fine.'

'Good man.' Ravenscroft grabbed his bag. 'Anyway. I'll see you tomorrow morning. Have a good night.' He got up and walked off through the incident room.

Leaving Marshall alone and a bit bamboozled.

It was only eleven o'clock, but it felt like he needed to get home and sleep.

Maybe he should. After all, what was the point in being the boss if you couldn't do that kind of thing?

Someone knocked on the door.

Kirsten was peering in. 'You are here, then?'

'Right. Just had a chat with Ravenscroft.'

'Commiserations. Saw him leave.'

Marshall smiled at her. 'So you are speaking to me, then?'

'Rob...'

'I mean it.'

'Of course I am.'

'You're annoyed with me because of all that stuff with Cath.'

'I am. But I'm here to update you. The DNA matches Pam's cat. So she definitely killed Jake. That, or Tigger did the deed himself.'

'Thank you. Any chance you could tell us where the body's stashed while you're at it?'

'Not my job. And someone will need to take that poor moggy in.'

'One, she's not a moggy like Zlatan. Two, I'm not taking in another cat.' Marshall pointed at the seat. 'Can we have a chat?'

Kirsten sat down, but with a great deal of reluctance. 'What's this about?'

'It's *that* chat, I'm afraid.'

'Rob...'

'Kirsten, come on. You owe me it. Admit it, you don't want to live together, do you?'

'Is it that obvious?'

'It is.'

'I've been thinking...' She nibbled at her lip. 'I was talking to Jen about the money you're lending to Cath.'

'So you are annoyed about it.'

'Yes. But maybe I was overreacting. Thing is, I was also *under*reacting too. If we are going to live together, then we need to make decisions like that as a couple.'

'It's the right thing to do. I can afford it and the house too.'

'You're missing my point. I... I think it's all getting too much for me. Us. Houses. Flats. Living together. I feel crowded. I like my own space.'

'So you want to split up?'

'I don't know how to say this.'

'Just say it, Kirsten. It's okay.'

'Okay. How about we continue as fuck buddies?'

Marshall felt a spear through his heart. 'Fuck buddies?'

'That sounds a lot crasser than I wanted. Friends with benefits, say? We see each other, but we have our own places.'

'To be brutally honest, I don't think I like the sound of that.'

'I'm serious, Rob. We still have a future together. I mean, the sex is really good and we're good mates and everything. I think we each need our own space for when things get too real.'

'And what if I want things to be too real?'

'Then maybe I'm not the girl for you.'

'Being fuck buddies… Is that really what you want?'

'It is.'

Marshall sat there. Nothing felt right and he was so bloody tired.

'Think about it. You buy that place in Melrose. Take out a mortgage and pay it off every month. Or somewhere else. Meanwhile, I'll stay in that flat and you're welcome to stay at mine whenever you want. And vice versa.'

Marshall sat back, puzzling it all through.

Fuck buddies.

Like they were daft twenty-year-olds.

He was thirty-nine in September and he needed stability in his life. Something real. Something concrete. Not being ghosted or ignored. Or living an hour away in a city. Not wondering who she was seeing.

Maybe she'd change her mind. Or maybe this would stabilise.

He also thought that her being on the job would mean she understood, but it actually made things worse. She knew what normal police officers were like, and he was far from normal.

The collisions at work made things worse.

How would he be knowing she was friends with benefits with someone else and still having to work with her?

Maybe the COE not coming to Borders was a blessing in disguise.

But then all the things they'd been through – trying to get pregnant and then failing to because of her condition… It was a lot. He should give her time and space, then see what happened.

No, he knew what he needed to do.

'We were going to buy a house together, but now you just want to be friends with benefits.'

'Aye. I've been clear about that.'

'But you haven't. You blow hot and cold, Kirsten. I want to do the right thing by you, but I can't figure out what that is.'

'Is this about Douglas?'

'No. It's nothing to do with that. Unless you're saying there's something.'

'There's not. Of course there's not.' She gritted her teeth. 'But I hear what you're saying, Rob. Don't worry about it. I hear you. Maybe we both just need to face it. We're finished, aren't we?'

AFTERWORD

First of all, a huge thanks to you for reading that – I really hope you enjoyed it – and for all the previous Marshall books too...

A lot went into this book and it's been yet another ordeal for me, but less of a painful one than the previous book thanks to not writing it when I'm suffering from hay fever, and to my new process.

It wouldn't be with you if it wasn't for a few great people.

Thanks as ever go to James Mackay for the help in developing the idea into a synopsis then an outline I could write. As ever, for punching the book hard in the nuts a few times to improve it, but let's not mention the wee trip to the woodshed the first-pass synopsis sorely needed this time...

Thanks also to John Rickards for copy-editing witchcraft, to Julia Gibbs for proofreading wizardry and to Angus King for the god-like audiobook narration (never, *ever* tell him I said that).

And a *massive* thank you to James Morrison for his insights into the world of PPU. It really helped develop the idea, from my joiner telling me about a rumour of someone who'd done a certain something living somewhere in Hawick, into the novel you've just read. All the mistakes are mine, not his!

A huge thank you to the brilliant author Craig Robertson for arranging for a load of us authors to visit Gartosh's Forensic Support labs… just as this book was being proofread, so I had tweak a few wee bits.

Also, thanks to all the Teries on my Facebook page who universally suggested the Teribus Arms – see you in there for a pint (without spit, thank you) and a game of pool (without a cue being cracked over my head, thank you). I hope I did your town proud…

Marshall will be back in *Our Debts to the Past* at the end of September 2025, or maybe sooner… Not that long to wait, really, but the ninth will be along not long after that and it'll launch something adjacent to these books that's very new (and maybe a wee bit old too). I'll be ramping up my production again after a wee blip there (for once it wasn't health-related) – I'm sure you'll soon be sick of my books!

I'll put the next novel on pre-order once it's done – this is a great way for you to support the books early, and my newsletter will always be the first way you hear of that. And remember, Amazon don't charge you until the book comes out…

Thanks again for reading – please leave a review on Amazon as it massively helps indie authors like me.

And now that's over, I'll be editing four Police Scotland novels (*Ghost in the Machine* through to *Stab in the Dark*) to bring the clunky text in line with *Dead in the Water*, which I reworked in October. It's all ahead of them coming out in audio from May… But they'll be much better for it – watch out for the wee 2025 edition "roundels" on the covers…

Finally – if you missed Shunty's second outing in *False Dawn*, well it came out between these books (and it may or may not feature a wee appearance from a certain Rob Marshall).

Cheers,
   Ed
   Scottish Borders, January 2025

MARSHALL WILL RETURN IN

Our Debts to the Past
Summer 2025

Sign up to my mailing list to be first to know when it's out...

ABOUT THE AUTHOR

Ed James is a Scottish author who writes crime fiction novels across multiple series and in multiple locations.

His latest series is set in the Scottish Borders, where Ed now lives, starring **DI Rob Marshall** – a criminal profiler turned detective, investigating serial murders in a beautiful landscape.

Set four hundred miles south on the gritty streets of East London, his bestselling **DI Fenchurch** series features a cop with little to lose and a kidnapped daughter to find..

His **Police Scotland** books are fronted by multiple detectives based in Edinburgh, including **Scott Cullen**, a young Edinburgh Detective investigating crimes from the bottom rung of the career ladder he's desperate to climb, and **Craig Hunter**, a detective shoved back into uniform who struggles to overcome his PTSD from his time in the army.

Putting Dundee on the tartan noir map, the **DS Vicky Dodds** books feature a driven female detective struggling to combine her complex home life with a heavy caseload.

Formerly an IT project manager, Ed filled his weekly commute to London by writing on planes, trains and automobiles. He now writes full-time and lives in the Scottish Borders with a menagerie of rescued animals.

Connect with Ed online:
Amazon Author page
Website

ED JAMES READERS CLUB

Available now for members of my Readers Club is FALSE START, a prequel ebook to my first new series in six years.

Sign up for FREE and get access to exclusive content and keep up-to-speed with all of my releases on a monthly basis.
https://geni.us/EJM1FS

Printed in Great Britain
by Amazon